Cloud Chamber

A NOVEL

MICHAEL DORRIS

SCRIBNER PAPERBACK FICTION
PUBLISHED BY SIMON & SCHUSTER

SCRIBNER PAPERBACK FICTION
Simon & Schuster Inc.
Rockefeller Center
1230 Avenue of the Americas
New York, NY 10020

Chapter 3 is adapted from "The Dark Snake," which originally appeared in *The Georgia Review*.
A version of this story also appeared in *Working Men* by Michael Dorris. Copyright © 1993
by Michael Dorris. Reprinted by arrangement with Henry Holt and Co.

First Scribner Paperback Fiction edition 1998
SCRIBNER PAPERBACK FICTION and design are trademarks of Simon & Schuster Inc.

DESIGNED BY ERICH HOBBING

Set in Garamond No. 3

Manufactured in the United States of America

1   3   5   7   9   10   8   6   4   2

The Library of Congress has cataloged the Scribner edition as follows:
Dorris, Michael.
Cloud Chamber : a novel / Michael Dorris.
p.   cm.
1. Irish Americans—Fiction. I. Title.
PS3554.O695C56   1997
813'.54—dc20   96-42544
CIP

ISBN 0-684-81567-2
0-684-83535-5 (Pbk)

For Louise
Who found the song
And gave me voice

ACKNOWLEDGMENTS

To Mary B. Dorris, Marion Burkhardt, Virginia Burkhardt, the late Katherine Smith, and the late Alice Burkhardt, my thanks for your courage, embrace, and indelible stories; to my rediscovered Irish cousins Eddie, Neil and Sean, my thanks for your generous welcome, and to Tom and Des Kenny of Kenny's Bookstore, Galway, my appreciation for your advice and good counsel; to my colleague, Sandi Campbell, my thanks for your unstinting encouragement; to Ken Robbins, my thanks for another inspiring image; to my agent, Charles Rembar, my thanks for being a tough grader; to my editor and publisher, Susan Moldow, my thanks for your sharp red pencil, trust and patience; and to Louise, my love and gratitude for all of it.

Cloud Chamber

CHAPTER ONE

THE DARK SNAKE

Rose

When I was still Rose Mannion and had the full use of myself, I was a force to behold. My hair's fine blackness was my signature, the legacy of a shipwrecked Spaniard off the Armada who washed onto Connemara and arrived, bedraggled and desperate, at the cottage door of some love-starved great-grandmother. In every generation that followed, it is said, there is but one like me. My mother used to call my mane a rain of Moorish silk as she brushed two hundred strokes before prayers. Never cut since birth, each wisp that pulled free she collected and worked into a dark snake she stored inside a wooden box. Now, ever since that terrible night, its lengthening coil I wind within a salver of Galway crystal, my constant souvenir of destruction. In the milky glow of lamplight it shifts and expands through the engraved cuts like a Hydra with many faces, each one of them Gerry Lynch.

What was there, back then, not to love about Gerry Lynch? It's true, I was a girl in the habit of measuring each person new to me by a tabulation of their natural imperfections: this one had too short an upper lip, that one unfortunate hair. This one was marred by the heaviness of the upper arm, that one by the gap of a missing tooth—the easier to place them the next time we met. But Gerry Lynch broke the mold.

You even had to adore his flaws. Too quick with the compliments, and those, too expansive to be absorbed without a shading of doubt. A tendency to sometimes withdraw into the depths of himself while feigning to listen politely. A furtiveness, *hesitancy* better describes it, and at the late-night meetings, when his turn to speak arrived, he once or twice in his enthusiasm seemed just that much off—brasher than need be, almost as if he took personally the injury that united us all in our resolve to remedy. An occasional bout of silliness, a touch boyish in a grown man.

But if these trifles be the beads on his Sorrowful Mysteries, think only of the Joyful, the Glorious! His devotion to the Cause. His bow-head humility at the Communion rail. His gait, so bouncing with natural exuberancy that who could fail to follow where he led? His clean town-smell, warm days and chill. The tenor voice that pulled the heart tight as the cross-stitch of a doubled thread. And for the Hail Holy Queen: that song he made up, that darling brave ballad that bore my name. He sang it to all who'd listen, his eyes twinkling merry—except when he'd glance into the crowd my way, and then, so serious that everyone but us two faded into nothing. I could not meet his eyes, and still draw breath.

There's no denying, that song set me off, elevated me you might say, beyond the already considerable pedestal of my own and the county's regard. I first heard it as dusk was falling outdoors, and it took me that much by surprise. I was wiping a table in the lounge of McGarry's Pub in Boyle, half-listening to Liza O'Connor, the other afternoon employee besides myself, expound on the injustices of the Ursulines, the cruel penances they extracted for her merest transgressions. It was too early for the supper crowd and there was little to occupy me. Out the window the post road was an empty lane, not even enough traffic to raise dust. The sweep and dip of the land, bisected and angled into small plots by stone fences, was a maze without escape—bricked in, I was, by the poor rectangles of Ireland. The walls had no gates—wood was too dear—and so each day a part of the structure had to be dismantled to let the sheep out or in, then built up again to ensure they would not stray.

Suddenly, from the adjoining common room there came a shout of laughter that piqued my attention. Why else tolerate the slave wages paid at McGarry's than to listen for the boys next door, to puzzle out the dazzle of their rowdiness, me with no brothers at hand of late for closer study?

"That would be Sean O'Beirn," Liza observed. He was her love interest of the moment.

"It's not the laugher I question," I said to deflate her, "but the one who inspires him." That shut her up.

Again, a round of loud urgings penetrated the thin wall. "Sing it," a chorus seemed to goad. "You dare not."

"I do, though," replied a familiar voice that instantly, in song, turned into such polished silver that a mist of quiet stilled the establishment, muted the clink of pints, the groan of chairs, the murmur of mundane conversation. The sound was pure music, so much so that I stopped my rag midway across the rough surface, listened below any search for the sense of it, content to float among its blending and overlapping tones. I looked in question to Liza at the serving table, who mouthed, careful not to irritate the perfumed chords with any grating noise: *Lynch.*

Of course, but a Lynch transformed. And then, like some echo that must reach the end of a distant valley before wafting back to earshot, the words revealed themselves.

> *I don't know when and I don't know how*
> *But I'll wed my Rosie Mannion.*
> *Hair as black as ravens' wings*
> *And eyes like forty-seven.*
>
> *Hair as black as a banshee's wail*
> *And eyes that hold my heaven.*

I don't know how and I don't know when
But I'll wed my Rosie Mannion.

A heat spread across my cheek, down my neck and arm to the hand that clutched the cleaning cloth as if it were a shroud I could yank over my own face. The presumption of it, I thought, but crouched behind the outrage lurked another assessment: the silken triumph.

I rapped last night upon her door
Expecting Rosie Mannion.
Her mother's ghost 'twas greeted me
With eyes so dark and gleaming.

The bald shock of it. To take her name in vain as if her loss were not a stone lodged in my heart. I would never forgive him. Liza covered her open mouth with her hand in solidarity.

Hark to me, she said, dear boy:
You'll never have my colleen
Unless you take her father's oath
And swear your life to Ireland.

My mind raced to its limits like a bird flown down the chimney, trapped in a room, beating its wings against a closed window. The audacity, the heedless jeopardy, to acknowledge the pact in daylight, in the company of who knows who? Was it courage Gerry Lynch possessed, or stupidity. Liza went white, her pallor I'm sure the mirror of my own. If the rooms were listening before, they were positively fixed in concentration now. And yet the lilt of the song, the innocence of it, the pitch and dangle of the jaunty voice, belied the seriousness, made life and death but backdrop to . . . me.

Wait. It was my father he was offering up in his laxity. My father who had read to me every night of my childhood, who had led me through the Classics, shown me the world.

I took charge of myself, burst through the swinging door of frosted glass like Joan of Arc herself and pushed my way into the men's assembly until I stood, trembling, face-to-face with Gerry Lynch. I was tall for a girl and he was taller but somehow in my agitation our size was equated and I could taste the whiskey breath of him on my own tongue.

"Have you gone moony?" I demanded of him. "My poor father's taken no oath. He's an innocent man, devout and simple, unfairly accused."

Gerry looked at me stupefied, almost as though surprised to be overheard, and then a smile—a smile his face pretended to fight but clearly he was too pleased with himself for having so summoned me. He nodded a bow, courtly as if we were but passing neighbors on a street corner, and kept in his throat whatever else remained of his song.

"It's only a ditty," he said. "It's nothing but a word that fits the meter, that makes the rhyme."

The bird flew to the opposite wall, smacked into it hard enough to unstun its brain.

"Nothing, is it? The oath is nothing? Ireland is nothing?" I looked around the room, the smoke dense as fog, the men bleary-eyed, torn between amusement and curiosity. The sight of them, safe and free, curled my lip. To hell with puny caution, with cleaning up the mess of dirty dishes and sloshed stout. Was I not Rose Mannion, my mother's daughter? My father's? My brothers' sister?

"I'll give you 'nothing,' " I said to his grinning face, and placed my right hand, still clawed around its rag, hard enough upon my breast to feel the thud of my heart beneath it. "There'll be no life for me, no wedding bells, no rest or haven, until the land I walk upon is mine." I cast my eyes accusing around the hall. "Is ours." My voice was bold and steady—I alone caught the quake. The wording may not have been exact but it was close enough. Those that knew, knew, and those that didn't, be damned.

"Rose." Martin Michael McGarry, the young nephew of the

house and himself a tall drink of water, gawky and half-formed, laid his big-knuckled hand upon my shoulder. "Enough."

I turned the blaze of my eyes at him. Who was he to stop me? "Am I clear in my meaning?"

"You are heard, dear girl," he said, and I knew for a fact that he was one of us, or rather, that I was now one of them. The room I had entered in my fury moments earlier was no longer the room in which I stood. It had become . . . how do I express it? . . . churchlike, sacred in its grave solemnity, and for that fleeting, solid instant, I was its priest.

Gerry Lynch broke the spell. "We're with you, Rose," he said abashed and sobered.

"I'm glad to hear it," I answered, and yet I didn't hear it from him, not quite, not like I heard it from Martin McGarry, but I chose to believe him all the same. It wasn't a matter that bore lies or exaggeration, after all, and every man who had witnessed my profession had witnessed Gerry Lynch's as well. We were full into it, united as if wed already.

After that day, when the ballad became our anthem, people couldn't turn their speculating eyes away from me. What was it about me, they asked in whispers or to themselves, that inspired such poetry and adoration, that herded the likes of Gerry Lynch into one yard and no other? That called forth promises before they were demanded? Promises that made the toes of some tap and the heels of others strike the ground in a satisfying rhythm? Pledges that caused the stanzas to proliferate with each refrain?

"Do you care if I sing it out just the one time more?" Gerry would ask my leave in mock apology for the frequent repetition. And I'd shrug or genuflect my head as if I could barely entertain the notion, so above it all I was. But in my mind, I answered bold enough to shake him in my embrace: "Sing it till the pixies dance and the sun rises and sets again. Sing it till there's no one living who doesn't echo every stanza in their bones. Fill the air with it, float it on the breezes that travel north to Donegal and south to

Clare. Sing it till the very hum of the earth joins in its melody, and every rose that blooms bears *my* name, and not me theirs."

"Pride goeth," the Scripture teaches, "before the fall," but pride is also its own fuel, its own reward, a vice easily mistaken for virtue. Pride was my basking mirror—and my blindfold. Pride was a beacon so bright and warming that I did not notice the approach of night. Pride was the stand-in for everything and everyone deprived from my life—father and mother and brothers and even Gerry Lynch, frequently absent from my company with no explanation save the lame excuse that he needed a solitude in which to pen another verse in praise of me. Pride was the sustenance of my loneliness, the succor of my dreams, the antidote for my uncertainty. Pride was my armor. Pride was my ax. And pride was my sorry defeat.

The night he visited—the night with which I thought to begin this tale but which ended its one sunny chapter, the night that forever separated illusion from reality I invited Gerry to my house for supper. It was time, I told myself. Sooner would have been too soon, suspect and the stuff of gossip. To wait longer would be flippant, cruel, coy—and I despised coyness.

I made ready the bed in which I myself had been conceived. I washed the flannel sheets, put fresh ticking in the pillows, aired the quilts atop the stone fence that ran behind the house. I swept the floor clean, put a jar of pansies on the old table and bought butter from Mrs. Tierney, who was famous for her churn. Six was the appointed hour of Gerry's arrival—proper dusk: no one could accuse us of subterfuge. I trimmed the lamp's wick for an even, flattering light—should illumination be needed. I doubted it would, till much later. If Gerry had the endurance to sit past sunset in my father's stiffback chair I had misjudged him. If he held back that long I might change my mind and strike the match myself.

I bathed in water strewn with petals—a conceit I had read of in some Frenchy book of my brothers. For once I studied myself, approved the blush of my skin, the fullness of my figure, the sprinkle of freckles that decorated my breasts even as stars accentuate the pitch of an inky sky. I was a virgin, of course, but I was not ignorant. I had heard the man stories of others and made up one of my own: how it would go for me and Gerry. So often had I anticipated the crush of him against me, the push and the pull, that it seemed as though our first togetherness was already over and done with. I was impatient to let the fact catch up to the fancy and be done with it.

But nothing about that evening went as I had sketched it. It was eight o'clock before I heard Gerry's footsteps in the lane. I was put out with waiting, threw open the door before he had the chance to knock, and confronted him with the full weight of my displeasure.

"Before you say a word." Gerry was out of breath and held up a warding hand. "I've run all the way from Boyle." His eyes glittered in the flames thrown off from the hearth. He had a tale, and in spite of myself I was caught by the excitement in his face, the urgency of his tone. I ushered him in, fetched a pot of tea that had grown so strong it had turned black. While I was pouring he noticed on the curio shelf the wooden box with my combings—its existence was well known. With that he laid his trap.

"Surely this must be the sole surviving snake in Ireland." He released the coil of my hair on the table spread with a lace cloth to disguise the wear of the wood. "Outsmarted St. Patrick himself, no doubt. It deserves a better castle." And with that he produced from the pocket of his great coat a bundle swathed in cloth. My hands trembled in the unwrapping, and there before me was a salver of the finest Galway crystal, sparkling in the lamplight. I refused to gauge the depth of my pleasure.

"A fancy notion," I said, then added "There are snakes and there are snakes in the grass. And what's my price for this?"

"Don't take on so serious, Rose." He was still worried at his tardiness and shifted his eyes to meet my own, anxious lest he had given more offense than tease. He wondered, no more than I, where the night would lead. "You know I can't resist your hair, nor anything else that ever was or ever will be a part of you."

Of course I knew. But what he didn't apprehend, what I hadn't yet let him realize in its entirety, was that the sentiment was more than a share returned. My eyes then were still beyond the ability to see clearly as far as one Gerald Cornelius Lynch was concerned. To study him was my secret pleasure, and even in the privacy of my bed I'd close my lids as if in prayer and drink in the lovely sight: the stand of sunlight hair, a wild growth of reeds in a windstorm; the eyes, changeable as the color of the sea off Sligo when the clouds blow fast above it; the lips that couldn't help but repose themselves into a sly smile; the clever chin; the neck above his jumper, long and pale and pulsing with the thick blood of him; the hands that ended in fingers agile for strumming, for tapping on keys, for playing any song I might yet yearn to hear. The whole of him, so different from any man of my acquaintance. The sum. The tender heart. But these were thoughts I didn't speak aloud.

"You black Mannions are a matched set," he went on. "Intent on draping airs about you like the Holy Virgin's mantle."

I gave him a look. He was strayed from the path I had laid out for him.

"Not without cause, I'd never venture that, but you can be touchy, overserious when it comes to yourselves."

The twist lay between us, spun of years, strong as rope. I let it do the talking for me.

"Is the braid to be part of your trousseau, then? Will it come hid amongst the linen sheets and embroidered napkins?"

"There'll be no weddings for myself till Ireland's free and whole again," I couldn't resist reminding him. My voice sought his contradiction. "You know the pledge."

"The famous pledge, with its added female codicil. Another example, as if one were needed. What other West Coast girl has felt compelled to swear a man's oath? None save you."

"None other had my provocation," I said, surrounding us with the awareness of my father and two brothers, rotting or worse in an English jail, ghosts in the walls of their own house. "Fortunate those girls are." And weak, I might have added. And cowardly.

"I meant no slight."

As suddenly as the silence settled about us I was jarred by the oddity of the situation. A girl of seventeen installed like an abandoned crone in her family house, saved from eviction by the barest charity of American cousins, entertaining a . . . yes, he was, Gerry Lynch was a gentleman . . . with no supervision or protection beyond herself. Deprived of a sainted mother struck down by a stray Queen's Regiment bullet, of a father and brothers brought short before they could exact their just revenge, captured in their nightshirts. While our root cellar was defiled, every edible bite of nature pissed and shat upon, every provision against our winter hunger wasted, they were forced to stand by, helpless and dazed. Afterward, they were dragged across the breadth of the island and then that of the sea to the Pandemonium of their oppressors.

I held my tongue, waited, and in that quiet, I did reel out the vision of myself wed to Gerry Lynch, did watch our boys and girls swing on the iron gate, did see them grown and wed come back to bring us grandchildren to admire. I did feel the palm of Gerry's hand gentle against my cheek, did blush at the roost of us beneath the blue and white squares of the quilt that waited for my marriage bed. All stretched within my reach, far side the piled stone walls of our enslavement.

We'd live here, no question. The Mannion house was not grand but it had a charm to itself, a coziness that made anything bigger seem too grand by comparison. The Lynches were Galway traders, their history smudged by wrong unions and compromises, a past not lost on Gerry who chose for himself the honesty of farm work, though he was so far from common that he recited Shakespeare to the cows.

"Which play?" I asked when he confided me this endearing habit.

He paused for a moment in thought. Was it to guess which tragedy would impress me the more, which verse I would find most pointed toward our particular circumstance? Was he breaking a Bible's spine in scheme that my finger would alight on the very line of Scripture that best forecast a future in his direction? Or did he truly not instantly recall, there being too many possibilities?

> "*Let us from point to point this story know,*" he began,
> "*To make the even truth in pleasure flow:*
> *Since thou beest yet a fresh uncropped flower,*
> *Choose thou thy husband, and I'll pay thy dower.*
> *For I can guess, that by thy honest aid,*
> *Thou kept a wife her self, thy self a Maid,*
> *Of that and all the progress more and less,*
> *Resolutely more leisure shall express:*
> *All yet seems well, and if it end so meet,*
> *The bitter past, more welcome is the sweet.*"

So the boast *was* design. So much the better. It confirmed my respect for his determined ambition.

" 'If,' " I corrected. I knew the comedies as well as he, better, and felt particular partiality to Helena in *All's Well*.

"If what?"

" 'If,' not 'Since.' '*If*' she beest still an uncropped flower."

That made him blanch. "But surely you don't imply. . . ." he stammered, gaping at me as though I were suddenly turned into a stranger. Two could frolic at manipulation.

"I merely quote the line as written," I answered guilelessly, and let him stew.

"Say you love me, then," he asked impatiently.

I could have denied it.

"I might."

"More than anything?"

I did not belittle this question, just let my silent agreement stand beside us in the flickering room.

"Because I'll now be putting you to the test." He reached out, took my hands in his, pulled me close enough to smell the sweet stout on his breath.

"There's no need." I saw it all. The grandbabies around us. Him in his cap, smoking his pipe. Me beaming at the back of his head.

"There is," Gerry answered in a voice that could have come from a pulpit, that formal. "There's a bond stronger than marriage vows, stronger than the link between mother and child. It can be ours if we dare it."

What was he speaking of? Did he mean the carnal knowledge of a man and a woman? He had that without all this rigmarole, if only he would be still and ask for it. I shifted to move even closer but he held me where I was. This business was about talk, not bodies.

"Dare me." I lingered in my innocence of him.

"Secrecy." He whispered the word, let it slither from his mouth like Satan's own serpent, and it was as if I could see a second surprise box wrapped in brown butcher paper and tied up with satin string. I wanted to pluck the bow. I wanted to know.

"What great secret do you have for me, Gerry Lynch?"

He fairly shivered, so het up was he, so full of what he was about to impart. But now that he felt confident he would not be rushed.

"First," he said. "I offer you my heart."

"And I accept it, and give you mine in return."

"You're bound to silence, then. Like a priest in Confession."

"It's not as your priest I see myself."

"In this matter only. Swear." He laid my right hand upon his breast. I could feel the inflation of his breath beneath my fingers, and deeper still, the pulse of his rushing blood.

"You frighten me." But in fact I was thrilled.

"Swear."

There was at that moment nothing Gerry could ask me I wouldn't avouch. "I do."

His lips stretched tight over the ridge of his teeth. "Right. Hear me out."

I nodded, matched his smile with my own, eager to join him in whatever room he was about to lead me.

"I'm not whom you think."

Still, the smile held, though I tipped my head to one side to show bemused confusion.

"The Gerry Lynch you see is but the easy half." He stopped my question with a shake of his head. "Hear me out," he reminded. "My day is coming. Our day. But this news will be hard for you."

I was used to hard. I thrived on hard.

"I am on the other side," he blurted.

His gaze held mine and his hands tightened their grasp while the words echoed between my ears, ricocheted against my clamped jaw. Trapped within the well of my body they raced the length of my arms and back, fell to my stomach, battered at my knees. Surely, this was some joke of his.

So I laughed.

His expression intensified. He was telling God's truth.

"I do it for Ireland," he urged upon me. "I see further than the rest of them, to the greater good. England will be our salvation. Trust me, woman. That's all you need to know for now."

I wanted to blot and smudge his words before they dried into permanence, but I was frozen in his cobra stare.

"Now you must protect me," he said. "My life is in your hands. Will you stay sealed?"

The blindness of his pride put mine to shame. The tide went out of me. This was some stranger clasping on to me. Worse than that. This was a man I hated as much as I wanted.

"Have you given up one of our own?" Such simple words in themselves. So cruel strung together. I had heard that betrayal was the price they extracted as treacherous proof of loyalty.

Gerry looked away.

"Who?" I asked. "Which ones."

"McGarry," he said. "Just Martin McGarry."

As if to ward off the poison of that name, he pushed me back against the table with such force that it skidded across the floor, rammed against the wall. Miraculously the salver didn't shatter, fot it landed on the cushion of my hair. The table, though, was a different story. So old was it, passed down as it was in the family, so many meals had it held, so many elbows, so many hands slapped down upon it in anger, that it could take no more, and a split spread like a forked stick across its center.

"I'll get you a new one," Gerry Lynch whispered suddenly at my side, and then he kissed me.

The hours that followed contained every event I had imagined in the days I had prepared for them. His touch was liquid gold, his lips sweet upon the crook of my arm, the back of my knee. We did not light the lamp, and so he didn't see the dullness of my eyes, the marble flatness.

"Thank you," he cried at some point. "My Rose," at another. My body responded of its own will, with its own ideas and schemes. It danced the merry dance with Gerry Lynch, matched him move for move, wanton enough to make the descriptions in that French book seem like Sunday dinner talk. If, as the Church averred, what we did together was wrong, a sin against the Sacrament of Matrimony, Gerry's treachery magnified the crime a thousandfold—and that made the pleasure of it all the better. Wickedness once released knows no natural bounds. It fills every moment to overflowing, drowns out all sound by the breadth of its own greedy desire, engorging on itself, shouting its bravado, never satisfied enough to pause in its demand for more. Compared to those hours with Gerry Lynch, the only time I would ever know him or any other man in fullness, my later wifely duties were so pale a reflection, so chaste, as to insult the memory. Even the acts of giving birth to my sons seemed too tame, the pain nothing against the remembered pleasure that was ever afterward denied and hence my Purgatory. Never before or since was I so completely alive to living.

And yet, a part of me also remained distant, even then, *in mediis*. While Gerry Lynch kissed and fondled my limbs, my mind watched behind a tree of thoughtfulness, contemplating my course. I was glad of our bodies' preoccupation, for it gave me a hiding place in which to think. A priest, he had asked me to be. A muzzled nun, more like it.

While Gerry sweated and wept and begged for mercy, I examined every road open to me, sufficiently traveled down each and determined that I had no possible destination but one. It was only after I had decided how and when, to whom and in what manner I must bring Gerry Lynch to justice, that I allowed myself to merge wholly into his mad embrace, to match his ardor unstinting, to lose my heart for all times, even as I closed off my mind and kept a cold and bitter clutch upon my soul.

CHAPTER TWO

THE SKIB

Martin

We served the poor in our fashion, a pint at a time. We wrote the bill in pencil light enough to fade with the memory of debt. We opened the doors of the public house when the first one knocked and didn't turn the lock until the last had stumbled out into the starry light. We were the county's secular church, the place where indulgences came with the stand of another round, where the saints were the ones buying and all the angels toiled in the kitchen.

Rose Mannion was one such, a girl whose halo surrounded the sum of her. She moved through a room like a jet of flame, a girl of such sweet purity, such oblivion to her own effect, that the longing looks that rained down upon her left her dry and untouched. She was young to work full hours, but strong and willing, and much in need. Her mother long departed, her father and brothers in chains, she was adrift, so unworldly that she did not recognize her vulnerable posture.

There were plenty of them anxious for the task of protecting her, plenty who slipped something extra into the pocket of her apron as she brushed by, plenty who would have gladly interposed themselves between the worthy Miss Mannion and any trouble she might encounter, expecting as payment only the mild nod of her head in their direction. There were some among the elderly who would have liked to take on her father's role, a few of the happily married who would have been her brothers, but for the rest, myself included, it was Rose's beloved we aspired to be, the man to whom she turned each night.

That was a far-fetched dream for me, for I was nothing to look at: a big head set on thin shoulders, hands broad as shovels, feet pigeon-toed and clumsy. If the world could have been privy to half the retorts I thought of too late to say I might have been considered middling clever, but as it was I came off tongue-tied and blushing, a bashful boy rattling around in a full-grown shape. I was missing an upper tooth on the right side so never opened my mouth too wide to smile or laugh, just pursed my lips as if every event I witnessed set me to thinking, slowly, how I felt about it while others were quick to make up their minds.

In the Movement I was given little of importance to do. I was the one who set up chairs in the meeting hall, who watched the door while others palavered, who voted "aye" on every question so as not to offend the man who had proposed the plan. I was a follower, no question, who believed in the general notion of the Cause—Ireland for the Irish—more than I struggled with the moral particulars of it. Duty was a lesson I learned from instruction rather than from that inner voice that some professed to hear. When I paid heed to myself, all I heard was the sound of my own listening, crisp and empty as the inside of a cast-iron kettle.

Where did the gumption come from then, I wonder, the day I stood up for Rose Mannion, there before the full complement at the pub? She was giving it fair to Gerry Lynch, putting him in his place after some misfired joke. All but waving the banner flag, was she, her face pink, her eyes bright with daring. I enjoyed the performance, but I worried as it went on: there could be present men who would take her words the wrong way—or the right—and report them outside our halls. Rose's family was suspect enough to generate interest even in the poppings-off of a fiery girl. And so I took it upon myself to voice caution, to still her tirade before it indicted her beyond repair.

"Enough," I said.

I half-expected she would turn on me—me who up till then must have been mere furniture to the likes of her, me the lanky poor relation of the house that paid her wages—and tell me to mind my own affairs. But instead she shone the full beam of her gaze into my face, nodded as solemn as a child just confided a grown-up secret, and did my bidding. I knew in that instant that she mistook my position, that she believed I spoke out of genuine authority, not impulse, that in confusion she placed me high in the clandestine chain. That she thought me . . . someone.

I called her "dear girl," and she tolerated the familiarity.

But then my moment was done and Rose saw only Lynch, who was everything I was not. He charmed her with his clever song, hoisted her above her rival, Liza, because Sean O'Beirn couldn't match Gerry's lilting tenor or easy banter. I watched it all, invisible in the mirror of her reflection, a part of the picture so taken for granted that I inscribed without awareness.

And yet, I was altered. It's an odd thing how your life can change in the wisp of a breeze. A tinder may ignite or a fire blow out, but either way a boundary has been breached, a threshold irrevocably crossed, a key to the door. Once envisioned in Rose's estimation, I had an image to uphold, a possibility to strive for. Of course I had been previously in sympathy to the goals of the Resistance—who could not be?—but now I conceived of taking an active part. My very ordinariness might afford me access to places a more prominent man would be denied entry. I could become a vessel for information: the floating bottle that contains a message, the skib that holds the dinner spuds, so common and everyday that it adorns the simplest table without ostentation. I had a good memory, I gave myself that, and a strong pair of legs. I could carry word and leave no scrap of evidence to be discovered, could fill my own emptiness with another's meaning. And so, the very next day I went to Sean O'Beirn—the one or near enough that Rose Mannion had assumed me to be, the one who spoke for us to other patriots—and offered him the use of me.

It was not for me to judge, but those scraps of message to which I was temporarily entrusted did not seem earthshaking.

"Tell O'Connell eight o'clock at the bridge," went the first one, nothing more.

I went to Roscommon Town, four hours it took me between the walking and the occasional ride on the back of a cart, found O'Connell at his smithy, repeated Sean's chit.

O'Connell, a big man with a full head of white hair, paused his hammer and squinted his eyes.

"Which bridge?" he asked. "Which night? Or is it morning?"

Well, there you go, I thought to myself. You can't even do the job of a carrier pigeon. I turned on my heel, hoofed it back toward Boyle—the sun was down low when I made it to the pub—and put O'Connell's questions to O'Beirn.

"Three hours hence, man," he shouted in irritation—but how could I have known? "At Ballymarene, of course."

My dad lent me the horse and I road like a banshee was behind me.

"It's tonight," I told O'Connell between breaths when I found him at his dinner table. "Ballymarene Bridge."

"Good God," he said and rushed from the house, taking my horse, leaving me to stare at his wife and children, their eyes round, their spoons stalled halfway to their open mouths. It was dawn before I made it home. I never learned what transpired, not even if the meeting took place, but I must not have been a total washout, for two days later O'Beirn dispatched me on another mission, this time to Sligo, this time in possession of all I needed to know.

And so it went, once or twice a week, in every direction of the compass, I crossed the Western counties of the north with words I didn't comprehend and gave them to men for whom I was but the echoed voice of my betters. I noticed no effects of my labors.

Nothing changed that I could see. Nothing blew up. No one disappeared. For all I knew I was involved in mere diversion, but still and all I was not nothing. Still and all I had earned the right to have told Rose Mannion, "Enough."

When Rose came to work as usual on the morning of April 18 I could tell immediately that something was amiss. Her complexion was gray as limestone, her eyes bloodshot and fierce, her lips pressed so tight against her face that you'd think her teeth would show through.

"We need to talk," she whispered to me the first moment we were alone in the kitchen. I must have looked surprised, which I was, for she took my arm roughly and steered me to a corner. I waited for her to speak while a long storm of silence passed between us. Whatever she had to tell she wasn't happy to impart.

"Gerald Lynch." The name was ground out, pushed through iron bars.

I nodded.

"He . . ." She drew a breath deep into herself, held it, then expelled it in a rush of air that carried words. "He gave you up."

My brain jerked in confusion. *For Lent?* was the first reply that sprang to mind but of course that was impossible. What was there of me that Gerry Lynch might do without for piety?

"Gave you up," Rose repeated, squeezing my arm where she gripped me.

It was as though she were speaking a foreign tongue.

Her impatience roared. "To the English."

So, she was still confused, still thought me important enough to betray. "You must be mistaken," I began, ready at last to announce my true station. "I'm only . . ."

She stopped my lips with the flat of her palm, not gently.

"What's this, what's this?" Sean O'Beirn walked to where we stood. "Has this lout said something he shouldn't, Rose?"

She shook her head, looked at him with some mistrust.

"It's all right," I told her. "Tell Sean what you've heard."

With some misgiving, Rose repeated her news.

"Where did you get such a thing, girl?" O'Beirn interrupted.

"He told me himself."

"Why would he confess? Why to you of all people?"

Rose looked away, set her jaw, let her muteness answer.

"But why *McGarry?*" Sean insisted, as if trying to find a reason to doubt her. *Why not me?* he left unspoken.

"I've told you what I know," she answered, irritated with what she took as his obtuseness. "What you do about it is in your hands."

There was a vibration about her like the side of a pot when the soup has reached a simmer. Her lips, normally so rosy and soft, were dry, seamed with cracks.

"You know the penalty for treason," Sean addressed her. "You know that the accuser must be present."

"I know."

"And you're prepared to do this? To confront Lynch with his crime and witness, if he's judged guilty, his punishment?"

Her trembling increased, strong enough to rattle the pot's lid.

"In my mother's name," Rose said, "I am."

A trap was laid. The next Saturday night in the pub Sean put away a good few more than his usual, seemed to relax his guard, bragged on me to all who would listen.

"Who would have thought our own Martin had it in him?" he said, slurring his words just enough and clapping me on the back. "Plain as turf, he is and that's his passkey. When he carries the plan to Tulsk on Wednesday not a soul will stop him, so unlikely a suspect. He'll fly unnoticed as the birds of the air."

Did Gerry's ears prick ever so slightly, or was it my imagination? I endeavored not to look at him directly but curiosity got the better of me, and when our eyes met, Lynch touched the peak of his cap in salute. It couldn't be, I told myself. Rose surely had got it wrong. And yet I stuck to the plan, recited the lines I had rehearsed.

"I'll be stopping in Kilnamanagh the evening prior," I announced. "Stopping over with my uncle at the old place. It's been too long since I tended the family plot and I'd better be about it before the grass takes over."

"You're a good lad," my father chimed in. "It's a lonely business, that graveyard. Full of ghosts. I'd clear it myself but there never seems to be the time. Give Eddie my greetings when you see him."

"And mine," said Sean. "But not a word to him or anyone beyond the walls of this room about the true nature of your mission, understand? Lives are at stake this time, Martin. Lives."

There was a nod all around, like a period put to the end of a sentence.

"I don't get home often enough." My dad, teary in his cups, was back to his earlier topic, the scheme eclipsed in his mind by a moon of guilt.

"You do your best," I consoled him. "Like the rest of us." But the whisper of other words washed within me.

"If Lynch is our Judas, he will have his Gethsemane," Sean had decided the night before when plotting with the boys who were sworn to watch over me. "If he shows his face on that windy hillside, it's as certain as a kiss."

For a thousand years, the story went, McGarrys had perched atop the farthest heights of Kilnamanagh, since the days when the monastery, the black church of the Ultonians in ruins before memory, tolled its bells for vespers. Once it must have been a proud spot, commanding as it did a wide and distant view of Kingsland. Pilgrims climbed here to deposit their prayers with the holy well of St. Patrick. Farmers gathered within the walls for safety. Generations of young men, young men who themselves would never father sons but rather recruited them through the Lord's intercession, fought their demons in this place, committed and confessed their sins of deed and more often of thought, toiled earth so barren and stony that no hope of abundance could be harbored, only a prayer for sufficiency, for enough to last till the next harvest.

The burial ground itself was a peaceful precinct, open to heaven and bound on all sides by crumbling stone. There, neighbors with the graves of priests long turned to dust, rested those McGarrys who had gone to their reward, arranged in death as they had lived in life, mother and father protecting those of their children who had died before reaching maturity, and, close by, those sons and daughters who had married and stayed in proximity. Compared to the grand design of the monastery, the lot of the McGarrys—and their neighboring families—was humble. You could chart the ebb and flow of hardship by the markers that shadowed the graves. In the bleakest of years there was little more than a stone, flattened by nature, thrust into the earth, its only artifice the faint scratches that once had formed a name or an epitaph carefully chosen for its aptness. Without the skills of a mason—who could afford such luxury when the crop failed or when sickness claimed too many in too short a span?—these words faded into meaninglessness with the thrash of a bad winter's storms. And while the bereaved vowed ever to recall those dearly departed, they did, of course, forget. The details of many lives merged into one, the exact placement of this Mary or that Seamus became confused and finally unknowable, the order of birth and death jumbled into a veil of sad impression whose sting, even when collected and totaled, was soon not sharp enough to draw forth a single tear in mourning.

Yet a duty fell to those midway on the soul's passage, in that short span when we dwelled between those planted in that ground and before our turn arrived to join them there for eternity. Who could begrudge it? It was little enough to ask for a man in his prime to keep the brambles at bay, to pry the blown grit from the shallow engravings, to remember, for an hour's sweat, if not the particular actors in life's drama at least the buzz of their modest assembly.

So absorbed was I in fulfilling this task once I had begun it that the night's subterfuge was all but pushed to the back of my awareness. I pulled at overgrown weeds, straightened tilted stones, whispered a *requiescat in pace* under my breath as I knelt at each probable tomb. The quiet that enveloped me was lush as the softest lamb's wool, the air weightless, the stars close and familiar. There's a feeling you get alone on a hilltop on a clear night—as though the music of a fine-tuned fiddle caresses and soothes your every thought—a feeling that you're above the reach of anything ugly or coarse, safe with the angels. The monks must have known this peace, I decided. It's what kept them here more than any churchly promise or stretch of faith. Beauty. No doubt such moments culled all mortal questions.

So concentrated was I in trying to translate this impression into words I could later repeat to myself that I didn't hear the footsteps of the two soldiers until they were upon me, and then it was too late to flee or even stand for my capture. They reached me still upon my knees, grabbed me under the arms and rousted me up.

"This is the one?" asked a voice stiff with England.

There was no answer.

"Speak."

"Yes."

It's odd how the sum of a man, all he has been and is and might be, can be fit into the cage of a single word. Gerry Lynch spoke from somewhere behind me. My eyes couldn't pick him out of the night's blackness, and so he filled it.

"Lay aside your weapons." Sean O'Beirn sounded more fatigued than angry. The man holding me tightened his grip and then, as the men who had been hiding behind the monastery's ruin passed the flame from one lantern to the next and it became clear that they surrounded us, he raised his arms.

"Please," he said as he was prodded off into the dark along with his partner. I could still feel the pressure of the man's fingers fading on my arms.

Somewhere to my right, a sudden running, a tumbling of pebbles, a thud as the stock of a shotgun met the back of a head.

"Come on." Sean O'Beirn set his hand gentle on my shoulder. "They'll be awaiting us at your uncle's."

The trial, if such closed an argument could be termed a trial, was blessed swift. The room was so crowded that smoke trailed from the hearth to pockets of breathed-out air that pressed at the ceiling. Gerry Lynch sat on a stool in the center of it all, shrunk in upon himself, a waterless fountain dwarfed in an overgrown arbor. Sean went through the motions, read the charge, asked for a plea—and you could see Gerry's eyes flicker toward excuse, almost hear the disclaiming words forming in his mind. But then, tucked in amongst us, he spied Rose Mannion. She stood, straight and grim, her accusation cocked, ready to shoot down any denial. Again, you could imagine the refute Gerry might fabricate—how this accusation was her revenge for his broken promise, how she not he should be examined for base motive. But before a sound escaped his lips he sighed and gave it up. To look at Rose was to know the truth without ever having heard it spoken. Her witness was unwilling, scraped out of her like a clam from its shell. Her pain was a living thing, embarrassing in its nakedness. Even if it were the only evidence—and of course it was not—it was sufficient.

In the end Gerry neither defended himself nor begged for clemency. He died there in that room, died though his lungs still breathed, his heart still beat. He died in the yieldless frost of Rose's stare. He died alone, or so he believed, long before the hangman's hood closed his eyes, before the rope's quick jerk, the final angry kick that dropped his left boot. It fell two feet. We heard its soft and empty knock upon the grass.

Only then did Rose cry out.

"My God, Gerry."

To my knowledge she never said his name aloud again. But put another way, she never from that moment bestilled its burnished clang.

*   *   *

The boys sunk Gerry's body in a bog as if it were no more than a sheep's carcass, then they piled gorse and holly above the spot. They passed the tale that he had set out to Australia on a sudden whim. Of the whereabouts of the two English soldiers I was told nothing—Sean said it was better that way because I was such a sad liar and there was no doubt that sooner or later all in the vicinity would be asked to account for their disappearance.

Rose took the whole affair quite terrible, strayed far from her right mind, in fact. It was she that insisted to chop Gerry down with a butcher knife, the same tool she had employed, face-to-face with him before he was led from the room, to snip a lock from the crown of his hair. I watched him watch while she tied it tight on both ends with white silk ribbons and tucked it within the fold of her blouse. She spared herself no part of what transpired, left unseen no sight, no sound unheard. Her face aged years in the span of hours. Her mouth in repose took on the shape of a spare and crooked string pulled from her right cheek toward the left edge of her chin, a grimace that distinguished her thereafter. The paleness of her brow was stark shale against the black soot of her mane, and her hands seemed to tighten in upon themselves, exposing every vein and bone in their intricate assemblage.

But her grave sorrow gave her the strength of ten, that piteous girl. Before dawn of the next day she fetched her father's ax and felled the ash bough from which Gerry had so briefly dangled. Hours later, she arranged for Paddy Murphy to divide its length into logs, deliver it to Elphin to be milled into the planks, turned into the curved staunch poles from which she commissioned Castor O'Connor to fashion the legs of a table. "A rush job," it was understood to be, "a priority," and it was finished without charge before the week was out. Then Rose sanded the planes herself, sanded them with such determined force that the stain of the blood from her knuckles deepened the gloss of the wood, brought out the pattern of the grain, polished the surface into a fine and glorious sheen.

No one put a question to her, of course. The very look that had blunted Gerry's protests was a shield—no, not a shield, for the purpose of a shield would have been to defend its bearer. Rather it was a shield turned bludgeon, a battering ram before which doors, sure to be burst through, meekly opened wide. Rose positioned its direction, followed in its wake, did what she needed done.

I, to my surprise, was her final task.

In the fortnight since Gerry's capture she had—quite naturally—kept her distance from the pub. Stumbling home late at night men reported that they saw light burning in the far recesses of her house, but she rarely was seen out and about. And then, one morning as I unbarred the door for the day, there Rose stood, dressed all in her black wool cloak and muslin bonnet, a weighty-looking satchel in her grip.

"I won't stay," she said. Then, "I choose not to go alone."

Was I the intended recipient of this news or was it merely that I was the first she encountered?

"Is it a trip you're taking?" I inquired. We had never, she and I, mentioned the events of that night and yet they stood between us sheer as the cliffs of Moher.

She made what some might call a laugh—more a kind of huff as you'd hear a pony exhale when urged against its will up a steep, unlikely path. "Trip," she repeated. "Trip. Yes, a 'trip.'" She unsheathed her glance, turned it on me full force. "I gave you your life," she stated. "Now I claim it."

"Are you saying . . . ?" I began, disbelieving the sense my brain made of her words.

"No, I'm not 'saying,'" Rose Mannion said. "I'm telling. You will go with me."

"To where?" I asked, thinking she meant at most Sligo. There and back would take the day but my dad would forgive the time.

"Away from this place," she said. "As far as the price of my house and all its contents will take me."

I looked beyond her and saw a small laden cart in the track.

"You can't be serious."

Her eyes were bullet holes in the target of her face.

"It would not be right," I argued. Here I was, still holding a twig broom, still in my feet, still half-dressed in my vest and hearing that my life was changed by Rose Mannion's will.

"We'll stop for the vows at the church in Strokestown. The priest there is one of us and has agreed to waive the bans."

"It's impossible," I said, and propped the broom against the wall to free my hands. I reached out for her, thinking to console an ache that had spilled into madness.

"They know," she said. "The English. They found the soldiers. They know it was you that done them."

"But I didn't," I assured her. "I never knew a thing about it. Why would they think it was me?"

"Because I told it them." Rose Mannion's voice was flat as the water of a well.

If there was one hope I had cherished for my life it was that I never be forced to live a day in any place but the county of Roscommon. True, many were blind to its beauties, many yearned to depart for the likes of Dublin or England or to put the ocean itself between them and the twisting lanes of home. But this was an ambition I never shared, never comprehended. For me, the views of my Western county were all I needed to see—the sounds of wind across the land, of rain on thatch, swans nesting in the flooded fields—of a saucy fiddle in a pub warmed by a turf fire on a late Saturday night were all I yearned to hear. There was no end to what a man could know about his surroundings when they were, in fact, his. No two meetings, even between the oldest of friends, the closest of cousins, the staunchest of rivals, were quite the same—each one branching oddly into the next, making way for the future revelations. The world was large—my books taught me that, as did the tales brought back by travelers from the Far Shore pleased with their adventures and all too willing to pass them along—but to one of its own, what Roscommon lacked in breadth it amply compensated in depth.

Somehow I always believed that safety lay in the choice for simplicity. To follow Horace, to value the Golden Mean rather than aspire to great wealth or power, seemed attainable, then maintainable. To accept with gratitude what grace was bestowed by birth was appropriate, proper, even laudable if not ambitious. And so, when I set my heart's desire on the path that stretched unbroken before me—a small life, anonymous by the world's measure, a balance of gain and retreat that rested neither too far in the margin of profit nor of loss was a conscious choice I made—though some would argue that I was merely accepting the inevitable without protest. I was satisfied with being satisfied, content with contentment, at peace with peace, and foresaw no obstacle to the smooth playing forth of that anticipation till, like all who had gone before me, I took my place in death beneath the very earth that had nurtured me in vitality.

I hadn't, however, counted on accidentally incurring an obligation to Rose Mannion. As an enactment of duty I traded that which I most realistically owned—a place to which I uncontestedly belonged—without hope of achieving that which, at least for a while, I dreamed I wanted more: a place of at least honor in her heart.

For the fact of the matter was, I was roused by Rose's demand that I accompany her, even as I was appalled by her means of achieving her coercion.

The leave-taking itself was a paltry affair. My weeping dad gave me his pocket watch and a fistful of coins. For the journey, Rose had sewn her hewn and polished table into a thick envelope of blue-and-white-checked quilts she stripped from her mother's bed. In her arms she lugged a wooden box housing a crystal salver—the one object she never set down, even in sleep—and the strapped case of clothes. I had little to carry but my father's watch, that parting extravagance, save the heaviness of my own sad sorrow. We neither of us possessed a photograph of family or town and so when we left, the only pictures available to us were those of dreams and memory. There was no question of ever returning—our names would soon be posted and our implication in the events of that hollow night would not likely be forgot in our lifetimes. We were banned from the very spot of earth I yearned to be, and so the pick of our ultimate destination mattered not at all to me. Wherever it was it would be, to me, not home.

Rose, of course, was as ever full of plans. She was never without a scheme, a set of blocks to move and arrange till they suited some distant purpose known only to herself. Some shirttail cousins who left Castlerea during the famine had written one letter back laced with a ten dollar bill from America and reported there was work to be had in a place called Kentucky, a place, they had added, green as Ireland herself with flat stones for fences and good land for sale cheap as rent.

Rose guarded this loose information—surely the stuff of bragging, of justifying desertion, of claiming to have arrived at a better version of the very place one had reluctantly quit—as if it were a map of buried treasure, revealed exclusively to herself. When people inquired were we were going, she lied convincingly. "Australia," she would sometimes reply. Or, "Boston." Then, "California."

"Why don't you tell the truth as you know it?" I asked her.

She gave me a look one might shed on a simpleton. "Do you want to be followed?" she retorted. "Do you want to be hunted down?"

But that wasn't her reason. She liked the mystery, the drama of having to disappear. Sometimes, in spite of all her loud weeping, her cries that her very soul was dying, I suspected she was more excited than anguished by the necessity and prospect of flight. More than once, she used the word "fugitive" to describe herself, and there was an undertow of relish in her tone, a glint, as if a hidden jewel had been betrayed by moonlight.

Who would suspect in those early years of youthful energy and expectation that I would end abed but decades later, stricken like so many others with the merciless influenza? Who would think as I ported Rose's precious table to Liverpool, guarded her trunk of clothes and momentos in steerage on the ship to Ellis, the ferry to Brooklyn, from there after a week's unwelcoming stay with her cousin Mary to the train depot, that my arms would waste with fever, my legs buckle as I tried to walk unaided across the creaking floor of my room to use the chamber pot? Who could predict that autumn of my twenty-third year when I first beheld the rolling green hills of western Kentucky, as close as kin in looks to the county of my birth, that its humid summers would prove to be the death of me?

Once cast into the river of my fate I was determined to go where it took me. If I was to be Rose Mannion's husband in this life, I would give her cause to be glad for the union. I was a worker when fueled by a goal, and to break Rose's grief, to raise the curtain she had draped around herself at the loss of Gerry Lynch, was the wood that burned to charcoal in the furnace of my heart.

We were poor as tenants in those first months, her pregnant with Andy, me desperate for any kind of work to be had, but Rose was undaunted, set her sights on a house on the highest rise in Thebes, a place called Bald Hill.

"In your dreams," I told her, believing at first she was but wistful.

"If you care for me at all," she commanded, holding out the hope that if I did as she asked she would embrace me in affection as surely as she consented each night in duty.

That was all the reason I needed. Hat in hand I knocked at the door of the landlord, struck a bargain of indenture with him: I would work like a slave for five years, do his every bidding dawn to dusk, in exchange for a down payment and mortgage on that weary frame house with a leaking roof and a slanting floor, a porch that ran like a belt full around, a porch on which Rose Mannion could set a rocker and survey her new domain.

The days passed one into the other, fitted tight as the planks of the parquet floor that was Rose's next project. He got full value of me, that Dutchman named Heinz, was sorry to see my sentence end.

"You're a Trojan, Martin," Heinz told me when he tore up the paper I had signed. "I hate to lose you. If it's wages that you're wanting, name the price."

"No, sir," I told him kindly, for he had not cheated me, just worked me like a plow horse. "It's my freedom I'm desiring."

"What will you do?" he asked. "To pay off the rest of the price?"

"The same as I've done in late evenings to furnish the place," I replied. "I'll pull my wagon through the alleys of Thebes, pick through the discards of one house to find the treasures of another. I'll be a cartman, the link between those who do not want something and those who do, and take my little percentage on every transaction."

"You're better than that," Heinz said half in his own self-interest in keeping me, half in seriousness.

"I'm no better than what I have to do," I told him. "A towhead son to feed and another bun in the oven. Besides, I like to be out and about, like to rummage in bins that never fail to yield a surprise. Once I found a lace tablecloth that needed but a night of the Missus's dexterity and a soak in bleach to repair. Once I came across a rectangle mirror framed in cherry, missing but half its crown of carved scroll. You never know before you look, like life itself."

Heinz clapped me on the shoulder. "Look in my trash from time to time," he advised me with a broad wink. "I know that house, know what your Rose might like."

"No charity," I warned him.

"Of course not. Anyone could take what I throw away. It might as well be you."

So intrigued was I by this suggestion that the next noon I stopped, cart empty, at the back of his fine house, and I couldn't believe my eyes. It was an upright piano I spied, its surface scarred but all the ivory keys intact. Surely this was not intended for me—but there was a note stuck protruding from the top: "Please haul away. The wife asked for a baby grand for her birthday and will not be denied."

With levers and wedges, I wrestled the instrument into the cart, careful not to injure it, and, hoisting the bars onto my shoulders, pulled it directly to the top of Bald Hill, barely able to contain myself in anticipation of Rose's reaction. I should have known better.

"What am I supposed to do with that monstrosity?" she demanded, coming out the front door and wiping her hands on her apron. She was large with child, appeared as big around as she was tall.

"The boy could learn to play," I said, out of breath equally with exertion and exasperation.

That gave her momentary pause. She had great plans for Andrew and perhaps—I saw the thought pass across her eyes—a talent for music lay hidden in his potential.

"Then buy him a new one." Nothing was too good for her or her son. "Not some castoff no one else wants."

"By the time I can afford the price of a new piano, his fingers will be too stiff to move." It was rare I lost my patience with her, dared to, but her disdain for this bonus was provocation.

Rose considered this reality, clenched her jaw at such further evidence of my failure as a provider. "All right, then, if you must," she finally allowed. "I reckon if I could turn a branch into a fine table"—ah, again that damnable table—"I can renew the stain on this machine. Don't scratch the moldings around the door as you bring it inside."

Machine, she called my gift. I was the machine. How I missed, in the span of that matrimonial transaction, all I had left behind in Ireland. My dad, the cool high watery air of Kilnamanagh, the laughter at the pub of a winter's evening.

Andy, hearing our voices, showed his face at the door. Rose refused to cut his hair and blond curls framed his sparkling eyes.

"What's that?" He pointed to the piano in my cart. "It's ugly. I hate it."

Rose threw me a knowing look, forcing me to drop my gaze. There was her stomach, my last hope for solace. "You," I said silently to the baby waiting to draw its first breath. "You, whoever you may be, will be mine—and not the child of a traitorous ghost. You will get my dad's watch."

CHAPTER THREE

ACT OF FAITH

———◆◆◆———

Rose

When Andrew left that morning in June, he called good-bye but as proof of mild annoyance I neglected to answer. His voice, barely changed in his forties from his boyhood tenor, hung loud in the air, mixing with the slam of the door. I hummed to myself above the noise, nodded my head, and remained at the table cleaning my ivory hairbrush. If I had looked up from my work, I might have watched Andrew bolt down the lane, through the gate, but instead, I was content to see him then as I have had to do thereafter, in clear imagination, as different from the rest of us as a bird to a school of fish. His small eyes are sharp sapphire jewels beneath a prominent brow, his shoulders knobby, his arms outgrown the shirt I stitched for him the year before he entered the seminary, his father's old tan shoes tightly laced. He was proud, straining to be ordinary, alert to parry every request out of my mouth, no matter how reasonable. Or I see him on the day of his first Mass, resplendent in the ornate vestments, his hair a halo, his eyes raised to the Sacred Host that he lifted for heaven's blessing. My tongue was the first to receive Holy Communion from his blessed fingers, a mother's right, and he laid the wafer upon me with the gentleness of a May breeze. I cast my eyes downward, was mortified to see dust on his shoes, and then shut them altogether, thanked the Lord Jesus for the grace of a priestly son, a son who would never leave me, never be distracted save by God Himself from his filial duties.

But that was long ago, before Andrew's loss of faith, before that Bridie confused his brain, before Robert made such to-do over his position with the railroad, before Andrew forsook his vows and chose to live as a common man. It could have been worse of course. Some that left did not return to their mother's house but went directly to the arms of a shameless woman. At least he had remained useful to me, if not my pride, in those weeks he moped around the house in his poor father's old clothes, caught somewhere between boy and man. In some ways it was like having him back as he once was, young and amiable, anxious out of guilt to please. But all things change, all things, and he grew restless, fidgety. Asked Robert too many questions, I see that now. Perked his ears at the sound of a distant train. It all comes clear in hindsight, but that day he left the house, that last day, I stopped myself from saying, "Tame your yellow mop into a part and button your coat." I didn't ask where he was going and when he would return—useless questions, I had recently discovered. In my own resentment, I spoke not at all—but prayed, as ever, that when he passed the church his senses would return, and so, then, would he.

From birth Andrew possessed a formality that required him to make announcements of his condition, of his pleasure or anguish, of his hunger or fatigue or good health. He reported on himself always, and as with the bulletins issued by mockingbirds beyond the windows, I eventually ceased to pay notice. He was like a clock that chimes the hour, and so I failed to hear in that morning's departure the slowing time. Failed to hear, and yet hear even now, hear ever since, unless I plan diversion.

From this vantage of a year I see what I should have known. Robert was not only brother but model, the years dividing him and Andrew a perpetual affront. For me, of course, the distance between the birth of my two sons, the first and the final of my children, seemed immense, a long closet filled with words. Conceived in my eighteenth year just before I left Ireland, Andrew was the last true hope I would cast into the world, the last advance before the long retreat I had witnessed so often in others and had prepared myself in Jesus to accept. He could never age in my eyes, never be other than a lad, impulsive and sweet. Robert, on the other hand, I bore as God's will.

I paid far too small attention to Andrew's interest in Robert's employment as a carpenter for the railroad. Certainly he had always evidenced a fascination for trains. For his seventh birthday I had made him a cap of striped ticking and a kerchief of red cotton, as if his ambition were nothing more than a costume fancy. I knew I had time to discourage his desire and at his Ordination my belief was confirmed. Those hiring agents must have been blind, must have observed him from behind, the outline of a man not adept in the world. They took his word that he had experience, they later claimed, they had no reason to doubt him, so tall and sure. They're sorry. They didn't know. They didn't think to look at his hands, smooth and unblemished as a fine lady's.

He must have gone directly to the station, must have set his watch to be there in time to board the eight o'clock. His menial job—after all his Latin and Greek, all his bookish education—was to shovel coal into an open fire. Bent double, his clean clothes surely black-smudged in minutes, his sleeves not yet rolled, he could not have seen out that high vacant window that allowed a square of breeze into the car. He was a hard worker when he wanted to be and on his first day would have pushed to prove his worth, to impress those average men whose ranks he yearned to join. Dauntless in his strength, he would have looked no further beyond the mechanical motion of his shovel than to search the red shifting heat of ashes for a hollow nest in which to fit another load.

I was changing sheets, stuffing a pillow into an embroidered case fresh from the line, when I heard a knock, one rap blunt as if a crow had flown blind into the side of the house. It came again, and I descended the stairs, smoothing loose strands against my scalp, searching in my apron pocket for a hairpin. It was unusual to have an afternoon caller, and so I was unprepared.

"Mrs. Martin McGarry?" A man in a black suit of clothes stood before me.

"I am."

"There's been a train accident." The lines in his face deepened, underscoring his message. His eyes were not without pity, but curious.

"Robert!" I reached behind to the banister for support.

The man shook his head. "It's the other one. The man who started just this morning. He never knew what hit him, it happened so fast."

I sat on the bottom step, watched his mouth.

"There was a cow on the tracks," he went on, as if this explained something. "Are you hearing me? A milk cow."

My mind in its denial flew anywhere and landed first in retort. *The train hit the cow, not the other way around,* I wanted to say. Yet this distinction was but temporary protection. I soon discovered anger as my shield, and then my sword.

"Do they pay you to dress up and bring bad news? Do they ask you when you return to that office that hired a priest how the mother took your message? Do they wonder if she cried before you, hid her hands in her skirts and covered her face? I shall give you no such satisfaction to report."

He shrank before my wrath, his nervous hands misshaping the brim of his hat.

"I don't know nothing about a preacher," he said, betraying himself as without education and not of the faith. "We've taken the liberty of having the remains removed to Koster's. The casket must be closed, of course."

"Of course." My voice was the haunt of itself.

"If there's anything I—or the company—can do . . ."

I stood in answer to his stupid sympathy, to his pale skin blotched from the drink he needed to fortify himself before facing me. I closed the door without another word and studied the inset panels, wooden windows stained a lighter brown than oak, and counted on my moving fingers the ones whom I must inform. With each name I removed from my coiled hair a silver clip and before I was done the famous braid hung below my waist, its weight pulling at the back of my neck, elevating the level of my vision.

I thought of shears. Let a cropped head speak for me. Let the smell of burning raven hair be incense for this empty house. There on the mantel sat my crystal salver, preserved without a nick all the way from Home. I wanted to hurl it into the stove. *The bitter past.*

After some time, the door opened and Robert appeared framed by afternoon sunlight and the green blur of front-yard trees stirred by wind. His throat was flushed with running, and his brown eyes were bright as creek stones. I waited while his breath slowed and did not help him find speech. I begrudged him the years he would live beyond Andrew's age. I begrudged him his choice of job, his rapid promotion—so irresistible a beacon. I begrudged him the ability to stand upright. I begrudged his wholeness, his worthless regret, his future, the pump of his healthy lungs.

"They've been here, then," he said, gathering this deduction from the sight of me. "I wanted to be the one, but I had no ride."

"It doesn't matter."

"It was a freak accident. A cow strayed from the field. It caught a hoof between the ties."

"Who told you?"

"The brakeman saw and threw the lever. The animal was never touched. The derailment was caused by the sudden stop, not by impact."

"Where is this cow? Who owns it?"

Robert shook his head as if to clear his thoughts, and pulled the end of his mustache with one hand.

"I think she was freed. She's gone home."

"And if this brakeman had done nothing? If he had driven into the cow? What then?"

"Her weight against the velocity of the train . . . it wouldn't have mattered much. A jolt to those on board."

I saw it clear, black and white as the picture shows in town each Friday evening. I watched the engine approach around a bend. The music of a piano rose. The cow pulled frantically, digging her hind legs into the gravel bed, twisting her horned head in effort. The whistle sounded, once, again, yet the turn of the wheels did not slacken. The cow's eyes rolled toward me, sapphire, sapphire, her thick lips moved to speak against the roar. All sight was lost in dust.

Andrew was always the kind who couldn't keep silent, who entrusted to me every passing thought, and that, I think, was the hardest part to bear. I missed his gossip, but worse, I could not drive from my mind the sureness that he was frustrated in his wish to confide his new experience. I listened hard, deep within myself, prepared to receive his Confession and absolve him. I made my mind a white sheet ready for his ink. I honed my inner hearing the way I've seen them tune a fiddle, running the notes through their extremes, eliminating till all that were left were the match to ideal memory, and then for an instant there would sound his voice, recognizable and distinct, forming words so much his own that my pulse signaled in reply. I'd catch fragments of sentences or the chorus of a summer church hymn, his voice pitched a familiar octave below my own, before it blurred.

"You'll never believe it," he began one morning just before the sun rose through my eastern window. And then he was gone.

"I saw . . ." he said another time, late, but the rest of the message was a shout from behind a high hill.

"Who?" I demanded back, piercing as a silent thought can be. "Who did you see there? My mother? Your papa?"

"Yes," I seemed to sense, with not a clue to which.

"Were they well? Are you peaceful in the Lord's embrace?"

I never spoke of these talks, not to my remaining son's duplicitous wife and my two baby granddaughters who came to make pies and clean cupboards, not to grim-faced neighbors who ate plates of food on the front porch, not even to Robert who was my cane throughout the wake. I desired no pamperings, no nods with eyebrows raised as though a mother's bereavement were the most familiar experience in the world. And in private I hesitated before summoning to my mind the image of Andrew's face, as if that click of perfect vision I insisted upon achieving before I surrendered to sleep were in an exhaustible supply. I feared to use up my ration of Andrew and so I parceled him as sparingly as fresh water on the boat from Ireland, once a day, and willed myself satisfied.

Yet I hated his loneliness worse than my own. He was nailed in pine, muted by packed earth, as dependent upon me for interpretation and words as he had been when, a helpless baby, I alone could read his thoughts. I knew to turn or change him, knew if he felt hot or chilled, knew the shape of his bad dreams and how to soothe his fears. From the instant of his delivery, I sensed his moods the way they say a severed hand feels pain.

So now, when I heard his muffled demand for justice, could I stop my ears?

There was but one enemy whose guilt was clear, and a single weapon at my disposal, but it was enough. I knew my course the moment the railroad president offered money.

"There will be expenses, I'm sure," he said to me even before the soft ground over Andrew had been hardened by the first night's dew. "We feel somehow responsible because we didn't check his story."

He gave me a white card that bore his name and address, and the name of the railroad, in raised script, and I slipped it into my glove, against my palm. I caught his fear on my tongue and made no reply that he could hear.

All that week I went to daily Mass and remained kneeling when others stood or sat. The monsignor who had replaced Andrew assumed that I prayed for my son and kept his eyes fixed on me during his right-handed blessings. He watched me as he raised the chalice, as he broke the consecrated wafer and summoned the Redeemer. On Sunday he spoke of the loss the Father felt for the Son's sacrifice, and asked the congregation to ponder Mary who never despaired that He would rise. He made no reference to Andrew's defection, but referred to him only as "Father Andrew," as if the weeks leading up to his death had never happened. Robert's fixy wife Bridie, at my side in the pew, touched my elbow at this deference lest I fail to be sufficiently thankful. I wore black tulle, my widow's mourning dress, and the skin of my arms gleamed beneath its shine. I draped net to conceal my eyes that never closed except in blinks, and feigned to listen, but easy comfort was not my object. I used those hours of quiet to sort choices, to foresee the years that remained me. If I were to conquer them, it would be through suffering.

The next week, still in my weeds, I walked to town, to the firm that drew my will, to Horace Wilton who had read my husband's own testament three years gone. Praise be that Martin did not live to crow this day. Horace's wall was hung with parchment diplomas, each framed in thin blond wood and protected by glass. He stood like a gentleman when I entered his rooms, ushered me to his desk, and waited on me before seating himself.

"Rose," he said. "It is God's tragedy, but a mercy that he went so quickly."

"I'm not here to talk of that," I replied.

"Well, then. If there's something else. How may we assist you?"

I opened my purse and extracted its solitary content.

"Ingersoll's card," Horace Wilton read and looked at me, confusion in his brow.

"Sue them," I said. "Ruin them."

He removed his rimless glasses, shook his head. "If there's a question of liability I'm sure we can reach a proper settlement. I know how badly those boys feel. I'm confident recompense can be arranged without resort to courts of law."

"It's not money I desire."

Horace seemed to see me for the first time that day, and pushed back his chair. "Have you considered carefully?" he asked in a deeper voice. "Have you discussed this move with Robert?"

"It is not his affair."

"But surely you realize that it will be Robert who bears the consequence. If you should embarrass the railroad it is his career in jeopardy."

I knew this, but I was not interested. Robert could protect himself, and at any rate, what kind of man would work in the employ of his elder brother's murderers?

"There are other jobs," I said.

"He's a married man with two daughters, your grandchildren. He can't just walk away. He's given them twenty years."

"A small number against a life."

"Robert is your son as well," Horace Wilton protested.

I asked myself, then answered aloud, the only mother's question that mattered. "I would do as much for him."

The day the writ was served Robert came to plead.

"I wouldn't ask for myself, Mama, but I will for Bridie and the girls."

I reached out my hand to him. His eyes were dull, full of the knowledge that his argument was useless. "There must be a balance to things. Were I to let Andrew go so peacefully as they wish, his life is forfeit, a thing not worth a weekly paycheck. Without a counterweight he is forgotten. Without my voice the cow becomes the story: 'The cow who caused a train wreck and, oh yes, I think a man was killed. *But the cow lived.*' A tale odd enough to be retold, and always the man will have no name."

Robert sat on my maroon plush couch, bent forward with elbows on his knees, his head low, but he listened.

"It must be different," I whispered. "The story will be instead that Andrew McGarry and his martyrdom brought down a railroad. You can't deny your brother that."

"I grieve him too, Mama. You're not alone in responsibility— or in your bereavement. But why add more sadness? This tale, that cow and our Andrew, will have escaped human memory in fifty years. Don't imagine our lives matter past their limit."

"Then what I do, I do for me," I said. "For me, if that's the only way you can understand. Tell that to your Bridie and let her complain. But ask how she would avenge her daughters, ask if there are boundaries. Ask *her* about Andrew's worth!"

Robert stood, turned brittle by my words, by my superior knowledge.

"I need ask her nothing about Andrew. There is nothing to tell."

I held my tongue, but I had lit a fire under Robert that was not ready to be quenched.

"Do you assume you are a mystery behind your veils?" he demanded in a hoarse voice. "You think only how you failed to keep Andy. But imagine your fury if he were merely injured. He lied to you. He deceived you. They say if the coals in the box had been piled less high that the train might have stopped more gently. It's true. It's accident that he's gone, but not that he left you. Andy was so in need to come back to this house a man and therefore to leave it—oh, I remember that need—that he stacked the coal to overflowing, stoked the furnace beyond its capacity. The engine was at racing speed, Mama, out of control. If there is blame, share it."

"Tell that to *her*," I shouted, poisoning his well. "If Andrew left me, where would that leave you?"

I turned from Robert, crossed the carpet on feet that trod so heavily they left impressions, and climbed the stairs. I turned the lock in my room and sat on the edge of the bed and didn't relax the muscles of my neck until I heard the front door open, then close with a final slam.

It is morning, the bread dough rising. As I sit on my porch working tangles from my braid a limping stranger pauses before my gate. He carries a red valise and leans on a polished wooden crosier for support.

"Hello," he waves. "I cannot help but notice your hair. I've seldom seen the like of it."

I never cease the sweep of my arm. I am heavy now, fill the seat of my rocker, yet I feel renewed in his vision.

In times past there was a steady stream of such men, ready to sell you potions or capture you in a photograph, tinkers and gypsies looking for a cool drink. This wanderer reminded me of another who knocked at our door the summer Andrew was ten. For a price he promised us immortality, our posed image recorded for all who came after. Long minutes in the heat we had to hold perfectly still, my husband and me sitting side by side, each bounded by a son. The insects were terrible, I remember, stinging and buzzing while we were frozen helpless.

"Your hair," the cripple repeats, and shifts his weight. "Where did you get it?"

"I take no credit for the Lord's blessing," I answer honestly, but I know what he means. Soon after the verdict of that juried trial, the new growth changed. Not to white, as you might expect in a woman of sixty-eight years, but to purest gold. More remarkable than that, whole tresses altered overnight, from root to end, and in this past twelve months the transformation was completed. Wherever I go I am pointed out, the subject of awe and conversation. There are those who ask for a lock, for luck, they say, but really it is for the oddness.

"It's amazing," the man marvels. He wants an invitation to sit, to share the shade of my roof, and contrives flattery. "Have you ever thought of going on the stage? In a carnival? It's that unusual. Angel hair crowning an old woman."

He intends his words as compliment, no doubt of that, but I stop my chair all the same. "There's work to be done," I say, and wait him out. In a moment he continues on his way and I go inside, pull the drapes. After this, in public I shall cover my head with a shawl.

But I will not be lonely. In my room, illuminated by the kerosene lamp that stands by the mirror next to the bolted front door, I comb the length of each strand with my spread hand, counting, weighing, and tell endlessly of the year's events: how it all happened as predicted. How I won a settlement of two thousand dollars and spent it every penny on a granite monument for your grave. It is a thing of beauty, a sight for all who visit. An armored angel stands guard above the carved words: "Not Gone." The railroad was dealt a blow and in return Robert lost his position. He and Bridie and my two young granddaughters soon left for Louisville. I hear he's sickly now, confined to bed.

In the cascade that spills over my shoulders, down my arms and over my breast I address and scold you in luxury—you whom no one else has recognized in its brazen shade.

The photograph is yellow too, spotted with dried water, bent at the edges, but not a night passes that I don't read its surface with my fingers. All that persists of my husband's head is a burst of light, a candle glow without flame. Behind him Robert stands as if obscured by a blowing gauze curtain. But due to some accident of paper the left side of the print is intact, clear as the day it was made. I am dark and you are fair, and we frown with identical expressions. Your hand on my shoulder is covered with my own. In the tumble of years you have returned again to that age of endless possibility, and so you will remain.

The house fills with sounds, with quick footsteps on the stairs, with babies' cries, with the share of grace before meals, and I talk into the early afternoon about little things, trifles hardly worth a mention. My voice carries strong to every corner, seals each window crack, awakens the fire. Sometimes we sing.

CHAPTER FOUR

BROKEN THINGS

———◆———

Robert

When I was dismissed from my employ at the railroad and my income abruptly failed, when I couldn't make the rent two months running, I duly received a notice of eviction.

Six weeks more of grace, I pleaded, and it was granted in recognition of my dependable record. Each morning I shaved and bathed, dressed in clothing Bridie had rewashed and steam-pressed the night before. I knocked on frosted glass doors, waited in anterooms, legibly wrote out my address and left it, should an opening occur. My unemployment should have been an easy hole to mend—the single pin missing from the cloak I had believed impermeable—yet the rend grew larger, the tear more jagged. At first there were no jobs the equal to the one I'd lost, nothing good enough for me, and then, no jobs at all.

Thanks to the blackball, my name alone disqualified me. No skill of mine was worth the offense my hire would provoke to a powerful man—for my ruin was the measure of his satisfaction, his revenge upon the insult of my mother's pride.

Finally, I resolved to quit Thebes, to take Bridie and girls and begin again in a city where my family lacked the curse of a history, where I would at least be no worse off than any other stranger.

There I would simply be the weight my muscles could lift, the span my arms could reach. I had come to the point where I would willingly trade ambition for survival, promotion for any occupation that paid wages. I was not yet old, after all, and able-bodied.

When I came to Bridie finally, laid this plan at her feet with no consolation, no prospect save flight, she withheld rebuke, turned her back.

Facing the wall, she asked how soon.

Five days remain on the extension, I pointlessly reminded her. Her calculations from the first put mine to shame. Like the long hand of a clock, they tracked moments.

She nodded her head and left the room. That night, I begged her forgiveness for my failure to prevent my mother's action, to survive it. She touched my brow, traced the worry line that ran east to west like the Ohio where it passed Thebes before turning south.

The decision was clear, but the mode of exodus gray. We were neither thieves in the night nor had we been invited to a promised land. Possessions were a nagging problem. When you don't know where you're going, you don't know what you'll need. Everything is guess, and a miscalculation either way is woefully expensive. Each piece of furniture was its own distinct decision: to take, to sell, to discard? We needed to travel light, for Bridie had the girls to manage, and so I would have to pack in my arms the sum of all we brought along. I made a ledger, then built a column of check marks. The obvious things were easy, the yes-and-no, much harder.

Today, after rising with no external destination on this, the last day of the allotted month, I pass through the stripped rooms of our house like a judge ordered to pronounce final sentence. There is a story to the acquisition of each object that remains us, a memory uniting plan and purchase. I can trace back a chair or a table to its maker, recall its mode of transport—more often than not strapped upon my own back—and follow the meandering route of its eventual placement within a given room.

I enjoy my possessions, not out of greed but rather because they stand for accomplishment, the X's on the calendar pages of my maturity. Property I take as solid, a bulwark against the wind of time. I buy and trade it the way, in a former age, a man might have crafted a tree by the skill of his own hands: with care and thought and increasing surety. I provided, and that persuaded me of my value.

But now, every capital crime past is apparent: an irreparable stain, a shattered dish no glue will long bind, a book already twice read. Weight matters, as does age and utility. Beauty alone is an insufficient criterion, and sentiment an unaffordable prize. Yet oddly it is the truly unjustifiable objects, those of no reasonable consideration beyond the desire or esteem of anyone but me, that are most painful to forsake. They cower in a corner of the attic, a pile of unkept resolutions. A sled with one runner, a bowl that leaked, a box of unpaired shoes.

I sit among them, my gaze lingering on one, then another. The afternoon light filters through the shuttered window and the air is close, flat, too long bereft of breeze. The floors below me are quiet, for Bridie has taken the girls to her mother's for a parting lunch of chicken and drop-batter biscuits. My name was not included in the note of invitation, the omission a badge proclaiming louder than any voiced accusation that my own mother was cause for the sad occasion.

At my right hand is Bridie's small blue ostrich skin suitcase, the pockmarked surface like an album photograph with brass wedges, its key long ago lost. I had proposed at the time to hire a locksmith—too costly, I was told. Well, then, we should break the lock, I had argued. It could always be closed by a rope—but Bridie had stood firm. We may yet find the key, she insisted, and then mourn the destruction. As always, she prevailed. For years the case remained in our closet, the pedestal for Bridie's Sunday shoes, but yesterday I had carried it up the stairs along with the other irreparably broken things, the other things it made no sense to keep.

All during the packing, I had watched for the missing key. The case was otherwise perfectly good, and dear, I knew, to Bridie. It had rested upon her knees as we rode the train to the 1904 World's Fair in St. Louis, our free passage a wedding gift from the railroad. The memory of those three days stirs a tenderness within my blood, a current such as sometimes moves deep into a dry well after a soaking storm.

It would be a crime not to try to salvage this, I think, and search the floor until I spot a thin bent nail. I imagine a brief shadow of sunlight flitting across Bridie's face if I succeed in producing an unexpected gain against so many losses. This move is more taxing for her, being younger than I, and sensitive. Even during good times my wife had about her such a fog of resignation, such a grim and general dissatisfaction, that it was said of me behind my back that I had married badly, married trouble.

In the spring of our union I blamed some failing in myself for her bouts of melancholia and enterprised to lure her into contentment. I spilled over with such a flood of forced good humor that occasionally, fatigued with resisting, she would feign to join in. I would waltz her, loose-limbed, around the kitchen, braying a lively old tune my mother claimed had been composed in her own honor, until my breath was exhausted.

Once, inspired, I tried to tease out Bridie's smiles by exaggerated imitations and pantomimes. "Who's this?" I demanded, then made as if brushing and preening my hair, pretending to gather it up between strokes and kiss its bundled tresses.

"Give me a hard one, why don't you?"

"This, then." I puffed out my stomach, patted the girth, rolled my eyes to heaven and sighed pitifully.

"It's Roy all over," she allowed, grinning in spite of herself, recognizing her pampered Lexington cousin, the one she boarded with before we were wed.

"Now who?" I folded my hands in prayer, closed my eyes, and hummed a few bars from the church hymnal. This was all, of course, long before the accident.

"You can't begin to capture Andrew," Bridie said. "Do yourself instead."

That stopped me. Where do you locate your own true key? Was I a too-thin man, arms and neck poking from a normal suit of clothes? Was I most myself awake or asleep, sitting or standing up, at rest or in motion? Finally, for lack of any better notion, I spread my arms to Bridie, opened my hands, presented myself for her inspection and approval.

She sniffed, was mildly amused. "To a T," she nodded. "To a T."

I expected children would lift her spirits, that motherhood would bring her fulfillment and pleasure, but Edna's birthing, my mother-in-law informed me in a fury, was long and arduous and unforgivable, and Marcella's arrival little improvement. After that labor, the doctor cautioned that Bridie could bear no other babies in safety, and so in a single sentence ended those merciful dark bursts of wrestled passion that my wife had previously suffered me, though refused later to acknowledge.

"Are you out to kill me?" she whispered, pushing me off the first night I turned toward her in longing. "Why not just strangle me and be done with it?" Marcella was nearly a year old and slept in the crib beside our bed. Bridie reached across and patted her firmly on the back as if to quiet her. Instead the baby woke, startled by the sudden jolt, and raised a cry. "See what you've done now?" Bridie accused, and lifted the girl to lie between us. "Shhh," she hushed, moving aside her gown and offering her breast. "Sleep now."

I had no choice but to accept the crash and swirl of Bridie's moods as an unalterable part of her nature. She despaired, she let me know in a hundred wordless ways, but she endured. I in turn settled for admiring her fortitude, though I didn't comprehend what private misfortune she used it to prevail against.

But now, I think, it's within my power to bring her some cheer, even on a day when she has every reason for bitterness. Above me, the attic beams climb in parallel rows, peaking in the center, the only channel where I can stand upright. Light lies in slats across the plank floor, and I place the case square in one of them while I tinker, tin in silver, seeking the hidden catch. After so much procrastination, the unlocking is surprisingly quick, not at all difficult. I hear a click, depress the button, and the latch snaps open. I raise the hood, half-listening for the creak of hinging long untested, but all is smooth, as if the case has been in daily use. The inside is stuffed with crumpled newspaper, arranged as a secure, unrattling nest around a central hollow in which reposes, secure and neat, a small stack of envelopes bound together by a white silk ribbon.

Careful not to disturb the packing—what instinct instructs my fingers?—I lift the contents, weigh them, notice that the top letter is addressed to Bridie in a strangely familiar hand, but at her sister's street number. The paper does not appear to be old. The envelope is slit neatly down the side and in my curiosity and confusion I shake out and unfold the page.

"My Darling," it reads. "I trust you remembered our promise not to unseal the flap of this letter until the miles have separated us. When you think of me from there, think of me yearning to be with you, then touch your tongue to the place my own has touched, kiss as if I were still kissing your own lips, and we will reach through distance, imperfectly but truly in our souls."

I nod, my brain frozen into confirmation of fact. The envelope was indeed still sealed. I read the paragraph again. "I trust," I read. "Us," I read. And, "still." The blue ink is smeared halfway through "imperfectly," blurred as though by water, rendering "imperfectly" imperfect. All this I see, as I begin to see. The script is writ in a seminarian's precise loops.

I release the paper into its stiff angles, slide it back into its narrow sheath, replace the whole in its hollow of crumpled newspaper, close the ostrich lid and secure the fastener. Only then, with the words quieted to a steady din, do I realize I have not turned the page, not sought to confirm the identity of the author, the one who offends God to call my Bridie "darling."

I twist the nail within the lock, embed the sharp point, then break the steel stem with the strength of my fingers. The case is closed beyond any natural reopening, and in benediction I speak but five short words: "She will love me again."

Memory is paradise denied. The garden was not the same lived as when recalled, and only when the gates forever close does the view between their bars achieve a true perspective.

Is it all illusion? I ask myself as I descend the stairs into the lower floors. Was the life that until this moment I took for granted ever real? Is the embrace into which I now yearn to retreat only a dream of my own devising, a state of grace too pure ever to have been or to be, a mere fantasy with which to torment myself because, with the validation of its absence, I can now conjecture it, appreciate it, wish for it, as I never could when I thought it normal? Is the curse of our Original Sin an easy banishment—the promise of return ours through salvation—or simply a vision, never attainable, of what might have been had we had the sense to grab it when offered the chance? Is it by nature unclear while its opportunity still avails?

Each question I hold for the duration of one oaken step, one solid thump of boot, no pause in my rhythm for an answer. I am not a man prone to profundity as some are, some who name this tendency "vocation" and elect the cloth as its protection. I am a man of nails and hammers, of levels and bubbles of spirit, of sawdust and bruises honestly earned. I leave my musings between the thin pages of my Milton and Tennyson, the reward of this final, drawling Sunday afternoon when at last I stretch out on the bare parlor floor after Bridie returns. She packs in the other room, pausing after each yanked drawer, each shifted crate. Edna and Marcella busy themselves with a forgotten box of paper dolls, discovered when a bed was moved, and I drift into the rhyme of couplets, extend my arms, soothe my brain that all truth can be confined to even meter.

There is no ceiling to the room. No roof. Only sky the color and brightness of a faded blue kitchen curtain spied at midnight from outside a sleepless house. I let my eyes play above the walls that enclose me until they light on a dot of pure white. I squint to focus. Stare harder. At last I can make out that it is, without question, a Dominican nun, her habit a moon reflecting the glare of an unseen sun. So sharp are her features, her beaked nose and jutting chin so starkly etched against the blankness, her opal eyes. A rosewood cross hangs about her neck, beads gird her waist, a smile hums upon her lips. She wears the expression of a woman sewing, a woman waiting for a pot to boil, a woman saying a mild Penance, confidant that every sin will be erased.

"How do you do it?" I call to her, cupping my hands to direct my voice.

"Faith," she replies in an ecstasy, though whispered, that falls upon me like a heavy drop of rain.

"Faith," I repeat . . . and then it comes to me that I know how, had once mastered the method.

Again, as before, I search in the clutter of my workbench and find a rectangle of glass not yet bound into a frame and hold it before my face. "I trust." My arms are spread wide, the pane its own horizon, as I peer through. The world I see is no different when filtered, all is as it had been, and yet, all is changed. I swing the glass above me, follow it steady with my gaze, until my field of vision is endless. There are no corners, no obstacles, no paths whose ends I cannot discern. I know I can fly if I believe I can, and I believe it, and I can, and I do.

I am up, faster than thought, speeding, accelerating into paler and paler space until I adjust the glass, bring it directly before me, and head west. I rush wherever I look, every compass point, and speed across a landscape of towns and forest, of shining rivers coiling amid plowed squares. These things I see obliquely for I sense, instinctively, that to look down is to invite the catastrophe of fear. Below me lies doubt, and even the suggestion of that stumbling question will cause me to fall, to tumble like Lucifer, so precipitously that I might forget to dismiss false anticipation, and, so, crash.

But I am strong. I know what I know. All choices are open to me: to hang and watch the world revolve; to race its roll or dive against its pull; to somersault or float among the trailing wisps of cloud.

I am a hawk just discovering the function of wings, a squirrel in an effortless leap between treetops, a comet losing no illumination in its streak among the stars. I am a note of music contained in sweetness, a pointing finger of lightning, a ship of cumulous puff sailing through a summer afternoon on a constant breeze.

Only one thing lacks me. To share this boundless joy, to record its marvel in the soul and heart of another. Briefly, I search for the nun, but she has disappeared off into her own necessities. My thoughts hone back to Bridie, my dear beloved. She must not miss this, must not, and I must be the one to show it to her.

I lower the glass, dare look down through the gathering clouds, and see below me, straight as a plumb line's path, my own house. Bridie scrapes carrots in the kitchen, her back bent into the chore, bowed, a stranger to surprise. Instantly I light beside her, so abruptly that she drops the paring knife by her chair.

"Stand behind me," I instruct. "Put your arms around my shoulders. Hold tight."

Amazingly, she does as bidden, asks no questions. She gasps as I raise the window glass and we shoot into morning.

"How?" she exhales against my ear.

I gently shake my head. I want her to breathe the day as I have breathed it and at the same time I worry that if I explain too much I may doubt myself and lose us both. But Bridie will not be denied.

"Is it the glass, some magic?" she demands. "A trick?"

"A miracle," I say. "That's it. A miracle."

"There are no miracles," she states, as sure in her absence of belief as I am in my hope of it, and we fall, a spiraling whirlpool cone through the clouds and the roof and the ceiling and the floor and drive into the hot earth like an iron spike.

I strained to come back to the world, to hear. Her mouth was moving and she was talking, but the words weren't the right ones. They were ordinary words, everyday words, delivered in a matter-of-fact tone, an efficient communication of useful information.

I watched her lips open and close, but it was as though I had become deaf to their sense. I looked at her eyes, and their glance was neutral, neither angry nor glad. Polite, her eyes were polite.

Somewhere, on some surface level, I must be understanding what she spoke, for I nodded at her pauses, raised my eyebrows in surprise or lowered them when appropriate to her text. But on another level I was shouting, keening, pleading all the while, for the eyes to change, for the words to suddenly resolve into the source of all the music, for her voice to say, and mean: "I'll never leave you. I crave your touch, only yours, your lips against my own."

She had in truth said all those things, perhaps not in the same conversation or even on the same day, but I recalled the words now as a composite, a litany I recited like a chant in my inner brain, as if the repetition would prompt their return, as if prodded by the concentration of my thought she would be urged to join in the melody, to reach out for me, to weep upon my breast and confess her confusion, proclaim the return of those defining truths.

"Will you be here for supper?" she asked, and my mind raced for a great purpose to her inquiry. A reconciliatory meal? A quiet dinner in which she would reach across the table, her hand dark against the pale linen of the cloth, to touch my face?

"I should think so," I heard myself reply. My voice carried no hint of my suspicion, not wanting to ruin her plan by its apprehension.

"There are leftovers from Friday in the icebox. I may be gone late."

Why? I kept myself from demanding. *Where are you off to? With whom?* But instead I simply sat up.

"I must carry the borrowed round table back to Mama's," I announced, daring to mention the source of our trial. "It was but a passing loan."

Bridie closed her eyes, opened them, speaking in that gesture all the chill she might yet sculpt in words, when she chose the time and circumstance to unleash it.

*   *   *

When, years earlier, I apprised that despite my most sincere efforts Bridie would never fully return my affections—that to do so would in fact compromise some essential and necessary part of herself—my first thought was to drink oblivion in such giant gulps that all pain would be forgot, until I too would forget and in forgetting be freed. It was as though each day she sanded a new layer of tenderness from my heart leaving the surface bare and raw, available to air. Contentment was an affront to Bridie, a denial of some mystery dear to her belief in herself. She fought it like an alien infection, like a heresy, like a seep of water that soils the basement wall. As its agent, its ally and second, I was enemy and criminal, the fire line of resistance. I represented all she feared to embrace and so she despised me, feared me, battled me on every front, resented her promise to cleave, was determined to prevail.

She succeeded. I accepted her assessment and loathed myself, mocked my modest offerings, ridiculed my weak resolve. I saw myself through her eyes, and was repelled, more even than she. She, after all, had at least the hope of escape. I was trapped into eternity, chained to myself, a perpetual and unwelcome companion.

Or so it seemed until our life-and-death struggle—her life, my death—arrived at its climax.

That night I did what I swore I would never again do, not after my father's desperate excess: I took to drink. Alone with the table, I set in its center the bottle we kept for the priest's visit, carefully positioning it to be equally distant from every point of the circumference while I debated with myself. If Bridie collected the girls, came home and found me drunk, there would be no going on with us. If Edna and Marcella saw me, as I had seen my own father, they wouldn't forget. I knew from experience that liquor made me sick, my body violently expelling with interest every drop I had consumed. Even Father Flaherty had railed temperance from the pulpit the Sunday past. His words came back, as if he had been speaking to me at this present moment: "Spirits solve nothing, only obscure duty."

Obscurity, however, was what I sought, what I required, what I yearned to achieve. To pull a hood across my mind, to darken those corners of insight brought irrevocably to light—that was my goal. I turned the bottle's cap, removed it to allow the aroma of sour mash to perfume the air. I had abstained since the night the jury's verdict had been read, and the smell brought back bleak despair. Light from the lamp penetrated the thick amber liquid, casting gold images on the wood's high sheen.

A drop, I told myself. A drop to still my nerves. More than that and my mother would eye me, superior in what she would not say, seeing me as my father as always, confirmed in her certainty.

I found a glass, tipped in a knuckle's worth, screwed back the top, replaced the bottle, arranged the glass to nestle within the warm glow. Altered its angle. Adjusted it. Lifted it.

Another drop and be done, I promised myself. One is but prelude, oil on the hinges.

This time I left the top open, ready. Tipped it again before the residue was gone. Just a spot more. And I felt it arrive, obscurity. No. Clarity. I must have more. It reveals an essence. I speak to myself. Aloud. What is so bad about wanting what a man wants? What distinguishes me from the normal course of events? Yes, I married a younger wife, deluded with her beauty. But now she's had two children, has matured. What right has she to persist in this high and mighty opinion of herself? Have we not finally become worthy of one another?

I poured again. The level now measured the label. No not quite. A bit more. Oh. Too much. I must now settle for the bottom of the paper, even, perfect. Clarity. I agree with myself. I nod. I know his name, that writer of sealed letters. I spell it, etch it, on my soul. I do not grieve his absence, do not regret. Faithless, damned. I deserve her and yet she died to me with him. Value me. See me. To hell with you all.

At a certain stage of drunk you crave music. You want to throw back your head and twirl with a partner beneath a ball that reflects light. You want to celebrate being in your life—to embrace it and dance, loving yourself and the woman you hold in your arms, and feel powerful and in step with the world and happy until your hangover. It's the moment in which you're in tune, each foot hitting the right base beat, all directions a circle. A smile carries you, carries you, to the place you live, the place you want to stay, the late-night haven where you are who you were supposed to be in your best dream, where you're above it and in it and full with it and can blend with whatever comes next, all rhythm and closed-eyes syncopation, and never die, never be old without being older, and the warbling voice is past and present and the ride into wherever that's good and you know it will turn out and you'll be sailing, sailing, sailing into the song you were meant to sing. And you don't want to wake up, to sober up, to remember—just to float with your head back, holding her, her holding you, around the floor and never come back, never land.

How to apologize, to make amends for our flaws—for our weak chins and nearsightedness, for our bad skin and crooked teeth, for not being all a woman could reasonably expect for herself, all she deserves, all that we wish we were or were not, had been or could be? All that she won't forgive. All that she sees with unblinking eyes while you smile a loose-lipped smile that she doesn't return, until you pass a mirror and see your hair lank on your forehead, your face white, your lips too red, your eyes flat and unfamiliar, and you wander out the door, you find a bush to hide behind, and you let it go, God you let it go, all of it, pure, emptying yourself until there's nothing left, except yourself, sorry, sad, shying from the memories, wincing at the words, guilty, alone, defenseless, worse than before, undone.

I hauled the table up Bald Hill, its curved side digging into my shoulder. My steps rambled, stumbled, traced a pattern random as a moth's flight. I surged and stopped, walked straight three serious paces, tripped back. I steadied my load, sighted with my left eye, set forth in a trot, slipped. Smashed my dad's watch. The table is all right, unbruised. The mud is nothing. Hoisted it. Set out for the light in the window.

She was waiting, of course.

"Drunk," she said, satisfied.

"A drop," I protested, "is all."

She inspected the table for nicks. Found one.

"I should never have loaned it," she said to herself. "Fine things go unappreciated."

Then to me: "I preserved this finish through steerage, through the toss of the sea, denied the begging of the infirm for a flat surface on which to stretch themselves."

I nodded, numb.

"It arrived with not a mar, not a gouge. Perfect as the day Castor O'Connor fit it together. Perfect as . . ." She paused, caught by her own thought.

"As what?"

"You'd never imagine. Look at this."

She presented me a tiny scratch, neat as if a thumbnail had been flicked perpendicular, bisecting the flat of the grain.

"It's always been there," I said in my own defense.

"Go on with you."

I studied the mark, which resembled a lowercase letter *c*. It could have occurred from the slip.

"It can be concealed," I said. "Wax."

"Wax." Her voice spat her estimation about the slipshod repairs effected by wax. "You would conceal deeper gouges than this with your refusals to see."

So she knew about Bridie, about Andy, without question.

"And look what it brings to you. Look at the loss we've suffered through your most grievous fault."

We beheld the scratch together. She had sucked the voice from me.

"It will remind me," my mother said at last. "Never again to trust you."

*   *   *

More than one in Thebes had observed that either by design or accident, I had gone and married my mother.

I, on the other hand, suspected that in Bridie I had done her one better. Rose McGarry was formidable, but she was set in her ways, absorbed in herself, a known and tested quantity. She was a mother, after all. When a boy grew into manhood he could by marriage or the clergy leave home—and Andrew's concession spared me the latter escape. When that occurred an unforgiving mother's presence changed from being a permanent condition to, on obliged visits, a season one could prepare for in advance and look forward to the conclusion of. A mother's grip was like winter, inevitable but predictable. You never knew how deep the snow would fall, how hard the wind would blow, how long the freeze would last, but you could depend upon and plan against the appearance of all three, sooner or later. As the cold weather—or a dinner at the house on Bald Hill—approached, a man knew to close shutters, to watch lest the fires go completely out, to don woolen clothing. And as the night drew on a faith could be permitted to arise. Six o'clock was darkest January, seven, February, and so forth, but by ten or so there was a clear promise of spring in the outside air. Jonquils stirred in their roots, ice began to melt in soggy patches, and the freedom of shirtsleeves beckoned just beyond the doorway.

With a bitter wife, however, there was no such respite, save work. If your beloved's eyes were full of expectation and surprise, anything was possible. If she possessed a summery soul, a man's life was one long gambol through green and grassy fields. Even if she were thoughtful and reserved, there was still the hearty comfort of color and the smoking fires of leaves.

But if she were Bridie, I learned from that day forward, a visit to my mother's could seem almost a welcome respite. In the wide swatch of my mother's dissatisfaction, I was but particle, whereas in the focused beam of my wife's displeasure, I was, I sometimes worried, the major obstacle.

There was no love lost between the two women who had mar-

ried into successive generations of McGarrys, that was clear from
the start. Early on, Rose McGarry recognized Bridie as a rival
abundant in those very qualities of will and determination in which
she herself took most pride. A demure daughter-in-law Rose could
have dominated, bullied, bent to her design. A daughter-in-law
whose claims to fame were traits Rose didn't value—babies or gar-
dening or home decoration—could be easily ignored or derided.
But a daughter-in-law who aspired to rule, who was accustomed to
and insistent upon being more envied and feared than cherished,
who took the subservience and catering of those who surrounded
her as simply proper due—this was a foe who must be opposed and
blocked at every juncture.

Perhaps, I parried thought when I witnessed them together,
each lost in fierce resentment of the other, Bridie's strength was
one of the qualities I most loved in her. I was not raised to be a
match for a woman—I conceded any battle before arms were
even drawn—but it was, at least at first, a heady flattery to be
fought over by two Olympians. If my mother was Catherine the
Great, my wife was Elizabeth the First. If my wife was a lioness,
she met a panther in Rose, and until our daughters were born I
dwelled in the delusion that I was in final default the sole prey for
which they vied, the excuse and subject of their struggle, the spoil
the survivor would utterly possess. True contestants in sport prefer the satisfaction of defeating another above the recognition of
victory. A trophy can be bought for a small sum in a store—it in
itself matters little except as proof. Cannibals in certain primitive
regions, I have heard, demonstrate their exploits by wearing on
their belts the shrunken heads of vanquished enemies. For my
mother and my wife, absent any other admittable prize, the only
parallel badge of value was me.

There was one precursor Tuesday dinner in particular in which
this observation first occurred to me. We sat, the three of us—
Andrew as always inconspicuously completed the square—at my
wife's table while Bridie stirred pots and slammed doors in the
kitchen. Grace had been said and we waited on the food.

Andrew's fingers were laced upon the chest of his black cassock, his praying hands collapsed into a priestly patience. My mother's face remained impassive, waiting for the opportunity to disap prove, while his eyes dashed from salt dish to water glass, from the fold of a napkin to search for the slightest rip in the lace of the tablecloth. Did they roam further? How did I miss their true direction? Fool that I was, I didn't look across the table but watched the door, fearful of the enemy unknown.

CHAPTER FIVE

THE VOW

— ◆ —

Bridie

I shall not forgive them, the sainted widowed mother and her vaunted holy son, him dead and rose again in her dark prayers. They stole from me what I didn't know I had to yield—the hope for a position in life, a connection between past and future that sat upon my head light and bold as a Sunday hat. The prospect of love.

I realized, of course, that a match with Robert carried risk. Junior to Andrew in age and ability, he would always be second in the world's esteem. Rose leaned on his steadiness the way she might sit on a flat stone for rest: oblivious and thankless. His drive to please was fueled by her refusal to derive pleasure, save from a mirror's reflection or from Andrew, the chosen scion. It took no seer to discern the preference. Gold over dross. The shining tiara. The blue eyes that could charm a saint back from paradise. Andy's gaze even once turned upon you forever left its stigma.

At twenty-two, my age at marriage, I was a child compared to the brothers. Andy was thirty-five, still a priest, and Robert nearly thirty. My waist could be cinched by the span of my father's hands. I took to wearing high-collared lace about my neck, a pearl ring, a cameo brooch passed down from my Dublin grandmother that boasted on its pink oval face a frieze of dancing graces. I was second born as well—a year behind faithful Kate—but unlike Robert, I was first to fly the nest. When the opportunity for a secretarial training course in Lexington arose, my valise was readied before I begged my papa's permission to go. I lodged with Kilkenny cousins—two sisters on their march toward spinsterhood, and their pampered brother, Roy—and came and went as I chose. One Sunday, I dared God by missing Mass, then withheld the mortal sin from Confession for a week's duration.

Though orphaned by the influenza, Mary and Bessie behaved as though they still lived under their parents' thumb: the Rosary each night after dinner, the house tidied before bed, the breakfast table laid out. They kept the place as though it were a museum preserved behind velvet ropes. "Mama and Papa's Room" was the chief exhibit: the never-to-be-worn-again clothes neatly pressed and hung, the bedspread smoothed, the knickknacks on the bureaus dusted, the lacy curtains muting the light that pushed through windowpanes scrubbed with vinegar and newspaper. There was a smell to the dwelling I noticed upon first entering, a clean staleness against which every exhaled breath was an intrusion. Cotton doilies dotted every conceivable surface and, true to the oppressive orderliness of the decor, each piece of heavy furniture, each cut-glass vase filled with silk flowers, each book, even, seemed as rooted to its assigned spot as if it had been glued there with flour paste. The three Kilkennys dwelled in their abode like obedient, old children who had just cleaned their rooms and awaited adult approval before disturbing the effect. Similarly, they addressed each other—and me as well, until I put a stop to the practice—as "dear," a habit that instantly grated on my nerves.

"Would you please pass the beaker of salt, Mary dear?"

"Of course, Bessie dear. Would you care for the pepper mill also?"

That was their route to a golden star in St. Peter's ledger. Their hands were immaculate, their clothing old-fashioned, well-kept and drab, their mousy hair pinned intricately in pointless designs that claimed what little imagination that they appeared to possess.

"It's only us here at the table," I exploded the third day. "No one is watching. If you want the salt, reach for it."

Instead of replying in kind, the girls hung their heads, stared into their prim laps, caught themselves but never quite broke the habit. From that day forward they were to each other "Bessie . . . d" and "Mary . . . d"—the latter a state neither of them ever managed to attain in life.

Roy, of course was used to being king of the roost. Fat and pink-faced, he need only look wistfully at an empty glass for it to be filled with iced tea, only sigh to himself to alert his sisters to some want or other that they hopped to satisfy. He tried that tactic early on with me, as we sat in the parlor after my welcoming dinner. A grandfather clock ticked solemnly and I found myself automatically counting the beats as one maddeningly pays attention to the drip of a drainpipe after a rainstorm. I would calcify in this place if I stayed too long.

One slice of coconut cake remained on the platter, and I saw Roy eye it. Bessie and Mary could barely contain their desire to scoop it onto his plate but, though I was quite satiated from the meal of roast and potatoes, I nipped his practiced scheme in the bud.

"I'll save the last piece of my cake"—there was no disputing in whose honor it had been baked—"for breakfast," I said sweetly. "Unless I would hurt the cook's feelings by not eating it now."

That got them coming and going. They were so busy assuring me that I was free to do as I wished that Roy's baleful stare went temporarily unnoticed. By the time he had sniffed and scooted back his chair, reclaiming his accustomed place as center of sisterly attention, it was too late. He took bets at the racetrack, I had earlier been told while he pursed his red lips in self-satisfaction. He had been sickly as a child and had a delicate constitution.

I looked at him that night, an overgrown baby stuffed into his blue suit, his nose marbleized with broken veins, his little tongue fairly poking toward a final sweet. Best to teach Roy his manners from the start. The cake had my name firmly writ on it, and I didn't offer to share a crumb.

After all the forced civility of my living situation, the secretarial college where I enrolled was an abiding whiff of freedom from family oversight. Students wore identical uniforms of starched white blouses and long navy skirts, and each of us pinned the watch we were required to possess above our left breast, the more efficient to consult. Otherwise we were permitted no jewelry—no rings or crosses or even my treasured brooch distinguished me from the others. With that vanity removed, I fell easily into the sorority of working girls. We were young careerists with limber fingers poised above keyboards, hands guiding our ink pens into the formation of uniform numerals—jaunty fives, crackling sevens, speculative, yawning nines.

Naturally I looked beyond the immediate, envisioned myself within a year's time presiding over an office of such diligent clerks and secretaries in Louisville or Chicago, strolling purposefully down the rows between their desks, stern yet indulgent of my favorites. I would insist upon absolute neatness, close attention to detail, punctuality and impeccable spelling. They would respect me, eventually grow to appreciate the standards I maintained, be loathe to leave my stewardship—but, well-trained, their services would be much in demand. I would hold no grudges if, after a suitable time, they departed for supervisory positions of their own.

Of course, first I had to master the basic skills myself, and so applied myself to the task. Bookkeeping came easily to me, it seemed. My accounts always balanced to the penny. Dictation, however, was another matter. I could barely conceal my contempt as Mr. Gruelich—an instructor imitating a future employer—droned on about "parties of the first part" and what had and had not yet "come to his attention." I studied him as he stood behind his desk, a long string bean, his eyeglasses ajar on his face, the right lens higher than the left. His hands were bloodless, deeply etched with pale lines, the fingers squared. The man had no literary style, and his diction was abominable. I took it upon myself to improve his language when I transcribed the letters, and for this helpful service I was castigated.

"I do not recall saying that I was 'devastated' by Perkins' failure to provide a receipt," the man chastised in clear hearing of my classmates. "And why is the word underscored?"

"For emphasis," I explained, but he was unpersuaded.

"It's not professional."

"But effective," I countered.

"Your job is to reproduce, not to embellish," he scolded. "You will not go far in the business world if you are headstrong."

I felt my cheeks flame. Headstrong! My letters would become legendary, if only he had the brains to foresee it. I averted my face, watched a mockingbird out the window until Mr. Gruelich moved on to the next girl in his piddling critique. Still, I remained shaken by the public reprimand when the school day ended. I turned down the street toward the Kilkennys' house, all the while mentally rehashing the incident, my retorts becoming ever more barbed. Years from now, when Mr. Gruelich was still repeating the same exercises, I would be long gone. If he was fortunate I might hire on a trial basis a top student or two from his school. The correspondence we would exchange on such occasions would be exemplary—original in its wording and punctuation.

Lexington in August was humid, the late sun a weight on the air. Overwatered flowers drooped on their stems as I walked down the lane, and every now and then the white sky momentarily brightened with a flash of heat lightning. It was during one of those periodic intensities that a familiar voice called my name.

"If it's not Bridie O'Gara in the flesh. Slow down and let a man catch up to you."

I looked and saw that it was no man, only Father Andrew McGarry from home. Yet away from Thebes he did seem a vivid presence in the dusky street. The McGarrys were neighbors of a sort, beneath us in class, immigrants from the West of Ireland. The father was a ragpicker and yet the mother put on airs because of her diocesan son. There was a younger brother, drab but presentable, who worked for the railroad. Like us they were parishioners at St. Brendan's, their pew close to the altar in deference to Father Andrew's pastoral duties.

"I'm in Lexington on the Church's business," he announced importantly.

"And what would that be, Father?" At that moment all men, even those of the cloth, were Gruelich to me.

He hesitated, cornered by the smallness of the truth. "I escorted Monsignor O'Brien to his mother's eightieth birthday celebration," he admitted with a disarming laugh. "He has been too unwell with gout to attempt the journey alone. Your mother asked that I look in on you, to tell her how you fare, so far from home."

I let him look. Bold girls in the parish school whispered about Father Andrew: his shock of yellow hair, his eyes the color of morning river spray, his hands so . . . spiritual as they held up the Eucharist for our contemplation after the Consecration. Not a few had scandalized themselves by imagining, in a private moment, his face superimposed upon a statue of some tall soldier or carpenter saint—or crowning the Sacred Heart Himself.

I realized I was as much looked at as being looked in on, and checked the collar of my blouse to make sure the top button was fastened. It wasn't. I left it that way and saw him notice my decision. He stepped back a pace, looked in on me even more intently. I continued to allow it.

"Your . . . family is well," he said at last. "They send you their greetings."

"I received a letter only yesterday," I replied. I didn't want to talk with him about my family.

"I'm here only today, tonight. After the festivities the monsignor must return directly to Thebes, so if you have anything to send along . . . ?"

Black suited him, I thought. It emphasized his natural assets. And how different it was to converse here on the street rather than in the dark of the Confessional or in the parade of worshippers leaving Mass. The altered setting called for topics of conversation other than sin and redemption.

"You'll be needing supper," I stated as if it were the most nat-

ural thing in the world. "My cousins will be pleased to provide it."
Of that I had no doubt. A priest was like royalty to Mary and
Bessie.

"It's too much trouble," Father Andrew . . . *Andrew,* I short-
ened him in the light of day . . . protested.

"No trouble to me," I said. "I board there myself, and there's
always extra." I imagined the look on Roy's face when he realized
there would be no second helpings tonight. His petulant self-pity
sweetened the prospect. "As I recall, the menu is pork chops."

"Pork chops," Andrew nodded, as if I had said something too
serious to be ignored.

"Red cabbage," I added. "Devil's food cake." *A dessert in need of
a priest,* I could have added if I dared.

He looked dazed at the sumptuousness of it all.

"A dessert in need of a priest."

His ears turned red, their blush offset by the brass of his hair.
"It seems fated, then," he conceded. "I couldn't leave you good
souls unprotected in the devil's company."

Such combustion. Mary, nervously peering as usual through the
parlor curtains in anticipation of my return, saw us first and was
unlatching the front door as I led Andrew up the stairs to the
porch.

"Is it Father McGarry you've brought home?" she asked
unnecessarily, all aflutter. I found it interesting that she recalled
his name, though her visits to Thebes had been few and far
between.

"I promised to feed him," I announced, and her eyes fairly
rolled up into her head at the excitement. She smoothed her dress
and did all but genuflect as she ushered him past her into the
dimness of the house.

"Bessie, come see who's come with Bridie," she called, her voice
pleased to be in the know.

Bessie looked out from the kitchen, blinked, then clapped her
hands together at the unexpected sight, causing a cloud of dredg-

ing flour to rise briefly in the air. "Saints preserve us," she prayed. "Won't our Roy be surprised?"

Won't he, though, I thought.

There was far more bustle than needed to lay an extra place at the table. Andrew stood back, his hands clasped together at his waist, beaming the way priests do toward their faithful house-keepers. I liked him better in the open air.

"There hasn't been a priest in this house since . . ." Mary began, then clamped off her sentence. *Since Papa's Extreme Unction,* all but screamed out of the silence. Andrew arranged his face into a sad, thoughtful expression.

"High time," I said to break the mood, and, no doubt of it, I caught a glint of relief from his eye. How tiring it must be, I realized, to be good all the time. How he must long to be himself.

"Come sit on the porch," I invited him. "Till the house cools off. Will you have something to drink?"

He hesitated, unsure what was permissible to request.

"A lemonade," I offered. "Or something stronger to take the edge off the day."

Oh, he was tempted. He wondered just what it was I had in mind. A lady's sherry or a gentleman's whiskey. The silence lengthened, so I reached into the lower shelf of the sideboard and produced Roy's bottle of "medicinal" bourbon. That brought a gasp of betrayal from Bessie, but before she could explain the existence of hard liquor in a Catholic house, Andrew tamped down a smile.

"Perhaps I shall indulge. The fatigue of the road, you know."

I reached for a glass and poured him the two fingers that my father always took. He didn't object, and I silenced the cousins with a look that rebuked any possible criticism of a man of the cloth. By the time Roy had dragged himself home, greeted us sourly, and allowed, by his presence, the food to be served, I had replenished Andrew's glass two more times, and he was feeling no pain.

The pork chops were picked to the bone, the red cabbage consumed, its juice sopped up with soda bread. The lemonade ran out and turned into water. The devil's food cake was rich and sticky. One thick, chocolate crumb rested on Andrew's starched clerical collar. It became him, like a beauty mark.

When we sat on the porch again later—the sisters busy in their tidying, Roy snoring on the couch—the day's heat steamed off the ground. I couldn't take my eyes from the crumb. It was the devil's flaw, that tiny imperfection that enhances beauty.

Andrew was feeling no pain thanks to the bourbon. He fairly lounged on the swing as I pushed it back and forth with one toe. Somehow, even in the dark, he shone.

"Do you ever get lonely, then?" I asked him—my boldness surprising both of us.

"I'm not allowed," he answered, admitting it.

"For a woman's company?"

He stilled the swing, turned to me. A quiet descended around us like a sheet flapped over a bed. His eyes were longing for me, seeing me, helpless.

"There is a crumb on your collar," I said, and leaned toward him until I was close enough to catch it with the tip of my tongue.

It would, of course, have been improper to dream acknowledgment beyond that special friendship that women—older than I, as a rule, to be sure—enjoyed with the clergy. Andrew, *Father* Andrew, was pledged to the Lord in body and soul. And yet I could not deny a certain . . . jealousy.

"You have so much—everything, the world," I prayed at Mass the next Sunday, appalling even myself—yet I held Eucharist firm and stiff on my tongue. "Why not yield this one prize to me?"

Beside me I sensed Mary nudge Bessie and knew, without raising my eyes to confirm it, that she drew attention to the flush on my cheeks. "A saint," I imagined them nodding to each other. "Transported in her devotion."

If they only knew.

After Andrew's visit—and the several that followed when he could finesse them—my interest in the business world ebbed.

Outwardly I presented the same determined and ambitious face but inwardly I began to see the drawbacks of a career. The likelihood of my being plucked from the gaggle of students, recognized for my promise if not my accomplishment—which still lagged behind other students in the performance of certain tedious skills—seemed to recede, to float away from my grasp the way the pleasure of an afternoon nap diminishes when supper must be set on the table. As I bent over my sums or transcriptions it struck me that there was another side to the bright coin I had tossed in the air. Either I would become the remarkable success I had so steadfastly imagined or—and there was no middle ground, it was either/or—I would in ten years find myself mired in a droning job, a woman forced to take pride in her appearance since no one else did, a woman who talked about her success with African violets, a woman standoffish, odd, furious. Alone with her secret memories.

I was not without my models in this forecast. The faculty of the secretarial college was composed largely of women who considered themselves experts superior to the ordinary run of office workers, and yet they were the very women I dreaded most to become. On the large scale their self-assurance was transparent to all but themselves, and on the small, each of them jostled the others for the post of queen, blind to the pettiness and parchedness of the land over which she believed herself to preside.

By and by, as I failed to distinguish myself in any eyes save my own, the thought occurred to me: if the pick of the litter is already spoken for, second best is the best there is. So when Christmas vacation sent me home to Thebes, I put myself in the path of the carpenter brother, of Robert McGarry.

Some would say that Andrew and Robert were more different than alike, dividing creation between them. One the sun, the other, earth. One the charm of summer leaves, the other the steadiness of a log. One impossible, the other . . . without challenge.

When I arrived dressed in my Lexington clothes, my watch pin the badge of the profession everyone instantly anointed me, my long brown hair gathered and puffed in a complicated twist, I was

the talk of the town. It was not necessary for me to embellish my
accomplishments—it was much more effective to respond to any
questions with humility, a lowered gaze, a dismissive shrug.
Nothing I could brag of myself equaled the envious imaginations
of those I had left behind. Their jealousies wrote whole novels of
my exciting and unmatchable life—I merely had to provide the
cover of the book, the display they couldn't bear to ignore.

Robert was taken more than most, his enthusiasm for the role I
portrayed magnified a thousandfold by his dawning awareness
that inexplicably I seemed to favor him above the younger, richer
boys available to me, boys more of my station. His eager devotion
was flattering, I'll grant him that, it set me off. But truly, if I be
honest, he was for me little more than an open doorway, a back
entrance into his brother's life.

When, after Christmas Mass Robert stumbled an invitation for
me to visit his family's house that afternoon for punch and carols,
I ascertained before accepting that of course Father Andrew
would be present. He, after all, was the pianist of the family, he
had the voice of an angel, he knew the words to every song yet
written, was dexterous enough to compensate for the broken
strings that his father had never had the wherewithal to have
properly restrung.

My first direct encounter with the mother, Rose, was a triumph—the awakening from which she never altogether recovered. She was famous in Thebes for her haughty rudeness, for the
airs she put on, the highfalutin vanities with which she cloaked
herself in spite of the fact that one and all knew the poverty of her
origins as well as the exactitude with which she counted her pen-
nies at the market. Still, it was a shock when she met me at the
door, her eyes shrewd and piercing, Spanishy in spite of her
rolling brogue.

"What is your business?" she demanded, blocking the foyer of
the small frame house on Bald Hill, her hands gripping either side
of the narrow jamb.

I presumed she referred to my recent professional training, and so replied, "Executive secretary."

Her avid expression didn't alter, but she brushed aside my career with a quick raise of her plump chin.

"Here?" she asked. "Your business here at my door?"

"I am invited." I could be as high and mighty as she. "I am your guest."

Somehow, without moving any part of herself, Rose solidified before me, fixed as a stone cross.

"Andrew?" she inquired, her voice sarcastic, her fury barely contained, as if she could see through me and had gleaned my secret.

I forced my face to register amazement at such an unthinkable suggestion. "Robert."

The wood of her frame softened, as if soaked in rain. I looked beyond her hunched shoulder, caught Robert's eye.

"Bridie," he called out. "Come in."

Rose and I confronted each other. Far across the parlor Andrew entered from what had to be the kitchen. He smiled at the sight of me.

I reached out my right hand as if to take Rose's in greeting, yet it was no neighborly cordiality that passed between us. The strength of my purpose in coming that day prevailed over hers in barring me, and so with the controlled, invisible power of a circus acrobat who makes even the most difficult maneuver seem effortless I wrenched her grasp away from its post and used it as a knob that I turned and pushed against. The hinges worked. She gave way, and I was through. For that victory, even at the moment I sensed there would be no forgiveness, but I didn't care. I was younger, and I was sure.

Andrew tied the knot, of course. Any other choice would have been suspect. And it suited me. It was to him I addressed my "I dos," to him I pledged the fidelity of my heart.

The mother stood in the first pew, gripping the rail, her eyes tearless and alert. She didn't know what she knew, but she knew she knew something. Robert, at my side, could not believe his good fortune, and looked at me in levels of disbelief as we inched closer and closer to Andrew's pronouncement. He was a dreamy sort to begin with and that day he was lost in the improbability of our union. I practically had to hold him up when he finally put his arms around me for the chaste, obligatory kiss. I met Andrew's eyes over his brother's shoulder. He knew whom I had truly married and he smiled, grim and sorry for himself. Robert was his stand-in. God's joke.

There were flowers festooning every wall of the church—but by my command, not a single rose.

For our wedding trip we took the train to St. Louis, Missouri. Robert, still dazed from the surprise of being my husband, was an uncomfortable passenger on a run he had often worked. The tickets were our bridal gift from the railroad—first-class all the way, the president had put it when he presented me with the envelope at the reception—but there was nothing relaxing or luxurious in watching Robert's gaze dart this way and that. Nothing, not the slightest arrangement of linen headrest, not the final tiny jerk of a gliding stop at the Cairo station, not the fit of the conductor's jacket, not the missed punctuality of our arrivals and departures from places in which we had no interest, not one detail satisfied his prissy standards.

He viewed me, of course, as the endlessly fascinated audience for his whispered critiques. His wife, I was now supposed to care what he thought.

"Look at the dust on that humidor," he accused, and looked at me for confirmation.

I brought my handkerchief to my mouth in mock horror. The sarcasm escaped him.

"Look! The porter stepped over that scrap of paper in the aisle. Just left it lying there."

"We must report him immediately."

Robert actually nodded. And him no more than a carpenter, a repairer of depots and ties.

I made an effort: "Dear, for today close your eyes to all of it. I'm afraid you're going to find something wrong with me next."

For a moment, I'm sure of it, he cast me an appraising glance. The gall! But then, seeing nothing to displease him he swallowed my small white hand in the jaws of his two hardened palms.

"Never worry about that, Bridie. To me, you are near perfection itself."

To *him!* *Near!* He implied that a husband's blindness overcame an objective eye, and even then there remained some minor flaw. I withdrew my hand, wiped it against the grain of the ostrich skin traveling case that rested on my lap, and stared out the window at the passing landscape. When he wouldn't stop poking at me to notice some new lapse in good service I finally shut my left eye— the one he could see—so that he'd believe me asleep. But my right eye remained open, staring into my bleak future, hypnotized by my yawning stupidity.

We stayed in the third-floor honeymoon suite at the railway hotel downtown. Drab and shabby it was, as if any polish that once adorned the furniture had been scuffed and worn away by heedless travelers. The sheets had a grayish tint to them, the pillows were permanently dented by the weight of too many sleeping heads. I opened a bureau drawer and discovered a Protestant Bible, which I opened at random for some divine opinion. Romans 6:16 confronted me. "Do you not know that if you yield yourselves to any one as obedient slaves, you are slaves of the one whom you obey, either of sin, which leads to death, or of obedience, which leads to righteousness."

I closed the book. I'd heard enough about obedience to last a lifetime. I did not escape my mother's law only to find myself subject to a husband's whim. I would obey myself, I decided. I would make my own commands and follow them.

Our windows faced out on the business district and the sounds that rose from the street awoke me. Impatient horns. Shouted instructions. The clatter of passing freights. As if summoned by a conjurer's spell, Andrew's face rose in my imagination. He looked bright and expectant as the day I had encountered him on the street in Lexington, full of unspoken promises he had no right to make.

I longed to explore the shops, to eat at the best restaurants, but Robert controlled the money and hated to part with a dime unless it was absolutely necessary. We received a special employees' discount at the hotel and so ate the plain, salty fare of its crowded dining room buffet: potatoes, beans, beets, pork roast. Country food, cooked the way my mother would make it.

Daily, we visited the grounds of the World's Fair. My Lexington-bought clothes, so elegant and distinctive in Thebes, were dowdy in comparison to the outfits worn by fine ladies at the exhibits, and yet I pretended not to notice. I clutched the bones of Robert's forearm with fingers pressed so hard that my nails turned white. I feigned an interest in the dances of China, the paintings of Germany, the oddities of India. My husband plodded beside me, nodded at whatever I pointed, engaged guides in earnest conversation, scrupulously collected handout literature for future study, all the while chewing unconsciously on the tips of his mustache. I thought I would lose my mind.

Whenever I had time to myself my thoughts flew to Andrew—wondering what he was doing, what delighted him today. What a different experience St. Louis would be if it were he at my side, him seeing the world's treasures, him making whispered jokes that only I could hear or understand.

"Too late," I inform Robert in my cruelty, my slaking calm after Marcella was born. "Once I loved you, but no more, never again." I had done my duty, more than that. I repeated the curse after Andrew's death, when there was no more point to pretense.

It's the "once" that hooks him to me, intricate and unyielding as the crochet stitch that binds squares secure across years of washing. If "once," he thinks, "then, perhaps, once again."

But the "once" is my lie. Oh, yes, once—when there was another within my reach—then Robert would do. But the shift in circumstance is not some fickleness of mine, subject to alteration as a warm day in March. The change is permanent. Andy is gone, and without the balance of his promise, Robert is a mere weight I drag, a reminder by his sheer size and bulk, by the space he intrudes in the small room of my life, of he who is absent.

My resistance, of course, is tinder to him, kindling an ardor he never previously possessed. We want most what is specifically denied us, and I withheld from my husband the single thing I owned and therefore the single thing he desired: my agreement to return his affection. He was so easy, too easy. I soon had him at that pitiable disadvantage—if one possessed pity—where the slightest curve of my lip ignited his hope, the most accidental brush of my hand against his arm unfolded behind his eyes scenes of approaching joy, of rapturous reversal, of a return to that fancy of matrimonial harmony which, he now forgot, we had never shared. So easy.

Did his torment give me pleasure? Did my misery find solace in the company of his own? Did his suffering endear him to me, make him even so close as a brother?

So he dreamed, and dreamed in vain. I despised his pliant love, spread it upon my breakfast toast and devoured it as he watched. In each episode between us, each encounter, I made careful to take slightly more than I gave. If I allowed him the use of my body, that night I wore my oldest, frayed flannel gown, declined to remove it completely, got up instantly afterward and made myself a tea. The next day . . . the next day I looked through him, diverted his hangdog eyes with talk of bills owed and the food staples we could not afford. Then, days later, when his despair threatened to tip over into enduring numbness, I would look up from my work, sweep the hair back from my brow, show my teeth in a smile, and whisper the talisman to show I remembered it all: "Tuesday." And he was mine once more, settling for less and less, the scope of his possibilities narrowed but still not closed. I allowed him his hollow belief. I dangled his wish. I taught my husband to beg, and I despised him for his weakness.

Andy would not have put up with such treatment, I told myself. Good luck to you, he would have said, and found another to love him. Sure'n, he needed no such excuse. From the time he wore long pants he attracted the glances of women the way a skittish colt lures riders burning to take the dare.

That last free night, my wedding's eve, when he passed the open door of the dining room, the candle flame brightening his eyes in the hallway gloom, I recognized my despair, then dismissed it before it could form into words. I would take what I could get. Did a storm possess its lightning? A river its current?

CHAPTER SIX

I AM A FATHER

◆

Robert

I awoke to a nurse's prod. The ceiling above me was white, the
carved wooden moldings coated with layers of brown paint. The
joist was poorly executed and cracks fell like spider webs against
the green walls.

The nurse unwrapped a tight bandage from my arm and wrote
upon a clipboard attached by a thin chain to the foot of my bed.
Her back to me, she pulled hard at some foundation garment
beneath her starched uniform and said, "Jesus, Mary, and Joseph."
A Catholic.

I cleared my throat so as not to startle her but she jumped all
the same, whirled with indignation on her face and a blush spread
on her neck.

"You're alert," she accused, angry at having been caught
unawares. Then, without another word she quit the room, left the
door ajar, her footsteps beating the floor like busy hammers. I
tried to raise myself on my elbows but was halted by weakness, by
a cough that pulled my stomach toward my chest, and I fell back.

In the hallway, a crowd approached at some speed. Their bustle
sucked the silence from my room the way an open drain invites
bathwater.

"I don't *know* how long." I recognized the nurse's voice. "Looking me up and down, and after all this time."

"Did you question him?" asked a man. "What did he say?"

Before she could reply they were all around me, four of them, staring, with uncertain smiles on their mouths, their glances straying from me to each other and back to me again.

"So. Methuselah awakens at last," said the man who had spoken before. He was portly, wore his white coat buttoned to the neck, and a stethoscope hung about his neck. Behind small spectacles his eyes were pale, watery, more curious than kind. "I am Doctor Henderson. But the question of the hour, sir, is who are you?"

They waited as if, but one square shy of a coverall, they expected the drop of a winning bingo number. I opened my mouth but no words issued from it, and when I concentrated, when I sought the information they required, I encountered only grayness. My memory was a bare room without furniture or decoration, and I was its prisoner and only occupant.

In panic I struggled once more to rise, but only resummoned the punishing cough. "Where am I?" I asked, when breath permitted.

"Where you've been for two weeks and three days," Henderson answered. "St. Anthony's Infirmary, Cincinnati, Ohio."

"Why?" I demanded. "What happened?"

"That's for you to tell us. You were discovered in a doorway not six blocks away, with no money, no identification save the clothes on your back, the bruises now healed, and a knot the size of a walnut on your forehead. No one in five adjacent counties has reported you missing."

Nothing. No face appeared to me, no picture within the frame.

"You may speak freely here," said another doctor—younger, made gentle by homeliness. He was tall and thin, all wrist and nose. He reminded me of someone, of something. The memory shimmered like a drop of oil on a rainslick street, its dark colors merging into each other. But as my concentration sharpened the spot turned opaque, liquid mercury that scattered then reabsorbed into itself, round as a platinum bead. And I knew, without benefit of any particular recollection, that I was a man who had been betrayed. More: that I had lived in silent knowledge of that betrayal, and that, like a minuscule dose of belladonna laced daily into ordinary food, the poison of that awareness had hollowed me out, left me as empty of feeling as I now was deprived of sense.

"Anything?" the gawky doctor prodded. "A name? A place? A next of kin? A date of birth?"

"What is it today?" I inquired in reply, as if trying to ascertain the length of my unconsciousness.

"September thirteenth," the man answered.

"My very birthday," I stated flatly.

He looked doubtful, but at least I was talking. "Very good," he said encouragingly. "What a coincidence. A place?"

I closed my eyes, watched for what appeared. A forest, sleek and white, draped with gray moss, run through with mirror streams.

"Are you from Cincinnati?" the old doctor asked.

The sky, where it showed through leaves and branches, was violet. I shook my head. "I am from far away," I told them. "I am a stranger here."

My physical ailments—my contusions and scrapes, my bandaged ribs and smashed fingertips—healed quickly enough under the professional care of those physicians. Like a baby just learning to be human, I was complimented on my appetite, on the movement of my bowels, on successes notable more for their contrast with the absence of other, more basic skills—I knew how to write if dictated to, knew that the capital of Illinois was Springfield, knew how to tie shoestrings—than for themselves. From time to time people would barge into my room, their faces tense with a wild conviction that drained out of them the instant they got a close look at me. I was not their missing James, not Bill, not Charlie announced a succession of dashed-hope women and indignant grown children. I was not, I was not.

And then one day, about a month gone into my stay, the door

opened and a woman filled the space. She stood still, studied me. She was squat, trussed in layers of clothing, her brown hair pinned back so tightly from her face that her features were sharpened into a grimace. Unlike all the others, there was no question in her eyes that crested into a wave of disappointment. If anything, the air in her went out, ripped by a foreboding turned into certainty.

"Robert," she said. Her voice was tight, joyless, a dam that held back a reservoir of anger.

"Madam," I acknowledged.

"You're saying you don't know me, then," she sneered. "That the name Bridie McGarry means nothing to you now?"

"I *don't* know you. Should I?"

She turned her face aside as from a possum crushed in the lane.

"Educate me," I beseeched her, both interested and dreadful about a past of mine in which such a woman had played a significant part.

The temptation to list my crimes appeared to be too much, and she drew a breath, long and narrow in preparation. Its exhalation would be a shelf sufficient to contain at least an index of my injuries to her. But before she could expel them, two girls pushed past her, paused briefly in delighted shock, and then threw themselves upon me where I lay. The younger, surely no more than twelve, could not stop repeating "Daddy" as she gathered the blanket into her white-knuckled fists and pushed her face into my neck as if to banish any distance between us. So compelling was her reaction, so demanding of attention and response—I stroked her curly hair and whispered "Shhhh"—that it was a moment before I noticed the older child. Tall and thin—I'd place her at fourteen—she held all interior what her sister—no question of that—proclaimed to the world. Her lips moved in some private conversation. In appearance, Marcella was clearly the woman's child, soft and round. Edna was more like me. Her brown eyes recorded my every feature while she waited her turn. She is used to deferring, I realized, but no less passionate. Something has taught her to hide, but she has not lost the ability to feel. I reached out the hand of my other arm and she took it, fiercely, and brought it to her cheek.

"I'm Edna," she whispered, staring at me unblinking, and then mouthed, voiceless but unmistakable, *"your favorite."*

Then I went with them, first in a taxicab to the railroad depot and then by train to Louisville. I sat between the children who were my daughters—what reason would they have to lie about such a thing?—and opposed to Bridie, the woman who had identified me as her husband. We rode in silence, the girls dozing in the relaxation of their quest, the woman lost in her own fury, me seeking through the window any familiar landmark.

I was Robert McGarry, they informed me. Carpenter by trade, once a layer of railroad track as far south as Alabama. I had disappeared suddenly a month ago and they had waited for some word, finally placing announcements in several newspapers and even hiring a detective—a retired policeman and distant cousin—to find me, living or dead. They had given up hope, regained it, given it up again. And then the call came that had brought them to Cincinnati.

We had been knocking on the door of being well-off. My work had been steady. I had built the house to which we were returning, though unless we found the money for its creditors it might soon belong to the bank. As soon as I recovered sufficiently from my ordeal I could resume my profession.

Did I remember, was their constant question of me. Did I remember the begonias below the porch? Did I remember the cake last Fourth of July (coconut), the color of my suit (blue), the number of our street address (10)? Did I know my age, the name of my dead brother, the Stations of the Cross?

And the odd thing was, I remembered everything save the personal. Facts, so long as they did not pertain to my own history, were unencumbered. It was as though I had subtracted myself from society and now, invisible and unaffecting, observed it through a peephole. If something had not happened to me, I knew of it. If I had supposedly been involved, it was obscured.

This selective incapacity was a source of frustration to the daughters and of outright disbelief to the mother. Whereas the former asked their questions in innocence, the latter put forward hers in sarcastic challenge. "Tell me you don't remember Beardsly," she dared, referring to a man to whom, according to her, I owed a large sum of money. "What were the last words I said to you before you . . ." She couldn't bring herself to finish. Before I what?

Ran away, was her implication.

Escaped, my guessed interpretation.

I was installed in an upstairs bedroom in the house I could not remember constructing. My carpenter's eye automatically sought out the seams of hinge-hung doors and the gloss of plaster, but though I admired the workmanship, I felt no echo of touch, no memory of problems well solved. Yet my body fit into the shallow hollow of the bedroom mattress, and in the faces that stared back at me from a tin-framed daguerreotype on the dresser I puzzled out elements to prefigure my own. Father Andrew, the brother they told me I had lost in tragedy.

"Papa," I said as I beheld another man's placid countenance. "Mama," as I lingered on the smiling woman who sat at the man's side. Only later did I realize how futile was my exercise.

"They are my parents, not yours," Bridie scoffed when I told her of the concordances I had discovered. "This is yours."

She rooted in a closet, pulled out a portrait held in a gray mat and tossed it on my lap. I held it before me, looked into the face of yet another stranger. She was handsome, generous in her features, defiant and proud in her expression. She wore dangling jet earrings, a cameo brooch, and her lips played a half-tease. If she could have spoken I was sure I would recognize the timbre of her voice. She was scheduled to visit me from Thebes when I was improved.

The wallpaper was cream colored, with vertical rows of ivy arranged in stripes, the bars of my cell. Light entered through a northern window, and a quilt of postage stamp blue and white checks was spread over muslin sheets. In the drawer of the table next to what I came to think of as my side of the bed—though Bridie deigned, to my relief, to sleep elsewhere—there was a jumble of items: small change, a harmonica, a pocketknife, a key tied round with a piece of string, an old watch, a small book of verse. Occasionally, in my solitude, I would finger these objects, one after the other, as if they might be the channel through which I could reenter the stream of my life. But they remained mute, foreign.

Marcella, as the younger child was called, read to me from books of her own choosing, romances and biographies of kings and queens. She would sit in the rocking chair, mesmerized by her characters' grand destinies, absorbed in their steady pace toward fame and fortune. As their ultimate fate revealed itself she would still the chair, stunned into immobility, pleased and encouraged in her own prospects. She confided that she never began a book before first browsing its final pages. If they were not happy and triumphant, she made another selection for, she explained, she was too tender-hearted for any sorrow that was not eventually relieved. My own condition, I knew, she regarded with similar optimism: my present circumstances were but prelude to a resumption of the life Marcella insisted upon and in which her solicitude would play a significant recuperative role. Already she basked in the anticipated congratulations that would rain upon her for her steadfast faith, her unflagging devotion, her resolute determination. She willed my recovery, believed in it with the fervor of a convert. It was necessary to her vision of herself, and therefore it must come to pass.

Edna seemed at first more stoic. Her care of me was offhand, casual, noncommittal. Get well or not as you will, was the attitude she affected. It's all the same to me. Marcella chided her sister unmercifully for this calmness, but Edna shrugged off the criticism. During her visits to my room she would read the job advertisements in the newspaper, circling those for which she deemed herself qualified. Without commotion or complaint she let me know that she would quit her education at the parish school and seek employment as soon as the right opening occurred. With me infirm, she was the obvious wage earner. Bridie bragged of high-level secretarial training but sighed that she could not in conscience leave an invalid in order to practice her trade. Now and then she took in washing and mending from sympathetic neighbors but clearly believed this occupation beneath her.

Sometimes Edna, professing exhaustion, lay upon the empty side of my bed and shut her eyes. I doubted that she actually slept, and was confirmed in my suspicions one late afternoon when I myself dozed off and then awoke quietly to find the girl kneeling by the headboard, her face pressed against the wood, her eyes squeezed shut, praying with a desperate intensity. Tears stood on her cheek, and her fingers were wound together in supplication so tightly that they had turned white, the blood cinched to a halt. "Take me, take me," she intoned. "Take me." I feigned slumber, peered through the slits of my closed eyes. I stood outside myself, imagined the feelings a father should have in hearing his child make such a selfless appeal on his behalf. If I were in my heart that father I would comfort her, say "No" a thousand times. But I was not, and wrapped in my own embarrassment, I kept silent. A short time later Edna resumed her position on the bed and lay like a board, her unwavering gaze fixed upon me.

As my recovery prolonged, it became apparent that the problems with my health stemmed from more than a knock on the head. The hacking cough once attributed—and thus dismissed—to a chill experienced during those days for which there was no accounting, was reevaluated when flecks of blood began to appear on the linen handkerchief with which I covered my mouth. Despite a diet of heavy, if tasteless, stews and soups, my weight continued to decline and my energy did not return. The doctor, when finally summoned to examine me, pronounced his diagnosis within moments: I had contracted consumption. I was being consumed.

If the woman had regarded me warily before, she now ministered me as though I were a wounded enemy soldier whose surrender had been grudgingly accepted. I was her duty, her burden, her cross. She ordered her daughters to stay away from me—in this I concurred out of fear of my own contagion—but whenever she was absent they ignored our warnings, breathed my air.

"I can't help it," Marcella excused and approved her weakness as she fluffed my pillow. "I have no control."

"If we're going to catch it we already have," Edna stated when I held my breath and turned my face from her morning kiss. "It's too late to worry."

My own response to the likelihood of my impending passing was detached. How could I regret departing an existence to which no memory or emotion bound me? At best I was a visitor who, I understood from the woman's coldness, had overstayed his welcome even before he had left the first time. Indeed, death struck me as the most convenient solution to the imposition my presence entailed. Unlike my unmoored life, my probable fatality was conventional, easily explained and accepted, normal. It provided a decent if abrupt ending to what would naturally become a story much repeated over the years by Marcella and Edna. Perhaps it would even constitute a sufficient balance of justice for the woman herself. My life for some reason was an affront to her, an insult. My death would be an appropriate apology.

This self-pity ceased absolutely, however, the first time, from the corner of my eye, I saw Edna duck her head, cover her mouth with the heel of her hand, and heave her chest four times in quick succession. In shock I realized: I had bequeathed her more than the color of my hair, the shape of her fingers, the wide set of her brown eyes.

Edna was aware of my notice and glared at me, half-angry to have been discovered. It was early evening and the smell of boiling cabbage penetrated from the kitchen.

"No," I said, stricken. Every rage at mortality absent in regard to my own condition surged back double strength when the terror magnified to this child.

Edna didn't insult me by denying the obvious.

"I'm headstrong," she said. "I shall survive it. You will, too."

I lacked the courage of her bluntness. "Yes," I agreed without conviction.

We looked at each other, locked in what we both believed was a lie, and suddenly it was as though she had become a spinning box, each side fronted by a mirror. In one she appeared as she was now, but in the others I saw her as an infant, as a child taking her first steps toward me, as a girl off to school with her lunch pail. I spiraled down the path of her life, the memories certain and sure, more real than the oak posts of my bed. Her childhood was a line from shore thrown out to a drowning man and I clung to it as the images shifted and played off each other, as she became all she had been, resolved in her fullness, growing more herself with each revolution, pulling me, swifter than my thoughts could calculate, into the current. It was dizzying, hypnotic. I seemed to catch glimmers not only of Edna as she had been but flashes of Edna as she would become— tall and austere, her young face lined old with regret.

I reached out my hands to her and she flew across the room, all the Ednas that ever were and ever might be, and fell hard against me, held me with arms whose strength was the match of my own, and we stayed that way as the light from the northern window dimmed and the cabbage smell grew strong, until the woman called my Edna's name, sharp and insistent, for a third time.

Did they follow, the parade of other memories? Not all at once, but more or less in drips and drabs in the hours and days that I lay staring at the ceiling as though it were the screen of a moving-picture house. The details of my life came back to me like a letter torn into shreds, unfinished sentences that had to be painstakingly fit together in order to garner sense. History materialized not as a full accounting but through iron chains unwinding off a pulley, sometimes fast as if dragged by a dropped anchor, sometimes laboriously, requiring the full muscle of my concentration to crank the wheel.

In certain cases, I experienced the emotion of events without a sufficiency of accompanying detail. I would look at a book, at a chair, and ache with a sorrow whose root I could not dig out. A bare space, invisible except through the eye of recollection, where something important had once reposed. In others, I could recite the facts of a past happening, but they were devoid of feeling. Bridie's hostility is an example. Her coldness, past or present, justified or manufactured, did not now touch me. I observed her glare as one watches falling snow through a thick windowpane while sitting dry in a warm room. I could reconstruct her winter's advent, chart the brief spring and summer of our marriage, its long fall. I could remember mornings when frost seemed to cover the bed we shared, gray days when her eyes were as lifeless as blossoms drooped by a night's chill. I knew that I had been caught, and often, in the wake of her gales and squalls, that I had been buffeted and lost in the swirl of her tempest, but since my reappearance I was safe from the impact of those moments, whether because I had so succumbed that I rested in blissful numbness or because I had of necessity enveloped myself in an impermeable coat, I could not say.

My aloofness to Bridie's moods at first provoked and then ultimately infuriated her. I could tell that she was used to my acceptance of her convictions, and I wondered if some major shortcoming or unpardonable crime had slipped my awareness, for nothing I could name seemed commensurate with her contempt.

"What did I do," I asked her early on, "to so stoke you? Was I unfaithful?"

Her body compressed, crowded by a docket of accumulated resentment.

"If only it were something so . . . easy," she replied at last. One strand of her hair had escaped her pins and floated light as a cobweb beside her head. Its lilt defined the carved stone of her set jaw. "It's not what you did or didn't do. It's not who you are—or were. It's who you aren't. Who you never could be."

The wisp caught her eye and she trapped it between her right forefinger and thumb, stuck it roughly into the warp that stretched her temples toward her crown.

"To think," she said. "I nailed myself to you of my own free will. You promised me paradise on earth." Her gaze surveyed the mortgaged room, came back to me. "Liar."

After that exchange she left me alone more than she had, but when after several days I showed no injury from those long self-conscious absences, she startled me by the needless slam of doors and drawers. She sold, without permission or apology, my carpenter's tools and used the money to buy a quilt from a country woman who knocked on the door, pawning off her possessions for whatever a stranger would pay. When I feigned no interest in her further recriminations against me—her endless list of my inadequacies great and small—she altered her audience, chanted the litanies to the girls in my presence. "If he won't remember for himself," she prefaced these bitter summations, "then you remember it *of* him."

Marcella covered her ears to these accusations, though not tightly. Edna heard them out, her eyes bold and unstraying from her mother's face, refusing to give the acknowledging nod Bridie's every pause demanded. It was not so much that Edna didn't believe the truth of my failures, but that she didn't care. My flaws only increased her instinct for protection. There was nothing she couldn't forgive so long as I loved her.

And I loved her.

In attempting to assess the degree of my own culpabilities, I picked at that curious hole in time which eclipsed the circumstances of my recent absence. Had I been beaten and robbed, my brain addled by a blow to the head? But what could I have owned worth stealing? What injury could I have committed to provoke such an attack? Or was the explanation more complicated?

Had I become aware of my illness and decided to disappear rather than be a burden on those responsible for me—or out of concern for the spread of infection? Had the pressure of my creditors become too heavy? Had I fallen in love? Had I decided to take my own life? Had I run away from something or toward it?

I had apparently left no note of farewell, nor taken with me anything save the change in my pocket—evidence which seemed to rule out premeditation. On the other hand, perhaps that was my intent all along, to make my vanishment inexplicable and thereby spare the girls guilt or false responsibility. Was I an innocent victim or a scoundrel, cowardly or courageous, guileless or conniving?

Such questions, when not canceled by matching answers, left me even more mysterious to myself when my memory partially returned than I had been without it. I knew almost everything about myself and yet did not comprehend myself at all. I was the summary resumé of a man, the perfectly cast shadow, the accumulation of some seventeen thousand days. The only part of me missing was me.

Did I announce this literal recovery, apprise my wife and daughters of my growing restoration? Never—for no sooner had I reconstructed the broad contour of my past than I became like a blind man who has regained some sight but finds it more compatible to remain unseeing. Did Edna realize that by her instigation memories had floated back to me? I didn't raise the question, nor did she. Perhaps she knew. I think so. I can't be sure.

As for the rest, they had their suspicions but, with one exception they had no proof. Try as she might to trap me into some inadvertent admission, Bridie could confirm nothing. I surmised that secretly Marcella preferred that I remain an enigma, for that oddity stood her apart from classmates and caused the nuns to regard her with unusual indulgence. The creditors were naturally dubious of any mental ailment that delayed their repayments, but they were ashamed to hound a man so undeniably ill. The doctor was preoccupied with my more immediate deterioration. The priest assured me that all would be clear in paradise.

Besides Edna, only my mother saw through me.

When she finally arrived in Louisville for a last look, as she put it, Rose Mannion McGarry was already well into her seventies. Stocky, she moved like a minor hill shifting with the slope of the earth's crust—inexorable, fueled by gravity as much as by intention. Her skin, however, was fresh as a girl's, fragrant and pink. Her eyes looked round the corners of what she saw. Her fingers constantly worried a rosary, a tic, I soon realized, rather than a devotion. And, of course, her hair: an eerie blond, the envy of Marcella, preened and braided into a heavy rope that capped her small but emphatic head.

She stood in the doorway of my room and blocked out everything beyond it—and thus it was a copper-topped silhouette and not a woman who confronted me. She did not bother to announce her name or her relationship to me as others, out of politeness, accorded. It was beyond my mother's conception that she could be forgotten.

"You do look like death," she stated, appraising me. "I'll be the last, then. The last to go."

Among those who once had mattered to her, she meant—her husband and two sons, her parents. The famously regretted lost love of her youth. The rest of the world was irrelevant.

Her self-centeredness suddenly galled me. "Not if you hurry," I replied. Oh, she came back to me all right. I remembered her too well, her allegiance to the past, her careless cruelty.

She started at my words, seemed to ponder them.

"The TB has improved you," she observed at last. "At least you don't whine."

"What does it matter what I do?"

"It doesn't." And yet, clearly, it did. I could tell that to her surprise my mother found me worthy of her interest.

"*She* sent for me. She said it might be a matter of days."

The "she" was the woman, my wife, Bridie, and I thrilled at the dismissal in my mother's voice. We were allies on this point, at least.

"Was it the brevity of time that moved you to come after all these years? What if *she* had said 'weeks'?"

My mother flexed her lips, conveying that she found my candor suitable. She was content not to have to pry the admission of my returned memory from me. Yet she caught herself, unwilling to give too much away.

"I could not be there for Andrew," she sniffed and produced from her black sleeve a dinner napkin which she used as a handkerchief to dab at the corners of her shrewd and measuring eyes.

"No," I agreed. "He eluded you."

Her fingers tightened around the cloth and her mouth hardened, but then, in spite of herself, she nodded. "So," she said. "You're not just McGarry's child after all. You're mine as well."

"We cannot choose our parents."

She settled herself onto the rocker, stuffed the napkin back up her sleeve. "You go too far."

"I have not even begun."

She looked around the room as if searching for some interruption. This was not the conversation she had anticipated or prepared for. She fended off my thrusts but, unusual for her, lacked a plan of attack, and this worried her.

"So," I continued, pressing my temporary advantage. "Have you come to beg forgiveness?"

My mother recoiled as if slapped, so great was her astonishment at my words.

"Forgiveness? Forgiveness for what?"

I braced myself with my elbows into a half-sitting position. Where to begin? I was speechless and the immensity of my anger so overwhelmed me that I slumped back onto my pillows.

"Forgiveness," I said, "for being who you are."

"Ah," she decided, confidant again. "It's the fever been talking all along. I should have guessed. I'm sorry," she drew out the word in a sarcastic sneer. "I'm so *sorry* for being myself."

There was no arguing with her. *"Teum absolvo,"* I intoned, the priest who heard her Confession in my own Extreme Unction. "You are forgiven."

Who would have imagined that so immense a body could

move so quickly? She was out of the chair and leaning over me before my words had dissipated into the walls.

"What right have you to judge me?" she demanded. "Sickly, puny. What did Andrew see in you worth imitating, worth his vocation? 'A man,' he called you. 'A man among men,' as if a priest, a man of God, were any less. He was a man *above* other men and he gave it up to be like . . ." She steadied herself with a hand against the bedpost. There was spittle on her lips and a deep flush spread down her neck. "Forgive *me?* You . . ."

"I'll never forgive you." Edna stood in the doorway, her hands balled into rocks that weighted her arms. "Leave him be."

My mother made a movement like a person sinking into a pothole. Her version of a curtsy.

"Oh, I'm begging your pardon, Missy," she mewled in her thickest brogue. "It's overstepping my bounds, I am, for sure, with your precious father."

"Look at him," Edna said, ignoring my mother's tone. "Look what you've done to him. He's lost all his color."

They both turned to stare at me and, paralyzed by fatigue, I had no choice but to allow it. A silence descended on the room, airless and dry. I could not breathe, gasped for oxygen, and when it came in a rush it activated that familiar tickle, that feather lodged deep in my throat that must be expelled. The cough rose, lava in a volcano, rose and rose until it lifted the cap of my clamped lips and found release. My eyes never closed, so I saw it all, watched as the faces of my mother and my daughter turned suddenly twin in their expressions of fear and ashamed disgust, watched as a flaming tongue of blood erupted from my mouth and sprayed upon the white sheet like a pan of butcher slops scattered on the snow for crows.

My mother insisted on taking me back to Thebes where, she maintained, the country air was better for my lungs. The journey on the train would be a trial, but I did not protest once I saw the distress this plan imposed on Bridie. It was not that she wanted me near, not that she mourned the loss of a portion of my remaining days, but rather that she worried what the neighbor women might say behind her back. When she stated this concern to me, accused more like it, I simply returned her look. We both knew that they could not say bad enough.

Marcella, whom I still hoped to save from the curse of my illness, chose to regard my exile as good news, an opportunity for her to occasionally visit, to be a city girl come to pay pitiful respects to her invalid father, a girl to be admired for the piety she could not help but inspire. But perhaps I do her an injustice. Perhaps she was merely an optimist, as she insisted, a person who saw the bright side of any event no matter how dark. Perhaps she concurred in the theory that the visit would be restorative for me.

Edna's reaction was swift and unambiguous.

"I'm coming, too, then," she stated immediately.

"You're needed here," Bridie countered. "With him infirm, it's time you went to work."

"I'll get a job in Thebes, send you my paycheck," Edna promised, but to no avail.

"You're the strong one," her mother said. "With no man in the house, we need you for lifting."

Edna looked to me for help but I could only reflect her helpless gaze. If I was not able to protect myself, how could I protect her? And so it was decided. The one woman got me, for a time, and the other got the girls. The divided spoils of a long war.

In Thebes my mother installed me on the porch, wrapped me in frayed quilts, fed me from the pot of stew she replenished daily. She had faith, she said, in sunlight, in vegetables, in the benefits of well water. This was her excuse. In fact, I was on display, a rebuff to those who had whispered accusations against her when she had caused me to lose my employment with the railroad.

"Robert is home at last," she announced to any passerby. "They asked me to come for him in his ailment and, against my own doctor's advice, I collected him back where he belongs."

The implication was that I had left out of some private folly, that I had deserted her but that she had graciously retrieved me—could an indulgent mother do less? Going or coming I was trouble to her, though she didn't complain, save for those casts of her eyes heavenward, those discreet, forced coughs that meant nothing, she insisted, and if they did, well, her health was a natural sacrifice, another in a progression that began with my birth.

We sustained the animosity but not the candor of our first encounter, she and I. I lacked the energy to constantly spar with her and once she realized this she lost all inclination.

In Thebes, I faced my mortality, walked the site of my grave, saw good-bye in the eyes of every visitor as the ties of almost fifty years frazzled and frayed. Further and further into my isolation— that state which always I had most feared—I discovered the peace of a rich man stripped of his wealth and yet still, surprisingly, himself. With the ultimate question answered beyond doubt, I lost my curiosity about details and instantly gained that advantage of distance which had previously eluded me.

As I lingered, sitting month after month at my mother's table sipping her bitter tea and pretending to listen to her never-ending loop of gossip, I traveled back where not closed off to me into the byways of my life, viewing events in the soft light of their origins rather than the glare of their hoped-for conclusions. It was easier to forgive the naiveté of early intention than the cold calculation that often explained success.

My mother complained of encroaching deafness, but privately I wondered. Whether by nature or convenient excuse, this infirmity allowed her to fully acknowledge only those announcements she made to herself. The comments of others—our questions, our opinions, our expressed ideas—for the most part did not penetrate her shield of self-fascination. And yet, some tidbits she obviously did hear for they turned up in the string of news she broadcast to the world, a chronicle as regular in its repetitions as the radio's hourly report on a day in which no events of significance transpired. To say that my mother talked to herself is to undertell the experience of her reluctant external audience: me, and anyone who happened by the porch to pay respects. She beat us down with her words, used them like pounding fists. Though superficially they were concerned with matters of mundane notice, they were charged with her malice and spite. Our ears were the only doorways my mother could still enter under her own power.

"They *say*," she would preamble, always twisting the "say" to emphasize her own suspicions of veracity, her own unresponsibility for what she was about to impart, and then launch forth her tirade.

"The new priest, Feeny, is nothing to our Andy. He mumbles through the Consecration. His sermons are a ledger of facts and figures. My cousin Catherine swears for a fact that she saw him take a dollar bill from the collection plate and put it in the pocket of his cassock. Of course, as I says to her, there's no telling what he might be needing it for. Reimbursement, don't you know, for something he paid from his own meager dole. Far be it from me to talk ill of the clergy. It's just that when you have a gold standard to measure against, all else is brass. And speaking of Catherine, her girl Deirdre is down sick, or so they *say*. At least she hasn't been seen around town of late. Though Joe Malloy swears it was Deirdre he saw in that fancy house in Evansville on Saturday last. I told him it couldn't be, not to repeat such a libel, but I can't control his tongue. I remember when he was just a boy. He bit the head off a sparrow. He claims he didn't, but he did. You have to watch him I told Margaret, his mother what died of drink, God rest her soul."

And on and on until we came again back to Father Feeny and began anew. The stories slid off me like oil drops, so familiar did they become, but it amused me to watch the panic in the eyes of unwary guests when they realized they were trapped in her net. She never even paused for breath, disguising her necessary inhalations with the cover of punctuating gasps. The faces of her listen-

ers soon began to sag, to grow dull with the onslaught. Their eye-
lids would flicker toward sleep until a training for politeness
jolted them open. People looked in vain for any scrap of paper to
read, and the inside of more than one cheek was bitten to main-
tain a posture of alertness.

It eventually became apparent to me that my mother took no
detailed notice of her retinue's behavior. All were obliged to nod
occasionally, to spend at least a decent interval in her presence
before backing off the porch, to bring her small tokens of jelly or
relish from their pantries. But to the conversation they were
required to make no contribution whatever.

There was one late Thursday when Bridie, huffing with exertion, paid a call.

"I have no time," she preambled. "It's a long trip and yet I do
my duty."

"How kind," my mother cooed, false and impatient as the Lady
of the Lake over Arthur.

"Just to see how he is," my wife spoke above my head.

"St. Ann bless you," my mother acknowledged. "And the
girls?"

"As well as can be expected, given the circumstances." A knife
to my heart. "I wish I had the means to bring them, but Edna is
already working a full shift."

My Edna. My own.

"You're good to take him," Bridie said.

"What else could I do? You have your own life. Besides, your
turn to do me a favor may arrive, to even the score."

Bridie, who could be as deaf as my mother when necessary,
ignored this threat. "Not that I don't think of him. Not that we
don't miss him. But the danger."

"He's home where he belongs."

Was I to have a voice? I waited for a question. It did not come.
I was like the Irish table, a thing between them, a thing each one
was determined to possess by outlasting the other.

"Do you have money?" my mother asked, offering none.

"I make do. Life keeps no promises."

"Because, if you have extra, his care is expensive. The doctor bills alone . . ."

"We scrape by. The bill collectors hound us."

Let me sink into the porch boards. Let my ears be stopped. Let Bridie be satisfied in her turning knife.

"You always were strong," Bridie conceded.

"Strong, yes, but not cruel. Never cruel."

They knew. Both of them.

"Judge not lest ye be judged," my wife warned.

"I judge myself," my mother replied. "More harshly than you could imagine."

They let the words settle like falling leaves between them. Neither would agree.

"Tell the girls I love them," I interposed, and four eyes turned to me.

"They know that already," my mother said.

"Get well and tell them yourself," my wife admonished. And then she left forever.

My spirit returned on the day my wife's cousin Roy from Lexington came to call and I was feeling especially alone. Halfway through my mother's familiar recital, I could stand it no longer and risked mayhem. Raising a napkin to my lips and making as though to wipe away some crumb, I spoke to Roy in a perfectly normal tone of voice.

"As long as you cover your mouth we can talk freely. She can't hear thunder."

His glance darted to me, to my mother, to me again, back to her. There had been no break in her string of words, not the slightest hesitation.

Roy, who was a large, elderly man, a butcher who fried up the fat he trimmed off pork and ate it by the pound, acted as though he was coughing, curved his fingers into a cylinder and brought his hand above his chin.

"Are you certain."

"I'll prove it." Up came the napkin. Looking directly into my mother's eyes and shaking my head slightly at the atrocity she was loathe to be revealing, I said, quite plainly, "God damn."

Roy started, but when my profanity produced no reaction in my mother, he began to giggle, his meaty shoulders quivering, his stomach rising and falling in abrupt bounces.

"Hell," I said. "Shit. Bastard."

Now Roy coughed in fact. His face had reddened alarmingly. "Stop," he begged me from behind his hamfist. "No more."

"There was a fine lady of France," I said. "Who lost at the market her pants."

Roy pushed back his chair, stunning my mother into ashen silence, and then fury.

"Sit down, Roy Kilkenny," she commanded. "You haven't even had lemonade yet."

And so he sat, miserable in his repressed hilarity, while my mother proceeded with her inventory of the local population and I with my profanity. What surprised me, long after Roy had been reduced to wheezes, to high, off-center trills and muted shrieks, was that I could last as long as she.

CHAPTER SEVEN

VOCATION

Edna

Years ago, before Papa got sick, I had visited the Ursuline convent in Samaria, Kentucky, on a seventh-grade outing from St. Cecilia's. We rode a bus south through the lush countryside, the road bordered by fishing ponds and tobacco fields. As we slowed down for the small Baptist towns along the way we were instructed by the proctors to duck our heads lest our brains be penetrated by some Protestant heresy floating on the dogwood-heavy air. I sat next to Madeline Evans, and while I counted the miles, each one a step away from the familiar and toward something that at least I hadn't seen before, she mumbled the Rosary incessantly, as if to prepare herself for the state of grace our destination required—there was to be a special afternoon distribution of Communion as the climax of our stay. In anticipation, we were told not to partake of the Sacrament at that morning's Mass, but I had forgotten and now could not receive the Host a second time.

It was all perfectly as it should have been, the waiting, and yet I felt a sense of fallenness as I watched others file up the aisle, kneel at the altar rail, and return with eyes lowered and lips tightly closed. I imagined that some of those elect stared at me, wondered if I had broken my fast, or what mortal sin I had committed and not yet confessed. I let myself wonder along with them: murdering my mother? Bearing false witness against her before the matrons of Our Lady's Auxiliary?

While we waited by the bus for the tour of the convent to begin, I watched, transfixed, as two lovely novices not much older than I knelt side by side—stiff-bristle brushes in their hands, a soapy bucket set between them, billowing sleeves rolled to the elbows—and scrubbed without visible effect a long flight of stone stairs. As they worked, uncomplaining, their lips moved in silent prayer, and within the space of my observation their task was completed. It was a warm day, so the water instantly evaporated. And then, from within the building, a door opened. A heavyset, older nun appeared with a pan of garbage from the kitchen and without apology threw the contents on the spotless steps.

I turned in horror to my teacher, Sister Sybilina. What was this about, my look demanded, and she seemed to understand.

"To teach humility," she stated. "To counter pride."

I didn't speak, but indulged in a silent contemplation. If someone had done that to me, I thought, I would scoop up the mess and toss it back in her face. Even as that triumphal scene played out in my daydreams, I realized that this meek order was not for me. I'd had enough tests of humility, enough domineering queens. I was ready for action, excitement, human contact. Let steps be washed by a downpour of rain. I preferred to be the one who dirtied them with the unconscious scuff of her shoes. I would be the one in charge.

Of course those thoughts came to an abrupt halt once Papa disappeared, and was found, and I had to leave school for paying work. My family could not afford the luxury of a vow of poverty.

The summer of 1930, the seventh year after Papa died, I was nineteen and Marcella was two years younger. That was the worst of the Depression, and I had almost lost my good job as a receptionist for the Lincoln Life Insurance company nine months before on the day the banks failed. Mr. Pitou, the office manager, had personally given me my salary check the previous Friday afternoon, the same as he did every other week, and on my Monday lunch hour I rushed over to Citizen's Fidelity Savings to cash it. Mama always waited for the money to balance out her accounts at the grocer's. When I got to the bank, however, the door was locked. I rattled the handle a few times, then noticed a well-dressed man sitting on the curb, cracking his knuckles one after the other.

"What's going on?" I asked him. "Is today a holiday or something?"

He looked up at me with eyes that made me tired just to see them. "Where have you been?" he demanded. "Mammoth Cave?"

"Don't get fresh," I said. I didn't like his tone of voice. "I just want to go to the bank and get back to work."

"You're out of luck, then. The stock market sank. They ran out of money."

"Don't be silly. I don't own any stocks. What do I care?" I knocked on the glass doors, squinted my eyes to peer through. Papers littered the floor and a chair had been left turned over. I had been in the file room all morning trying to sort through a bunch of policies sent up from the Nashville office and hadn't spoken to a soul.

"You don't believe me, turn on the radio," the man said. He shook his head, lost interest in me.

"Hold on." I reached out to touch his shoulder, then drew back my hand. I got a feeling like the one that tells me a migraine is on the way and can't be stopped. "How do I cash my check?"

"You don't. I told you, there isn't any more money."

I was carrying a shoulder bag that day, and as I turned it knocked against my hip. I walked slowly back to the office and paid no attention to the conversations that were raging from one desk to the other. They fell around me like rain showers as I marched directly to the glass window of Mr. Pitou's private office, turned the knob and walked in. He was sitting in his green leather chair, facing away from his desk and toward the wall.

"Excuse me," I said. When he didn't answer, I said it again, louder.

He rotated his chair. He had much the same look as the man on the curb—worn out, shell-shocked the way some of the boys had come home from the war. "Yes?"

"I didn't cash my check on Friday," I told him in as ordinary a voice as I could find. "Now there's some problem with the bank. My mama's counting on my salary, so this once I'd rather get paid directly. I unsnapped my bag, fished out the pale blue check for sixteen dollars, and held it out to him across the broad wooden expanse of his desk.

"You are . . . ?" he asked, trying to place me.

"Edna McGarry. I've worked here three years," I added unnecessarily.

"You're the sickly little girl whose father was taken."

The check arched stiff between my fingers, like half a drawbridge.

"It's sixteen dollars," I said. "Even."

"But surely you're aware . . ." Mr. Pitou began, then he closed his eyes, opened them. "I don't suppose you follow the market?"

The headache was building from my neck, flooding into my brain like the sea over a dike.

"It's madness," Mr. Pitou went on. "The whole country's gone crazy and you're telling me to give you sixteen bucks?"

"Not give," I corrected him. "I earned it. I need it."

He paid me out of his own pocket, counting the bills, snapping them between his fingers to make sure no two were stuck together.

Mr. Pitou let me keep my job, though some weeks he could only afford a portion of my salary.

"You're so thin," he said more than once. "And that head cold. You've got to get it seen to."

He had no children of his own and he wanted to be my father, but I wouldn't play along. Papa had been father enough and now I had taken his place as provider. I kept Mama afloat, kept Marcella in

school. I was grateful for Mr. Pitou's kindness but would take no
more than was due me, and as with that first day, I took that in cash.

It all changed, of course, with the flood two years later, the
rains that washed the Ohio beyond its banks and into the streets,
that closed the city, kept me from work, sent a chill through my
body that carried forth the seeds of illness that for years I had
guarded and hidden from view with every ounce of my will. It
was a shock to learn that Marcella had done the same. The waters
eventually subsided but our coughing did not. We went to the
public clinic together.

I remember how the doctor looked at me when he read the
results of my tests: as if I were already a corpse.

"You're young," he said, his words contradicting the expression
of stoic acceptance in his eyes.

"And it helps that you found it early on," I added to encourage
him.

"Well," he said. "Not that early. You've probably been a low-
level case for years, perhaps even since your father. There's no way
to firmly establish a chain of infection, or even the primary carrier."

"He would never cause me harm." This was a thought so horri-
fying I recoiled from the sound of my own words. I had already
forgiven Papa in my heart, decided to think that his germs kept
him alive in me somehow.

"Possibly you were all three exposed to the same source. Has
anyone else in your family fallen sick in the past few years? Is your
mother well?"

"She's fine."

"It's one of those unknowables," the doctor shrugged. "Some
people have a natural immunity. Others can have the disease
without ever showing a sign of it. They're the dangerous ones
because they are completely unaware."

He glanced at his watch, then carefully back at me. I was taking more of his time than he had allotted, but then compared to
me he had all the time in the world. At least I wasn't one of the
dangerous ones.

"Who's worse?" I asked. "Me or Marcella."

While he thought about the question, I wondered what answer I hoped to hear. Marcella and I always had this "more" competition between us and she almost always won. It would be fair that she win this one as well—she had bested me in so many others.

"You are," he said. "I'll monitor her for now—there's such a shortage of beds—but you have to go to the hospital. You're highly contagious."

If I expected sympathy from my sister, I was out of luck.

"TB is a terrible stigmata," she accused. "How will I face my friends?"

"But your condition is so mild they needn't worry."

"My case?" She was outraged. "Of course I'm not going to tell anyone about my case. I mean you. How will I explain your disappearance? People will guess. It was bad enough with Papa, but that was a long time ago. And besides . . ."

She stopped herself, aware that she was going far even for her.

"At least he had the courtesy to die in Thebes," I finished the sentence for her.

"I didn't mean it like that. I loved Papa. I miss him every day of my life."

I knew this was true, in Marcella's own way, so I didn't continue. "Tell them I've gone to New York City," I suggested. "That I've become a stage actress. Tell them I was summoned by the Pope. Tell them I've become a nun."

She liked the last suggestion. "Do you think they'd fall for it? I mean, you are devout."

As Marcella well knew, I had long privately flirted with the notion of taking the veil. I was attracted to the severe uniform, to the purposefulness of stern devotion, to the relief of a world populated entirely by women yet with all the unbearable rituals of femininity put aside. As the bride of Christ, there was no "death us do part" to worry about. I would never have to follow Mama into bitter widowhood.

"Whatever you want," I said. I instantly regretted all the lives I would now never have, so she might as well choose one of them. "But promise to visit me on Sundays."

"I'll just say I'm going to the novitiate at St. Catherine's." Marcella already had her story fully worked out. "I'll tell them that only the immediate family is allowed to come."

I will not remember that first year before my release. I will not allow one empty moment of despair to interrupt the flow of my life. It was a time out of time, unhooked to any moment worth recalling. I coughed blood until I simply coughed, until I stopped, until I was pronounced in remission and released to free my bed for someone sicker. It was a year in which nothing happened. A year of sleep. A year of holding the moment I left in order to resume it the minute after. It was a year of shut eyes, swallowed pills, fervent prayer. It was year of letting go of Papa, being Papa, saying good-bye. I did not age. I did not decline. I did not fully recover, but I recovered enough to fool them. It was a year in which I refused to fail because failure was impossible. It was a year I have forgotten, a year that happened to another Edna, a year of holding my breath until I could breathe again.

When I was released and pronounced cured that first time, I found work as the appointment secretary to a prominent doctor who knew the truth of my situation but wasn't bothered by it. Marcella had long since graduated high school and worked as the operator of a comptometer at Colgate Palmolive. Her illness had never flared up, and she was convinced that the initial diagnosis had been a mistake, that her sputum had been confused with that of a sick woman.

I moved back into my old room, tried to resume a life that had a hole in its center. I was twenty-three by then, and had missed too much to ever fill the gap.

For eleven months and two weeks during those middle years Marcella and I put aside from our salaries what cash Mama and we could spare. Before we got sick the second time and were taken out of circulation again we always tried to take an exotic vacation together to relieve the monotony of our lives.

For me, the trips served a hidden purpose. My wanderlust percolated through the endless months of office work, of waiting for the crowded trolley in the early mornings and late afternoons, of washing and pressing the same wardrobe, eating the same seven meals in unvarying order for dinner each week—Sunday, roast; Monday, hash; Tuesday, casserole; Wednesday, pork and cabbage; Thursday, soup; Friday, fish; Saturday, chicken and gravy—all the while making the same small talk with the same people. Every Saturday afternoon in the dusk of the Confessional I admitted to a litany of sins so recurring that I might as well have given up all pretense of willpower and simply conceded them: pride, envy, a lack of true forgiveness.

One September we had sailed to Havana, Cuba, on a tramp steamer run by the United Fruit Company. Marcella fell in love with the Norwegian ship captain, and my film was exposed by a dashing policeman after I had snapped my sister posed in front of a foreign battleship anchored in the harbor. On the bus ride back to Louisville from New Orleans, the port of call at which we debarked, we had left between us only enough change for four bowls of bean soup, which we shared along the way in Jackson, Memphis, Nashville, and Elizabethtown. Another fall we went to New York City after all, and took a double room at the YWCA in Greenpoint, Brooklyn, close to the railroad apartment of our great-aunt Mary from Ireland.

Marcella and I arranged for our vacation breaks to coincide, though there was precious little in the till in those years for luxury travel. The second-to-last summer before my breakdown the most we could muster was to rent a cabin—a shack, really—on Corn Island off the Indiana bank of the Ohio. At night, looking across to the south, we could practically see the light in Mama's window but that didn't stop us from pretending that we were far away, on our own. And, being close had its advantages, we convinced ourselves. Friends could drop over on a hot evening, sit in shallow water, and tell us the latest from work. Even in the most humid weather the mud was cool, and the breeze off the water kept the bugs at bay. One moonless devil-may-care night Marcella, on my dare, swam out into the current and slipped off her bathing suit. It was the highlight of her stay, she confided thereafter to one and all.

"You should try it, Edna," she encouraged me. "I can't describe the feeling. No part of you is confined, nothing separates you from life."

Privately, I had some doubt that Marcella had actually carried out her boast—it was so dark I had to take on faith what she claimed she'd done.

"Weren't you afraid you'd drop your suit?" I inquired the next morning at breakfast. "Then what?"

Marcella's blush was convincing.

"You know, at that moment I don't think I would have given a hoot," she said. "At that moment, I felt as free as a bird."

"A fish," I corrected.

"A flying fish, then. I can't explain, I can't even try. Did you know that your breasts float? Oh," she stopped herself. "Sorry."

Breasts were not a subject we discussed since, in our early teens, Marcella had blossomed and I had remained flat chested.

"Well, Mae West, at least you were in no danger of drowning," I said to restore the mood.

"Edna, what you say!"

"I'm not the one who played mermaid."

"That's *it*." Marcella clapped her hands for emphasis. "That's just what I felt like. Like a creature of the sea."

I looked over at her. Her eyes were closed as she was imagining herself. There was a glow to her face, the beginnings of the smile with which she would greet disbelieving sailors before she lured them to the briny depths. The drama Marcella perpetually imparted to the events of her everyday life sometimes drove me crazy, but other times, if I let myself be an appreciative audience to it, I was charmed. All the trials of her enforced routine—the backbiting at work, Mama's nagging, the way we had to scrimp to just get by, much less stay in fashion—fell away from her and Marcella became a princess, a movie star, a debutante at the Pendennis Club whose dance card was filled before the music started.

"Most of the time, you don't pay attention to your skin," Marcella announced from wherever she was. "You forget it can talk to you the same as words can. And there are parts of my skin that never get to say anything."

"So what did they say last night?"

Marcella's smile widened. She stretched her arms above her head, then bent her elbows, combed her fingers through her long black curly hair. She was wearing a blue halter top with white polka dots and shorts the same shade of red her toenails were painted.

"They said 'Vinny Callahan,'" she said. "They positively shouted that name loud and clear."

Vinny Callahan was the current candidate in Marcella's long line of impossible heartthrobs. He worked in the soap factory's accounting office and to my sister's mind she and he formed a kind of essential team: he provided the figures and she added them up. He was tall, a few years older than she and, we had learned two days ago from one of our drop-in guests, was presently unattached since he had just broken off with his longtime girlfriend, Francine Ryan.

"Did your skin also get a premonition of deep, painful scratches in itself?" I asked. "Because I think Francine's skin is still saying the same name."

"Francine." Marcella sniffed dismissively, sat up straighter and opened her eyes. "They were never right for each other. She can't fox-trot."

"I don't think ballroom dancing forms the basis of their relationship." Vinny and Francine had once been observed in midafternoon kissing in the Grotto of St. Bernadette, one of the side chapels of St. Louis Bertrand church. They later claimed they had gone there to light a candle so that Vinny would get a raise.

"Edna, you *have* no . . ." Marcella couldn't put her finger on what exactly it was that I lacked, or else she was reluctant to translate it into words. The funny thing was, I knew what she meant, and she was right: I *had* no.

"Sense of adventure," she decided at last.

I assumed that this was the most polite way she could phrase the compromise I had made with myself that too often excluded the clarion call of romance.

"Where would it get me if I did?" I asked her. Corn Island, no matter how you dreamed it up, was no Hawaiian paradise. Flat and so dry in August that even the morning grass was dusty, it was the only retreat we could afford but it looked for the world like an untended backyard. Our accommodations—eight dollars a week—had one lightbulb, four canvass army cots, a card table and six folding chairs. Marcella had plugged a rip in the screen door with a snagged pair of her hose. The greatest daytime source of activity and excitement in the immediate vicinity was the presence of a wasp nest under one of the eaves. Besides, there was always the aura of my "stigmata," as Marcella had originally put it. Once sick, always sick, was the common opinion.

"You see," Marcella said. "That's just what I mean, that kind of question. Go on, ask a real one."

"Would it get me a new life?"

"Yes indeedy," Marcella answered without the slightest hesitation. "If that's your heart's desire, yes indeedy-do. Just plunge in."

"With or without a swimming suit?"

Marcella blushed again. Maybe she had been telling the truth. "Stark naked," she said. "It's the only way."

That last summer, when I could feel in my chest the familiar constriction but chose to ignore it, to postpone the inevitable as long as possible, I went to Duluth, Minnesota, to finally explore the possibility of my vocation.

It had been a great relief when Lucille Andriott, a friend from church, proposed that we visit her cousin, Sister Mary Agnes, who was stationed in Minnesota, a place which, since I had never been there, sounded intriguing. We could all bunk at the mother-house for free, Lucille promised, and use the resources we saved by starting off with a round-trip to Canada on the overnight Lake Superior ferry. Thunder Bay might not be Santo Domingo but a cruise was a cruise and Canada did legally qualify as a foreign country. You never knew what might happen once you found yourself overseas.

For me, the trip would serve a hidden purpose as well. My "sense of adventure" had been tapping on my shoulder for atten-tion ever since Marcella had brought it up. Of course, my idea of "plunging in" was a far cry from the flights of fancy she would from time to time concoct for herself: ball gowns and fur coats, standing beauty-parlor appointments and boys, each one holding a shiny silver car key in his hand, lined up at the front door. For me, all I hoped for was an alternative to a return to Waverly Hills sanitarium, a haven where I could be sick surrounded by solici-tous sisters and the scent of incense.

I could have happily stayed in Chicago, where we changed trains on our way north. We had time on our hands—from four until ten p.m. To kill it, we walked downtown and took the elevator to the top of the Ambassador Hotel, where they ran a restaurant. We each ordered an orangeade and read Carl Sandburg's poem aloud as we stood on the lookout and peered through a telescope south toward the stockyards. Chicago was to Louisville as Louisville was to Thebes: it gave safety a bad name. It was a city you could get lost in. A city too preoccupied to remark on hem lengths or bobbed hair, a city full of foreigners who felt right at home, no apologies.

"Edna, don't," was the constant refrain I heard from Lucille and Marcella. "Edna don't jaywalk." "Edna don't order a beer." "Edna don't speak to that bum looking for a dime." "Edna don't stand in the window in your slip." "Edna don't stay up." "Edna don't lie in bed while the world's awake."

But to me, Chicago was one long invitation to break the rules for the first and last time. For every "don't" I found a "do."

There were limits to my imagination, I knew that. What seemed extreme to me and wild in the horrified eyes of my sister was everyday to someone with more experience in life. Still, each step forward allowed a person to see further, and you could only go one at a time, even running, so I didn't judge myself too harshly. I was on my way somewhere, destination unspecified, and I tried not to look back, tried not to worry about Mama alone in the house, tried not to feel guilty. Tried to believe I was well.

The Greyhound bus from St. Paul, where we had changed from Chicago, pulled into Duluth only an hour before the ferry was scheduled to depart, so with the rush of collecting our suitcases, buying our tickets, calling Lucille's cousin Sister Mary Agnes to let her know we had arrived in one piece and would see her soon, there was no real chance to notice the city. One minute we were in a frenzy of activity and the next: a blast of a foghorn, a chugging of engines, and we were afloat. We only had money enough for a single cabin, but that was all right because I preferred to sit up on the deck all night, watching the stars and listening to the orchestra, the Northern Lights, that played nonstop in the ballroom. It was like Waverly on water, with a loud radio.

I had thought Lake Michigan was big when I saw it in Chicago. It had waves, and there was a horizon line straight as a ruler. But somehow it seemed tamer than Superior. With Michigan you could make out both sides. It was like seeing the bottom of a teardrop or a beaker. The water sort of sloshed. Superior was more like the sky turned on its end. It took up half of everything, seemed bigger and wider than the land that tiptoed against it on the shore we had just left. Before us, its tides rolled with the weight of long momentum. We could be shipping off to anywhere, to anywhere at all.

I had noted that on this whole trip Marcella had not exactly been herself. Usually she was the first to improvise a new outfit, to try out a hairstyle no one else would dare, to march up to the best-looking beau and ask him to teach her how to swim or to send Morse code or to play the harmonica. But these last days she had seemed subdued—I'd say "thoughtful" if it wasn't Marcella, worn out. Now, of all things, she claimed to be seasick.

"How can you be nauseous on a lake?" I asked her. "Your stomach was settled during a hurricane in the Atlantic Ocean, the only one on board. You can stand on your head for five minutes. You can digest anything—I remember when you ate an ice cream and cheese sundae and string beans.

"Stop it, Edna."

She did look green around the gills.

"That darn bus ride took it out of her," Lucille sympathized. "All those curves, those twists and turns as we worked our way ever up the highway. Back and forth. Back and forth. Left, right, left, right. Zig, zag, zig . . ."

Marcella put her hands over her ears, squashing her hair flat against the side of her head. "If you two don't be quiet I'm going to throw myself overboard," she threatened in a high-pitched voice. "Then you'll be sorry."

That sounded more like the Marcella I knew.

"You're just angling for the first mate to dive in and save you," I joked her. "Or else you want the cabin all to yourself."

"I'm deadly serious, Edna."

"Shall we leave her in peace?" I asked Lucille.

"You go ahead," Lucille said, ever faithful to Marcella. They had shared too many beauty secrets, too many hours under hair dryers, to be rent asunder over a little bout of mal de mer. "I'm going to bathe her head with a rag soaked in warm milk."

"No!" pleaded Marcella.

"It works like a charm," Lucille promised. "You just hang on, honey. I'll find the kitchen. You want anything to eat while I'm there? Tuna fish?"

Marcella bent her index finger and bit on the knuckle while she breathed heavily through her nose. "Leave. Me. Be," she implored through the sides of her mouth, then added: "I'll get you both for this."

"I think she'll live," observed Lucille, betraying the slightest bit of impatience. This was, after all, the advertised highlight of our whole vacation and unfairly it was all about Marcella's queasiness.

"Touch and go," I agreed. "I think I'll prowl the deck for a while. Maybe I'll meet the Ancient Mariner and ask him to waltz."

"Age doesn't matter a bit with a man," Lucille repeated one of her many golden rules. "But make sure he shows you the signed certificate of ownership to his boat before you say 'I do.' "

I climbed a metal staircase to the upper deck. It was quieter there, and with nothing to obstruct a breeze, the wind lifted my hair behind me as though I were running very fast. I drew into my lungs just enough sea air to not make me cough, and struggled for a moment with my scarf—then gave up and abandoned myself to the experience. Isadora Duncan had advised doing just that when I saw her perform at McCauley's in Louisville. Even from the highest seats in the top balcony you could see her aban-doning herself to experience. No doubt she did it every night of her life—and before hundreds of paying customers—until one night her scarf caught in the tire of a car she was riding in and broke her neck. A person like me, though, didn't get the chance all that often, so I snatched it. Suddenly something heavy and damp fell over me, shutting out my field of vision.

"Relax, relax," a male voice said from behind me. "We keep these as spares for just such emergencies."

I pushed the thing off my face—it was some kind of canvass raincoat with a hood—and whipped around to tell this man that when I wanted to be smothered he'd be the first to know. But before I got the words out I saw, even in the moonlight, who I was talking to: Saint John the Baptist, the spitting image. They could have been brothers, this sailor and the head on Salome's plate in the tableau in my illustrated book of New Testament stories. Same doleful eyes, same scraggly wet beard, same dark lips peeking out from behind it. The difference, of course, was that this man's head was attached to a body. A big, strong body dressed in a black turtleneck sweater and boots. And this man's head had a smile on its face.

"I . . ." I said, brilliant as usual.

"First crossing?"

I was tempted to say that no, I did it all the time, that international borders were nothing to me, that there was a brass band of Canadians waiting to welcome me when we landed.

I shook my head. I didn't want to appear inexperienced.

"Then you can appreciate this weather. It's a precious calm one tonight."

I automatically glanced at his ring finger. Not even a band of pale skin.

"It gets worse than this?"

"Ha," he replied. "She can be a mean one."

I was still thinking of his finger. "Who can?"

"She. The lake. She can be a holy terror."

Mother Most Amiable. The words came back to me from the Blessed Virgin's Litany, my favorite one, and I answered aloud without thinking. "Have mercy on us."

"She did," the man said cheerfully. "Look at that. You could skip a coin clear to Nipigon. Like window glass."

It was. A reflection of the moon danced on its twinkling plane.

"So," the man went on. "You heading home like the rest of us weary pilgrims?"

It took a moment for the realization to penetrate: he actually believed I was a Canadian—a foreigner. I felt instantly different—as inscrutable as Theda Bara at her vampiest.

"I reside in the United States, now," I announced, leaving him to imagine the broad contours of my life story.

"Not Duluth, surely," he said.

Why the *surely,* I wondered.

"Chicago, Illinois. I stay at the Ambassador Hotel when I'm at home."

From the silence which greeted this announcement I could tell he hadn't decided to be impressed with my story or skeptical of it. After a long pause, he spoke again.

"And what do you do for a living in Illinois? What line of work? Or are you a rich married lady what's forgot to wear her five-carat ring?"

He had noticed.

"I guess you could accuse me of being a career gal," I laughed. "Married to my job, a slave."

"What kind of job?"

At any moment Lucille's hairdo might flutter at the top of the ladder as she came looking for me. Without intending it, she'd put a lie to whatever stray from the truth I might concoct.

"Oh, nothing so interesting as sailing the seven seas," I said.

"Lakes," he corrected. "And there's five of them: Superior, Michigan, Huron, Erie and Ontario."

"Fascinating," I gushed. How romantic, a geography lesson. "And what exactly is your particular . . . function?"

"I rescue damsels in distress," he said. "Then take them out to a three-course supper in Thunder Bay."

"You might reconsider that invitation in the bright light of day," I warned him. I thought it better to get the bad news over with before it started to collect.

"Let me be the judge of that." Before I knew what was happening he produced a powerful flashlight and shone it directly into my face. I squinted my eyes, threw up my hands to cover myself.

"Quite the something, aren't you?" he said.

I opened one eye. "Am I?"

"Oh, *quite* the something." He sighed. "You'll be wanting a looksee of your own I expect. Turnabout is fair play. Steel yourself."

With that he focused the beam on himself and let me gawk.

"Run for your life," he said. From his tone I could tell that someone must have done just that. But why on earth?

"You remind me of a man I used to know," I told him, even more startled at his resemblance to St. John the Baptist.

"In Chicago?"

"No. He was from abroad."

"Was?"

"He's deceased now. It's been a long time."

"You were sweet on him, is that it?"

"Oh, no. I'm over it." We were verging on the blasphemous. "He was involved with someone else. That's what got him in trouble."

The man took off his knitted cap out of respect for the departed.

"My name's Edna," I told him.

"Call me Jack."

Mary Mother of God.

"Jack what?" I held my breath.

"Johnson. Jack F-for-Frank Johnson." He saluted me. "At your service."

When Jack discovered that my girlfriends and I would not be tarrying in Canada—just window-shopping during the day and returning on the same boat tomorrow night—he switched our rendezvous, and changed dinner to breakfast, which he offered to fix for me himself immediately after our arrival.

"You've got to let me bring a contribution."

"Well, if you insist, pick up a slab of Canadian bacon," he suggested. "You can't get the real McCoy in Minnesota. You supply that and leave the rest up to me. Eggs, toast, coffee, orange juice." He reeled off the menu with such gusto that I was struck with a pang of hunger.

"I make unforgettable fried potatoes," he promised me, and touched my arm. "You've never tasted anything like them."

"What's your trick?" I asked to make conversation. His fingers were warm, even through the fabric of my dress and the wool of my sweater. I didn't want him to move.

"P-a-p-r-i-k-a." He spelled it out in a whisper and gave me a slight squeeze, then let go and slapped his forehead with the palm of his hand. "It must be love," he declared. "I've spilled my one and only secret. There's nothing left for you to wonder about."

I put my finger to my lips. "They'll never get it out of me," I swore. "They can roast me on a spit, gore out my eyes, have me torn apart by wild beasts while the crowds roar . . ."

I noticed Jack was regarding me with alarm.

"Like they did to the martyrs," I explained. "You know, the saints who went straight to heaven for enduring pain? Baptism of blood?"

"I was raised Methodist." He sounded prim, as though this fact elevated him to a higher level of civilization. I tried to remember what beef Methodists had with the Church but couldn't place it. Presbyterians were convinced of predestination—good works didn't matter. Greek Orthodoxes didn't approve of statues, which they called graven images, just flat pictures. Episcopalians allowed Henry the Eighth to keep on getting divorced and remarried. Baptists didn't kneel and took every word of the Bible literally. But Methodists? The name John Wesley came into my mind but I didn't want to betray my ignorance so I dropped the subject.

"Well," I went on in a calmer tone. "The word"—and I silently mouthed PAPRIKA—"will never cross my lips. Shhh. . . ." Then, at that exact moment of maximum puckering, two things happened: Jack F-as-in-Frank Johnson kissed me, and Lucille Andriott called from below, "Edna? Are you up there? Marcella needs you to give her an enema."

After that moment of supreme humiliation—I was down the ladder faster than a fireman at Mrs. O'Leary's barn—I didn't know if Jack would ever speak to me again.

Lucille was prostrate with apology and embarrassment. "I had no idea you were with a man," she said once we were all three squeezed into the tiny cabin, its narrow door securely bolted, its single porthole locked, Marcella resting, peaceful at last, on the lower bunk bed.

"You and your enemas," I said in exasperation. My sister had ever been a firm believer in the power of purgation to cure any and all ills, from a sore throat to a backache, and carried her travel kit, consisting of tubes and bags and rubber syringes, in her purse, just in case.

"It stands to reason, Edna," Marcella answered languidly in her own defense. "If the alimentary canal is empty it has nothing to be upset from. I am living proof. I know how to deal with myself." She raised her head from the pillow to demonstrate her new immunity from the rock of the boat.

"You're insane."

"Who was the sailor?" Lucille wanted to know. She sat on the upper, and swung her legs, first one, then the other, admiring how her nylon stockings shaped her calves.

"Just . . . someone," I answered evasively. "Ships that pass in the night."

"Quite a ship, it seems to me," Lucille observed.

"Well, I'll never be able to face him again," I said. "Thanks to your big mouth."

"Do you think it's too large?" Lucille frowned in vexation. "For my nose, I mean. In proportion to my face."

"I wouldn't wear my lipstick too red," Marcella advised.

"Don't forget the bacon," were Jack's final words of advice as I stepped off the ship into a country that required me to present my birth certificate.

I didn't, and I ate that humiliating breakfast at his rooming house as though it were my last meal as a lay person, as a woman who could have a midnight flirtation. Two paths lay before me, and they were both solitary roads: a sanitarium or a convent. When I finished washing the dishes I gave Jack the address of the Ambassador Hotel so that he'd never find me. I didn't want him to know he might have been kissed by death.

According to Lucille's cousin, the nuns in Duluth were nothing like the Ursulines or Dominicans we knew. They ran a home for pregnant, unwed girls and daily visited the city courthouse in search of needy cases to shepherd. They took for themselves the names of energetic saints, busybody saints—Ann, Elizabeth of Hungary, Martha—not the doe-eyed Roman virgins who welcomed torture and waited for the angels to carry them up to heaven. They were tomboy nuns, exception-making nuns, nuns with wisps of hastily cropped hair escaping from their cowls. They ate spaghetti, wore kneesocks instead of cotton stockings, were organized into a softball team that played in a secular league that included professed Lutherans and postal employees.

From the moment I met her, Mary Agnes—that's what she told me to call her—was more like a sister than a Sister. She was tall like me, sturdy under her navy blue habit, and you could tell that in real life she'd be a redhead, she had that kind of natural peaches-and-cream complexion. Behind her rimless glasses, which were so spotlessly clean that they reflected the light like two round mirrors, her eyes were China blue, accented by bloodshot streaks of exhaustion. She had a pale mustache, unperoxided, and large lower teeth that were prominent when she smiled. Her hands were chapped and big, and her waist was the same girth as her hips. On some that would seem boyish, but on Mary Agnes it was simply an indication of strength.

When Mary Agnes listened to you, she listened. She cocked her head to the left, held her lips tense and slightly open as if she was so interested in what you had to say she could hardly wait to reply. She punctuated your speech, nodding once curtly at the conclusion of each sentence, and bobbing her head energetically as you neared the end of what you were saying, as if she were getting a running start at her comeback. She paid such close attention to you that she heard behind the words, heard your inner thoughts, and that's what she answered.

"Edna, don't resist," was her first command to me.

"Resist what?" Marcella wanted to know. She was miffed that though Lucille had introduced both of us in the same breath, I was the one Mary Agnes greeted.

Mary Agnes winked at me—winked!—and turned to Marcella. "Surely she's told you," she said. "But even if not, how could you not have guessed?"

Marcella had been rolling the high heel of one shoe in impatience, and at Mary Agnes's words she lost her balance just enough to stumble. "I don't know what you're talking about," she said.

Mary Agnes winked at me again, no mistaking, and kept talking to Marcella. "Please. I don't want to let the cat out of the bag, to steal Edna's thunder. I'm sure she'll tell the world when she's good and ready."

She gave me the briefest of smiles and, I couldn't help myself, I smiled back. We were conspirators without ever exchanging a confidence because I knew she knew I was thinking about becoming a nun, and she knew I knew she knew.

"Let's get you settled," she said, and led us down a narrow corridor. I noticed in relief that the floor had not been mopped in some time.

"Your cousin's strange," Marcella whispered to Lucille. "No offense."

"None taken." Lucille patted her permanent. In our crowd she was known as the pretty one and so no insult bothered her as long as it didn't bat at that target.

"What on earth was she talking about?" Marcella demanded of me.

"It beats me," I lied.

"Strange," Marcella repeated as though she was beholding a footprint in the sand and had counted six toes.

After supper—macaroni and cheese—the nuns disappeared. There were six of them, and in the flurry of the excitement of the first night in a new place, I barely distinguished between them. From the back they all looked alike anyway, rectangular as shoe boxes, and they made a collective impression of being worn out. Some nuns you could imagine going to their cells and praying for the conversion of Russia. These nuns, you felt, closed their doors and threw themselves flat across their mattresses, too tired to even put on a nightgown or untie a lace.

We went to our rooms, too, each identical in its furnishing: a single bed with an army blanket folded at the bottom of white muslin sheets; one pillow; a metal writing desk and chair; a crucifix on one wall and a small print in a frame on the other. There were a few mission magazines stacked on my table and I regarded them with despair for they were all I had to read and it was only eight o'clock. Before picking them up, though, I stood in front of the picture and tried to guess the identity of the saint.

"Louise de Marillac."

I spun around to find Mary Agnes standing in the doorway. "I guess I should have knocked," she said. "But I assumed you were expecting me."

Was I? I wondered to myself. Certainly I wasn't surprised, but still, what did we have to say to each other.

"What's her story?" I asked, turning back to study the picture.

"French, seventeeth century, rich as Croesus. Widowed at thirty-four, gave up the glamour life to join one of those orders where you can't talk except to sing hymns, but it drove her crazy. In Confession, she asked Vincent de Paul what to do and he had the sense to tell her to get up off her knees and go to work. Eventually she founded the Daughters of Charity, a radical sort of religious community—for its day. 'Our convent is the sickroom, and our cloister is the streets,' she was quoted as saying. No vows, talk your heads off. She organized orphanages, schools. Florence Nightingale cited her as a major inspiration."

"I never heard of her."

"She was ahead of her time, Louise was. Besides, nothing terrible happened to her, nothing to warn her to be helpless, to surrender, to swoon in the face of danger. She's all but invisible in the canon of saints because she was a woman's woman—men had very little part in what she did and therefore show very little interest in it to this day."

"What about St. Vincent de Paul? Wasn't the whole thing his idea?"

"Ah, Vincent. He didn't know who he was dealing with. I'm not criticizing him, really, but if you read his story closely you'll see that rich widows with religious mania were the major source of his funding. He probably had Louise pegged as good for beaucoup de francs. Instead, she wound up out–Vincent de Pauling Vincent de Paul."

I concentrated on the picture again. "She seems so . . . petite."

"Big things come in small packages," Mary Agnes said, then, taking me in, added, "and in big ones, too. Look at me. Look at you. Look at us. Don't judge a book by its cover."

"You've got a lot of sayings," I said automatically, then cringed inside. Mary Agnes made you forget you were talking to a nun.

"A dime a dozen," Mary Agnes said, laughing. "You'll get used to me once you're here for a while."

"We're only here for four days."

"Edna, don't you think I know why you've come? You have 'vocation' written all over you. You've come home, dear. I can even tell you what your new name will be."

Things were moving faster than I could keep track of. One minute I was Lucille's friend, the next my life was changed. Slow down, I wanted to tell her. Whoa. But curiosity got the better of me. "What?"

"Sister Catherine of Alexandria," Mary Agnes said with certainty. "Clearly."

All these new saints, a whole sorority of them.

"Was she an Egyptian or something?"

"What a story. A queen who refused to marry Maxentius, the emperor of Rome—said she'd rather marry the Christ child and spend her life reading. You can imagine what that did to his ego, so Max puts together a team of fifty pagan philosophers to talk her out of it."

"What happened?"

"Presto, she converts every one of them."

"The emperor must have loved that."

"Yes, well. Instant martyrdom for the philosophers, but Max still wanted Catherine and proposed again. When she refused . . . well, it's not a pretty story, as these things generally aren't."

"I can take it."

"Okay. First he stretches her on a spiked wheel . . ."

My namesake! I felt the pricks against my back.

"But the angels came down and busted it up. Then, of course, she was beheaded."

"Horrible."

"I'm not finished. Does Catherine bleed? Not a drop of blood. Milk."

"Milk?"

"Milk."

I went over and sat on the bed. "I don't get it."

"You know, a miracle."

"But she was dead, right?"

"Yes."

"And why milk? What does milk mean?"

An expression of annoyance contracted Mary Agnes's features, but it was instantly chased off by one of a suspicion confirmed.

"I *knew* you were Catherine. You've got her logic!"

And a neck full of milk, I thought.

"It's late," Mary Agnes said. "We'll talk turkey tomorrow."

Once the door was closed—there were no locks, not even a hook and eye—I stayed seated, glad that there was no mirror in the room. I would have been tempted to look at myself and afraid to have seen Catherine of Alexandria's headless body staring back. It was disconcerting, Mary Agnes's sureness. Nobody since Papa had been interested enough in me to tell me what to do with my life. Mama bossed me around, it was part of her nature, but with a distracted air. She couldn't help issuing edicts but then she didn't pay attention as to whether or not they were ever followed. "Wear the pink," she would tell me when I got up in the morning to go to work, but then not notice when I wore the green. Marcella, being Marcella, saw only those aspects of the world that applied directly to herself, and what I did with me mostly wasn't one of them. The friends I had made at Waverly Hills had their own futures—or lack of futures—to worry about and I only drew their intense scrutiny if I coughed in their presence.

But Mary Agnes was different. It was as though she had been waiting for me—or *a* me, was more like it—someone she could slip under her wing, who would be her protégé, her find, her little sister. I was flattered, but more than that, I was intrigued. Maybe she knew what she was talking about. Maybe I should become a social worker nun. After all, I had plenty of firsthand experience with sickrooms. The unwed mother business I'd have to learn, and I decided that I had better do just that before I let myself be buffaloed into seriously considering Mary Agnes's version of my future life. I felt a kind of excitement at this thought, an anticipation, a sense of being close to a major discovery. I lay back on the bed light-headed. A pulse pounded and automatically I touched my index finger to my carotid artery beneath my ear to test the strength. Churning, I thought. And then I thought: butter.

I awoke late to a gray, foggy morning, and seemed to be the only one left on the premises. I had missed Mass, missed breakfast, missed the exodus of nuns to their various good works, missed joining Lucille and Marcella, who had apparently gone downtown to sightsee. I was just as glad.

After I washed my face and brushed my hair I found a copy of the Duluth telephone book and looked in the Yellow Pages under "Pregnancy Counseling and Information." There was a Mother Seton Center in Superior, Wisconsin, the next town. That was where Mary Agnes worked, so that was out. But I ran my finger up the column and found a second listing: Lutheran Social Services of Minnesota, right in Duluth. There would be no chance of bumping into her amid wayward non-Catholic girls. I called a taxicab and when it arrived gave the driver the address. He swiveled around to regard me with an odd look. "Quite the popular destination these days."

"I'm simply applying for a job," I informed him, as if it were any of his business. It was, after all, halfway the truth.

"Right, lady. So are they all."

We drove on a causeway that had buildings on the left and the lake on the right. After my adventures, it looked to me like an old friend.

"Do people ever swim in that?" I asked the taxi driver.

"Don't try it," he advised, going faster. His voice had taken on a tone of concern. "Keep your appointment. It's always darkest before the dawn."

The force of the car's acceleration pushed me back against the cushions. What was it about people in Duluth and talking in maxims?

"I told you, it's for a job," I said to put his mind at rest. "I'm a Catholic."

His eyes met mine in the rearview mirror. They were sympathetic. I noticed he wore a St. Christopher medal on a silver chain around his neck. "Father wouldn't even come along," he muttered to himself.

"Father who?" I hadn't seen any priests at the convent.

"The baby's."

"*What* baby's?"

The driver hunched his shoulders over the steering wheel. "We'll be there in two shakes. They've heard it all before." He thought for a minute, then looked up at my reflected eyes again and went on, confidingly. "The wife and me? We adopted. Cutest little trick you ever saw. Bright? She can sing 'Hello My Darling.' Knows all the words. Acts them out. We'll always be grateful to the mother. Don't judge her a bit. She gave us our angel girl."

"You misunderstand," I said. "I'm thinking about becoming a nun."

"Oh, my." He shook his head. "That's going too far. No need to give up your life over one night's mistake. Think it over. A few months from now, you can make a fresh start. Nobody's the wiser."

I could have screamed. I leaned forward, clutched the back of the front seat for balance. "Listen," I yelled directly into his ear, "I am a virgin." The word filled the car, shocking both of us.

He stopped at a traffic light, twisted his head to look at me head-on. "So was Mary," he said. "But tell that one to Joseph."

I felt slightly illicit being in a Lutheran facility. If someone were to come up to me and demand to know the last words of the Lord's Prayer I reminded myself to say "for Thine is the kingdom and the power and the glory." Lutherans were legitimately baptized, I recalled. They questioned Papal authority but otherwise they weren't dangerous.

I pushed through a heavy oak door into a waiting room area with green walls and a homemade-looking painting of a pine tree that hung above the secretary's desk.

"Can I help you?" The receptionist was grandmotherly, her hair curled just so, her nail polish pink, a prominent diamond on her ring finger. I'll bet *that* puts girls in trouble at ease, I thought.

"I'm just . . . looking," I stalled, as if I were browsing in a millinery shop. I had planned to work out my story on the ride, but all the talk with the taxicab driver—who had waved cheerfully and with some relief when he let me off, then waited by the curb until I was inside—had left me flat-footed.

"For . . . ?" The woman, whose name, according to a small brass plaque on her desk, was Mrs. Lars Norquist, led me with her pause.

"For . . ." I repeated, scrambling for an idea. "For . . . Sally." I don't know where the name came from.

"You mean Sarah."

"Oh. Is that what you call her?"

Mrs. Norquist was affronted that Sarah, whoever she was, had a friend who was permitted to use a nickname. "Not just me. Everybody calls her Sarah."

"Well, I don't."

Mrs. Norquist straightened herself in her chair the way a hen distributes herself over a nestful of eggs. "She's interviewing a client. Won't be free for an hour."

I said a prayer of thanks to St. Jude, the patron of impossible causes, and promised to eat no dessert with my dinner in payment. Even as I did so I realized that this was a small sacrifice. Dessert at the convent was, according to Lucille, always Jell-O. It was one of the few drawbacks of staying there.

"I'll wait, if you don't mind."

Mrs. Lars Norquist minded, she truly did, but what could she say? She became busy with papers, patting them into neatly squared stacks like playing cards. I sat on a chair and leafed through a pamphlet listing the many social services available to Lutherans in greater Duluth.

"Have you known Sarah long?" Mrs. Norquist demanded.

"Ages," I said, and then, after a pause I averted my eyes and added, "Sally."

A desk drawer slammed, a chair scraped the floor and I watched as Mrs. Norquist's feet, housed in sensible old-lady shoes, minced to a door that led to the inner office.

"I'm in the next room," she said forebodingly, and then hesitated before making her prediction come true. What did she think I'd steal?

"Did you paint the tree?" I asked innocently.

"As a matter of fact, I did," she answered, mollified that I had noticed and ready to dispute a compliment.

"I thought so." When I didn't say anything else, Mrs. Norquist turned the knob, marched through the entrance, slamming the door behind her. It sported a window of opaque glass so I could see her watchful outline, hovering just on the other side. I took an emery board out of my purse and began to file my nails. I didn't know what to do with myself, but I figured I had the better part of an hour to do it in.

I guessed wrong. I heard a door open down the hall, running feet. Mrs. Norquist's image blurred, disappeared as she got out of the way. The office door was wrenched open as a woman ran out, her face streaked with tears. My sister. Marcella.

"Edna!" She was more shocked to see me than I was to see her. "You followed me!"

"No." I stood up, shook my head in denial.

"You did!"

"No," I repeated. "I came . . . I came to see . . . Sarah."

"I'm Sarah," an out-of-breath voice said. Marcella and I both turned our attention to the doorway where a frazzled-looking woman leaned on the frame for support. "But you'll have to wait your turn. Elizabeth," she went on, addressing Marcella. "I want you to calm down and come back into my office. There are things I have to explain to you."

"Elizabeth?" I asked.

"This one says she calls you 'Sally,' " Mrs. Lars Norquist chimed in. "I told her you were 'Sarah.' "

"You know Sarah?" Marcella's glance ricocheted off Sarah and struck me hard in the face. "Have you been listening in on my private telephone calls, too?"

"Don't be silly," I said in my calmest voice. "I just came here today because it wasn't the other place, the Mother Seton Home, where Mary Agnes works."

"That's why *I* came here." Marcella did not like being upstaged. "I got here first."

Her assertion was so petulant, so like a little girl stamping her foot, that it made me laugh. I shrugged my shoulders, held up my hands palms out, fingers spread. "I overslept. Sue me."

Now it was my sister's turn to smile in spite of herself. "I told Lucille I wanted to visit the Iron Ore Museum. It was the only way I could think to get rid of her. I told her I had always had a passion for smelting."

I gave a serious nod. "That beats my excuse. I couldn't convince the taxi driver I wasn't pregnant!"

"Top that," my eyes challenged, and then the silence dragged, defined itself, toppled against me like a hard wind. I knew why *I* was here.

"You aren't, are you?" Marcella barely whispered her question, so much did she want me to say yes.

I shook my head once, almost sadly. "But you are."

She drew in a hiss of air and her staring eyes seemed to press against her lids. She turned to Sarah, who had stood by silently while Marcella and I had ranted at each other like two monkeys in a small cage.

"Elizabeth is a bit confused about her bodily functions," she said. "She's made a wise choice to come here."

"Her name isn't Elizabeth," I insisted, as if this news flash would invalidate all that had come before. "We aren't residents of Duluth—just visitors. We aren't even Lutherans. I'm thinking of becoming a nun."

"*What?*" Marcella was outraged not to have heard this idea first—her sisterly right.

"I was going to tell you."

"When? Next Christmas?"

"Oh, I don't know. Maybe after you . . ."

We both looked at Marcella's flat stomach.

"You are? Really?"

"Unlikely," Sarah inserted.

"Vinny," Marcella said, anticipating my next question and not bothering to argue about answering it. "He said—you know?— that he loved me."

"But he just married Francine a . . ." I counted back the weeks.

"A month ago," Marcella finished my arithmetic for me.

"Does he know? Does Mama?"

"Ladies," Sarah interrupted. "It is simply impossible. That is *not* the way a child is conceived. Shall we continue this conversation in my office?" She gestured with her hand that we should precede her down the hall, and an expression of deep frustration crossed Mrs. Lars Norquist's rouged and powdered face.

CHAPTER EIGHT

THE PORCH

Marcella

I like to lie on the long south-facing solarium off the porch in the late afternoons. When I make my lists of Why I Am Nevertheless a Fortunate Person, I include the fact that if I have to experience a disease I am lucky to suffer from the one I do. I could be a leper, after all—that would be difficult to find a positive side of. I could have that weight disorder that turns you into an elephant. But instead I have a curse that you often see reference to at the movies when beautiful actresses get a little cough, a troubled expression. As they waste away in Switzerland they only become more glamorous. I have an illness whose cure can be something as simple as fresh air and six glasses of water every day. I get actual compliments on my breathing, imagine that, especially after they had to collapse one lung by pneumothorax in order to reduce the strain on it and allow it to heal unstressed. I feel proud of myself, virtuous, every time I inhale without coughing. I contain the air inside of me, cherish it, feel myself cleansed by its natural purity.

I hate the empty beds in the private rooms though, the reminders that all the oxygen in the world sometimes doesn't prevent a final breakdown. I hate the way the radio station personalities who visit cover their noses and mouths with handkerchiefs, believing that the flimsy cloth will protect them from becoming infected. Several of the nurses do that, too, the ones who weren't patients before they joined the staff. A few of the interns from U of L. They act as if I am poison, as if a mere whiff of me will kill them. I wish it could, sometimes. I wish I could be like one of those gorgeous tropical flowers that emit a cloud of scent that knocks out a nosy insect—which they then consume as nourishment. I wish I had that kind of power. I wish I wasn't here. I wish I wasn't going to die young.

No. That is precisely the wrong attitude and I shall not tolerate it, I shall not, I shall not, I shall not. Draw the cool air in, treasure it, release. Draw, treasure, release. I am nevertheless a fortunate person. My hair is curly. I am pretty. I am not as ill as Edna, certainly not as stricken as Papa, may he rest in peace. My whole life is ahead of me. My lung will be allowed to reinflate when it is ready, when it is good as new.

This is the last season I shall be here, surely. Here, in this place, I mean. Next year I'll be back at work in an office at Colgate Palmolive, talking to my girlfriends, meeting boys who need never know about this interruption in my life, never. No one will notice when I breathe. No one will look up in alarm when I clear my throat.

Draw.

Treasure.

Release.

Why me is a question I cannot help asking, even if it does make me unpopular with the other girls on the floor. But really, *why* me? I asked the doctor at St. Elizabeth's Hospital that October afternoon when he diagnosed me and sent me home alone on the streetcar. Not that I was surprised. Edna was already back here for the second time by then and I had countless times taken the Sunday jitney out to visit her. This place held no mystery for me, no terror. Some people got well, there were documented cases reported in the *Courier-Journal*. I would get well or go into remission like Edna had—for years. I was annoyed, that was all.

When I walked in the house I could tell Mama knew. They must have called her. She didn't mention it, of course, the disturbing news, but she did seem more irritated with life than usual. My dinner was cold. The laundry she took in for income needed folding. I felt sorry to be such a trouble to her, a further disappointment after Papa and Edna, but we didn't bring up the subject. We both knew that they would call when a bed at Waverly became available, just as they had with Edna, and then Mama would be alone, deserted by her husband and children. The neighbors would help out for a while, but they'd worry. Had Mama truly escaped the White Plague, or had she only stubbornly refused to be tested? Did she hold in her coughs by an act of sheer determination?

It was a silent week between us. I prayed a nightly novena in the green light of St. Louis Bertrand's, kneeling straight without even resting my elbows on the pew in front. I promised sacrifices—no more chocolate, ever. No more pecan pie. I would devote the rest of my life to generosity if only it were returned to me. Mama kept her own counsel. The neighbors' clothes she scrubbed on the washboard were never cleaner than they were during those days.

I don't blame Papa, though Mama does. How can you hold the dead accountable, I ask her? How can he apologize even if you prove your point? "Forgive and forget" is my motto because I am physically incapable of holding a grudge—my mind is like a sieve that way. I only remember the good—and the bad . . . it rises like steam from a hot iron on a damp shirt. I tell Mama to think of Papa as a possible agent of fate, the means through which Edna's and my characters were tested. There's no sin without intent, and I know he loved me, his baby. I could see it in his eyes. There are those who thought of Papa as my cross, but to me, truly, he was just the means to my end.

The phone call came on a wet afternoon. The car from Waverly would be by at eight that night, after dark, like a boy collecting me for a weekend date. One small suitcase—a nightgown, robe and slippers were all the clothes I would need for now—and storage space for patients was at a premium. The good news: I would share a double with Edna.

I dawdled over packing, folding and refolding my clothes, tucking in a few momentos to brighten up my . . . our . . . room—a pressed corsage from my eighth-grade prom, a birthday greeting from Thebes, a sapphire rhinestone pin in the shape of a fern. I squared the corners of my sheet, smoothed my maroon bedspread, tilted the yellow shade of my reading lamp so that the portrait of the Blessed Virgin would be illuminated, and I left the light turned on. After I had seen to everything I could think of I stood in the center of my oval rug. My room was small, tidy, decorated in shades of beige, my favorite color. Each significant object had a name that only I knew, and to each I said good-bye . . . or rather, until we meet again, because I would be back here, of that I had no doubt. I would pass the test. I would prevail. I closed the door and turned the key in the lock. I would be back before my lightbulb burned out.

There were no sad good-byes between Mama and me. She was busy in the kitchen, her arms floured, her apron splotched with batter. "What are you cooking?" I asked her at seven-thirty.

"Pineapple upside-down," she answered. Her party cake. For me to take with me, to Edna? I waited for her to tell me that.

"Mmmm," I gushed. "Your crowning jewel."

"Mrs. Schuler asked for it," Mama said. "She heard how fluffy mine comes out. Her daughter Ermine is getting engaged."

I watched for the headlights through the parlor curtains, and exactly at eight they arrived, stopped in front of the house, did not extinguish.

"My ride's here," I called to the back.

No answer, but I knew Mama was suffering, afraid of the aloneness that would follow the close of the front door. I could feel her beating the dough.

"I'll be fine," I promised her. "Home before Christmas." The house smelled of pineapple.

She sighed. I know I heard it through the door. She sighed deeply and I wanted to go console her but the car was idling. I picked up my suitcase, waited for anything Mama might need to tell me, stepped into the night. The air was cold. I was letting out the heat. The latch snapped behind me.

I rode in the backseat, like in a taxicab, and didn't make small talk with the elderly driver who gave up his attempts after five minutes. I thought it odd that he brought along his dog, a yappy little terrier named Cherry who barked at every passing car and in between glowered back at me as if I was an intruder.

"He's cute," I said, hoping to shut up both the driver and the dog. But it didn't work.

"Guess how old he is?" the driver demanded.

I looked at the dog and the dog looked at me. He could be any age and anyway, who cared?

"Three?"

"Ha! Guess again."

Here I was leaving home, heading into the unknown and I was supposed to play quiz games about some mutt. I have nothing against dogs—we had a nice one once—but this creature had cold eyes that reflected the streetlights.

"Twelve?" I tried. I figured I'd shorten his life span.

"Older," the driver proudly announced. "He's the oldest dog in the world but he never ages a day."

"How lucky," I said and then sat back in the seat, closed my eyes, breathed deeply and pretended to sleep. The trip took almost an hour. And then I was here.

When you come to Waverly as a visitor or a new arrival they drive you up the winding path to the front door. When you leave feet-first they take you down through the tunnel so as not to discourage the other patients, at least they did that with everyone but me, but I'm getting ahead of myself. That first night the lights were blazing—you could see the building from Dixie Highway, floating like a castle in the sky. In those Greek fable books Papa used to read to us, Persephone, the goddess of springtime, went down to the underworld where she fell in love with the handsome Hades, but here I was going to what looked like the overworld, like that Protestant hymn about heaven. Either way, you were cut off, though, out of the normal flow of events, preserved in eternal youth.

"What happens when we get there?" I asked the driver as he put the car in first gear for the zigzag trip up the long driveway. At the sound of my voice Cherry hopped up, angled his head around as if he had forgotten my existence.

"It's like the best hotel you ever stayed in," he said. "Everything top-drawer. No expense spared thanks to the taxpayers. You're going to get spoiled, Missy, spoiled rotten, just you wait."

A nice man, I decided. I should have talked more on the way out here. I reached forward and scratched Cherry behind the ears. Now that we had arrived at our destination he seemed calmer, more at peace.

"What about the food?"

"Oh my dear Lord," the driver said, and shook his head in disbelief. "Pork chops an inch thick. Mashed potatoes and farm butter. Fried chicken for Sunday dinner. And the pies. . . . It's enough to make me want to get sick for the meals alone."

I thought this was going just a bit far, but still his descriptions made me hungry and I wondered if I was too late for a midnight snack.

"Buttermilk," the driver went on. Once he got started he wouldn't turn off. "Angel food cake. Oatmeal and eggs for breakfast, with sausages. They come around to the rooms with trays of hot chocolate and sugar cookies. Ambrosia salad."

"Stop," I said. "You're making me starve to death." Cherry licked my hand in sympathy.

But, no. "Doughnuts the size of softballs. Meatloaf. Corn on the cob. Ice cream any flavor your heart desires. And mind you, I just get the leftovers. Who knows what's so good that they eat it all up and don't leave any for the hired help?"

I felt faint, dizzy with a mix of good and bad anticipation, by the time we pulled up to the foyer doors. Two nurses in starched white dresses came out to greet me. One of them carried my bag, Susie she said her name was. The other one shook my hand.

"Hon," she said. "I'm Mabel Pigg but everybody just calls me Pigg. We were beginning to think you'd had the cure and turned back for home. But come on in and get out of those clothes. I hope you're hungry because the girls on your wing made a little welcome party for you and I'm afraid they overdid it. Do you like cobbler? Lemon chiffon?"

The driver gave me a meaningful glance full of the word "See!" Cherry propped his little paws up on the rolled-down window and barked an annoyed good-bye, as if to say, "Are we here already? Just when we were getting to be friends."

And then I glanced up and there was Edna, standing like a thin, backlit paperdoll at a second-floor window.

It didn't take long to fall into a routine at Waverly—there wasn't that much to do. You woke up, ate, read, ate, napped, ate, listened to the radio, ate, took a bath, ate, and went to bed. If it weren't for the disease that was doing its best to waste us all away, we would have weighed a ton. As it was, TB and the diet sort of balanced each other off, which I suppose was the general idea. I found it hard to get used to sleeping outdoors or, if the weather was truly awful, with the double doors open, but we got so bundled up with scarves around our heads and comforters piled over blankets that you could pretend you were on a cruise ship going to Norway or somewhere like that and that you were on a vacation.

Of course the ward was alive with gossip, mostly about the imaginary romances going on between this or that girl and this or that boy on the third floor where the men were. It was like a movie magazine to me at first because when you checked in they didn't let you out of bed for a month, so I didn't have dining room or rec room privileges and could only picture the love interests from the whispered descriptions. Let me tell you, once I was allowed to behold most of those fellows in the flesh the expression "love is blind" took on a new meaning. That's unkind. They were sick, after all, so what could you expect? I suppose none of us were exactly beauty queens, mostly padding around in our flannel nightgowns and sensible robes, limited to one permanent wave a month. The winter air did put roses in our cheeks, but without a lot of powder that only made the rest of our skin look more pale. The whole hospital—well, that *is* what it is, let's face it—was like some kind of vanilla milkshake: unnaturally white people, white staff uniforms, white walls, snow on the landscape. No wonder we were served rice pudding at least three times a week.

You'd think that being stuck in such a place with your sister as the only constant company would have brought Edna and me closer, but the opposite was the case. The differences that had always divided us became even more pronounced. When I felt blue, Edna wouldn't tolerate a complaint. When I worried what would become of us, she told me to keep a stiff upper lip. When I found an interesting tidbit about hairdos or society functions in one of my magazines, she acted as though she couldn't care less. The only thing we shared on a regular basis was the Rosary, her calling out the Mysteries and the first half of the prayers and me responding, following her lead one bead at a time. But even in prayer we were poles apart. I prayed for the return of good health, she prayed for peace in Europe, for orphans in Abyssinia whom, she announced, had it far worse off than we did.

Edna's company made me lonely. We might be bound together by blood and circumstance but, I realized for the millionth time, we'd never be girlfriends. Her mind was closed in on itself, stubborn, maddening in its willpower. It was as though she was a wall of positive thinking so thick that you never knew what lay behind. Mama was like that in a way, except her wall was made of unbreakable glass. You knew everything she was thinking but you couldn't reach it. With Edna her secrets, if she had any, were a closed book.

Maybe that's too extreme. Wherever she was, as long as I could remember, Edna always found herself one special soul mate, and then they became inseparable. It wasn't so much that they talked to each other, but they seemed so intensely connected that they merged into a single being. Edna took on their personality traits and made them her own—stronger versions of the originals. She drove them like a car, these girls she adored—and that is the word for it. She dressed like they did, argued for their tastes in style, changed her appearance to get as close to being their twin as nature allowed. Me, I always preferred the company of men to women, but not Edna. For her, men, with the big exception of Papa, were like animals in a zoo: interesting for a visit but not something you'd choose to take home with you.

By the time I arrived at Waverly Edna had already found her current idol, a blond named Naomi who came from a good family in Covington. She was a beauty, I'll give her that. Willowy, with Paulette Goddard looks and what I call coat-hanger shoulders— no matter what she wore, it fell in a straight line. She was a rebel, too: she smoked Lucky Strikes in the broom closet even though the doctors said that if a TB case put a cigarette between her lips she might as well make out her last will and testament and sign on the dotted line. Tell that to Naomi, with her best interests at heart, and she'd laugh in your face.

"I'm immortal, haven't you heard?" she informed me the third day of my residence. "I'm not actually sick at all. I was causing too much heck at home so my daddy paid a doctor for a diagnosis and shipped me off here. It's just a matter of time until the lie is exposed, but in the meanwhile I make my own rules. I always have."

Edna listened to this hooey as if it was the gospel truth, nodding her head and hanging on every word. But you only had to look at Naomi's pasty-faced complexion to know she was anemic, and the coughs that came from her room—a single across from ours—were caused by advanced consumption—and not the type that stemmed from Kentucky leaf tobacco, either.

But Edna was willfully blind, deaf and dumb. To her, Naomi

made the moon and could do no wrong. When they had a contest for Waverly princess, Edna campaigned for Naomi as if her life depended on it, and when Naomi won and the coronation picture was in the paper, there was Edna in the royal court, a lady-in-waiting.

At first, I admit it, my jealous bone acted up. Why should my own sister be more interested in the health and welfare of a total stranger—and an Episcopalian, at that—instead of me. Not that I would have garnered the most votes if she had been in my corner. Probably I hadn't been around long enough to be that popular even though my hair was naturally wavy and I was often confused with Margaret Sullivan in appearance. But, still, where was the loyalty? After Papa died Edna was for all intents and purposes the head of the family and you'd think she'd watch out for me. Yet, I forgave her Naomi because even I could see she was a lost cause. Some days she didn't emerge from her single until late afternoon, and from the amount of time the nurses spent in there behind closed doors you knew she was fading. There was no earthly reason why Edna should have seemed so shocked at the end. You'd think it was me who had died—or Edna herself—the way she carried on. She didn't even take comfort from my offer of a shoulder to cry on. She just lay on her twin bed, her face turned to the screen partition, and refused to share her feelings.

"You're going to go into a decline," I warned her.

"There's no place to decline *to*," was all she answered.

"It's not as though you were in love with Naomi," I said. "Think what it must have been like for Mama when Papa's health failed."

That made her prop up on her elbow and look at me.

"You're serious, aren't you?" she asked in a tone of voice I didn't care for one bit.

"You wouldn't understand in a million years," I told Edna as she looked at me accusingly. Her face was a mask of Papa's. I wanted to just turn it off like a radio program I didn't want to hear—the news of the world or something. "Of course I'm serious."

"You've been rolling up your pin curls too tight," Edna said, changing the subject, and lay back down.

I touched my bangs, frizzed them out with my fingers. "Do you think so?" I asked. "I used those tissue papers that are supposed to add body."

But before Edna could voice an opinion, a nurse appeared with our lunch trays—corn beef hash and lima beans, with raspberry Jell-O on the side—and by the time I checked in with my mirror I looked all right to me.

I've got to say, though, that after Naomi some of the light went out of Edna's eyes, some of the spunk. She seemed resigned to her fate, passive, a different person, and that couldn't help but infect my own attitude and outlook. Watching Edna mope I became depressed, downhearted. I thought about all I was missing, stuck out here, a pariah of society. I'd had two or three weekend visitors—boys I'd gone out with before I got sick—but they sat in the lounge twisting their hats in their hands, less sympathetic than ambulance chasers, less amorous than horrified, less enamored with me than they were nosey observers. When Mama came—which was rarely— all she could talk about was the long ride, the crowded bus, the hardships she was enduring because we weren't there to help her. It was as though I had become invisible, a see-through image of myself. Or maybe more like a mirror. Well people stared at me and caught a reflection of what might happen to them if their luck ran sour.

It was about that time that I began the morning practice of making lists about Why I Am Nevertheless A Fortunate Person, but as the days blended into each other, as Christmas passed and Easter passed, as the air on the porch got warmer and more humid, as the azaleas bloomed and the honeysuckle perfumed the air, the number of reasons got shorter. I am alive. I have not been assigned to a single room. I have not expectorated blood overnight.

It wasn't that much to go on. I needed more than not being dead to live for.

*　　　*　　　*

Every afternoon I see the young colored boy—Earl, I've heard him called—pull up in his Ford truck, and wonder what he's brought us for supper. How lucky, I think, that there is a grocery in Louisville that will deliver to us here, a grocery that is not afraid that it will lose customers if the word gets out that someone associated with the establishment has been in direct contact with Waverly Hills Tuberculosis Sanitarium. I do not remind myself that no white grocer will come within a mile of us and so we have to rely on poverty rather than charity, on the coloreds rather than one of our own.

By pure chance, I am the only one taking the late sun today. The solarium is my island and I am its queen. The plank floor is painted gray, weathered by the polish of the seasons. The panorama before me is green and leafy.

Edna and the rest of the southside patients are at an all-day bingo game in the cafeteria but I begged off by claiming to have cramps. The fact is, for once I craved solitude. I didn't want to feel sorrier for anybody than I felt for myself.

I watch as Earl carries his boxes into the back door of the kitchen. He's a strong boy. I have twenty-twenty vision so I can see the muscles of his arms bulge when he lifts a crate of oranges. He wears a flat cap with a short brim, a white shirt with sleeves rolled up to his elbows and denim overalls. His skin has a sheen to it, like a lemon-polished banister. Truly, now that I think of it, he's a Michelangelo statue come to life. "The First Man" would be the title. "Adam," though of course that would be impossible. In every picture I ever saw of the Garden of Eden Adam and Eve were not even white, they were as pink as we used to get in summers at Corn Island after the first day roasting in the hot sun.

People can sometimes feel your eyes upon them, insistent as a tap on the back, and Earl glances up, sees me looking at him. He tips his hat.

"Ma'am," he says.

His voice carries, deep, soft as warm water.

"Marcella," I inform him impulsively. I'm not *that* much older than he is.

He smiles—does he ever—as though I've just told him a private thought with which he strongly concurs.

"I have a cousin named Marcella," he says. "So I'll remember."

That information throws me for a moment. I've never known any other Marcellas. Papa picked the name out of one of his poetry books and I've always felt unique. Now suddenly there's this woman running around . . .

"Is she pretty?" I ask.

"She's not hard on the eyes," Earl allows, but from the way his gaze lingers I know he thinks I'm the prettier. I give him a smile back as reward, then catch myself. This is the first personal conversation I've ever had with a Negro, and yet I don't feel odd in the least. I realize that I'm flirting, the same as I would with any other boy. Except Earl is not any other boy, and I don't mean because of his race. He's beautiful.

We're like a scene out of *Romeo and Juliet,* me on the balcony and him standing down below. Luckily I'm wearing the quilted satin robe I brought from home. I can tell from his expression that he's as confused by what's going on as I am, but that he's not ready for it to stop. We're both being dangerous and we know it. A train rumbles by in the distance, like a curtain going up.

"Wherefore art thou?" I emote dramatically.

"Marcella," Earl says. "I art right here."

"I know," I say. "I art right here, too."

We're both embarrassed, don't know what to do next. He glances over at his truck as if the horn has just blown, then we both speak at the same time.

"Do you own . . . ?" I start.

"How sick . . . ?" he begins.

"You first." He's polite as can be.

"I wondered if you were the owner of the grocery store."

"No, my daddy. Ernest L. Taylor, Senior. I help out sometimes, but my ambitions aim in another direction."

"Which one?"

"Ambition, or direction?"

"Aren't they the same thing?"

He rubs his chin as if my idea makes profound sense to him. "I swan they do," he agrees, "if it all works out."

I wait for him to add more. I've got no place to go, and at this moment there's nothing I'd rather do than hear the direction of Earl Taylor's ambition.

"I'd like to study veterinary medicine," he confides. "Learn to take care of animals."

"I had a dog." I am sure this news will elevate my standing in Earl's opinion. "Trixie. A cocker spaniel."

"They can be mean." He looks worried for my safety.

"Not Trixie," I laugh. "She was too lazy to be nasty." All the while my mind is racing a mile a minute. A doctor. Likes animals. Looks like a statue. If Earl weren't off-limits he'd be the most attractive man I'd ever talked to. "Your question?" I say finally, to return the favor.

"My . . . oh. I was only going to inquire about your health, your being here and all."

"My health?" As I formulate an answer two facts become instantly and indisputably clear to me. I am going to die. And before I do, I intend to kiss Earl Taylor on the lips. "I'm not a bit sick," I say. "I was causing too much heck at home and my papa paid off a doctor for a fake diagnosis. Any day now the lie will be exposed and they'll kick me out."

"I'm glad." Earl smiles again, bright as a Chinese lantern, looks from side to side. "If I didn't know better I'd ask if you were lonely up there all by yourself."

"If I didn't know better I'd say I was. I'd say nobody is due back here for at least two hours." I get up from the bed, cinch my quilted robe tight about my waist, and walk over to the rail. "My voice is getting hoarse from all this shouting," I say softly. "There's a fire escape emergency stairway around the corner."

"If I didn't know better . . ." Earl begins.

"Just this once," I interrupt him, "don't."

*   *   *

Despite my excellent long-distance eyesight, I was unprepared for Earl Taylor up close. I mentally changed the name of his statue from "Man" to "God." He had long lashes—an attribute I have secretly envied, delicately flared nostrils, and a mouth you could get lost in. "Cupid's bow" does not begin to describe it—it was carved as if out of the most tender wood. He smelled like Palmolive soap—a scent with which I was familiar and nostalgic from my previous employment—and when he removed his cap his closely cropped head was shaped like the Pharaoh in the illustrated Bible who wouldn't listen to Moses' warnings. Next to Earl Taylor I felt . . . dowdy, pale, washed-out.

"So. Marcella." The way Earl pronounced my name, it came out new. My family, my friends, I myself, we all said "Mar*cell*a," which now sounded fussy, sort of like a finger shaking in my face. Earl, though, took his time: Mar-cell-a, with maybe just the slightest more emphasis on the Mar. My name in his voice wrapped me up in an alpaca sweater. I never wanted to hear it any other way.

"Ear-ul," I tried to stretch him out too, but to me I just sounded like my Thebes country bumpkin cousins, so I tried again: "Mister Taylor." That was better. That ignited the smile I was hoping for.

We were standing about two feet apart but nevertheless his presence made all those dime novels I'd been reading come true. He did send off heat. My knees did feel weak. I did experience a magnetic attraction. He must have seen it in my face.

"Do you know what you're doing?" he asked softly—which warned me off a little until he added, "Mar-cell-a?"

"Sweet pie," I said. "I have utterly lost my mind." I took a step toward him, another. I reached my arms around his big shoulders, pressed my hair against his big chest, heard his big heart beating fast. We remained that way for a moment, him still a statue, me waiting. And then Earl Taylor turned into a man.

They say that running a slight fever increases passion. If that's so, we both must have been under the weather. They say a single bed is too crowded for two people. I say there's no such thing as too crowded. They say that the first time hurts a woman, that it's a disappointment. They couldn't be more wrong. They say that lovemaking before marriage is a sin for which you'll burn forever in hell. I say what we did was worth every minute of eternity. They say it's wrong for a white woman and a Negro man to be together. I say don't knock it until you've tried it. They say a man only wants one thing and when he gets it he loses all respect for you, leaves you in the lurch. I say Earl Taylor made even better love to me after we made love than he did during it—and that was a feat I wouldn't have believed possible. They say you feel ashamed when you slip. I say, ashamed? Are you kidding?

"Are you all right?" Earl asked finally when we came up for air.

"Am I all right, who?" I like my candy.

He whispered in my ear: "Mar-cell-a."

I got goose bumps all over my body. "I'm just fine," I said.

"Fine, who?"

"Mister Earl Taylor."

He kissed my neck.

But then I did feel guilty—awful in fact. I sat up, practically knocking him off the bed. "I lied to you," I said. "I've risked your life. I am sick."

"No you're not," Earl said, and gently pulled me back down to him. "Not anymore. You're right as rain. Love medicine cures all ailments."

And you know what? I believed him. And you know what else? It turned out to be absolutely true.

Earl and I were a modern-day Romeo and Juliet, but now that I had come back to life I wasn't about to kill myself. On grocery delivery days I did everything but yell "Fire!" to clear the porch, but mostly I only managed to recreate our original rendezvous twice, a month apart, and otherwise we didn't do more than wave to each other.

The days at Waverly, which had always seemed long, got

longer, but they were peanuts compared to the nights. My future was all of a sudden filled with "what if's." What if I got well? What if Earl lost interest? What if he was already married or had a girlfriend? What if somebody found out about us? What if—and here was the worst one—we were never together again? I was going nuts with unanswered questions until a day when everything became clear. The doctor told me that my X rays showed dramatic improvement and that if this continued he believed I could go home by September, and a letter arrived for me with no return address. It was from Earl, who had Palmer penmanship, and it contained the words I wanted to read: "I've got to see you."

I wracked my brain but came up empty-handed. In a ward full of girls nothing was private, and I couldn't exactly stroll out of the hospital and claim I was going down to the drugstore for a cherry coke. I needed a coconspirator and the obvious choice, the only choice, had to be Edna. There was one thing I knew about her without any question: she could keep her mouth shut.

That night, after lights-out, I whispered, "Edna, are you awake?"

"No."

"This is serious. I'm in love."

Silence.

"Did you hear me?"

"Which doctor?"

"He's not a doctor, but he's going to be."

"Which med student?"

"Not a human doctor."

A pause. "Let me get this straight. You're in love with a non-human who's going to be a doctor? Did your fever spike?"

"An animal doctor. A vet."

"What, did you see his picture in the paper? Go to sleep Marcella."

"Edna?"

"What?"

"I more than saw his picture."

"How much more?"

"Remember the day of the bingo tournament?"

"Yes."

"Well, let's just say I won the coverall."

Her blankets rustled as she sat up. I heard her feet hit the floor, both at the same time, and then she plopped down beside me.

"Come again?"

"You heard me."

"Do you mean what I think you mean? Didn't you learn your lesson with Vinny? I thought that Sarah explained the facts of life to you in Duluth."

"This is the fact of life."

Edna felt my forehead with the back of her hand. "Cool," she observed in her nurse's aide voice. Then, "So, does he . . ."

There was a question in her voice.

"Earl."

"Does Earl think it's the real thing?"

"Yes."

"And he's free?"

"Of course. Oh, you mean is he married? Of course not."

"Look," Edna said. She was interested now, in spite of herself. "If it's real it will hold. You get out in two months."

"It won't hold that long."

"If it's true love it will." She was a romantic.

"It's me that won't hold. I missed my period."

"Marcella! You swore to Father Rooney never to take a chance."

"That was before Earl."

Deep sigh. Edna was thinking. "Okay. I guess we could arrange a wedding here in the chapel. We'd have some explaining to do, but . . ."

"That wouldn't work."

"Why in heaven's name not?"

"Earl is a Negro."

"Earl is a Negro," she repeated.

166

"Um hmm. Younger than me, a little."

"My stars."

"Wait till you meet him, Edna. Don't judge me."

"Am I asleep?" Edna asked the dark. "Am I in a dream?"

"So will you help me?"

"Help you?"

"I have to figure out a way to see him, a place for us to get together and talk. We have to make plans."

"Are you going to give up this baby?"

"No. I'm going to marry Earl."

"Not in Kentucky you're not. It's against the law."

"I don't care where, as long as it's soon, before I show."

"Are you going to tell Mama?"

"Eventually." That was a worry too big to worry about.

"Marcella, have you thought this out? Are you sure? This could spoil your whole life."

"If I don't do it, I'll never be happy."

"You can't know that. Be realistic. This is purely physical."

"Edna. I've never been more sure of anything. I need you. You're the only one I can turn to. You can manage anything, I know you can. Help us. Find a place."

I could picture Edna sitting in the inky night. There were a few stars but no moon and the air was full of the clematis that grew up the sides of the building. I knew her eyes were closed, that her mind was spinning. I knew that she wouldn't say no.

"Edna, I'll owe you forever. I'll never be mad at you again."

Edna's wall was cracking, I could feel it, caving in against the pressure of the sea. I knew her teeth were gritted. I knew her hands were fists, her body rigid, but her heart, her heart was pure mush.

"Please."

The water gushed through. "I already have. The bottom of the tunnel."

"Where they bring out the dead bodies?" I was horrified, but I had to admit, it was the last place anyone would expect.

"It seems appropriate enough to me," Edna muttered, but she didn't mean it. She was hooked, an accessory after the fact, as they say sometimes on *The Shadow*.

"You're a genius." I sat up and hugged her till her back relaxed. "If it's a girl we'll name her Edna."

"If it's a girl, I wish her luck. Or a boy."

"I know it's a girl," I said. "I can feel it, and my feelings are never wrong."

CHAPTER NINE

THE TUNNEL

———————

Edna

I abused and betrayed the trust placed in me. As a nurse's aide I had been given a set of master keys that passed me through any door in Waverly Hills—and out of concern for Marcella I broke the cardinal rule and opened the lock to the tunnel.

In fact, the night she told me about Earl I half-believed—because I wanted to believe—that Marcella had slipped unnoticeably into a state of mild dementia. It was, after all, a lot to digest in one bite: a man, who was a Negro, who was Marcella's boyfriend, who was the father of her imminent child, whom she wanted to meet in order to plan their forbidden wedding. I'd heard of people who concocted fantasies in the clear shining aura that preceded their entry into paradise. Some patients before their deaths imagined whole unlived lives. But even for my sister, who wasn't that sick, this story was too improbable not to be true.

I should have told her to get her head examined—or some other part of her anatomy—but Marcella was usually so full of herself, so utterly convinced of her own high value, that it was impossible to resist her when she sounded doubtful. And that night she talked to me it was fear I heard mixed with her usual bravado, uncertainty flavoring the greed to have her every desire instantly fulfilled. What she wanted was impossible, unthinkable, foolishly romantic. Of course, I fell for it in a heartbeat.

The tunnel was the eighth wonder of the world. From an ordinary-looking doorway in the basement of the sanitarium it dropped underground almost a quarter of a mile in a series of concrete stairs to open into a garagelike building at the foot of the hill, where there was a loading dock large enough for the hearses to back up. The lighting was harsh—bare bulbs did not produce a flattering hue—but privacy was assured as long as no corpse was scheduled to be collected. It was a place where Naomi, God rest her sweet soul, had snuck a smoke, and somehow with its combination of death and drama it reminded me of those Roman catacombs the early Christians hid out in. A priest friend of ours, Father Rooney, made a pilgrimage once to Vatican City and when he came home he regaled us with stories of martyrs' bones that could be viewed behind inset glass windows, of flickering candlelight and narrow passageways. There was something, too, about being deep beneath the earth's surface that suspended everyday rules—at least that was how I explained to myself my involvement in the conspiracy.

It's not as though the tunnel had never before been used for illicit trysts. A few of the nurses claimed to find it eerily exciting to spoon with an eligible young doctor on the very slab where cadavers rested before being carted off to the mortuary. It was sort of a variation on that old canard, "I had too much to drink and I don't remember a thing," except in these cases the explanation went a bit further: I was dead. Some old hands even claimed that once a nervous intern who hadn't gotten the word that his date was off—for the obvious reason—had made precisely that mistake, not discovering his error until matters had proceeded well beyond second base.

But what Marcella was talking about wasn't a fling, it was a leap into thin air. However nice this Earl Taylor might be—and who knew? Marcella was a mantrap confined to a country without men. Anybody in pants might look good to her at this point—how nice could he be? Could he be worth turning every-body's life upside down? Could he be worth the trouble? Could any man?

"Reserve judgment," Marcella begged me, and I tried. My philosophy was naturally live and let live because, after Naomi, I knew that any of us could die tomorrow. Who was I to envy my sister a flash of happiness if this was the real thing? Or even if it wasn't? Beyond a certain point a person's responsibility—even an older sister's—was more interference than kindness. I could lay out the case against Earl Taylor, tick off the reasons why not on the fingers of two hands, but if in Marcella's mind that didn't add up to "no," then I was either with her or against her. And I couldn't be against her.

So I mailed a letter to Earl Taylor, told him the date and time I would use my key to unlock the door in the dark of night. I helped Marcella assemble a trousseau of sorts—it was heavy on nightgowns and light on traveling outfits—raided our savings accounts for enough money for train tickets, made up my mind to face the consequences of my actions. What I couldn't do was go along with Marcella's phony justifications.

"I'm doing this for both of us, Edna," she told me the day before the breakout. "It's our chance."

"It's your chance," I reminded her. "I'm the one left to clean up the mess."

"Think of Little Edna!" Marcella didn't play fair. We both knew that a niece might well be as close as I ever got to having a child of my own.

"Think of Mama." That was a conversation-stopper. Marcella's face turned to stone. Well, maybe not stone—closer to the very dense clay we used in our rehab classes to fashion off-center ash-trays and flower pots.

"Mama married herself. She'll understand."

It's funny how words can be intended to mean one thing but when you interpret them they describe an entirely different idea. *Mama. Married. Herself.* It was as though Marcella had through no fault of her own turned into the Oracle at Delphi, because I realized without any question that she had spoken a deep truth. Mama *had* married herself—Papa had simply been left out of the equation. It explained everything. I just wondered if Papa had ever realized it. Maybe he had. Maybe that was why he had left in the first place. Maybe that was why he had never fully come back. He had married Mama—and Mama had married Mama, too. He was in the way.

"Edna, where have you gone to?" Marcella had a sixth sense that alerted her when a person's attention had strayed from her problems.

"I'm thinking," I said.

"Good." She assumed, of course, that I was mentally working out the details of her honeymoon, but in fact she was the last thing on my mind. I am just like Papa—everyone said so—but I didn't want to wind up as alone as he did, the third wheel on a bicycle. There was one clear way to avoid turning out like that. I had two parents to choose as my examples: I could marry myself, too—and not implicate another human being's emotions. In the speed of thought the union was proposed and accepted. "I do," I said for the solitary time in my life, and from that moment on, with more relief than regret, I did.

"Shhh!" I told Marcella, who kept whispering in my ear about her second thoughts.

"But what if I'm making a mistake," she insisted.

"You'll come home. Sadder but wiser."

"What about Little Edna?"

"There's always Duluth. Meanwhile keep quiet. If the night nurse hears us the decision will be out of your hands and you'll never know what you missed."

"What if I'm supposed to miss it? What if my guardian angel is trying to stop me?"

"Isn't this a little late to worry about your guardian angel? Where was she those times with Earl on the porch?" I pictured

Marcella's guardian angel, eyes squeezed shut, hands over her ears, wings folded tight.

The basement hallway was dimly lit, and we threaded our way between crates of shredded wheat and shelves of stacked sheets. I carried Marcella's packed valise in one hand and the tunnel door key in the other. She had a box of her personal items brought from home. Thank God no one had passed away in the last twenty-four hours—the coast should be clear, and Earl was set to be at the lower entrance at midnight sharp.

The lock turned smoothly and we were on our way. The steps descended in a continuous stream, angling back and forth like the edge of an open accordion. At each landing there was a switch that illuminated the one below and extinguished the one above, so we were always in a spotlight, always the one passing flame in an ever deeper darkness. Unconsciously our footsteps adopted a common syncopation, regular as a metronome, as if we were in military formation, as if only one person was marching to an inaudible drum. The very hollowness of the space pressed words out of our brains. We were pulled by the force of gravity. We were buckets lowered into a well. We were approaching the end of who we had always been to each other—for once Marcella left with Earl and I remained behind, an unbridgeable rift would divide us. Marcella would become my elder in experience, I forever after her junior in hesitation. I was at once Marcella's past and my own future, and yet we never paused, even with our weakened lungs never rested to catch our breaths, just went on, rapids toward the brink of the falls, fearless as if our journey would never end.

"Thank the dear Lord!" Marcella exclaimed when we reached the bottom landing. "I hate to think of you having to climb that mess."

"I have all the time in the world," I said. "I have till breakfast before bed-check."

"Well, don't exert yourself, you hear?"

A knock sounded on the far side of the door.

"He came!" cried Marcella, and ran from my side to lift the latch.

*   *   *

I had seen Earl before, of course from a distance, but on the other hand I had not really *seen* him. Now, in that small space, emerging from night, he was everything Marcella had said—and more. The "more" was that, no matter what else there was to say about him, Earl Taylor worshipped the very sight of my sister. He was nobody's mistake.

I averted my eyes from their kiss, which both shocked and thrilled me.

"You came," he said to her once they allowed a space of inches to separate them.

"I had nothing better to do. My cotillion dance card was unaccountably empty." The silly words didn't match the catch in her voice, the longing.

I glanced up and Earl was looking at me.

"I'm Edna," I introduced myself. "The matron of honor." Impulsively I pressed into his hand the only wedding gift that seemed good enough—the pocket watch Papa had made me take the last time I saw him. Earl snapped the lid, admired the Spartan dial with its Roman numerals.

"It's old," I told him. "And was once broken. But now it keeps perfect time."

"Thank you," Earl said. His eyes were like currents of electricity, yet being so much younger he was shy around me, unsure in spite of his imposing size, his maleness.

"Do you have the tickets?" I became all businesslike to cover my own awkwardness. "First to St. Louis, then change trains and on to San Francisco?"

Earl patted his pocket. "After Kansas City we can ride together."

"Make sure you have a chaperone." I laughed as if this were the most amusing joke—what else could I do? I felt like the worst kind of ninny. I was about to be related to this man by marriage and I couldn't think of anything halfway intelligent to say to him.

"I'd never know you were sisters."

He did not mean this unkindly, but all the same I drew in upon myself. "I favor my father's side," I said. "Marcella, our mother's."

Just the mention of her name snagged Earl back into Marcella's orbit and she smiled as she felt the glow of his return.

"Then that's a lady whose acquaintance I'd like to make," he said automatically.

In the stunned silence that followed this pronouncement, we all imagined the scene. I don't know what horror Earl saw, what hysteria blanched Marcella's mind, but me, I simply heard Mama say, "Take off your hat when you're indoors." She'd deal with the rest of him later, in her own sweet time.

Over the next two years my news from Marcella arrived in drips and drabs in the form of notes that were more style than substance. A typical paragraph, taking up almost a whole page in my sister's loopy scrawl: "I bought the smartest red suit on sale in Sacramento. It's got a tucked waist, a form-fitted bodice, and the skirt is completely lined. Earl enlisted in the army before he got drafted, but he's stationed close by in Marysville so I get to see him whenever he has leave. Elgin's talking a blue streak—yesterday he said, "Mama, you're 'bootiville.' " What a little charmer, just like his daddy. We get a few hard looks when I take him out in his tailor-tot but nothing like it would be there."

I wrote back volumes of questions that never got answered, begged her to contact Mama more often, gave her the good report on my clean bill of health, but I might as well have put my letters in bottles and set them adrift in the ocean, for all the response I got. Every now and again Marcella would breeze over some fact that indicated she had at least read one of my weekly epistles, but that was as close as I got to any proof that my messages had been received. I told myself that in an emergency she would waste no time in getting in touch with me, and so each flighty aside I took as reassuring, a sign that all was well in California.

At least Marcella did enclose photographs in most of her letters. Whenever a new one would arrive I'd drop by Woolworth's on the way home from work and pick up a frame. They always came with stand-in pictures—a movie star, a happy couple, a scenic view—

which I'd discard and replace with Elgin, my nephew who Marcella said had been named in honor of my wedding present since he obviously couldn't be the promised Little Edna.

It was strange: I didn't particularly miss Marcella—I knew her so well and so long that I could chat forever with her in my imagination as though she were in the same room. Sometimes in these idle conversations she'd even surprise me by saying something I couldn't have predicted in advance, like a real person. No, the one I missed was Elgin, even though, or perhaps because of the fact that, I had never met him. As the gallery of his babyhood grew on the wall of my bedroom—Mama called it his shrine—I studied his face, looked deeply into his dark eyes, tried to figure out the befores and afters of the instant when the shutter had clicked. Here he was, my one toe in the door of the future, and he was an utter mystery to me. Every time I'd hear a baby cry in a store or on the streetcar I'd wonder, does Elgin sound like that? I took to browsing in the toddler section of Stewarts' department store and try and guess his size—that was one of those questions Marcella always forgot to answer. I picked out special greeting cards for every holiday—Valentine's, St. Patrick's, Easter, Halloween, Thanksgiving—and stopped by the bank for a brand new dollar bill to tuck inside the envelope. I addressed them to Master Elgin Taylor c/o Private and Mrs. Earl Taylor and hoped that Marcella had the sense to open a savings account in his name. A one-way connection was better than no connection at all, I consoled myself, and was confirmed in this conviction the day a photo arrived of Elgin on his first birthday. Serious as ever, he stared over an iced cake and into the camera. On his head, nestled into his black curls, was a pointed party hat. He wore a special bib with a yellow duck swimming in a pool of blue water. Best of all, though: in his fist he clutched the very card I had sent him—"To A Dear Nephew"—as if it was his favorite present.

For all Mama's ranting when Marcella ran off with Earl, she could no more resist the notion of Elgin than I could. Marcella and especially Earl were at a safe enough distance to allow Mama the occasional brag to her friends at the Saturday afternoon meetings of the Sodality of Mary.

"My grandson at only eighteen months knows a dozen words of the English language—and three of them are 'please' and 'thank you,' " she informed Mrs. Flaherty the day her own granddaughter Mary Elizabeth took two cookies from Mama's treatplate without asking.

"Too bad his darling mother never brings him to see you," Mrs. Flaherty sniffed back.

Mama bristled, not to be outdone. "Unlike some, I don't believe in interfering in my grown children's lives. I raised my girls to stand on their own feet, to fly the nest."

I busied myself with folding napkins as I felt both pairs of eyes turn toward me. Would Rita Flaherty have the gall to point up the discrepancy I represented? Would Mama explain away my continued presence with some trumped-up excuse? But no, this time they let me pass unscathed.

What *was* I doing here, anyway, I asked myself when we came home after Benediction that night. No air moved in the room but through the open window came the scent of freshly mowed grass. I remained kneeling by the side of my bed, my face cupped in my hands, my head bent. The blue and white patch quilt reeked faintly of mothballs. Beneath the braided rag rug, the floor was ungiving and my knees ached, but I was determined to resolve this question before I rose. I wore a green cotton nightgown and slippers fashioned to look like Indian moccasins. My hair was wrapped in a nylon scarf turban to save my permanent. It didn't matter to anyone but me when I got into bed, and I could think better in an upright position.

There was no denying that I now found myself on the far side of some invisible boundary without ever realizing I had been approaching it, some indelible line as thin but as significant as the meandering weave of a river through a road map. No passport, no visa had been demanded as I passed on my one-way ticket from young to not-young, from girl to lady. But the signs were plain: a teenaged salesclerk addressed me as "ma'am," a man offered me his seat on the bus, my figure required apparel that could only be described as matronly. Suddenly my marriage would have been more surprising than my remaining unwed, and I was even beyond the age at which the discovery of a religious vocation would be accepted without a supercilious remark. Suddenly I was, in the world's estimation, who I was going to be, a sealed package, a closed door, a perpetual "Miss."

I stood up, walked across the room and switched on the fan. It moved back and forth in a narrow arc, creating its false breeze, blowing the hair away from my face in one minute intervals. It stirred my gown, awoke sensation in my breasts until I folded my arms in front of me. I remained that way, alternately cooled and at rest, until I felt the welcome embrace of drowsiness, until I knew that when I gave in and lay down on my bed, I would be able to sleep.

Of course I had my career, if you could give my job such an exalted title. I did the books for a company that manufactured and sold rubber tires, a small family-owned operation that had been the only place willing or desperate enough to hire me when I finally left Waverly Hills for the last time. I had gone from interview to interview, my resumé carefully obscured, my two stints at the sanitarium accounted for by "nurse's aide"—and fooled no one. It was as though I had dropped through a pair of rips in my life and disappeared from view. I was a character from H. G. Wells's *The Time Machine,* someone who twice left the real world, had a whole set of experiences, and then reentered not a day older than when she departed. Except the real world had not stood still waiting for me. I was the same but it had moved on—and it knew perfectly well where I had been.

But the Al E. Keppler Company didn't care. The rumor was that constant fumes of cooking rubber ruined a person's lungs anyway, even if she worked in an adjacent office, even if on the humid days of midsummer she wore a surgeon's mask while she added her columns of figures. To tell you the truth, I didn't much worry about further hazards to my health. The way I saw it, my lungs had nowhere to go but up and if anything they would benefit from the addition of thin rubber linings. I knew their shape well from all my X rays, and after my first year at Al E. Keppler's I pictured them sturdy as inner tubes: black, yes, but so fully inflated they could float on water or resist the pricks of ordinary punctures.

When I first started I thought of the job as a stepping-stone. Everyone must start at the bottom, I reasoned, and the main thing was the weekly paycheck that kept Mama and me paid up on our expenses. As time went on, however, and no other opportunities presented themselves, I stopped waiting for surprises. I became trusted, depended upon, a fixture. I told myself that I was one of those essential workers in war-related industries that President Roosevelt depended upon, that I was doing my little bit against Hitler, helping out the boys overseas. I bought a U.S. savings bond every month and named Elgin as my co-beneficiary. I traveled down Dixie Highway to Fort Knox on Friday nights—even though it meant passing by the entrance to Waverly—to serve punch and change records on the Victrola for the USO dances. I was a good listener those evenings, a shoulder for love-sick boys to cry on, an older sister—safe and comfortable as a soft divan.

Civilian customers, some of them quite well known personalities, stopped in my office to check their accounts and eventually came to call me by my first name. Sometimes on a slow day they even confided their troubles between complaints about faulty treads or expired warranties.

"My husband, the old fool, wants to mortgage us up to our ears and start a restaurant," one woman said. "He thinks I'll go along with it if he names it after me, but I told him it was his baby."

"Can I run a tab on those new snow tires?" one of the richest men in the city wanted to know. "I never like to pay cash in full. Follow that advice and you'll never go hungry."

Sometimes over the phone a client would get flirtatious just to see how far along with the idea I'd go, but I was always suspicious. If his car was a station wagon or a four-door sedan that meant married and if it was a roadster that meant wild. I kept waiting for an invitation from a two-door hardtop in mint condition, but it never came.

One day as I was balancing a monthly bank statement I had a shock. My hand, gripping the yellow lead pencil, had turned into Papa's. All those months I had sat by his side, stroking his wrist while he drifted between wakefulness and sleep I had grown to know the design of his veins, the articulation of each finger, the half-moon of each nail—and now there it was, replicated on the end of my own arm. At first I was disturbed—women were supposed to use lotions and polish, were supposed to emblazon their fingers with diamond rings and golden bands. Their hands were supposed to look delicate and soft and mine, sure in its grip, was just the opposite. A hand that had known work and hard water. A hand that had no time for itself. A hand that didn't ask for holding. But after a while I gave myself a break. My hand brought Papa back in a rush of memory. My hand knew what it was doing. My hand was the one you'd reach for if you needed help.

Which, after an absence of almost four years, is exactly what Marcella did, except she did it over the phone. The call came in the middle of the night, an insistent ring that startled me out of sleep and drew me down the dark stairs in bare feet, shivering in the chill.

"Hello?" Let it be a wrong number, dear Jesus.

"Earl's killed." Marcella's voice was strangely calm, accustomed to the idea, as if I was not the first person who had heard her news.

"Killed who? Whom?"

"Been killed. In a boat accident overseas. I'm a widow."

I held the receiver to my ear with one hand and wrapped the other arm tight around my waist. "Mercy on us."

"They're shipping his effects back by airplane—I got a telegram of condolence from his commanding officer."

"Marcella!"

"I've got no time to feel sorry for myself, Edna," she said. "Not tonight. I'm not going to let go until after the funeral—they'll have a memorial service for him out here at a military cemetery where they don't make distinctions. I'll wait to fall apart till I come home."

"Sure, honey. You want to talk to Mama?"

"You tell her. She never even met Earl. She didn't know him. She didn't want to know him." There were splinters in Marcella's tone, long and sharp, so deep under the skin that no ordinary needle would pry them loose.

"Should I come?" I'd be on the next train if she asked for me.

"Get my room ready, and fix up the sewing room for Elgin. He eats cornflakes for breakfast . . . and applesauce."

It was as though Marcella was an automatic washing machine, chugging back and forth within a confined space. "Don't ask me not to be normal," I read between her spoken lines. "Don't make me feel anything."

"I'll lay in a supply. When . . . ?"

"Today is the twenty-third," Marcella said, and I knew for both of us that conjunction two and three would ever after be marked with an indelible "x" on our calendars. "I'll plan to be home on the first."

"Where will we put them all?" Mama looked around the kitchen, surveyed the white metal cabinets, the blue linoleum floor, the table set for two breakfasts.

"This house was built for four," I reminded her. "We'll manage fine."

She shook her head in irritation. "How are we going to explain the child?"

"We'll tell him that his daddy loved him and God took him early. We'll tell him that everything will be all right."

Mama bugged her eyes at my obtuseness.

"Not *to* the child. The *child*."

I swallowed the words that struggled for release. Almost all of them.

"Your grandson has a name."

She gave me an accusatory glare. "You can't hide your head in the sand, Edna."

As if that's what we all hadn't done. As if we didn't know how.

"In some of those pictures you've got plastered on your wall he could be . . . Italian?"

"More Jewish, I think," I said and watched the denial cross her face like a storm cloud.

"This is not a joking matter."

"He's a baby," I said. "A precious treasure we don't deserve. You'll hold him in the rocker. You'll tell him stories. You'll teach him to say his prayers."

She nodded. She could see herself doing these things. She could feel his little body snuggled on her lap. She could smell his hair. She could see how much he'd adore her.

"We'll cross the other bridges when we come to them," I went on. "One at a time."

"How's my Marcella?" Mama finally asked, pitiful.

"Bearing up. She's got a spine of steel under all that frou-frou."

Mama smiled to herself, claiming the credit. "She can stand on her own two feet after all."

But I didn't care. I mourned Earl—he had seemed like a nice enough man. I would guide Marcella through her grief. I would take care of them both. I could do anything that was necessary, because when the dust finally settled, for years and years, I got Elgin Taylor. I got my boy.

CHAPTER TEN

OIL PAINTINGS
FROM BAVARIA

Elgin

My father could sleep with his eyes open. That's one of the things I've heard about him. That he knew how to order at a restaurant, is another, and that he was a good ballroom dancer. And yes, he was Black. He had his army uniforms specially tailored to emphasize his small waist and broad shoulders, and he was decorated with a bronze star for a gunshot wound in the leg he suffered at a baseball game when the private seated a row ahead of him was careless with a rifle.

He wore a ruby ring that the army didn't return with the rest of his effects, but what did come back to my mother was a steamer trunk containing her father's pocket watch, four oil paintings and many sets of crystal glasses my father had plundered from Germany. My mother put the watch in her jewelry box and hung the paintings on the living room wall in a rectangular arrangement: on the top row was a blue and white scene of crashing surf and a picture of a fountain in a town square, and below them were a homey pair of mountain chalets, one with a week's laundry strung on a line from the porch to a tree and the other with a window box filled with red flowers. When I was sixteen, I copied the identical signature at the lower right corners of the canvasses, then checked the name against an artists' directory at the library in case we were in possession of valuable masterpieces. I did so without hope, for even I could see that my father had bequeathed us the work of an amateur.

The crystal glasses were stored in a locked cabinet, and rarely dusted. Each individual glass was quite beautiful—delicate, some with a hint of amber or aquamarine, some accompanied by a decanter—but there were no complete sets. In one case, there were three matching wine goblets, in another, seven miniature brandy snifters. I came to suspect—because it's what I would do—that the original owners, forced to leave their belongings behind as they fled before the advancing American army, had deliberately smashed one of each set. But their gesture had no meaning. We didn't drink.

I kept my personal legacy from my father in a tin box: his bronze star, pinned to dark velvet; a cigarette case inlaid with a mother-of-pearl map of Germany, each city marked by a lapis lazuli. Inside were two stale Egyptian cigarettes that my father had failed to smoke. There were a scatter of uniform insignia, stitched lightning bolts and numbers, and a variety of multicolored ribbon pins that signaled some achievement, either his or that of a slain German officer, I couldn't tell which. Folded into its envelope was a letter my father had written to my mother the second Christmas after my birth. He was homesick. Security prevented his revealing his exact whereabouts. Beneath his signature he had drawn a horizontal "S", then slashed two short perpendicular lines through the midpoint. I thought this was a private code, something between my parents, until I recalled noticing the same thing under the name of John Hancock on the Declaration of Independence. My father made no mention of me.

Loneliness or battle fatigue—those were factors used to rationalize my father's accident, only two days prior to his scheduled repatriation. He was rowing a boat at midnight on the Danube

River. He overturned and his body was not recovered. Where was he coming from, alone, at that hour, or going? Whose face was in his mind? To whom did he call for help?

I occasionally try to sleep with my eyes open. I stare at an object and let my mind go blank, but when my tears dry, I blink. Whenever I notice a man of approximately the age my father would have been who seems to look at nothing while standing in line or waiting in a bus terminal, I observe him closely to see if he's unconscious. It's often impossible to say.

When I was nine, my mother came close to marrying Albert Fitzpatrick, a man who looked like Dwight Eisenhower, the president at the time, and who worked for the L & N railroad at the switch station in Versailles, Kentucky. Fitz, which is what everyone called him, was in his forties, smelled of brilliantine and had always lived with his sister in the house where they had grown up. He courted my mother in the booths of restaurants while I drank ice cream sodas, and it was clear to all of us that if I didn't actively oppose him, my mother would say yes.

Fitz was shaped like a suit of clothes on a padded hanger or a three-storey house with a fat central chimney. His cheeks were pink beneath the powder he patted on after shaving, and his eyes were bright as the blue rhinestone on my mother's favorite pin. He was a man who took care of himself, who cut his fingernails square and kept them clean, who tucked a toothbrush in the inside pocket of his sports coat, who could be depended upon to produce a clean, ironed white handkerchief if one was needed. My mother was his last chance, he told her, and he hers. He told her that, too, and he was right. He argued that a boy needed a father. He understood about me, he promised. He didn't hold me against her.

When my mother and I went out on dates with Fitz, I rode in the backseat of his Buick sedan, and positioned myself so that I could watch Fitz's face in the rearview mirror. He drove with one hand, sometimes the left, when he put his hand on my mother's knee, but more often the right. Those times he crooked his elbow out the window and drummed his fingers on the chrome in tune with whatever music was on the radio. Now and then he'd glance at my reflection in the mirror, hoping, I imagined, that he wouldn't see what he saw.

He couldn't quite sit still: his foot would tap, or he'd scratch behind his ear, or, while he was listening to someone talk or waiting for a waiter to appear, he'd compress his lips, open and shut his mouth absently, and make a popping sound like water dripping from a faucet in the middle of the night. I told my mother he made me nervous. I told her Fitz was ordinary.

Among the women who raised me there was a constant hum, a buzz of mutual affirmation or longstanding feud. Even the most mundane pronouncement was greeted with incredulity— "There's a white sale at Kaufman's." "Really?!"—and gasps of amazement. No silence was permitted to penetrate their exchanges. Rather, words and sounds overlapped the evenings like shingles on a roof, creating a solid wall in which difficult thought, true controversy, contemplation, could find no port of entry. Few candid utterances ever had the space to form.

I lived as if inside a room of benign mosquitoes—all whine and no bite. I learned to tune out their conversation, to answer without hearing the occasional questions directed at me, to treat the drone of their voices the way a man who lives by the ocean incorporates the crash of waves—it became my base, the boat in which I floated.

Eventually at night, when at last my mother and Aunt Edna knelt by their twin beds and said their prayers before sleep, the shock of silence would sometimes startle me into insomnia.

I loved them and I was confused by them, as they, I was sure, felt toward me. The feelings were scrambled together, the whites and the yellows of them surfacing in random order. The banalities beaten into a foam of genuine goodness, the insistent focus on inconsequential topics cooked in a sizzling butter of repressed pain. I was lulled by the nights of sitcoms on televisions—shows we followed as diligently as if they held the key to wisdom, by the formality of dressing up for Mass on Sunday only to endure another vapid sermon from the pulpit, by the sameness of the food we ate, the predictability of opinions we expressed to each other, by the trivialities that were taken seriously and the desperately important matters from which we shied away—pleading ignorance or too great a sensitivity or distaste.

Secretly I yearned for toughness, unbending views. I imagined that such things existed among men, but I knew no men well enough to insert myself into their company and learn otherwise. I grew frustrated even as I perfected my social graces. I resisted the feminine swooning of the Church even as I took daily Communion. I stood at the door of my life even as I became increasingly reluctant to knock.

Now and then a spark would ignite in Aunt Edna—she would be roused by a political speech, moved by a segment of the nightly news—and that kindled in me a sense that with her there was the possibility of engagement. She had an edge, a serration which, to my mother's shock and dismay, she occasionally unsheathed in pique or fatigue. At such moments, my mind clicked on, raced, but before I could join the revolt, my grandmother's admonishment—"Edna!"—would spew guilt like water from a fire hose and douse my aunt's brief flame.

It wasn't that I resented their pleasure or wished them ill. It was only that I felt so isolated, so gagged, so stifled in the limited range of emotions that they sanctioned, so wrapped in protective plastic. And yet I was enough their product, sufficiently under their influence, that I suppressed my protest, accepted their norms as the direction manual for my operation, berated myself for my minor dissatisfactions and complaints. In Confession I sought penance for my transgressions of thought, acknowledged my lapses of respect, begged divine forgiveness for my rebellious nature—and then purged my soul through the immediate recitation of an assigned seven Hail Marys or one Hail Holy Queen or three Memorares—the very prayer, my mother had told me more than once, that she had chanted during the onset of her labor with me, right up until the gas she insisted upon put her under.

"Remember O most gracious Virgin Mary, that never was it known that anyone who fled to thy protection, implored thy help or sought thine intercession, was left unaided. Inspired by this confidence I fly unto thee, O Virgin of Virgins, my Mother. To thee I come; before thee I stand, sinful and sorrowful. O Mother of the Word Incarnate! Despise not my petition, but in thy mercy hear and answer me. Amen."

I wonder what my life would have been like had my father not died. We wouldn't have lived in Louisville, for one thing, where he and my mother were, in the beginning, against the law and later at the very least would have been frowned upon. If my father had lived I would have been a Negro and not simply "exotic looking" as my mother and aunt insisted. As a flesh-and-blood presence he could not have passed for anything but what he was, not for Sicilian or Greek or Spanish with a touch of the tar brush, as my grandmother had once described him to a woman who stared at me too long on the day of my first Holy Communion. We drove home from church in complete silence, but when we got out of the car my mother stopped by the snowball bush in the side yard. That was the only time I ever heard her angry.

"Mama, bite your tongue." She spat out the words as if they were caps in my cowboy pistol.

"Mind your manners, Marcella. What do you expect me to say? Darkie?"

"If you ever, ever again use a word like that in front of Elgin I will leave this house and never look back."

I was stuck between them, just below the bosoms of their Sunday dresses. My mother's was a flowered jersey, my grandmother's a black crepe. I was wearing a white short-pants suit for the occasion and looked down at my Buster Brown saddle oxfords. A new clear-glass bead rosary still twined in my fingers. Yesterday I had made my first Confession and so my soul was spotlessly clean, as white as it would ever be, for I had reached the age of reason and would now be held responsible by God for all my future sins. Father Vance had called us, my whole second-grade class at Holy Name, little seraphims. My mother never before raised her voice and now she frightened me. I shut my eyes and entreated my guardian angel for protection.

"Don't you dare address me in that tone." My grandmother was not used to being crossed by anyone, much less by my mother.

"The she-lion defends her cub," my Aunt Edna dressed in a navy blue suit, weighed in with a raised-eyebrow voice. Now I was surrounded by tight-girdled hips, penned by a triangle of women arguing over my head.

"You stay out of this Edna," my mother and grandmother barked at the same time, surprising my aunt into temporary silence, then they turned back to each other.

"It's that dang white suit in the bright sunlight," my grandmother went on. "You might as well rent a billboard and advertise."

The only prayer that came to my mind was the Act of Contrition that we had to memorize perfectly for Confession, so I recited it silently, over and over.

"Elgin has a beautiful suntan." Aunt Edna had recovered and come in on my mother's side. "Everybody envies it."

"All winter long?" My grandmother, once challenged, was not about to be appeased.

"What do you want, Mama?" my mother demanded. "Tell me. What?"

"You put us through this," my grandmother answered.

"She was in 'love.' " The way Aunt Edna said the word it sounded like curdled milk.

"At least somebody wanted me back. At least I'm not an old maid." My mother was so unused to the emotion of rage that she didn't know how to control its direction. She was a spinning firecracker, a pinball machine with all the lights and bells and buzzers going off at once.

"Hush up." My grandmother refused to let this be an argument that didn't include her at its center. But I was the one, forgotten, in the middle and finally it was too much for me, too awful, and even though I was a big boy now with Jesus Christ in my stomach I couldn't help myself.

For a moment my crying was the only noise in the daffodil spring morning. As I drew in big sniffs of air I could smell the tinge of the honeysuckle that grew near the alley, the mixed fragrance of three colognes: lilac for my grandmother, lily of the valley for my aunt, violet for my mother. Cars drove by on the street, birds called to each other, the sun beat down from a cloudless sky.

Suddenly my mother, my aunt and my grandmother were all on their knees—no thought to grass stains on their dresses, no concern for runs in their hose, their worried, horrified faces at my level.

"Honey," said my mother.

"Doll Baby," said my aunt.

"Sugar Pie," said my grandmother.

Their arms fought each other for the right to embrace me but in the end they wove together tight as a robin's nest and I was crushed in softness, washed by breaths sweetened by Lifesavers—lemon for my grandmother, orange for my aunt, cherry for my mother, buffeted by hair stiffened into peaks by aerosol spray.

"Don't listen to us biddies," my aunt said.

"Dry your beautiful green eyes," my mother said.

"My little man," said my grandmother. "I got up before dawn and baked you your special cinnamon rolls. Come on now, smile for your grandma."

"Let me see where you lost that tooth." My aunt tickled me under my ribs, her fingers gentle.

"We are so proud of you today." My mother asserted her rights and pulled me into her lap, stroked my short hair, rocked me in her arms. "An angel straight from heaven."

"And you look like a dreamboat," my aunt agreed.

"Cinnamon rolls," my grandmother intoned, but we took a

while before going in for them. Instead, in a time out of time so unusual that I never forgot it, we sat on the ground holding on to each other. Nobody worried what the neighbors might think. Nobody complained about anything. Nobody got bitten by a mosquito or stung by a bee or stuck by a rock. We just rode the earth together as it whirled around the sun, and after a while my grandmother began to sing in her choir-trained voice, "Oh Mary, we crown thee with blossoms today." My aunt and my mother joined in, harmonizing, "Queen of the Angels," and looked at me expectantly, happily, until I added in my high soprano, "Queen of the May."

We shared a wide-ranging secret life, my family and I. There were the after-dark visits to the West End where my father's cousin ran a small grocery store, a place where, for an hour or two every week I was a Negro. My grandparents were in the Lord's hands, but in the crowded rooms behind the counter, the walls were covered with photographs of them: getting married, posed with my father as a little boy, in his army uniform—that picture was bordered by a black satin ribbon. He was their only child, the miracle baby who arrived after they had given up hope, my cousin loved to tell. Their pride and joy who could do no wrong in their eyes.

"They didn't even mind about . . . you know," my dad's cousin, who had the same first name as my mother, told me when I was old enough to understand. "They accepted her as God's will be done. They took her into their hearts like they would any . . . you know. And when you came along, they took you into their hearts, too."

While she told me this, I was looking at the album that was normally hidden in the piano bench, the album with the photographs of my mother and father at their wedding in California, of my father in a sleeveless undershirt holding me in his muscular arms before he was sent overseas the last time. I turned back a page and regarded my grandparents in their old age. My grandmother was tall and straight—"Creek Indian blood," my cousin explained as she peered over my shoulder. "Just look at that nose." My grandfather was rounder, plump as an easy chair. His hair was gray but his eyes looked ready to laugh at a joke. I was between them, barely able to stand, too young to remember. Somehow in the pictures of me in that album I seemed darker, different. Once I stared so hard into the mirror over my cousin's bedroom dresser that she laughed.

"Who do you see, Shug?" she wanted to know.

"Just me," I told her, embarrassed to be caught.

"And who is that, Mister Smartypants?"

"Elgin Taylor."

"My oh my, aren't you the one?" She laughed and came over to stand beside me. You could see a resemblance in the shape of our lips, the curve of our chins, the set of our heads on our necks. As I watched, her face turned serious. "I remember your daddy when he was your age," she told me.

"Tell me."

"Spoiled, that goes without saying." She didn't mean it. "Sharp as a tack, though, no denying that. And he had a mouth on him that would whip cream."

"Am I like him?"

She cocked her head, turned her eyes on me and in the reflection we appraised me at the same time. She smelled like the chicken she was frying, like the shampoo in her hair, like peach lipstick.

"Shug, you were right the first time. You're just you, a one-of-a-kind."

"Then I'm not? Like him?"

"You need to grow some. Earl was big, powerful, but weak underneath. The bravest thing he ever did was to marry your mama. It's not fair to make comparisons. Give yourself time to grow into him, then beyond."

I felt slight enough to be knocked over by a stiff breeze.

"But you got his brains. You got . . . you got the sense of him, I don't know how else to explain it. I mean, just standing with you in the room brings me back, reminds me. You don't have to say anything. It's just kind of a presence you inherited. Like, you know, the way one thing will make an idea about another thing pop into your head? You got that."

She put her arm around my shoulder, hugged me against her. "He would have loved you, baby. Loved you to pure distraction."

I imagined it was him holding me, his face next to mine. I imagined he loved me to pure distraction, answered all my questions, told me what to do, who to be. I imagined staying with my cousin forever, working in the store where he worked, growing into him. But when Aunt Edna knocked on the back door and she and my cousin said their wary, uncomfortable hellos and good-byes, I picked up my plaid wool coat and went on home.

We didn't talk much about my father at our house, except to be generally grateful to him for contributing toward the production of me. My mother had her own private photo album stashed in the back of her closet and I was allowed a few pictures which I kept in a box on my bedside table, but when someone—a sociable teacher, a lonely priest, someone who couldn't be denied—paid a call, my mother would drag out a framed portrait of a soldier who looked like a combination of Anthony Quinn and Lena Horne and claim he was her deceased husband, born and raised in New Orleans, Louisiana—and buried there as well. People would glance from the picture to me and back to the picture again, trying to believe her, not knowing why they didn't, and admire his "Mediterranean" handsomeness.

"Tall, dark and handsome," my mother always described my father to outsiders. "He swept me right off my feet."

"That's the understatement of the week," Aunt Edna said one evening after an assistant pastor, hoping we would help sponsor a missionary in the Belgian Congo, had left with five dollars.

"It's the honest truth," my mother answered. "Earl was tall. He was dark. He was handsome."

"And you were good and swept," Aunt Edna added.

"Behave," my grandmother admonished, though I didn't want them to stop. I wished they'd tell me the whole story.

But mostly, except for women my mother and aunt knew from work or long ago, few outsiders entered our domain. The parents of my schoolmates, sensing that something wasn't quite right about us—the rumor circulated for a while in the sixth grade that my mother was secretly divorced or, just as bad, had never been married at all—discouraged their children from my friendship. As time went on, I ceased to mind, preferring the unsuspicious company of my mother, aunt and grandmother—or of myself— to the effort it took to lie.

We made the most of our time, turning even the most ordinary event into a production. Before bed at night we'd call the kitchen table "The Stork Club" and pretend that our chocolate milk and cups of tea were dry martinis. Before Sunday dinner we locked the doors, pulled down the shades and dressed up: me in a sports coat and tie, my mother and aunt in evening gowns from their youth now stored in keepsake trunks, my grandmother in her best hat, and act as though we were eating our meatloaf, mashed potatoes and green beans with ham at the fanciest restaurant in town. We spent evenings painting by numbers, playing Monopoly, or watching the tiny screen of our television set, but whatever it was we did, the four of us did it together. We were like the remnants of an endangered tribe—hostile to strangers, reluctantly accommodating of each other, in solid agreement as to the external boundaries of our available territory. They—especially my mother and aunt—were girls who had never quite grown up and I was a boy who had never quite been a child. And it suited us all just fine.

I never grew into my father, but eventually I became impossible to conceal. In ninth grade a boy who didn't like me because I wouldn't let him cheat off my answer sheet, Charles Bartlett, called me "nigger lips." In tenth grade my geometry teacher asked my mother at a PTA meeting how old I had been when she adopted me. In eleventh grade no one would be my date for the junior prom. In twelfth grade I was refused service in a restaurant. The waitress pointed to a sign that read "We reserve the right to select our clientele," and asked me to leave.

That day, instead of going home, I drove directly to my cousin's grocery.

"What's wrong, Shug?" She had grown heavy in her late middle age, weary with the repetitions of her life, the constant small reorders of evaporated milk and loaves of bread, chewing tobacco and root beer, Tabasco sauce and canned corn. The unpaid running tabs of the customers she carried out of kindness.

"God-damned shit," was all I could say I was so mad.

"God-*damned* shit," she agreed without question or hesitation.

"Who do they think they are?"

"Say it, child."

"Shit!" My vocabulary condensed into a single, shouted word.

"Mmm-hmm," she nodded with such earnestness that my anger was pushed out by amusement.

"Aren't you even wondering why I'm so pissed off?"

"Do *I* need to ask? I'm just surprised it took you so long."

"So what do I do? What do you do?"

"You do what you have to do or you do what Earl did."

The mention of my father's name always came as a surprise to me, as if a door suddenly opened in a blank wall.

"You join the army, Shug. It's your ticket out of town."

"That didn't save him from being killed," I said. Even I could hear the bitterness in my voice.

"That may be, that may be," my cousin allowed. "But I do believe it saved him from killing somebody himself."

As if they knew that I would be arriving to make an important announcement, my mother, aunt and grandmother were assembled in the living room and saying the Rosary when I walked through the door.

"The Second Joyful Mystery," Aunt Edna droned as she had ten thousand times before, "The Visitation. Our Father Who art in heaven . . ."

"I need to talk to you," I said.

"Don't interrupt the Holy Rosary." My grandmother shot me a righteous glare.

I leaned back against the wall, raised my eyes and looked at the paintings: the churning sea, the clean clothes flapping in the Alpine air. He saw those pictures, liked them enough to steal them. It was as though I was finally waking up.

". . . on earth as it is in heaven," my aunt concluded.

"Give us this day our daily bread . . ." my mother and grand-mother responded.

"I'm not Italian," I broke in.

They stopped, turned to me as though I were about to provide the solution to a crossword puzzle clue.

"Elgin," my mother began.

"I'm not Greek."

"You're Irish," Aunt Edna insisted. There was a quaver to her voice, buried beneath its certainty. "Irish as Paddy's pig."

I couldn't help it, I smiled at her. "Black Irish?"

"The Spanish armada," my grandmother said, and began to recite the familiar family tale. "A shipwrecked sailor arrived at your great-great-great-grandmother's door."

"And a man delivering groceries glanced up to a porch." I spoke for once only to my mother. "And there you were."

"Elgin," she repeated, asking me not to go further.

"And here I am," I said softly.

Her eyes met mine, and I knew for just that instant when she looked at me she saw my father as he had been the first day she had met him. It was as though she had fallen back in time, back to before, when nothing had seemed impossible.

CHAPTER ELEVEN

SOLE SURVIVING SON

Marcella

You'd think it would be more than enough for a woman to sacrifice a husband to war. Even the U.S. government agreed with me and awarded Elgin a draft status of 4-A, sole surviving son, that exempted him from military service. You'd think a boy as smart as he was would take advantage of the one material legacy he received from his father—a safe passage through Vietnam—but no, he comes back from that cousin of his, that other Marcella in the West End who has been the very bane of my existence since the first day I heard her name—determined to enlist in the armed forces.

Couldn't he see the look on Mama's face when he spoke the words? Couldn't he hear my heart breaking?

Edna was no help at all. "Why?" was all she asked him.

"It's time," Elgin answered, as if that made any sense on earth.

"Isn't there another way? College?" Edna asked.

He shook his head. "I've got to find out who I am."

Hippies, that's who influenced him. All that "know yourself" mumbo jumbo they talk on TV. "Be free!" Who's "free" I'd like to know? Am I free?

"Who you *are?*" Mama was stalled at Elgin's response.

"Grandma," he said. "You know what I mean."

But of course she didn't, as he well understood.

"Where did this crazy idea come from?" I asked—and out of nowhere I had that experience, what do they call it?, déjà view, where you think you've been in it before. It was as though my words were an echo, and then I remembered, clear as day: I had repeated an exact quote of my question to Earl the day he enlisted.

At least my late husband had a comprehensible answer: "Because otherwise I'll be drafted and this way I have some choice about what I do."

"And that is . . . ?"

"The cavalry," he said. "It'll give me a chance to work around horses so that when I get out, when the war is over, I'll have some background for vet school."

"I didn't know they still had a cavalry." All the cowboy and Indian movies I had ever seen raced across the screen. Bugles blowing, blue-shirted riders charging, flags flying. Earl galloping on a palomino. I liked the idea of the cavalry.

"These days it's more for show," Earl said, bursting my bubble. "Safer than combat, which is a concern what with Elgin and all."

Thank you very much, I thought to myself. Don't be safe for me or anything. "Have you informed your parents of this decision?" Earl remained close to his family, even from a distance.

"They approve."

Thank you very much again. "So you're not asking for my opinion on this? It's an after the fact."

"A what?"

"You've already signed the papers?"

"Be with me on this, baby. It's the only thing to do. Marcella?"

It never failed, that tone of voice. My insides turned to butterscotch pudding. This, this anger wasn't about Earl not asking my okay. It was about Earl being gone, about Earl being in any kind of danger, about losing control of what mattered to me.

"You know I am."

"I know, baby."

We each took a step toward each other, another, until every inch of me was pressed against him, until I could feel the creases in his pants upon my thighs. His neck was warm against my cheek, his large, wide-spread hands completely covered my back. I kicked off my shoes and stood on his feet—that was the way we danced to Guy Lombardo on the radio in the dark some nights. The brass buckle of his belt dug into my ribs and I rubbed against it. I wanted to feel it, wanted a scar that would last until he came home.

"Where do they keep these horses?" I murmured to Earl's chest.

"They travel around," he said. And with that his hands began travels of their own. "They go north and they stay there for a while. Then they head south."

When Earl touched me like this the word "no" disappeared from my active vocabulary.

"They roam east."

They did.

"Then they roam west."

They did that, too. If he kept this up much longer I might whinny. "Don't they ever like, you know, bed down?" I asked.

"On occasion they don't even bother with a bed," Earl said.

And sure enough, they didn't.

"Mom?" Elgin's voice broke into my reverie. "You all right?"

"I'm not a bit all right," I told him. "Not one iota."

"Don't dramatize, Marcella." This from my dear sister Edna.

"I'll do anything I want. I'll be *free* like everybody else!" See how they like it.

"First my husband, then my son-in-law"—Mama was stretching that one, even for her—"then my grandson, all gone before me."

"I'm not dead, Grandma," Elgin reminded her, but Mama was off on a tear.

"Left alone. If I had . . ." she paused for effect, made sure we were all listening to what she wasn't supposed to say. ". . . Andy would never . . ." Then she swung her head abruptly to the side, the equivalent of clapping her hand over her mouth. We weren't supposed to know about her romance with someone named Andy long before she married Papa, but he cropped up in every grocery list of her woes.

"Then you should have married him," Edna said sharply, violating our unspoken pact of silence on the subject of Andy.

Mama smarted as if struck on the cheek. "What did you say, Miss?"

"You should have married Andy instead of Papa, had his children instead of us, had a better life all around."

The look on Mama's face was like a poker player whose biggest bluff had just been called. All her chips were in the pot—she had nothing left to raise. A rare silence settled onto her, obscuring as one of those lead shields they use when you get an X-ray treatment. From within its protection she spoke the truth.

"I would have if I could have."

There, it was out. She'd trade us all—Papa, Edna, Elgin, me, our years together, our decades of the Christmas and Mother's Day and birthday gifts we had meticulously selected for her, the forgiveness, the laughter, the hurricane of words that had blown through this house—for someone who was just a first name.

"Who was he, anyway?" Elgin asked. "Somebody from Thebes?"

Mama's face flushed, her right ear a bright crimson, and she lifted her chin in refusal to answer.

"Do you know if he's even alive?" I asked, my hurts multiplying to the second and third powers.

"He left me first," Mama said, and dabbed at her eyes with the corner of her apron. But then her back straightened. She looked directly at me. "I never left him."

I glanced at Elgin, who was out of his league in this battle among women. Here he had come in, ready to knock us over with his big announcement, and in a matter of minutes the momentum had shifted, had gravitated like a ball of mercury to the lowest ground. The epic poems of our family's history were carved in granite stone by rivers of blood. The past ruled over the present with unsympathetic dominion. Whatever Elgin might do or not do mattered less in our secret councils than the deeds of Edna and me, and we ourselves were mere asides compared to the grand escapades of Mama and Papa—and now this Andy. And all of us, every one, paled before the incandescent sun of my late grandmother, Rose Mannion, the founder and the source of us all. Every item she had touched and which still endured—the crystal salver, the handmade Irish table, even the tune of the song written specially for her—was invested with myth, sacred relics of a Titanic age beyond our memory but which ruled our imagination. She was, I realized in a grace of intuition, the only possible trump to Mama's hand.

"I suppose Grandma knew about your Andy?" I asked her brazenly.

Mama froze. Her cheeks contracted around her clenched jaws and she turned toward me with the full force of her bitterness.

"She killed him," she said. "To keep us apart."

Our living room was a tableau. It lost a dimension, as though we were transformed into an oil painting titled "Stunned Surprise." This Andy, previously only a sigh of regret, of missed opportunity, an unrealized threat, had in the span of a conversation risen like a midday moon and blotted out our combined existence. It was as though each of us, one at a time, had been smudged and erased by the soft end of a hard pencil. Mama's declaration, so absolute in its unthinkability, left no room for ordinary retort. One couldn't say, "Huh?" or "What do you mean?" or "Could you please explain that further?" The only balancing response would have been to scream "Liar!" but what did we know? Maybe it wasn't a lie. Maybe *we* were. And so we remained immobile, each of us in our own sad definition: me, the widow; Edna, the orphaned; Elgin, who didn't know who he was. Mama, denied her true love. Only Rose was absent, and her lips were sealed.

I was lying on the twin bed I used in my upstairs bedroom. The furniture was a suite we had inherited from Mama's Lexington cousins who had died out without direct heirs. It was raining hard, one of those lashing Louisville storms that seem to swat at the earth rather than merely drench it. The drumming on the shingle roof came in angry waves. I had retired while it was still dusk and failed to turn on a lamp, so now the only illumination came from the streetlight through the slats of Venetian blinds. I thought I might never go downstairs again if I could help it.

There was a knock at the open door, which meant it was Elgin. Neither my mother nor my sister would extend me such courtesy.

"Come in, Honey."

He trod heavily across the floor—setting Mama and Edna, still downstairs, to wonder why he had come to see me.

"Can we talk, Mom?"

"I'm listening."

The mattress on the other twin bed groaned as it absorbed his full weight. For a while we let the quiet settle.

"Are you mad at me?" he asked. His face was striped with light and dark.

Elgin had the ability to hold my heart with the innocence of his questions. He acted as though my feelings, mad, glad, sad, were important, worth worrying about. He acted as though I *had* feelings. And for that simple and unique reason, I could never hold anything against him for long.

"I'm mad at life."

"I know. But are you mad at me? For joining up?"

Just the mention of it made me mad at him all over.

"It's like you're choosing your father over me."

"I didn't *choose* anything," Elgin said, low and slurred as if he were talking in his sleep. "I was an accident. Admit it."

"Did that other Marcella put such foolishness in your head?" I

202

could strangle her. "Accident" was not a concept I associated with Earl Taylor.

"She didn't have to. I only have to look in the mirror."

"Are you ashamed of who you are? Elgin, is that how we raised you?"

"Mama, can we talk straight, here for once. Can we just drop the bullshit? Excuse me, the . . . pretending? Who are we protecting?"

"We're protecting me," I answered. "And you. And Mama. And Edna."

"From what? Who do you think is fooled?"

"It's not a question of fooling, it's a question of faith. We can't see God, but we believe in Him."

"Yeah, well, people can see me. And when they do, they don't see an Italian by the name of Taylor."

"Elgin, I was not ashamed of your father. We lived openly in California, proudly. He was the sweetest man I ever knew. Handsome, quick as a whip, full of plans. There was nothing to apologize for about Earl."

"Then stop. You broke the rules, Mom, and I'm exhibit 'A.' You and Aunt Edna and Grandma have never made me feel bad about myself, but the world is bigger than this house and I've got to live in it as who I am. I've got to learn how. Not as a white boy who goes black on vacation. Not as a Greek. Not as the band leader in the St. Patrick's Day parade. I'm who I say I am. I'm who you say I am. But I'm also who everybody else on earth says I am, and somehow that's got to add up to a single sum."

I closed my eyes, took a breath. I was capable of talking without . . . pretending. I just didn't ordinarily elect to do so. Real life can be sordid, disappointing, so why sink to its level on a day-to-day basis? But all right, my son wanted honesty and I'd give it to him.

"This is the thing, Elgin. You're like—now don't take offense because I mean it in the best possible way—you're like a lion raised in captivity, like that Elsa. What happens if you return to the wild? Do you possess the instinct for survival? Is it any more . . . 'bullshit' "—that expression had never before crossed my lips but I wanted to show Elgin that I could speak that hippie talk as well as the next one—"for you to pretend you're a Negro? How would you ever pull it off?"

"Mom, what do you think I've been doing for the past few years? A person acts like he's treated. It's not a talent, it's a survival skill. Do you think anybody is a 'Negro?' Do you think my father was some sort of exception? The only people I have to act differently around are white people because they assume I'm stupid or dangerous or harmless. As a Negro I can be me. It's as a white man I have to apologize."

"Oh, sweetheart. If it were only that easy."

"Come on, Mom. What do you know about it?"

My little Elgin believes he has grown up into a man. Well, let him hear it all. "Try being a woman, just for a day, will you do me that favor? I have perfected the impersonation, I admit, but give me credit. I learned early on how to play the role. I am a human being cast in a dramatic production, just like you, just like everyone. You don't step out of character, you don't suspend disbelief. I know everything a woman has to know. I am a woman. Don't tell me your identity crisis. I've lived mine since the day I learned how to attract my papa's attention."

Elgin didn't say anything for a moment, and I was halfway out of breath. Finally he spoke.

"Hello? Who is this person I'm talking to? Just exactly where has she been for the past nineteen some years?"

"I art right here," I couldn't resist saying, and smiled in the dark at the memory.

"You're what?"

"You think it doesn't take strength to be me? Marcella, the helpless one. Marcella, the simpering fashion plate. Marcella, who depends upon the world."

"Then why do you do it?"

"Oh, Elgin. Oh, darling. By the time I was old enough to

know what was what, Edna had the corner on independence. She was Papa's clear favorite, before and after his disappearance. So I was left with Mama to charm and there was only one way: to be the girl she expected, the girl she needed. And I did it to perfection. I have ever since. You want honesty in the dark, young man, you'll have it, but I'll never admit to any of this after tonight. This is your one audience with your mother without her makeup on, so listen carefully. I'm not as dumb as you think. You see Edna as your ally, Edna as your champion, Edna as the one who will love you no matter what. Well, she will, I'll be the first to admit it. Edna would lay down her life for you in ten seconds flat, I give her that. But, Honey, Edna wasn't the one who took a chance and had you. Edna wasn't the one who gave you birth and didn't for an instant consider the invitation of your dear other Marcella to surrender you up to be raised by strangers. Edna wasn't the one who bore the gossip, who was deaf to the whispers, who laughed in the faces of every friend who wouldn't go along with her story. Edna wasn't the one who came home to Mama with her tail between her legs because it was the best thing for you. Edna loves you, Elgin, more than she loves anything else on earth. But so do I. So do I."

The bedsprings gave as Elgin rose. It took only two steps for him to cross the distance between us, and then I was in his arms as I had not been in the arms of a man since the last time Earl left with his cheery, "See you later, gorgeous." And I let myself be held. I let his tears of recognition course down my neck. I took his "I'm sorries" for the sincerity they were worth. And I let him go, the boy I had lived with and lived through and lived for.

"You," I said to Elgin when he had quieted down. "You don't ever be ashamed of me either, hear?"

"Never," he promised with the innocence of the untested. "Never in a million years, Mom."

We'll see, I thought without saying it. We'll see.

I've got to say, Elgin was a better correspondent than his father had been. His letters described the miseries of basic training, the rage he felt at the lectures about how the Vietnamese weren't fully human, the fear. Throughout it all, though, even from APO address overseas, he kept the promise I had extracted at his departure: Don't ever tell me anything that will upset me too much. And what could I respond in return? I had nothing of substance to report on, so I filled my envelopes with meringue and gossip, minor priestly misconducts and nuns who left the convent, Mama's outrageous remarks and Edna's stiff-necked stands. I clipped items from the *Courier-Journal* about his high school and sent him reports about the Derby. Mama baked him cookies and I wrapped them in the paper of the season. And when he called with the news that he was being sent overseas, I told him I was proud of him, that his daddy would be proud, that I was in his corner all the way. I told him that and trilled my laughter through the rest of the connection and then cried myself to sleep. I know Edna did the same. If we lost Elgin, we lost our reason for life, pure and simple. If we lost Elgin I would never forgive Earl for giving him to me. If we lost Elgin I would never forgive Mama for bringing me into this world. If we lost Elgin I would never forgive God. If we lost Elgin, I would never forgive myself for letting him go.

I'll never know what he saw over there in Europe. He never talked about it and I never pressed him. All I know is that once Elgin returned after his first tour of duty I decided that I would not grudge him any happiness he could find in this life, that I would never again pressure him or criticize him or try to fit him into any mold but his own. He looked ravaged, older than Earl at his last good-bye, like Papa in his final days. He had experienced something that hurt him, something he couldn't talk about, and now he had to fill in the blanks between that and where he started, any way he could. He had a right, my precious son, to make up for lost time.

Where did I go, I wondered sometimes late at night. Where was the life I had been promised? Was it all lived in those three years off and on with Earl, the sum total? Was the rule that you lived the first half of your life for your parents and the second half of your life for your child and if you could manage to squeeze a vacation or two in the middle for yourself you should count your-self fortunate.

Yes, I guess the answer is, at least I think so when I contemplate Edna. She had been squeezed shorter than I. She went directly from Papa to Mama to Elgin, no intermission, no time for herself, no lightning strikes of pleasure when it was all about her, nobody else. I counted myself among the blessed. Draw. Treasure. Release.

I first saw Christine's name on a Christmas card in 1971, post-marked Seattle, Washington. "To Mother"—which Elgin *never* called me—"from Us."

Us?

And there was this name, sprawled across the bottom of the page like she owned it. "Love CHRISTINE and Elgin."

"Who's Christine?" My first question on the Christmas Eve long-distance phone call.

"Just . . . somebody."

"Somebody who?"

"Somebody I met out here."

"A nice girl?"

"Nice enough."

"What does that mean?"

"It means nice enough."

"Is she there?"

He hesitated. "Yes . . ."

"Put her on."

"No. Next time."

"Why not?"

"She's indisposed."

"In where?"

"Disposed. Bide your time, Mom. Is Aunt Edna standing next to you?"

Of course she was, so I had to wait. Christine. The name sounded respectable enough. But where does a soldier meet a respectable girl? Christine. All the things I didn't ask about her. Was she a Catholic? What color was she? Was she a virgin—Elgin wouldn't answer that. He'd say, "Oh, Mom, give me a break." But a mother had a right to know.

I wouldn't let her name alone. Every time I'd talk to Elgin—which was weekly now that he had completed his double stint in the service and had chosen to be discharged for reasons unbeknownst to me at Fort Lewis, outside Tacoma, I would bring her up.

"So how's Christine?"

"She's okay, I guess."

"You guess? Haven't you seen her?"

"Sure I've seen her."

"Well, then you'd know how she is."

"Fine. Christine is fine."

"I sense something here, Elgin. I sense something serious."

"You'll be the first to know," he promised me.

"Before her?" I asked.

"The second, okay?"

I didn't answer. Already I was second place.

"Okay, the first."

"Thank you. I'm just a mother."

"Oh, you are that."

"I beg your pardon."

"You're a mother. You are a mother. Believe me."

"I know I'm a mother. It's what I am."

"It is what you are."

"And I *am* proud of it."

"And you *are* proud of it."

"Good-bye, Elgin. I love you."

"I love you."

Click.

So it was no surprise when he finally admitted to the engagement.

"I've always wanted a daughter," I told him.

"I know."

"I don't mean instead of you."

"Uh-huh."

"In addition. I want a picture."

"She doesn't like pictures."

"Then bring her to visit, to meet her new mother."

"I think her current mother is all she can handle."

"What's that supposed to mean?"

"There isn't time for a visit. Mom, she's, uh, in the family way."

I shut my eyes, opened them. Who was I to judge, and he was going to marry the girl.

"How wonderful. Tell me about her."

"She's an Indian."

"An Indian?"

"An Indian. From Montana."

I thought of Earl in the cavalry. It seemed right.

"How wonderful."

Edna, on the extension phone, chimed in. "Is she a Democrat?"

I heard him say, off to the side, "Hey, Christine. Did you vote for Kennedy?"

"Of course," said a voice I tried to place. "He's cute." Cigarettes, definitely. Older than Elgin possibly. Not fresh out of the gate in any case.

"Yes," Elgin said.

"Thank God." Edna was relieved.

"Was she raised Catholic?" I had to ask, for Mama's sake.

"Were you raised Catholic?" Elgin asked the invisible Christine.

"Mostly."

"Yes."

"Can I say hello to my future daughter-in-law?"

"Next time," Elgin said evasively.

"Why not?"

He whispered into the phone. "Well, Mom, she assumes you're, you know, black."

"I'll set her straight."

"I don't think that would be advisable at this time."

"Elgin are you ashamed of your roots?" Edna was indignant.

"Me, too," he said, and hung up.

No one was going to deny me a bridal shower, even if the bride deigned not to be present. I had my friends to consider and Elgin deserved a proper send-off. I didn't care if she was an Indian or a Mexican. I had only one child and I insisted upon the ceremony.

"Send me a photo of Christine," I nagged Elgin every time he called. "Nothing special, just so I get the general idea of her."

"She hates having her picture taken, Mom."

"An old one, then. Her college yearbook." A mother could hope.

"She didn't go to college."

"High school, then."

"She doesn't have it with her."

"Then give me her mother's address. I'll write. It's good we make a connection, anyway."

There were all these unexplained blackouts in my conversations with Elgin about his Christine.

"I don't think her mother," he said, finally. "She does have a friend, though. Back where she comes from. You could write to him."

Him? "An old boyfriend?" I did not approve of prolonged relationships.

"Nothing like that. Just a friend. Dayton Nickles is his name. A friend of her brother's."

"She has a brother?"

"He was missing in action in the war."

Even though Elgin was fully discharged those words still sent a chill through me.

"Mail me his address," I asked. "I'll write to Dayton."

"He sounds like a good guy," Elgin said. "I'll bet he'll answer."

"Dear Mr. Nickles," I wrote in my best penmanship. "You don't know me but my son Elgin Taylor is going to marry your missing friend's sister, Christine, and it has been suggested to me that you might have a photograph of Christine that I might use for the announcement. I would surely appreciate a quick reply."

I wondered if he interpreted the meaning of "quick."

Whether or not he did, he wrote back by return mail and enclosed a cutout from his yearbook.

"Dear Mrs. Taylor, Unfortunately this is the only photo of Christine in my possession, but you are welcome to it. I apologize for the inconvenience of the writing but inasmuch as it goes across Christine's face I cannot remove it with Wite-out without obscuring her features. All best wishes, Dayton Nickles."

A nice boy, I decided, well-bred.

The picture was another matter. There was this over-made-up face, all eyebrow pencil and lipstick, staring out at me. Christine looked hard for a high school senior, older than her years, older than Elgin. Her black hair was permed within an inch of its life. Her eyes were—and there's no other way to express it—cold. Her lips were pulled back to reveal evenly spaced teeth. She was trying to look like that Annette Funicello whom Elgin used to pine over on *The Mickey Mouse Club*. Worst of all, catty-corner across her forehead she had written in thick script: "To Dayton. Eat your heart out. Love, Christine."

How did I explain that?

"She means Ohio," I informed my sodality ladies. "She had a full academic scholarship to the University of Dayton, a Catholic school, which she turned down in order to attend the College of Great Falls, Montana, which as you know is run by nuns."

" 'Eat your heart out,' " Rita Flaherty quoted. "Isn't that a little . . . extreme?"

"They really wanted her," I told Rita in a superior tone. "All expenses. They brought her to campus twice."

The event was a wedding shower in our dining room with Christine's framed photograph in the middle of the table. If we couldn't host the real thing, at least we could honor her image. I served Vienna sausages, toast with the crust cut off, pimento cheese spread, kulka coffee cake from the German bakery, and iced tea. A regular feast. I couldn't help it if Elgin's Christine looked like low-rent, looked like somebody you wouldn't want to know, looked like a Presbyterian on the make. Preordained for my son.

"She's a lovely girl," I lied. "She calls me 'Mother.' "

"How dear," said Rita Flaherty in her bearing-false-witness-against-her-neighbor voice.

"They're going to name their first baby, should they be so fortunate, after me," I said for added impact. "My middle name, Diane."

"When is it due?" Madeline asked in mock speculation.

"At least a year after the wedding, unlike some premature infants," I responded pointedly. Let *her* explain her own little apple-of-her-eye grandchild, Aloysius, who had appeared in record time after Mary Elizabeth's hasty, bansless nuptials to Peter Daley.

Before we opened the gifts I brought out a punch bowl filled with a concoction of ginger ale and Hawaiian punch—very festive—and a miniature wedding cake with a bride and groom on top. It goes without saying that the tiny statues bore little resemblance to Elgin and Christine, but it's the thought that counts. I had informed Elgin of the exact hour of the party—counting in the time zone changes—and hoped in the back of my head that he and his fiancée would call in order to join in, but the telephone remained silent.

"Here's to the happy couple," I toasted, and everyone clinked plastic glasses. The gifts were the usual fare: a toaster, a set of steak knives, a baby blanket—from Rita, of course—a heavy glass vase, a box of stationery. I unwrapped them carefully one at a time, slitting the Scotch tape with my thumbnail, and we all exclaimed as if we'd never seen such treasures before in our lives.

"I'm going to wrap these back up in their original paper," I told the group when we were done, "and ship them off to Elgin first-class mail. That way he and Christine can have the pleasure of surprise."

At the mention of her name, all eyes were drawn to Christine's pouty face. You could almost hear her saying, "Eat your heart out," as she beheld the set of silver-plate coasters, the enamel pie server, the book I had contributed: *The New Bride's Guide to Creating a Happy Home.*

"She'll be floored," I assured the girls. "I'll bet she'll use some of this pastel notepaper to thank each of you individually." I could always disguise my handwriting—they'd have nothing to compare it to. I'd explain the local postmark by saying that Christine had sent them all to me personally in a Manila envelope and asked that I pass them on.

"Is she Italian, too?" Rita asked sweetly. "I mean, she seems almost as dark complected as Elgin. Their children will get such lovely tans in the summer, and not have to use a drop of sun lotion. I envy them, I truly do. Me, I turn red as a beet after a half-hour's exposure."

"No wonder you always look so peaked," Edna commented, coming to my rescue.

"In the olden days a lady never went outside without her parasol," Rita countered. "A genteel pallor was considered the mark of high society."

"Would that high society have been in County Cork?" Mama asked from the sidelines. "And how did they manage to dig potatoes and hold an umbrella all at the same time?"

"I'll have you know . . ." Rita began.

"More punch?" I offered, and used a soup ladle to replenish the refreshments.

I was so desperate to forge some kind of bond to my son's new family that I wrote letters to all concerned: to Christine, to her mother (whose address I had finally wormed out of Elgin), even to Dayton Nickles to thank him for supplying the photograph. He was the only one who answered, and over time he and I struck up a sporadic but friendly correspondence. He was a teacher on the Indian reservation where Christine had been born, and seemed like a most pleasant young man. I tried not to wonder why Christine hadn't chosen him rather than Elgin—tried not to because the answer might well be that Dayton hadn't chosen *her* for reasons unknown.

In any event, Dayton Nickles became my lifeline of information. It was he who informed me that Elgin and Christine had been wed in a civil ceremony, he who broke the news that their child, a little girl, had been born and named some foolishness— Ramona—but that at least she also bore my own second name, Diane—another one of Papa's romantic flights of fancy—as a tribute. And it was Dayton, over the years, whose little hints betrayed my worst suspicion: that there was trouble in paradise, that Elgin and Christine were not getting along as well as they should. There was nothing I could do to help. Elgin seemed determined to keep me from even talking to his wife.

"She thinks you still live in California," he told me.

"Why would she think that?"

"She just got that idea."

"Well, set her straight."

"It's not just that. She, you know like I told you. . . . The black thing."

"You mean *Negro?*"

"Black, Mom. Times have changed."

I looked away from the phone, put the receiver against my chest while I gained control over my reaction. "Damn you, Earl," I whispered. Finally I spoke again.

"This will come as some surprise to your grandmother and Edna."

"What does it matter, Mom? Why rock the boat? We aren't even living together at the moment. What do you care what she thinks?"

"Where's little Diane?"

"Ray's with Christine, mostly. I'm working odd shifts at the post office. I see her on Sundays and whenever . . ." He paused, obviously about to conceal from me some pertinent fact.

"Whenever what?" I prompted.

"Whenever Christine is under the weather. She's delicate."

I looked over at Eat Your Heart Out on the mantel. I didn't believe "delicate" for a minute.

"Do you want me to come out there to help?" I asked. "What's a grandmother for?"

"No. Mom, no." Elgin's response was too quick and too certain to allow any objection. "But thanks. I'll let you know if it gets to that point, really. Everything's fine—just a little lover's quarrel."

There was this Lana Turner movie, *Imitation of Life,* that I saw twice when it ran at the Rialto downtown. Lana's colored maid had a daughter who turned out light skinned and when she grew up she passed herself off as white. She never admitted the truth until her poor mother worked herself to death. Then the guilty daughter threw herself on her mother's coffin and begged for forgiveness, too late to matter. I wondered, would Elgin do that with me? Admit where he came from?

"Have you figured out who you are yet?" I asked him in a cold tone of voice.

"I'm a work in progress, Mom," he said. "Bear with me, okay?"

"Just don't ever show her that other Marcella's picture and claim it's me," I warned him.

"Come on, Mom. What a crazy idea. What do you take me for?"

Every hollow, false word he uttered told me that he had done that very thing.

The fiction ended one summer when Elgin called all upset.

"Mom, can you and Edna take care of Ray for a couple of weeks if I fly her out there? I can't miss any more work and Christine's in the hospital. I don't want to leave Ray with strangers again and . . . it's time you met her."

"When?" I asked, my heart thudding. I looked around, began mental lists of all the preparations I would have to make. Coloring books, Chinese checkers, homogenized milk. We could take her to the zoo. I could sew her a whole new wardrobe.

"I'm calling from Chicago," Elgin said. "Between planes. We'll be there in about two hours. Can you pick us up at the airport?"

When I didn't reply, too amazed to say anything, Elgin added, "This is an emergency, Mom. I wouldn't ask if it wasn't."

"Will she recognize me?" I asked. Was she expecting his cousin to be waiting at the gate?

"She knows," Elgin said, defeated. "She thinks you look like a movie star."

I left Edna and Mama to clean the house and make up the other twin bed in my room, then stopped at a toy store on the way to Standiford Field. I couldn't greet my granddaughter empty-handed. I love to shop and when I'd make up her Christmas or birthday boxes I'd prowl the aisles for inspiration before settling on a present. This time I didn't have the luxury, so I snatched up the first possibility that caught my eye, a Raggedy Ann doll with a stitched-on smile that could brighten a room. I was holding it in front of me when I spotted Elgin's head above the crowd of passengers. I was glad I saw him before he saw me, because it gave me time to compose myself. My baby had aged in the seven years since I'd seen him. There were threads of gray in his hair, lines that didn't come from laughter that ran from the sides of his nose down past his lips. His eyes lacked their sparkle. That green color: there was more of me in Elgin than of Earl. Earl had a vibrancy, a spring, a twinkle that his early death had preserved in my memory. Elgin had outlived his father in more respects than years, and it pained me to see it. Then he picked me out of the crowd and his face lit up, just like it used to. He reached down and when he stood back up he was holding a wiry little girl, all big hair and wide smile and spindly legs, and gesturing for her to look at me. I waved Raggedy Ann in her direction, and the next thing I knew my grandbaby was in my arms, smelling of Juicy Fruit, talking a mile a minute.

CHAPTER TWELVE

INDOOR STARS

<hr>

Elgin

You can't see the stars from Louisville on summer evenings. An industrial haze overcasts the night sky, diffusing back to earth the colored lights of the Colgate Palmolive clock, the top of the Heyburn Building and all the other proud illuminations. From a distance, approaching from the east especially, the city appears enclosed in a paperweight, like a colony on the moon. Whatever happened below has its reflection above, and for the space of miles it's clear where those long-dead astronomers got the idea that we're all protected by a curved roof arching overhead.

There used to be a movie house downtown, Loews, with a violet blue ceiling sprinkled with points of light, each accurately positioned. It was a comforting place to rest, an indoor amphitheater, a drive-in without cars. As the film credits began to roll the sun would go down and for two hours you had your choice: Hollywood or heaven, or a combination of the two. Sometimes when I was small and still Italian I could go there at night with my hat pulled down, my collar turned up, in the company of my mother. When I got older, of course, I was not permitted inside.

Real stars came as a shock to me when I went to boot camp, far beyond the natural boundary of that smoke screen. They weren't as bright or as close to where I sat as they were at Loews, but there were damn more of them. They spilled down the walls of the sky and even got mirrored in the black water of the lake where we did our aquatic training. Outdoors at night, I felt as though they must be spotting my skin, turning it red like a flashlight does to your finger when you hold it over the bulb.

The way I saw it, the day I signed up I was a clean-washed blackboard, all previous writing erased. I could be anyone, my own floating definition, a walking collection of expectations that I didn't have to choose to complicate. In Louisville, growing up, I had been hard to miss, the face in every family photograph to which eyes were instantly drawn. In the service, however, I was invisible—another brother, vague about my background, watchful, blended in. "Army brat," I would say if pressed, but few questioned me. At last I was one in a crowd.

Of course, I had been so busy trying to escape the shadows of my past I didn't pay enough attention to the future I was buying into. When I declined my deferment, rejected the only legacies besides a death pension and a bronze star my father left me, I only vaguely looked ahead. I was prepared for geographic dislocations, a loss of control over my movements. I had absorbed all the sitcom and old TV movie stereotypes about loud-mouthed sergeants, pompous protocol, the antics of barracks life. I was ready to shout "Sir" at the slightest provocation, ready to learn how to make a bed that could bounce a dime, ready to crawl under barbed wire during basic training. I think, based on my father's example, I was even ready to die. What I wasn't ready for was being sent to Germany and assigned to wait tables at the officers' club.

I had no skills, it was explained to me, no special talents, no killer instinct. I couldn't disassemble a gun and put it back together again fast enough to suit my supervisor. I couldn't take it seriously when they asked me to yell and stick a bayonet into a stuffed dummy. What I had, the powers that be finally decided, were good manners. "You're unusually well-spoken," I was told more than once. "Polite." They didn't add "for a black person" but we both knew that's what they meant. Some of the guys in my unit added those words and came up with a total of "Uncle Tom," but in my heart I knew the answer was more like "Aunt Edna." I had been trained to be considerate and deferential; it was a strain not to be. I'd listen to black soldiers from Detroit or New York or D.C., feel the anger that steamed and bubbled like boiling water, listen to their stories of mistreatment and racism, of brutalities on the streets and off them. I'd nod, learn the vocabulary, say the right "right ons." What else was I going to do? Reminisce about our dress-up Sunday dinners, about my phony Italian childhood, gripe about being valued, treasured, loved so hard it hurt? The truth of the matter was, I had a confusing past, painful to me in small ways, but not a bad one, not compared to anyone I was compared to. It's easier, at eighteen, to admit to adversity than to kindness, however misguided. Sympathy beats envy every time as an icebreaker. I could fake a lot of things, but rage wasn't one of them. Pissed off was about as bad as I got, and that didn't qualify me as mean, lean, fighting-machine material. Finally the only camouflage I was offered was a starched white shirt, black pants and patent leather shoes. The only weapon at which I was expected to be an expert was a carving knife, the only strategies had to do with matching the right wine with the right entrée, the only infiltration maneuvers involved refilling water glasses without interrupting table conversation.

My mother, grandmother and aunt had a mixed reaction to my assignment, which they decided was safe but beneath me. My cousin Marcella took a harder line, convincing me that she would have made a better soldier than I. "Spit in the food before you serve it to them," she advised me. "That's what the house slaves used to do. Those officers may be the ones sitting down, but you're standing up. So you *stand* up."

When I got to the base in Germany and started at the club, I stood, but I couldn't bring myself to spit on good food. I did my job, quickly got a reputation for efficiency. The rest of the staff marked me as standoffish or shy, depending. A loner. In the evenings I took advantage of the night classes offered at the rec center and started taking German. As long as I was here, I figured, I might as well understand what people were saying behind my back.

The coincidence of winding up in the very country my father died trying to defeat was not lost on me. I'd look at German men my father's age and wonder if they had shot at him. In less than twenty years, the span of my life, we had officially gone from being enemies to being friends, and yet I couldn't forgive them for what they had taken from me, couldn't pass a crowded beer hall, the laughter and music shouting out at the street, without walking in my father's shoes, hearing what he couldn't hear. Lots of the soldiers at the base had German girlfriends, wild, blond-headed women whose English always sounded suggestive, even when they were saying the most ordinary things. But I kept to myself, resisted being fixed up. I studied Germans the same way I studied everybody else: white Americans, black Americans, even Italian or Greek Americans. If I watched them closely enough I could blend in and become invisible.

There was one officer, a black captain from Seattle, "Jenkins" according to his nameplate, who took an interest in me. He usually ate alone and when I'd come to take his order he'd make small talk—the where are you from, do you have brothers and sisters chitchat you hear all the time, except with this guy he listened to my answers and would remember them at the next meal. That way we made progress, you could say. He accumulated knowledge about me the way you'd fill out a questionnaire at the first visit to a doctor's office. It wasn't long before he'd open up with something like "Have you heard from your mother in Louisville?" or "Where in Germany, exactly, was your dad's accident?"

He told me stuff about himself too. How he loved Seattle, rain and all. How it was the place to be, the future. Mountains and ocean and how the group that had it hard out there were Indians, not people like us. "You've got to see it, Elgin," he said, "to believe it."

He showed me pictures of his ex-wife, his two kids, both girls. Bragged on their grades, their piano-playing lessons. It got so I started to look forward to him coming in, missed him on the days he didn't. I started to wonder why he rarely shared a table, and when he did—and acted more formal toward me—I halfway resented it. He must have been about thirty-five, one of those spit and polish career men who pin all their ribbons on straight as a row of stair steps. He had kind eyes behind his wire-rimmed glasses, a sly smile when he broke the rules and left me a fat tip. And unlike most of the rest of the people who ate at the club, Jenkins treated me with respect, as if I were more than ears and feet and hands whose only reason for existence was to make their orders appear hot and on time. He was, I realized after a while, considerate, and that made him feel like home to me.

It did not escape the notice of my coworkers that I spent more time at Jenkins's table than absolutely necessary.

"Taylor's got a boyfriend," one of them—Darrel Spencer, a total asshole—stage-whispered one day across the steam table. Several of the others laughed, but at first I didn't know what he was talking about. Halfway out the door with a plate of French fries the meaning hit me and I turned around, crossed over to Spencer and pushed the potatoes, not even a minute out of the deep hot oil, into his dare-you face. "You fool nigger," he shouted, swatting at his skin with a damp dish towel. "Fool!" But he never said another word to me about Jenkins and neither did anyone else.

Still, his remark set me wondering. Pure friendship was not an emotion I found it easy to trust. What did Jenkins see in me, want from me, expect? I found myself pulling back, answering his casual questions with a single "yes" or "no" and cutting him off when he began to talk about himself. "Today's a bitch," I'd say. "I'm back-ordered three tables," and then hide out in the kitchen. One evening, while I was doing this, the door swung wide and I caught a glimpse of Jenkins sitting at his table. He was staring at the plate, lost in some private thought, and looked up when a waiter passed. *He hoped it would be me,* I realized when I saw the disappointment register on his face. Jenkins was the only person in a three-thousand-mile radius who gave a shit about me and here I was, running away from him because I was afraid that somebody like Spencer would razz me. Screw that. I pushed through the door with a shrimp cocktail, on the house, and set it before him.

"So what's happening, sir?" I asked. "Long time, no talk."

Jenkins looked up at me with that wide and unbelieving smile of his, a smile that held back laughter like a damn contains water.

"The name's Paul," he said, "and can the 'sir.' "

"Consider it tuna fish," I said. "Paul."

Fact is, I hadn't had all that many friends. I mean, you could count them on no fingers. Maybe my definition was off. I had lots of "heys," a few "what you up tos?" and one or two "I'll call yous" but nobody outside my immediate family to whom I felt connected, responsible to, responsible for. I had no right, no right whatsoever, to think of Paul that way and yet he gave me cause. Yes, I was the waiter and he was the waitee. He had the rank and I had the "no skills." He was older, had been around and I was dumb as dirt. But there was some place we saw through each other to, some candle fire through a keyhole, that balanced off all the inequalities. I didn't believe he wanted a thing from me beyond that steady gaze. What more was there to want in this world? He was the father I didn't have, the brother, the soul mate. His calm patience welcomed me to tell him anything, to let down my force field, to establish contact, and relief passed through me like the memory of a special birthday cake every time I said his first name.

"So if I'm Paul," he said later that evening when I took him up on his offer to stroll around the fence line, "you're . . . ?"

"Elgin."

"Like the watch?"

"You could say that," I allowed, "but it's also the case that the boys in my family all get names starting with the letter 'E.' My father, for instance, was an Earl."

"He's the one that was killed over here."

"Not so far away, so it happens," I said. I tilted my head south. "He was on a river, alone in a boat. It capsized. He could have floated anywhere."

"Have you been there?" Paul asked. "To the place? To pay respects."

The thought had not occurred to me, but once he mentioned it, it seemed like fate, like the right thing to do.

"I will," I said. "First leave I get I'll get myself a ticket and visit the spot. I never knew him."

"Would you . . ." Paul began, then stopped himself.

"Would I what?"

"No. It's too personal. We don't know each other. I have no right to ask."

"Ask," I said, more curious than anything else.

"No, I just thought . . ." Paul stopped on the road, looked through the wire mesh.

"That?"

"You know, I mean, I could take you. Save you the fare. It might not be a place you want to go alone—but I'm sure there are people you're close to, people you'd feel more comfortable with."

I thought about what he offered, and it was as though my father's arm had dropped around my shoulders—a sensation of which I had dreamed but never before experienced. To not go alone, to be able to choose that.

"Are you serious?" I asked—but the question was a marker of time, nothing more. I knew he was serious, and I knew I'd say yes.

"Are you?" Paul asked with a voice that was broader than what I was prepared to answer.

"I'd like you to come," I said, bringing us back to my limits. "If you have the time."

"I have the time," Paul said, and we walked further, letting the silence settle back into itself.

I telephoned my mother one afternoon, calculating that I'd catch her somewhere between *Green Acres* and bed.

"What's wrong?" was her first response.

"Nothing," I said. "All's well. It's just I've got a leave coming up and I thought I'd go to that place where my Dad was drowned."

"Earl?" she interrupted me, as if trying to identify who I was talking about.

"It was in the mountains, right?"

"The German and Austrian border," my mother said. "The blue Danube River, like the waltz. That's what his commanding officer wrote me."

"Would you want me to get you anything from there?" I asked. "A keepsake?"

"Get me a crucifix," my mother said. "On a chain. To wear. And take pictures, so I can see. Do you have your camera? Wait!" she commanded before I could answer. "Let me run get Edna. She'll have a spasm if she doesn't get to hear your voice."

"Mom," I said, but there was nobody listening. I could picture my mother racing through our house, excited, ignited at the thought of an overseas phone call.

"Elgin!" It was my grandmother, alarmed. "How much does this cost?"

"How are you doing, Grandma?"

"Edna's in the bathroom. She's coming out, hang on."

"Elgin?" Aunt Edna was out of breath. Her voice was a mixture of amazed and delighted. "You always catch me when I'm on the throne. It's an unerring instinct."

She didn't mean a word of it.

"Did Grandma get off?"

"She's watching the second hand move around the clock." It was my mother, on the upstairs extension they had installed for me on my fifteenth birthday. I could see the blue Princess phone with its lighted dial.

"What's the problem?" Aunt Edna asked my mother from downstairs.

"He wants to go see where Earl was killed," my mother answered.

"For heaven's sake, why?"

"Don't ask me," my mother said. They were in the middle of a conversation in which I had little part beyond starting it.

"Hello?" I said.

"Elgin!" they simultaneously exclaimed, as though they had forgotten I was on the line.

"So where was it?"

"Let me look it up," Aunt Edna said.

"She's getting the map," my mother informed me. "We have it circled, the town."

We waited, not saying anything. This is stupid, I thought. "So, Mom," I finally said. "How are things, really?"

There she was with no protection, no Edna or Grandma to deflect the "really" part. Trapped by a direct question. But, no. She was no amateur at evasion.

"How are *you?* Have you made lots of new friends over there?"

"One," I said.

"What's her name?" My mother sounded coy, girlish, and at the same time irritated.

"His. Paul Jenkins. He's an officer."

"An officer!" This was major news. *Elgin,* I could hear her telling her friend Ruth Ann, *has befriended an officer. They're thick as thieves.*

"Here it is!" Aunt Edna was back, her finger on a map. "It's down in Bavaria, Passau, south of Munich."

"That's right," I said, remembering as she said the name of the town.

"He's going to get me a crucifix," my mother bragged.

"He's a sweet lamb," Aunt Edna answered. "Always was. Thoughtful of his mother."

"I'd better go," I told them. "Grandma must be getting pretty antsy about the phone bill."

"She's had a stroke and died," my mother said.

"Out cold," Aunt Edna added. "She'll never get over it. All the way from Europe."

"Give her a kiss from me," I said, and could picture their startled expressions. I'd lay odds that neither one of them had ever kissed their mother in living memory.

"You be good," my mother said.

"And *write*," Aunt Edna commanded. "We read your letters as divine revelation."

"I promise," I said. "Love you."

"Honey," my mother said.

"Sweetheart," Aunt Edna said, waiting, pointedly, to be last. But she wasn't, quite. Before I got cut off I could hear my grandmother in the background. "Hang up that dang receiver," she ordered one of them, "or I'm pulling this cord out of the wall."

Paul Jenkins was as good as his word. In late October I had a weekend free and he arranged to drive me south to the Austrian border. When he pulled up to the door of my quarters in his car, a Mercedes, I realized I had never before seen him in civilian clothes—and he was a cool dresser. He wore a loose-knit cashmere sweater over a purple silk shirt, jeans, and hiking boots. His eyes were concealed by a pair of expensive shades.

"Hop in." He leaned over and opened the passenger door. "Next stop, the Alps."

It hit me: this was reality. Being on the base, working in the restaurant, I could have still been in Kentucky. But I wasn't. I was in Europe. I was going to where my dad was killed. In a fancy car with a man whom I couldn't figure out.

"You look good." The sunglasses made Paul's eyes big as a grasshopper's and just as unreadable. "What kind of music do you like? You pick."

I turned the dial of the radio away from anything American and stopped at what sounded to me like church music.

"Opera?" Paul shook his head in a pleased way. "Elgin, you are positively full of surprises."

I didn't want to spoil his favorable impression and tell him that he was wrong, that I wasn't full of surprises, just dumb.

"Verdi can be a little over the top," he commented.

"Yeah," I said, pulling up a line from *American Bandstand*. "I'd give it a seventy-two. Good to dance to but the lyrics are hard to understand."

The grasshopper eyes turned to me in confusion.

"Kidding," I assured him. "I'm just excited to be seeing something at last. This is like the first time I've been off American soil."

The car roared along, faster than I was used to. We passed towns that looked like they should be subtitled "Figure 6: A hamlet in Central Europe" in a tenth-grade geography textbook. The hills got steeper the further south we drove. Patches of snow began to appear high up on the sides of them. The music, whatever it was, didn't seem a bit over the top to me. It was just right, a kind of sound track for the travelogue that was unfolding like Cinerama before the windshield.

"Reach behind you," Paul said after we had driven about twenty miles just listening to the voices trill at each other. "I packed a light lunch to save time. You want to get to Passau before dark, right. To look around."

Sure enough, there was a regular picnic basket and an ice chest sitting on the rear seat. The sight of it took me back to the outings at the graveyard in Thebes my grandmother, mother, aunt and I annually shared. "Visiting the past," my grandmother once said, "is a way to guarantee your own immortality." Even though I was young when she told me that I understood her meaning perfectly: *you* had better come see *me* when I'm gone. A picnic basket made me miss people I only knew by their names and dates, made me miss May in Kentucky, the sound of bees in the air, water cold from a well bucket.

"I hope you don't mind," Paul said, worried about my long hesitation.

There was no way I could explain to him what I was thinking, so I opened the lid. Instead of fried chicken and angel food cake, potato salad and biscuits, there was a long stiff loaf of French bread, a bunch of different kinds of cheeses in odd shapes wrapped in cellophane, green grapes, a small tin can that at first I thought was tuna but turned out to read "pâté," a big chocolate bar.

"Wow." What else could I say. Was this what other people ate for lunch?

"Just to tide us over," Paul said. "We'll find a good café in the town, I'm sure. Maybe there'll be one in the hotel."

The hotel. I hadn't much thought about where we were going to stay and now I couldn't get my mind off it. Two rooms or one? All night. Nervousness wrapped around me like wet rope. Spencer's face flashed in my imagination, his head back, laughing.

"There's wine on ice," Paul went on. "Alsatian. When in Rome, like they say."

How did he get to know so much stuff. "Do they teach you about all this high-tone living in Seattle?" I asked, picturing a whole city full of finicky eaters.

"I wasn't born to fine things," Paul said, "but I've learned to enjoy them. You take your small pleasures where you can find them in this life. Commit those words to memory, Elgin."

It wasn't his small pleasures that worried me—but we rounded a turn and there were the real mountains, craggy and bright against a sky of deepening blue. I had never seen anything like them and I wanted to bang my head against the window glass to register the impression. Instead I blurted out, "Holy shit!"

Paul slapped the steering wheel with his hands, laughed his rich dark laugh. "You are too much, man. Everything's new. I love it. It takes me back to me at your age, makes me feel young."

I barely heard him, the view was that obliterating. The view and the music and the loaf of bread and car and the wine with the dog's name. And yes, and Paul Jenkins, too, in his sweater and expensive shoes and his kindness to me. I didn't know what *he* wanted himself to be to me, but I knew what I wanted him to be. My dad, my big brother, my best friend—all the men who had never dropped in on my life, all the men I had missed and wished for, all the men who would show me how to act, how to talk, how to be like them. Sitting on that leather seat, racing fast, I felt for the first time I could remember almost . . . calm. As though I had landed in the place I should be, as though I could rest, as though I could fit in like I always imagined other people fit in: a jigsaw puzzle piece you didn't have to squeeze and lean on to make it fill the hole.

"Thank you," I said to Paul, said to God, said to my father for bringing me here.

Right on schedule we arrived in Passau before the light failed. I had dozed off the last thirty miles or so—a combination of excitement and anticipation canceling each other out—but the cessation of forward motion woke me up.

"We're here," Paul said.

I opened my eyes, shut them, opened them again. I couldn't believe it: I was looking directly at the view in one of the oil paintings that hung in our living room. A kind of chalet with a balcony, and a mountain with the same unmistakable shape behind it. Even the flower boxes with geraniums were unchanged.

"It's impossible," I said aloud, but to myself.

"No, this is it," Paul said. "The central town square." He pointed to his left toward a sign.

But it wasn't the sign I saw, it was another one of the paintings, the smaller one of two houses with a clothesline strung on a pulley between them. There it was. I felt like I had entered the Twilight Zone, like Rod Serling's voice was about to boom out: "This is the story of one Elgin A. Taylor. A GI in Europe, out on a drive with his buddy."

"If it wasn't impossible," Paul said, "I'd say you had gone pale. What's the matter?"

I turned my head all the way to the right, and this time I wasn't surprised. There was the third painting: a fountain ringed by flowers. The artist must have sat exactly where we were parked. It was as though I had walked through one of the pictures I had looked at without seeing every day of my childhood and crossed into the midst of one of the last sights my father had ever seen. Crossed. The fourth picture. Choppy waves on the ocean. My brain was whirling, the thoughts bumping into themselves.

"Come on." Paul jostled my arm. "You look like a man in need of a serious brew. There's a place we just passed. We'll sit down, order, and then you can tell me what's going on."

"So you're saying it's like déjà vu." Paul was trying to understand. "Like you've been here before."

"No," I said. "It's like having my living room come to life in 3-D." I thought of the other large picture on the wall in Louisville: Jesus opening His robe to reveal a Sacred Heart ringed by a crown of thorns with a little gas fire underneath it. Was He going to turn up next?

"It makes a kind of sense," Paul said. "I mean, this is the last place where he was. Maybe he had just gotten the pictures before . . ."

"But they aren't even pretty," I told him. "That's the part that always stumped me. Why rip off ugly paintings?"

"There's no accounting for taste," Paul commented and glanced around the restaurant where we were sitting. It was done up like the set of a bad movie, all beer steins and coats of arms. "Do you get the feeling we, shall we say, stand out in this place a tad bit?"

"Now that you mention it." Ever since we came in we'd been getting fishy looks. Several of the locals would glance at us, look hard, then dart their eyes away fast.

"It happens over here out in the sticks," Paul said. "They're not used to seeing . . . Americans."

"Americans?" He did make me smile.

"Americans of a certain hue."

One man in particular—a guy in his midfifties, big stomach, bushy brows and mustache—couldn't let go of his fascination. It was as though he was trying to memorize my face in particular, his glances going back and forth like the pendulum of a cuckoo clock. It ticked me off, and I waited him out, watching for the next checkout and deliberately making eye contact. "Something I can do for you, sir?" I said loud enough for the whole place to hear.

To my surprise, instead of being embarrassed his whole face beamed. He slid off of his bar stool and made a beeline for our table, holding out his red hand to be shook. His eyes were the color blue of a 1957 Bel Air Chevrolet, my mother's favorite car.

"My English is stinking," he said in a heavy accent.

"Not as stinking as my German," I said back in German just to show off my studying.

"Ach, Sie sprechen Deutsch!" And then he was off a mile a minute, into some long involved story.

Every once in a while I'd catch a word that sounded familiar but by the time I mentally translated he was past it. He kept gesturing to my face, opening his arms as if to express amazement, asking several of his friends to agree with him from time to time, and they'd go "Yah, Yah" right on cue.

I shook my head, raised up my palms. "I don't *sprechen* that well. Can you do that again in English?"

The guy did a mea culpa pound of his fist to his heart in apology. "I am silly," he said, meaning sorry, "but it's the . . . *Ähnlichkeit.*" He waited for one of his friends to translate.

"You look like someone we know," the bartender explained. "Very much."

"Somebody *here?*" Paul's voice was as disbelieving as I felt. Were they making a joke of us?

"His niece," the bartender added. "Veronica."

"You stay," the heavyset man said, shaking his head in encouragement and pointing to the chairs we were sitting in. "You drink beer, my treat. I call Veronica."

Paul and I looked at each other. This we had to see.

"Sure," I said. "Don't mind if I do."

"You stay!" the man repeated and went to the phone on the bar. He dialed a number, spoke excitedly to whoever answered. More "Yah-ing."

When he got off he carried two mugs of beer to our table. "She work," he said, beaming. "She come. You stay."

"We stay," Paul said, and lifted his beer in a toast. "Cheers."

"Yah!"

"I told you this place was weird," I said to Paul when the guy went back to talk to his pals.

"It must be your flaxen hair," Paul decided. "Your rosy cheeks." His knee brushed mine under the table, and the word "Hotel" flashed neon in my mind.

"Listen . . ." I began, not knowing what to say next, but I was saved from figuring it out because behind me the door burst open and I saw Paul's eyes widen in surprise.

"I don't believe it," he said.

I swung around, curious and amused, and looked into a face that could have been mine in a mirror. It even had the same expression: stunned. Her mouth dropped open, she blinked, drew her head back, stared. She was me as a girl, I was her as a boy: same nose, same lips, same shaped eyes. Ears, too. It wasn't that either of us looked so special, we just looked average in exactly the same way.

The men at the bar slapped the counter and laughed, enjoying our reaction.

"No way," I said to this Veronica, and she said something back in German that must have been the equivalent.

"Do you speak English?" I asked.

"Yes," she said. "I studied it in school."

"This is unreal. I thought that guy was kidding." I gestured to the man who first spoke to us.

"My uncle," Veronica said. "He did not exaggerate. The likeness is . . ." She searched her vocabulary lists for the right word. "Unnerving."

Her English was better than mine.

"You want to sit down?" I invited.

She nodded to Paul and pulled up a chair.

"So," Paul asked to make conversation. "What's a sister doing way over here."

"A sister?" Her instructor obviously had not brushed up on blackfolk talk.

"You," Paul said, indicating her hand, the color of her skin.

"Ah," she said. "My pigmentation. My father was American. In the army like you at first but then he settled here when he married my mother. He didn't want to return to the . . . racistisim in America. My father helped him."

"Was?" I asked.

"He died three years ago," Veronica said. You could tell from the way she said it that they had been close, that she missed him.

"What did he do for a living?" Paul kept looking from my face to Veronica's, comparing features.

"We are grocers," Veronica explained. "My grandfather, my uncle. My father worked in their business. I work there now."

"Where was he from in the States?" Paul was going somewhere with his questions.

"Kentucky," Veronica said. "His original name was Earl Taylor before he changed it here, to Hans."

I knew I was gazing at something without seeing it, really seeing it, and when I heard what she said, I focused. It was the gold chain around Veronica's neck. It was the ruby ring suspended from the end of it. It was the ruby ring. The ruby ring.

I guess I got up so fast I knocked over my chair. I guess I bolted out of the restaurant, ran down the narrow street making cars stop to let me by. I guess I got back to Paul's car, found it locked, beat on the windows until I felt his hands on my shoulders, heard his voice urging me to calm down. I guess that's what I did because that's what he told me and he had no reason to make it up.

"He didn't die!" I shouted into the shiny metal of the Mercedes. "He fucking did not die. All this time, here he was living another life, being a father."

"Shhh. Shhh." Paul's hands were strong, his body warm against my back. "Let it out, Elgin. Let it out."

"Damn," I said. "God damn." I sounded as though I was laughing at the funniest joke I had ever heard, but tears were running down my cheeks.

"Hey, Veronica's kind of freaked, too," Paul said when my breathing slowed. "You know who she is but she doesn't know you're her brother. Let's go back, talk to her."

Her brother. I was a brother. I had a sister. I had a father—until three years ago.

"He couldn't get out of the grocery," I said, still talking to the roof of the car. "He was going to be a vet but he wound up where he started."

"Come on."

Paul's voice was soft, understanding. How could he have left his daughters, this otherwise nice man?

"I'm just glad I'm here for you, Elgin," he said. "Lean on me, man. You don't have to go through this alone."

I let him move me away from where I stood, let him point me in the direction I had run from, let him put his comforting arm around my shoulder. And I leaned on Paul Jenkins. I leaned on him every step of the way.

The rest of that day was a blur. My father wasn't dead but he *was* dead. Veronica had a sister away at some university so I had two half-sisters, not just one. In the confusion of the situation her English deteriorated, words failed us. She could comprehend the news that the once upon a time Hans Earl Taylor was my father before he was hers but she didn't know how to ask the questions that came to her—the hows and the whys and the why nots. So mostly we just looked at each other, shocked and sad, but still with one more human connection than either of us had ever before suspected we possessed. At one point, she took my hand. At another, she fished a photograph out of her purse—and there he was, portly, middle-aged, dressed in foreign clothes. Not a bit like the picture of him in uniform that had sat on my dresser the whole time I was growing up. Not a bit like the young man my mother described meeting for the first time when she was on the balcony at Waverly Hills. Not at all the same man, and yet . . . the same man. He didn't even tell his parents, my grandparents, that he was alive. Neither of the Marcellas in his life had the slightest suspicion. But didn't he wonder about us all, I wondered. Didn't he wish he knew how we were?

"Do you want to meet my mother?" Veronica asked. Outside it was dark. The crowd in the bar had thinned out without ever getting the full story of what was going on. They could wait, they had decided. They'd know it all eventually if they bided their time.

Did I? The woman Earl left my mother to be with?

I shook my head. "Your sister, maybe, someday," I said. "For today, you're enough for me to handle."

She nodded, looked from Paul to me. "It must be a good thing to live in a place where you are not so . . ." She gestured to herself. "Unusual."

I thought of being Greek, of being Italian. "I wouldn't know," I said. "I've always been pretty unusual, too."

"I mean, here I am the wrong color," she explained.

"Blame it on Earl," I told her. "That was his thing, wrong colors."

She didn't get it and I didn't want to spoil her memories. There was no point. I knew for a solid fact that I would never tell any of this to my mother or Aunt Edna—or to Marcella. Let Earl be who everybody needed him to be, to have been. That was my return gift to him for my life. The way I counted it, that paid him back in full with compound interest, whoever the hell he really was.

"Do you need a place to stay for the night?" Veronica asked. The ruby ring glinted in the lamplight.

"We're at the hotel," I told her, and didn't catch Paul's eye. "We have to leave early in the morning. But write down your address and phone number. We'll keep in touch. I'll call you next week, once we've both gotten used to all this."

"It is wise," Veronica said in her stilted school English, and did as I asked. She got up, reached for her handbag, but before she left she came around the table, kissed Paul on his cheek, kissed me on both of mine. "I am happy," Veronica announced. "I am not alone."

"Neither are you," Paul said when she was gone, as we were walking back to the hotel. And all that night, like a brother, like the best friend you could have when you needed the best friend that could be, like a loving father, he held me in his arms and stroked my head and didn't ask for a thing more than helping me. And he did.

When everything you believed to be true turns out to be false you have two choices: you can go back and reexamine each memory, sift it through the sieve of fact, and reconstruct your life as best you can; or you can kiss the whole mess good-bye, give birth to your own new self, and go from there. I wound up doing more of the second choice than of the first, maybe because I was too afraid of betraying away the secret to my family if I spent too much time with them, maybe because it was simply easier. My letters home were written less frequently, and I could feel the hurt and upset in the long communications I received from Louisville. Why hadn't I gotten my mother the cross she asked for from Germany? Why didn't I send pictures so that they could better imagine my life? My mother, aunt and grandmother would all write their own versions of the same events—you wouldn't think three sets of eyes could view the world so differently—and Marcella kept sending postcards with messages like, "Something's wrong. I can feel it. What?"

"You've gone *vague* on us, Elgin," Aunt Edna accused in my birthday card, underlining the key word. "Your mother's heart is at risk. I hope somebody got you a cake. Love, Aunt Edna."

I had gone vague on *me*. When I'd meet new people I'd improvise a history on the spot. I was from California, had two sisters, that kind of thing. I was anybody they expected, no surprises. I told them what they needed to hear and they liked me for it. I was Mr. Nice Guy, well-spoken, a no problem. I was nobody at all you had to think twice about.

I signed up for a second hitch in the army because I wasn't ready to go home—like father like son, I suppose—and became the headwaiter. Sometimes people would ask me if I had ever served a tour in 'Nam and I'd answer, "Yeah," and leave it at that, as if my experiences were too painful to recount. They appreciated not having to hear about it, not having their ears bent with stories they'd been beat up with a hundred times before. I was "deep," strangers complimented, an "enigma." I'd just lower my eyes, letting them know they'd got my number. They never guessed my true identity: a son not worth coming home to meet.

After our one night in a hotel together—"nothing happened" as they say after a night of too much boozing, but in fact a lot happened, a lot of stuff there's no names for, no laws against, no limits to, almost more than I could handle happened—Paul Jenkins and I got standoffish. From my side it was because he was the one person on earth who knew the story I was trying to forget, and from his side—well, maybe I wasn't the one he was looking for after all and he was nervous that I knew it. We stayed friendly enough, from a distance, and because of him I maintained a favorable impression of the city of Seattle, so much so that I chose to be discharged there when the time came. It was as good as anyplace else, I figured, and I somehow expected to do nothing but eat fancy food and be understood.

So I'm out, I'm in some bar that a guy I knew recommended, just having a scotch, keeping to myself as usual. Nothing to do, nowhere to go, two thousand miles from a home I didn't feel at home in anymore. Blue. Adrift. And in walks this compact little woman—Asian I pegged her—obviously not aware that she's made a mistake and come into a soul place. She looks lost, out of it. The way I probably appeared at that beer joint in Germany. Everybody stares at her—like they did at Paul and me. What's she doing here? What's she want? She orders a drink. I see it register on her face that she doesn't belong. She doesn't seem as though she belongs anywhere but dares somebody to say so. I like that, the dare part. She doesn't leave. Gutsy. What the hell, I go up to her, call her pretty. We sit down at my table. Is she a hooker, I wonder. Is she dangerous?

No. She's just shell-shocked. Shows me a letter somebody wrote to say her brother's missing in action in Vietnam. I tell her I've been there, meaning I've had my share of being knocked off my feet, but she misinterprets, thinks I mean I've served in 'Nam. I let her think it if it makes her feel better, what's to lose. Tell her that her brother will turn up. That's what I do to people, promise them the moon. Worse they can be is disappointed, after all when I'm long gone. She takes my words as gospel, proposes that we repair to my place. What the hell, part two. On the way she tells me she's an Indian, pure-blood. I've never been with one of those before—reminds me I'm supposed to have a Creek great-grandmother on my dad's side—don't know what to expect. Her name's Christine something or other. She's open-throttle need and that starts my ignition. We get back to my room. She creates me, her need creates me, brings me to life like I haven't been before. Every move is new. This Christine is the first person I've met since Germany who's more heart-wasted than I am and it warms my blood. I can give instead of take. And I give. And she takes. And she gives. And I take. And it isn't just another one-nighter, it's the beginning of something unpredictable, unreasonable, uncontrollable. And she asks me to promise that I'll never leave her. And I do. And I mean it when I say it. I cross my heart. I mean it. Christine. I love you.

CHAPTER THIRTEEN

LAST RITES

———◆◆◆———

Edna

"This is it." Mama nods with solemn regret, agreeing with herself.

"You say that every year," Marcella replies, as she herself, in fact replies every year. Her voice is preoccupied with a mental checklist of preparations for our annual graveyard picnic. I can almost see the items scrolling behind her eyes: fried chicken, orange-iced angel food cake, lemonade, potato salad, tablecloth, plastic utensils, napkins . . .

"Don't forget the cups this time," I remind her.

"Bless your soul, Edna," Marcella exclaims. "I knew I was leaving out something."

"You'll be sorry you made fun of me," Mama intones as if looking forward to our grief over her future absence.

"Yes," I say. "I expect we will. We'll bring an extra bouquet for your tombstone to make up."

"Irises," Mama instructs. "No roses. They cheapen the arrangement."

I roll my eyes. I am long beyond the age when past grievances or rituals hold significance. Paying respects to the dead on Decoration Day had been a heartbreak in the decade after Papa went, a responsibility after Grandma passed away, a pleasure when

Elgin was a boy running through the plots trying to figure out who was who, but now it is just one of those things we do, my sister, my mother and I, out of habit. Like putting up a Christmas tree, hanging out Earl's flag on the Fourth of July, eating turkey at Thanksgiving, sending each other birthday cards. Markers of time passing, like retracing a route on a road map that you follow without fail or detour. Once I had been a person who believed she could do almost anything. Now I'm an old maid who does the least that's expected of her.

"I just feel," Marcella begins tuning up—another predictable event—"that I should be at Earl's side. There he was, memorialized at the military cemetery clear across the country, all alone."

"He's not even there," I remind her. "Somebody will stick a flag in the ground. It's his due as a vet."

"Still," she goes on. "A flag is not a living object of beauty, like a mum."

"Cut flowers are dead," I say. "They just look alive for a brief span." Like us, I could add, but don't. Like us without Elgin.

"Edna you have no . . ." Marcella searches for the right word, not too insulting but still equipped with a sting. "Romance," she decides, for the millionth time.

"But I do remember cups," I tell her. "The lack of romance has its compensations."

"Next year," Mama butts in, "when you kneel in prayer, just remember this day. And who, Miss Edna McGarry, is going to mourn *your* passing."

I have to admit it: age has not diminished Mama's aim.

"You will," I say. "When you have nobody to complain about."

Marcella, in a rare act of sisterly solidarity, protrudes her lower lip in appreciation.

"Heartless," Mama says. "It wasn't lungs they collapsed on you girls, it was a more vital organ."

"Nothing beats breath," I tell her. "It's like running water. Once you lack it you never fail to appreciate its availability."

"Throw it up to me," Mama pouts. "Your father didn't even

give that to me, the consumption. No. He passed that on to you along with everything else."

I smile. Thank you, Papa, I think, and see his sweet, caved-in face. Everything you gave me was a gift.

The graveyard at Thebes has a smaller attendance every Memorial Day—and a larger area of occupation. Last year's visitors turn into next year's residents with the persistence of the drip of a faucet, and we're just backed up the pipe, awaiting our turn. For all Mama's carrying-on, someday she *will* join Papa and his brother Father Andrew in the rectangle demarcated by a line of Indiana marble. The joke of her demise will become a reality and then no one will stand between Marcella and me—me, really, being the elder—and the reserved space. Will Elgin come to call? Will his Christine allow him? Of course not. We'll be as forgotten as Pompeii. Elgin probably wouldn't even be comfortable to visit this lily white cemetery now that he's full grown.

I've thought of ashes, of course, but don't want to shock Mama. Ashes blown across the waters of Lake Superior, across the Caribbean Sea, across, at least, the Ohio River—some major body of water that will enliven them like the dehydrated Swiss steak I read the astronauts brought along to outer space. But the Church is still iffy on the subject of cremation and any such decision on my part will embarrass my survivors. Better to fall apart beside Papa, to blend into the same earth, to nourish the same weeds.

Marcella is riffling through her closet to choose today's ensemble and pauses at a plastic zipper bag. "I want to be laid to rest in my wedding dress," she announces, and pulls out her rose two-piece suit on its satin hanger. "I still fit it, I'll have you know, and I still like the color scheme."

"You want the hat with the veil, too?" I ask.

"Why not? And makeup. Eye shadow."

"Go ahead, laugh at an old woman." Mama will not leave off. "But there's things you don't know."

When pressed for the center of attention, Mama always gets mysterious.

"Such as?" Marcella bites.

Mama plays the line, bound to silence by some promise unknown to us.

"You can't just say that and hold your tongue," Marcella persists. "Is it juicy, Mama? Tell! Pretty please."

Mama slides her eyes from one side to the other, as if leary of being overheard. "It's terrible," she whispers, "a scandal."

Now she has me hooked. "How terrible can it be?"

"It concerns your Grandmother Rose Mannion McGarry, may she rest in peace."

"She's haunting us," I guess. "Didn't get in the last word."

Mama shakes her head, firmly in possession of information not yet imparted.

"She's not there," she says cryptically.

"Where?" Marcella wants to know

"There," Mama repeats. "In the ground."

Marcella and I look at each other. This is news.

"Where is she, then?" I inquire.

"In this very room, all along."

We glance around, spying for our grandmother's presence. It's hard to believe she could have been here without actively interfering in our lives.

"There." Mama points to the Irish glass salver, capped with wax to preserve my grandmother's hairbrush savings.

"That's just her hair," I object.

Mama assumes a superior expression, her favorite.

"Isn't it?" Marcella knocks.

Mama stretches out the moment. "That's what I always *said*," she admits. "But . . ."

"But . . . ?" I prod.

"It's *her*," Mama exhales. "Rose reduced to her pure essence."

"What?" Marcella is spooked.

"She wouldn't be buried next to her husband," Mama says.

"Positively refused. The coffin is empty. She was . . . burned up."

"Cremated?" This was impossible.

"That's the word," Mama confirms.

"Why on earth?" Marcella is equally in the dark.

"It was her dying wish," Mama whispers. "She asked me to take her back to Ireland, to sprinkle her under a certain tree near Boyle. But I never found the opportunity, so I pass the responsibility on to you. It's too late for me."

Marcella and I eye the famous oblong vase with horror. All this time we assumed it was Grandma's hair, decomposed, when in fact it was herself in our living room, overhearing every word.

"What happened to her lovely hair?" Marcella asks.

"She wanted it incinerated with her, all mixed together, past, present and future."

"So, who have we been putting flowers on next to Grandpa, there in between Papa and his brother the priest?" I demand.

"Worms," Mama says.

"Nobody's there?" I insist.

"I will be," Mama announces. "Where I belong."

"You're on the other side of Papa," Marcella corrects. "The square we bought to reserve it."

"That's Edna," Mama says as if presenting me with a birthday surprise. "So she won't be alone."

"And Grandma?" Marcella hasn't taken her gaze off the clouded glass.

"Take her home. When I'm gone. She never left, after all. Take her back where she came from. It will make a nice vacation trip for you, to distract your minds from missing me."

The drive to Thebes is quiet and takes a fraction of the time that it used to now that the interstate highway is completed. The dogwoods are out, coloring the greenery along the road like splotches of pastel paint. We keep the windows of Marcella's Mercury rolled up so that Mama won't get a crick in her neck from wind,

243

and listen to a station that plays one sad love song after another. Everybody in them wants someone who doesn't want them back. I'm glad to be beyond all that.

I have the backseat to myself, just me and the picnic basket and the smell of chicken, and I rest my face against the glass pretending to sleep. I don't really mind these excursions. Thebes is like the clasp on a necklace with many strands of pearls, the place where everything starts and stops as the years loop forward. The place where I began this life, the place where I'll wind up when it's over. Even though she hasn't lived there in more than sixty years, Mama still refers to it as "home"—not with nostalgia, but with resentment. It's the home she was driven from because of Grandma's lawsuit against the railroad. When she was growing up, she had always yearned to leave it for Lexington or some other city, but she hated that the choice of departure had been deprived her. The charm of a place was apparent to Mama only when she was denied the ability to disdain it.

I ponder the announcement that I am destined to take Mama's plot, to lie on Papa's right with nothing on the other side of me but a stand of willow trees. It's a comforting thought. It reminds me of the afternoons during his illness when I lay in his bed reading and rereading his green-bound Tennyson, his lips moving in silent recitation of the words. Where else would I rather be for eternity? Finally, I do doze off, lulled by the hum of the tires, the steady vibration of the engine, the hardness of the glass. I dream, as is so often the case, that I am doing exactly what I am doing: riding in a car, going home to Papa, counting the miles.

I awake. We're there.

"Edna," Mama fusses as we get out and stretch our legs, "the whole right side of your hair is flattened out, straight as when you were a little girl. I hope you have a brush."

"Who's going to see me, Mama? Who gives a hot damn about my hair?"

"Don't swear!" Marcella is next to speechless. "Think where we are!"

I hold out the sides of my skirt and curtsey to the nearest tombstone, which happens to read Hector A. Posey. "I beg your pardon, Hector," I say. "But I expect you've heard worse, on this side or the other."

"The Poseys are decent people," Mama shushes me. "You're a grown woman, Edna. Don't be so smart."

"I'm goofy from sleep," I apologize. "The gravel road must have loosened my brains."

Marcella and Mama exchange a look that suggests they accept my explanation as a scientific fact.

"Time's a-wasting," Mama says and starts off dutifully for her parents' ground—she'll join us at Papa's presently. She has always looked the same to me, a short, stout woman with thick upper arms and narrow wrists. Her gray hair is firmly pinned into a bun at her neck. Her mouth, at rest, turns down at each end as though she has just heard a remark too beneath her to answer. Her hazel eyes, behind clear-rimmed glasses, are the eyes of an alert, clever robin. She walks slowly, deliberately—not a kind of constant forward-falling like most people on flat land, but as full of effort as if she is making a steep climb. She's ageless, I think to myself, but watching her progress, I know better: she's aged. This probably won't be her last visit to this place before her final one, but it could be. I feel a pang of tenderness. She doesn't give an inch, never has, and there's an anguish to that quality. She takes so much credit for having endured hardship that the real hardships she's suffered get overlooked. She's like a rock in the path that you trip over so often it becomes familiar. You depend on it being there. The path wouldn't be the same without it, wouldn't be a challenge, wouldn't be interesting. She carries three bouquets of snowballs, plucked from the bush in the side yard. The metal vases are built into the ground, part of the burial package Thebes provides to its tenants.

"I'll go draw some water from the well," Marcella volunteers. Which leaves me to carry the basket, the jug of lemonade, the tablecloth and some blankets to sit on. My sister, I notice, has once again neglected to bring cups. At least now we'll have a topic of conversation over lunch.

It's an odd experience to stand at Grandma's grave and know it's empty. That rectangle of earth labeled

ROSE MANNION McGARRY
Born 1852, Cty. Roscommon
Died 1941, Thebes, Ky.
REUNITED AT LAST

seems hollow, a tunnel of vacancy that pierces the earth to its core. She and I had never been close—Papa stood between us, a solid wall seen differently from either side—but she had a presence that took up space. I sat on her tomb and looked over to where Grandpa rested.

MARTIN MICHAEL McGARRY
Born 1852, Cty. Roscommon
Died 1918, Thebes, Ky.
HUSBAND AND FATHER

I barely remembered him, just stories.

Poor as a poor box, Grandma said often enough. Started out as a ragman, dragging his cart around the town looking for throwaways. Worked himself to such weakness that when the influenza came he was among the first to succumb. Left me with two boys to raise, a piano with broken strings, a house with no plumbing.

"And taught me the love of books," Papa interrupted her once. "He was a good man, a kind soul."

Grandma had sniffed her dismissal of this compliment. Reading she considered a waste of time, a lazy man's pleasure.

Papa, who so rarely provoked his mother, didn't give up easily that day. "He loved you dearly, Mother," he said. "He devoted his life to you."

"As well he should have. It was I, after all, who gave him that life. He owed me a debt beyond repayment."

The words lingered in my memory. So many stories half-told, so many important secrecies now meaningless. My grandfather lay alone in his final marriage bed, beneath foreign soil. He had never made something up to Grandma, who knew what? But what, then, did Grandma's "reunited at last" signify? Certainly not with her husband. With God Himself?

"Are you thinking what I'm thinking?" Marcella has returned with the water and has come to sit beside me.

"I don't know," I say. "What are you thinking?"

"An extra space!" Marcella stage-whispers. "Who'll get the use of it?"

The cast of characters in our family drama was limited. Mama was bound and determined to be between Papa and the priest. I was on Papa's other side. That left Marcella—who had long stated her intention to be shipped west to symbolically join Earl—and Elgin, who might well decide to stick with Christine, even though they were currently separated. And then there was their daughter, Rayona, whom we had only seen that one summer. I couldn't imagine her happy in Thebes. No likely candidate for the last plot.

"Of course, there's no law that says we have to tell," Marcella points out. "As far as the world knows, Grandma's where she's supposed to be. Still . . ."

I can sense her sentimental side coming out, and beat her to it. "You feel bad for Grandpa having no company."

Marcella opens her mouth and firmly shuts it again. I have stolen her very words and she resents it. "I expect he's used to it by now," she says finally.

If anyone overheard our conversation they'd call for the padded wagon. Yet, it makes a certain kind of sense. The dead never really are quite gone in our family. The influence of their deeds and personalities is always pushing and nudging us one way or the other.

"I expect, from what I hear, he was used to it in this life as well," I say. "Miss Rose could be a terror."

Marcella laughs at my irreverence. "I'll bet you wouldn't dare say that if she was here under your feet."

She's right.

"What's Mama busy about?" I ask.

"She's plucking weeds behind Father McGarry. I never have figured out why he wasn't interred in a church cemetery. I didn't know they let them—the religious—mingle with regular people. You'd never catch a nun out here in the public domain especially with such a giant headstone."

It's a good question and I'm surprised it has never occurred to me before. "Mama," I call to her. "Why isn't Papa's brother buried somewhere with other priests?"

"His mother wanted him handy," Mama shouts back, two graves hence. "And she always got her way. Besides, at the time of his death in the train accident he was at the point of leaving the clergy. His death saved his mother from humiliation."

"Don't tell me he'd fallen in love?" I say sarcastically. You hear about a lot of priests getting married these days, but I thought that back then they couldn't do that.

Mama ignores me, but keeps complaining about Grandma. "After all that combustion to get him here, you'd think *she'd* have the courtesy to stay. But no. The High and Mighty must return to Ireland. Had the nerve to ask *me* to take her. The gall. I've got a good mind to spill her right here where she belongs, but then I'd have to put up with her till the end of time."

"And we'd miss out on our vacation," I remind her. "We'd be stuck in Louisville, grieving over you."

"You always have to be a smart aleck, Edna," Mama says. She's not hurt, not even annoyed, just reconciled to my shortcomings. "And see where it got you."

"Why do we have to stop here?" Mama complains. "All the times I took the bus, I thought I'd never have to lay eyes on Waverly Hills again."

"Old time's sake," I say. "I hear it's for sale. They're going to tear it down and build the tallest statue of Jesus Christ in the United States on the ruins."

"Who is?" Mama asks.

"Baptists," I confess. "But ecumenical ones."

"I read about it in the paper. It's like those praying hands in Oklahoma." Marcella folds her hands as an illustration.

"Only bigger," I said. "It will be Louisville's signature. You'll be able to see Him from Indiana and Tennessee on a clear night. Airplanes flying over will dip their wings. It'll probably have to have a red light on its head. Anyway before they demolish Waverly, I want to see it once more."

"Hasn't the day been long enough already?" Marcella never liked the graveyard. It reminds her she's a widow.

"Are you saying you don't have good memories?" I ask her. "All those years outdoors."

"I don't need memories," she answers unkindly. "I have Elgin as proof."

"And when did you hear from him last?" I can play that game if she wants.

"He's busy. Christine's sick, he said the last time on the phone. Real sick. Gone home to her mother and took the little girl along with her. He sounded worried."

"Busy," Mama echoes, ignoring, as usual, the existence of Elgin's difficult ex-wife. "They're always busy."

"Papa wasn't too busy to read poetry," I say.

"Reading's reading." Mama is unimpressed. "Doing's something else again."

"He *did*," Marcella chimes in a flash of daughterhood. "He did a lot."

"More than you think, more than you'll ever imagine."

"Stop it, Mama," I say.

"There's the turnoff," Marcella points, and we take a sharp right behind a new Krogers supermarket and up the narrow winding road. "I swore I'd never come back a second time like you did."

"It's like a magnet," I say. "It draws you as though you had never left. As though you're a ghost who got free."

It is sad, that's the only word for it, sad. Overgrown and unmaintained. Wild. Vines snaking over the road. Tree trunks unremoved. We park the car as high as we can drive, leave Mama with the radio on, and Marcella and I trudge the rest of the way on foot.

"Criminal." Marcella is awestruck at the decay. "When I think of how beautiful, how well kept it always was."

"The mansion that TB built." Through the trees I catch my first glimpse of the building itself and look away in disbelief. "Marcella," I say and take her arm. "Up there."

We don't speak. There's nothing to say. A breeze moves the higher tree limbs and reveals the once-familiar sight, the place where we spent years of our lives, the place we didn't want to come to and never expected to leave, the place where Marcella found Earl. The place where Naomi died.

It's as though Waverly has been bombed in a war we haven't heard about. The windows are shattered. The porches are sagging. Missing shingles write indecipherable words on the roof.

"Have mercy," Marcella breathes.

We continue our climb. A rusted gate hangs open and we pass through. The air smells wild, foresty, a thousand miles from the turnoff we have just made from Dixie Highway. Birds chatter above our heads. Without thinking of it, without quite meaning to, my sister and I begin to hold hands. Our grip increases when we come out of the trees to what was once the circular driveway where we each in our turn, alone late at night, me twice, her once, were dropped off from the jitney cab. The building has no door.

"It makes you want to cry," says Marcella, crying.

"It makes me plain mad," I say, but I am crying, too.

"It's like we're the last survivors," Marcella goes on. "Like victims of a natural disaster. The only ones who remember the way things were."

"Then let's remember," I urge her, wanting to blot out with the sound of our voices the vision of destruction that confronts us. "What's the first thing that comes to your mind?"

"My quilted satin robe," Marcella begins. "Three-quarters length with a silk sash. An off-pink. Rhinestone buttons. It was my salvation."

"I can see you in it. Your hair fanned out on the pillow, the sunlight pouring down. You were a beauty."

"I was," Marcella says with no special congratulation in her voice. "I always looked younger than my years. I was wasted out here when I should have been in my prime."

"Not entirely wasted."

"No." She laughs to herself. "Mohammed came to the mountain after all. It was like a fairy tale that day. Thank goodness I was wearing that robe and had just done my nails."

"I don't think it was your nails that first attracted Earl."

Marcella shakes her head. "I just mean, if he had gotten up close and then at the last moment noticed a flaw, an imperfection, the magic might have flickered. That's all it would have taken, a flicker, and we'd have both come back to our senses."

"But there were no flickers," I say. "For once."

"No flickers at all," she agrees. "For years."

We listen to the silence, to the wind that moves without obstruction through the gaping windows of the facade. Your vision can play tricks on you, substituting wish for reality. As I cast my mind back it's as though a movie screen has been pulled down before me, and on it projected the Waverly we used to jokingly call our private resort hotel.

"Your turn," Marcella says after a while. "Where are you?"

"That silly contest when you were here," I confess. "The Princess of the Mountain pageant, remember?"

She nods, there with me.

"She was so lovely that day, Naomi. I can see her plain as day."

"Smoking her Lucky Strikes," Marcella nods again and gives my hand an extra squeeze.

"Think how old she'd be now, but as it is she stayed young." I squeeze back. "I don't know why they didn't call me at the end. They knew how close we were. They knew."

"I'm sure you were in her prayers," Marcella consoles me.

"As she's been in mine, every night since. I guess you could say I loved her."

The mention of the word love, a word that never passed either of our lips except in relation to Jesus or Mary, wakes us up, reminds us that we are making contact with each other's skin, a circumstance we avoid at all costs. Simultaneously, we drop our connection. Marcella fiddles with her wedding ring for an excuse and I crack my knuckles.

"Well, this will be our last view of our flaming youth," I say to lighten the tone. "By next summer Waverly Hills will be replaced by that Baptist statue."

"I won't look at it," Marcella vows. "I positively refuse. I won't even remember today. In my mind Waverly is going to stay exactly as it always was, forever and ever, amen."

"We'd better get back to Mama," I say. "She'll be fit to be tied."

"We'll stop on the way home for pie. That'll mollify her. There's that nice little place near Audubon Park. I hope they have some coconut cream left."

Sometimes I think my sister is, without realizing it, the bravest woman I ever knew. And sometimes I think she's just in another world altogether.

Mama gets the last laugh: we do miss her when she dies that winter. You'd open your mouth to offer some excuse and then realize that she hadn't been there to make the criticism. You'd put silverware at her place at the table, just a fork, before her absence hit you. You'd tiptoe by her bedroom so as not to disturb her, you'd watch her favorite programs on television, wait for her voice during the Rosary, leave a space for her in the pew at Mass. After her funeral, Marcella and I walked around in a kind of trance for weeks, starting sentences and not finishing them, isolated in our separate grieving. With Mama present we seemed to have a purpose, a function, in living together. With her gone we're just two retired old ladies on social security, biding our time, following meaningless routines, eating and sleeping and waking up and going to the bathroom. It isn't bad, it isn't good. We live for Elgin's occasional Sunday morning calls, beg him to write, make lists of news items to mention to him. But really, we're going nowhere slower and slower, waiting, breathing, waiting not to breathe.

One morning I look at the calendar and realize that another Decoration Day is around the corner. By rights we should go and pay Mama and all the rest of them proper respects, but it isn't necessary, really. We've been to the cemetery once a month for five months on the anniversary day of Mama's funeral.

"Do you want to go to Thebes on Memorial Day?" I ask Marcella.

She mutes the volume of the Weather Channel, her constant companion. She claims she needs to know what the temperature is like out in Seattle where Elgin lives. If there's some extreme, some avalanche or flood, it will be an excuse to call and warn him, to make sure he's safe.

"Come again?"

"Decoration Day," I repeat. "What's the plan."

She sighs. Puts the sound back on. "Might as well, but it won't be the same. Two deaths in the span of twelve months. First Mama and then Christine. I regret we never got to meet her in this life."

I let my eyes roam the living room. There are Earl's oil paintings of Alpine chalets and roaring surf. There's the Sacred Heart. There is Mama's collection of imitation Hummel statues set out on the Irish table. No amount of polish can disguise the scratch Papa was supposed to have made. There's Grandpa's clock, wound nightly, its pendulum the metronome of our lives. Concentrating, I can hear its click-click-click. There is . . . there is Grandma!

"I've got a better idea," I say and rise from my lounger so quickly that Marcella activates the lever and sits straight up in hers. "Turn that thing off," I instruct.

"You're flushed," she announces.

"We've got something to do," I tell her. "A wish to make come true. A holy crusade."

"You must have dozed off," Marcella says. "Edna, wake up!"

"It's now or never," I insist, pointing at the old carved glass container. "If Grandma's going to get where she wanted to go, we can't just sit here turning to stone."

"Ireland?" Some of the old flash darts across Marcella's stunned expression. It brings back the times we'd set out on our adventures long ago—bus trips to New Orleans, cruises on tramp steamers, the false alarm in Duluth, Chicago, the time we drove across the country to bring Rayona home.

"What's stopping us?" My mind races, finds what it's searching for. I rummage through a stack of newspapers on the coffee table, locate the last issue of the weekly *Kentucky Irish American,* page through until I come to the ad that caught my eye. "Look at this."

Marcella wears her reading glasses on a gold chain, like a necklace, and raises them to her face. "Pilgrimage to the Shrine of Our Lady of Knock," she reads. "County Mayo, Ireland." She looks up at me, her eyes enlarged by the magnifying lenses. "Join a group tour?" she asks as if I'm proposing a blastoff on the space shuttle. She goes back to the paper. "Ten days. All expenses, airfare and transfers included." She puts the paper on her lap, thinks. "What are transfers?"

"It must be like on a bus," I say, worldly wise. "You know, they give you a slip that probably lets you on the connecting plane."

"Ireland. Aren't we too old?"

"I'm older than you, and I'm not."

"It's a lot of money, a fortune."

"We've got it, gathering dust in the bank."

She regards the paper a third time. "It says it departs in three weeks. We don't have passports."

"We'll apply for them."

She's stumped, has run out of practical objections. She lets her glasses drop to her bosom, licks her lips, raises her eyes to meet mine. Smiles.

"Call," she says. "I dare you."

"Read me the number." I reach for the phone. Grandma is as good as home.

"They look so Irish," Marcella whispers in my ear as one of the stewardesses prances by. "Regular colleens."

"They *are* Irish," I remind her. "This is Irish Airlines."

"Still," Marcella says. It's the middle of the night and we are halfway across the Atlantic Ocean on our way to Shannon Airport. We sit in the middle of a group of thirty ladies done up in their traveling clothes and four men, three of them husbands and one widower, who have banded together relieved at first sight of each other. Father Herlihy is seated at the front, the captain of our ship, the keeper of our passports, the veteran who has been to Ireland six previous times with tours like ours. Across the aisle Lucille Andriott, whom we have talked into going, is sleeping with her mouth ajar.

"It'll be just like old times," I persuaded her.

"I'm older than old times," she had replied, but she came anyway, and dragged along Sister Mary Agnes, her nun cousin from Duluth, who was officially retired. "I don't want to be stuck with just any roommate," she explained. "At least I know Mary Agnes can take care of herself."

And then some, I thought, remembering how close I came to being caught into a vocation that time we went to Minnesota when Marcella wasn't pregnant.

The plan is, we are to land early in the morning, go through customs, ride a bus up past Galway directly to Knock, where we will make the outdoor Stations of the Cross, go to an afternoon Mass, have tea, as they call supper over here, and have the late afternoon and evening "free" to browse in the gift shops, sleep, or pray. It is during that window of opportunity that the four of us will mount our expedition to Boyle, see if we can locate the tree were Grandma wanted to be dumped, and sprinkle her. I pat my emerald green travel case, part of our bonus package for paying in advance and emblazoned with the word "Getaway!" in bold white script, and feel the lump of the crystal salver, bubble-wrapped and masking-taped to ensure its safe passage. Once we fulfill our obligation we'll be free to sightsee without guilt.

When we land in a hazy rain Marcella insists that we wait in our seats until all other passengers have deplaned.

"I hate to be rushed," she explains, looking into the mirror of her compact and drawing bright red lipstick over her pursed mouth. Mary Agnes, hauling Lucille behind her, is the first one to set foot on the olde sodde.

"Where do you get these rules?" I ask Marcella, as we wait while even the wheelchair cases roll by.

"Life is too short to be racing around."

"Life is too short—our lives in particular—not to be!"

Now she's finger-curling her bangs.

"We're going to miss the bus," I say and get up.

She surveys the empty aisle. "Tell me this isn't better," she demands. "Besides, now we'll make an entrance."

"To the baggage claim?" I am exasperated beyond words and decide to sit with Mary Agnes, for whom lack of a full night's sleep seems to have worked as a stimulant.

Outside the bus windows the landscape, if you eliminate the occasional view of the ocean to the left and the infrequent castles on the right, looks amazingly like the countryside around Thebes. Long, well-built stone fences, a palette of greens that blend into each other, rolling hills. The road is narrow and we're driving at a fast clip on the wrong side—Marcella, I notice, has her eyes squeezed shut and is moving her lips in silent supplication—but for me the moment is thrilling, a throwback to my younger days. I tune out the drone of Father Herlihy's voice over the loud-speaker. He's reading from a guidebook, telling us what to look at and what to think about it. I don't care about any of that. I don't need to be educated. I just need to *be,* and there are few enough opportunities.

We stop for lunch—dry cheese sandwiches and tea with too much cream. The clouds seem to be lifting and now and then a patch of sunlight will shoot to earth like a laser beam, illuminating a house or a tree. No wonder they made up those legends about pots of gold.

Half the bus is dead to the world by the time we stop at Knock, and I've got to say the place strikes me as something of a tourist trap. Rows of outdoor faucets dispensing blessed holy water. Shop after shop along the one main street, each one hawking the same sets of religious-oriented souvenirs—plaster statues, key chains, miraculous medals, holy cards. I won't miss the browsing. Still, the sign giving the history of the place intrigues me. "On 21st August, 1879, fifteen people of varying ages witnessed, over a period of two hours, the apparition of Our Lady, St. Joseph and St. John the Evagelist on the gable of the church."

Part of me wonders what my grandparents made of this—it must have been big news—but another part is transported back almost half a century to the top deck of a ship crossing Lake Superior and my own personal miraculous apparition of St. John the Baptist; Jack F—as-in-Frank Johnson. Did he ever tell anyone else his secret ingredient? Did he ever write to me at the Ambassador Hotel?

The shrine itself is laid out over spacious grounds—a church, a residency, a chapel, and life-size stations placed evenly apart along a paved walkway. A tinny microphone voice with a thick brogue calls us to the first stop, "Jesus is condemned to death. O Jesus, Thou didst desire to die for me that I may receive sanctifying grace, and become a child of God. Teach me to appreciate it more and more."

The four of us make half-genuflections—a concession to our age and the long bus ride, cross ourselves and ponder the words.

"Look there," Mary Agnes says, and we see a group of nuns dressed up in the old-fashioned way. "I never could have stood that. Even forty years ago, our order was progressive, didn't believe women had to be covered in black from head to toe in order to lead a life of devotion."

We proceed at a fairly rapid clip from station to station—there is another tour behind us waiting to start. At the eighth, the invisible priest intones: "Jesus speaks to the women. O Jesus, Thou didst teach the women of Jerusalem to weep for their sins rather than for Thee. Make me weep over my sins which caused Thy sufferings and the loss of my friendship with Thee."

My sins: what are they? My monthly Confessions are like a tape recording of themselves with few exceptions: a lack of charity toward Mama and Marcella, and lately just toward Marcella. Pride. Unkind thoughts about people I don't like or Republicans. Those are the easy ones to explain, the laundry list recited so often that it is like a description of who I am rather than a chronicle of the shortcomings I seek to improve. The other, graver sins I have only tried to confess once, years ago at Waverly when Naomi had died and when I assumed I would join her within the year. The visiting pastor stopped by my bed on the porch, positioned his ear close to my mouth for privacy, and composed himself.

I stared at the slate gray sky, sunk into the silence of his anticipation and then began. "Bless me father for I have sinned. It has been a week since my last Confession." I paused, dove into the depths of my soul.

"Go on, my child," the priest urged, sneaking a glance at his watch.

"I don't believe a word of it," I spoke into the side of his head. There was a spot on his cheek which he had missed while shaving, a patch of bristly stubble in the shape of Indiana.

"I beg your pardon?"

"God. Redemption. Heaven. Not a word."

"My child, you are suffering from a crisis of faith." Now I had his attention. "Ask for grace."

"What kind of a sin is it, a crisis of faith?" I inquired. "Venial or mortal."

"If it persists, mortal. It is the unforgivable sin. Who is your patron saint?"

"I don't know."

"The saint on whose feast day you were born."

That, of course, I knew. October 25. The information had been drummed into me since second grade. "Saints Chrysanthus and Daria," I informed him. "A husband and wife buried alive for their faith by one of the Roman emperors."

"Let them be your examples," the priest told me. "Compared to them, your present suffering is mild indeed."

"They had each other," I said. "They didn't have to die alone."

"Despair is also a sin."

"What isn't a sin?"

"Acceptance," he said primly. "The acceptance of God's will."

"I don't accept it," I said. "It's not fair." I thought of Papa, of having to quit school, of Naomi. "I could do better myself."

"Blasphemy!" This was developing into the most interesting Confession the priest had encountered in some time and his voice betrayed his barely repressed excitement. "I cannot absolve you until you express true contrition."

He wasn't hearing me, couldn't hear me. I was wasting both of our time. I shut my eyes, drew a shallow breath. "Oh, all right," I said. "I am heartily sorry."

"That's better. For your Penance say the "Credo" three times and say a special Rosary in thanksgiving to St. Chrysanthus for interceding on your behalf."

"What about St. Daria?"

"Her, too, of course." He began his mumbled *"absolvo te"* in Latin, making the sign of the cross over my face, which I had turned away.

Thank you, I thought to myself, for being buried alive on my birthday.

"The trip was too much for her." Lucille Andriott's voice penetrates my reverie. "She's dead on her feet."

The whole tour has moved on to the next station and are halfway through Jesus falling for the third time. Marcella's expression is a cross between concerned, vexed and embarrassed.

"I'm fine," I say. "Just daydreaming."

"Maybe we ought to sit out the rest of the stations," Mary Agnes proposes. "The good Lord knows we can recite them by heart. I'm sure He or She will forgive us."

Mary Agnes is as current as today's news as far as church doctrine is concerned. Very up on the latest advances, but she hasn't worked out all the kinks. "If it's a 'She,' " I am tempted to ask her, "is She still a 'Lord'? Not a 'Lady'?"

"You know," Lucille says, studying our printed itinerary. "There is another Mass here in the morning. We could save time by skipping the one this afternoon, renting the car right now, and heading over to the next county to find that place your poor mother wanted you to visit."

We haven't confided the point of our visit to Lucille and Mary Agnes. The right opportunity has never presented itself.

"I vote for that," Marcella announces. "The sooner that little excursion is behind me the better I'll feel."

"Who's going to drive?" Lucille inquires.

"I never learned how, but I can navigate," Mary Agnes volunteers.

"Not me. I'd get confused by being on the wrong side of the road and your lives would be in danger." Marcella is adamant.

"I'll drive," I say, as they all know I will. "Let's find that rental place and head for Boyle. It looks as though it's only an hour or so away."

It's odd to see the directions in Mama's Catholic School handwriting. She copied them down from Grandma's dictation only days before Miss Rose's death, yet they are as precise and exact as if they have been issued by an auto club. "From Boyle go south seven miles. Take the road to the right just past the stone chapel. Follow it along beyond the graveyard at Kilnamanagh ('where your grandfather was born,' Mama had inserted within parentheses) until you come to a large open field dominated by a tree whose trunk is thick as a house. You can't miss it. Go to the west side of the tree. Find a gnarl about chest high. It's on the ground below where I wish to be."

Marcella and Lucille sit scrunched in the back of the compact Japanese car we have leased for twenty-four hours, and Mary Agnes occupies the passenger seat and watches the speedometer.

"This thing measures in kilowatts," she complains. "How do we know what a mile is?"

"Kilometers," I correct her. "You multiply one of them, miles or kilometers, by .6."

"Just watch for the stone chapel," Marcella advises. We ride in silence, our eyes sharp at every crossroads.

"Could that be it?" Mary Agnes points to a crumbly little building, no roof but indeed with a stone foundation.

I slow down. There is in fact a narrow road to the right, a lane more like it, barely wide enough for a single car.

"What if we meet someone going the other way?" Marcella worries aloud.

"One of us will have to back up," Lucille answers.

"I can do this forward but not in reverse," I warn them.

"Take a chance," Mary Agnes urges, and I turn cautiously. We're all nervous as cats.

"I know," Marcella bursts out. "Let's sing Grandma's song. Proclaim her triumphant return!" Without waiting for agreement, she begins the familiar tune in her alto voice.

> *I don't know when and I don't know how*
> *But I'll wed my Rosie Mannion.*
> *Hair as black as ravens' wings*
> *And eyes like forty-seven.*

"What's this?" Mary Agnes wants to know. "Your grandmother had a song written about her."

"And never let you forget it," I say. "It goes on and on."

"Did your grandfather write it?"

"Who but," I prevaricate. "Nobody else had the courage to marry the woman. I guess she must have been something in her day."

"She was something right along," Marcella comments from behind me. "A holy terror. But what are 'the eyes of '47'?"

"Haunted," I tell her. "Like all of them during the Great Hunger."

"I think it's real romantic," Lucille says. "To inspire poetry from a loved one."

"In later years, the way I recall it, she inspired more fear than devotion." I'll never forgive her for not loving Papa more than she did, as much as he deserved.

"That could be a cemetery," Mary Agnes observes, craning her neck to look up a hillside. "There's a fence around it and what look like some markers."

I think of Grandpa, what little I can remember of him. I remember large hands, rough nails, the smell of tobacco. "He wore long johns," I say aloud, surprised to know this. "All year around."

"A strange epitaph," Marcella says. "Surely we know more than that."

"Papa loved him," I remind her. "Said he had a melancholy nature."

"Who wouldn't, with your grandmother," Lucille says. She met Grandma a few times and was taken with her coldness. I hear Marcella gasp and know what she's thinking: Grandma is right here in my Getaway bag. Lucille is taking her life in her hands.

"There!" Mary Agnes is enthusiastic, vindicated. "That has to be it."

The tree is huge, the only vertical object in a wide meadow of grass. As we get closer I see that the trunk is rippled, like a water-fall of bark flowing from the top into the earth. Thick branches spread a pool of shade the circumference of the crown.

I pull the car into what looks like a wagon path and cut the engine. The sudden stillness is sobering. It's like listening to a seashell.

"All right, girls, shall we?" Mary Agnes is halfway out the door when I stop her.

"This may sound . . . look. Marcella and I, I think we should do this alone, if it won't hurt your feelings, you and Lucille. It's kind of a family thing, you know. It won't take five minutes."

"It's fine with me," Lucille says. "I'm content to just sit here and watch the grass grow. It's the first time we've stopped since we got off that plane."

Mary Agnes, though, is hurt at being left out. Her face wears a pout and she lifts her chin. "Take as long as you want. I have to say my devotions anyway. I just don't know why you brought us along if we have to be exiled in the car."

"Get off your high horse," Lucille admonishes her cousin. She taps my shoulder. "Don't mind her," Lucille tells me. "She has to be in on everything. It comes from all those years of social work."

"I'll have you know . . ." Mary Agnes counters and I grab my flight bag, make my escape, leave them to hash out their differences in peace. Marcella is waiting on the other side of the car.

The field is spongy. "I guess this is what they call 'turf,' " Marcella says. "It's going to be a nightmare to get my shoes clean, and I only brought the two pair."

"It's a small sacrifice for Grandma," I say. "Offer it up for the poor souls."

"Mary Agnes says that they don't give indulgences anymore. What do you think happened to all those years of Purgatory we eliminated when they did?"

"I'm sure it's not retroactive," I console her. "They still count."

"I should hope so."

The tree looms larger and larger before us. You can see where one branch has long ago been sawed off and then the stump healed like an amputated arm.

"I'll bet that's what Grandpa made that table out of," Marcella says. "Remember? Grandma always claimed it had come from this very tree."

"Who knows?" It sounded too much like a story to be believable as far as I was concerned.

"So where's this gnarly part?" We walk slowly around the tree watching for the patch at chest level. Finally we get back to where we started without locating it.

"Do you think this is the wrong tree?" Marcella wonders.

"It has to be the right one. Let's look again." Then it comes to me. "Marcella, think how tall Grandma was at the end."

"As round as she was high," she says. "Oh! You mean her chest would be lower than ours!"

"Here it is." I'm at the side away from the road. Our rental car is hidden from view. The bark in the tree comes together like a whirlpool, a knot deep in its center. I unzip the bag, take out the package and hand it to my sister.

"You did a good job on this," she praises me while peeling off layers of tape and bubble wrap. "Not a scratch. Now what?"

"I guess this is it," I say. "How do we get the wax off of the top?"

"There's a stick." Marcella touches a fallen branch with her toe and I pick it up. "You do the honors," she says. "You're the older."

"Grandma liked you better." She doesn't deny it, but still hands me the salver.

"I'm too . . ." she begins. "You do it. I'll sing that verse of the song again. Make this more churchlike."

She begins, *"I don't know when and I don't know how . . ."* while I pry at the melted cap using the stick as a lever. It comes off with surprising ease, revealing the gray contents.

"Okay, Grandma," I say. "You got your wish at last. Welcome home." I stand by the gnarl, beneath the overhang of a thick branch, and tip the salver enough that a stream of pale dust pours out. The first portion reaches the ground, blends with the soil, but then a breeze whips up from nowhere and catches the rest. As we watch, the fine ash lifts and glitters in the late afternoon light, then borne by the wind it spreads like a puff of dandelion seeds, falling and blowing across the field back north toward Kilnamanagh and Boyle, west toward the sea, becoming a part of Ireland indistinguishable from all the rest.

Marcella and I stand speechless as Grandma disperses. Finally my sister breaks the silence.

"It's as though she was flying." I see tears in Marcella's eyes and my heart melts. She can do that to me, can be so beautiful in her vision that she carries me with her, but then she always comes back to earth. "What are we going to do with that nice vase, now?"

I look at the empty salver, our companion since childhood.

"We can't just leave it here for somebody to claim," Marcella goes on. "It would be a shame."

"You want to bring it home?" I ask.

"Just think how pretty it would look filled with flowers," Marcella says. "It needs a good run through the dishwasher, of course, but . . ."

I smile at her, shock her by stepping close and kissing her cheek before she can avoid me. "You're Mama's daughter, you know that, don't you?" I say with real affection. "Mama all over."

Marcella blushes, not sure whether or not I mean this as a compliment, then decides that I do. "And you're Papa's. Always were. I guess that's why we make a good team."

That's as close to a profession of love as I've ever received from my little sister, closer, I know, than I'll ever get again, so I take it, savor it, turn it over in my mind.

"We are a good team," I agree. "We've done the right thing."

"We do the best we can with what we've got."

"And your best," I say to Marcella as she reuses the bubble wrap to protect the old, fragile glass, as we walk back to the car where Mary Agnes and Lucille are still feuding, "is damn good."

"Edna!" The shock in her voice is pure show. There's a spring in Marcella's step as she crosses the field, a bounce that has no concern for mud or old age or jet lag, a halting lilt that's close to a rumba.

CHAPTER FOURTEEN

THE ORIGINAL RECIPE

Rayona

I am a rose am a rose am a rose am a rose. Am Rose. Or at least I'm going to be, in two days, Saturday. The batteries are slowing down on my Walkman so I've turned it off and chant the name like a mantra to give rhythm to my blading. Only in Montana does Robert Burns come out sounding like an after-powwow forty-nine song. A Rose Rose Rose, hey-yah, hey-yah, hey-yah-yah-yah. A steady beat, a late-night smoky-fires tired-singers-leaning-against-each-other pulse that goes perfectly with the winter-scarred and unresurfaced grade of the road. I keep an eye out for potholes and pickups full of joyriding cowboys, but really it's just me and the Bear Paws this time of day, so I think, I listen to my thoughts, I blade to them, left, right, bringing one boot in directly under my weight while pushing off to the side with the other. It's like riding on a bumpy assembly line belt, one of those chocolates that Lucy has to eat on Nick at Nite because she doesn't have time to wrap them, just moving ahead under its own power, accelerating. My hair, loose and wild, does a kind of swing dance. The silver turtle ring on my finger catches the sunlight in a laser flash. The mountains are blue dreams, in a row of sideways right angles at the edge of the valley. The air smells green and yellow, and the only sound is the eight little wheels beneath me, whirling on their new Singapore bearings, sanding at the asphalt. The sun is behind me so my shadow goes ahead, leading the way, and in shadow I look good—graceful and long, bigger than myself, a shifting pattern on the grayness of the road. In shadow I could be anybody, fill-in-the-blank anybody. In shadow I'm the dancing, flickering image of an overhead cloud whizzing across the land, going anywhere fast, wherever the wind blows.

In real life, however, I'm dressed inappropriately—as my grandmother Aunt Ida pointed out without saying a word, just by the screwdriver she let me feel penetrate her heart at the very sight of me. A maroon spandex sports bra and black running shorts, not your everyday reservation attire.

"In Seattle this is the uniform," I told her. "Go to any park. Along Lake Washington. Bike paths at U-Dub. It's high style."

"Sea-at-tle." Every frowning opinion she possesses, gleaned during her one and only visit to the city of my birth condensed into three syllables. She looked away, as if deeply pained at what people will say, but I don't buy it. She'd wear this, too, if she could get away with it. In paisley.

"Want me to buzz by Aunt Pauline's on the way home?" I asked, twirling the car keys on their peyote-stitch chain as I prepared to go out the door.

Aunt Ida swallowed her smile, pushed it down like an unchewed piece of gristly stew meat, but I knew the satisfying vision of her sister's shock that rose behind her eyes. I knew the joy it gave her that I was me, in spite of everything she tried to do to convince me to conform. I had Aunt Ida's number and she didn't fault that—though she'd never admit it—one bit.

I never could get into jogging or bicycling or any of those other good-for-you exercise things, though now and then I tried them out because they were supposed to be healthy and because I forgot how much I didn't like them the last time. So there I'd be, legs pumping, my heart rate putt-putting to its aerobic ideal, accessorized to the max, and in under thirty seconds the thought would arise: Where to? What's all this rushing, this energy, about if it's not taking me to someplace I need to go in a hurry? I don't know, maybe I never hit the "wall" that psycho-runners and marathoners always brag about passing through. Maybe I never pushed myself until my endorphins got fuel-injected into my animal brain. Maybe there was already enough of heading nowhere in my life—but speeding around in a big circle made me feel dopey as a hamster panting it out on a treadmill. You look at one of those idiots in a pet store and want to ask, "What's the point, dude? Where's the fire?" Which is basically what I said to myself after about the first six blocks down Broadway.

But blading . . . blading is a whole different story. The first moment on a dare that I stood on top of eight little wheels and rolled it was like how some women describe childbirth with an epidural: all the pleasure and none of the pain. Sometimes it was as though I was a passenger on my own sailboat, and other times I seemed to be the only stationary object in the universe. The world just whizzed by when I pressed fast-forward. On blades I made a muggy day windy, a cloudy day bright. And with a sound track, with my eardrums plugged into my personal favorite accompanist, Patti LaBelle—the woman must shift her feet while she sings she's got the rhythm so right—the path just opens up before me and I usually get back to a totally different place from the one I left. Usually, but not today. Today I was attached to a rubber band with Aunt Ida's name on it.

"Pick your own name," she had told me when I asked her who I was supposed to be at my naming ceremony. "Be anybody you want." That was sort of her philosophy of the whole event, of human existence, that she was the boss and could give permission. Girls didn't usually have formal naming ceremonies, much less grown-up mixed-bloods who were raised off reservation. And even if they did, somebody else, some elder or whatever, had to provide a name they had inherited the use of or dreamed or otherwise owned. You never got to name yourself to give yourself your grown up identity—except when Aunt Ida was the host, the single supplier of all giveaway blankets, pots, pans and five-dollar bills, the cook and defroster of all food, the personal fryer of every round of bread, the exclusive renter of the grounds. Except when Aunt Ida was herself. Nobody would dare to challenge any interpretation or invention of tradition she chose to make—and when it suited her, she generally improvised as she went along. Every now and then people—visitors or anthropologist-types who didn't know better—would clear their throats and prepare to correct her, to point out some well-researched and collected ethnographic fact that contradicted her pronouncement. There was the time she told some skinny woman from the University of Colorado who was getting on her nerves that "my people say you must drink from of mixture of the waters of life—where you've been, where you are and where you're going."

I was translating and fetched the cup in the dish-dryer on the sink Aunt Ida pointed to.

Without taking her eyes off the woman, Aunt Ida spat into bottom, then handed the cup over. "Drink," she instructed, as if she was bestowing a great favor.

The woman was at a loss. You could see her debating: germs versus losing Aunt Ida's respect—and an unending source of previously unpublished information. But finally she couldn't pull it off.

"Fascinating," she tried.

Aunt Ida's face closed up like a slammed door. She raised the cup to her own lips and drained it. Interview over. When Aunt Ida wanted to make the rules, she made them. As far as she was concerned, she owned history. I liked that about her, as long as her choices and my wishes lived in the same neighborhood.

So, when she announced it was "traditional" that I could have a welcoming ceremony and, coincidentally, pick out my own name, it was okay by me. How many chances do you get for a complete makeover, absolutely free of charge? As the day of Aunt Ida's first annual powwow approached, I paged through fashion magazines, went over to my friend Daisy's house to watch MTV on her satellite dish, read novels from the mission school library, looking for a possible new me.

Lots of the churchy ladies thought I should automatically become my mom, Christine, out of respect for her recent death. They thought this very, very hard, though during her lifetime these same purse-lipped women wouldn't have crossed the street to help her up off it. In her lifetime they passed her by tut-tutting away to themselves about how the world was going to hell in a handbasket and Mom was Exhibit A to prove their point. So what did I care what they thought I should do? *That* wasn't the reason I gave choosing "Christine" my serious consideration. No, it was because I missed Mom, missed her every time I had a funny idea and wanted to tell somebody who would appreciate it, missed her when I wanted somebody not to care if I stayed up all night as long as she could stay up with me and girl-talk, missed her when I drove a car making a million mistakes because she had taught me "her way" not according to the manual. For sentimental reasons I never shifted gears without stripping them, just a little.

But I couldn't be Christine. Mom had retired the jersey. Her number was Hall of Fame, one of a kind. She had been a "very unique individual" as my Aunt Pauline put it in the remarks she read from a recipe index card at the funeral, and then she had looked pleased with her own generous nature for saying so. Mom was all the Christine the world could handle, so I was truly free in my options, or so I imagined.

I was going up an incline now and could feel the altitude in my calves, but still on blades it was more of an "Excuse me?" than a "Whoa!" I had never dared to shoot the hills in Seattle figuring that on Pike, for instance, it would be like one of those scenes from *What's Up Doc?* where a couple of guys are carrying a huge plate glass rectangle across the street just as I'm on the downslope. But here in Montana if my brakes failed . . . well, hello North Dakota.

*   *   *

"I hear this powwow is a special occasion," Dad had said on the phone from Seattle. "I plan to be there."

You know how news can come at you from two directions at once, like wind in a tornado? Well, when he announced his impending visit it was like that for me. From the south came this little gust of pleasure. I imagined his dark face glad at the sight of me, his head nodding encouragement. He'd no doubt appear in some understated Indian-themed vest or belt buckle to advertise his right to be present, a little caption that communicated "Married In." There were times when Mom would have liked to add her own parentheses—Divorced Out—but in the end she forgave him the same as she forgave everybody and everything else—me, Aunt Ida, Dayton, life, God, Bobby Goldsboro for writing songs like "Tie a Yellow Ribbon" she couldn't get out of her head once the painkillers kicked in. Dad was my link to Mom, the only other person besides me who could remember those rare and amazing times when the three of us were a family. And, to be honest, he was more than that, too. He *was* family.

Then, from the north I felt the blow of an Alberta clipper, a rush of close-the-shutters wind barreling down the Rockies that could pick up and transport any object not nailed down. Dad and Aunt Ida, together, the wind howled. Cover your head.

"Great," I said to Dad. He had noticed the pause before I responded, and paused back to let me realize that he wasn't going to draw my attention to it.

"What's this business about you getting a new name? What happens to your old one?"

"It's an extra name, Dad." I've explained this to him twice already so I assume he has a hidden agenda in asking, yet I go through the motions. "It's like when you get to a certain age you get to become *.* . . yourself. A whole bunch of people come, sing songs, dance, and you give *them* presents."

"You give *them* presents?"

"To thank them for coming." Personally, I'd give them presents not to come, but I keep this to myself.

"So who are you going to be?"

Was he pushing for Christine, too? Not likely. I had heard a million times how he had originally wanted to call me Diane, his mother's middle name.

"Diane is out," I informed him. "I'm already named that, anyway." We both knew that the most publicity I ever gave that fact was, when absolutely required, the letter D tucked in between the Rayona and the Taylor.

"I know, I know," he said. "But since this is a traditional kind of thing, right? This naming business? I thought maybe you could dig way back, you know, reclaim some of your lost heritage."

I knew next to nothing about Dad's background. His own father had died when I was too small to remember and his mom, the sole white member of our own personal ethnic rainbow coalition, was an old lady who lived with her sister and sent me a five-dollar bill in a card on my birthday and a big box of presents at Christmas.

"Which one?" I asked him. "Black or white?"

"Well, believe it or not, my mother's people were known as the black Irish," he confided smoothly.

"Pre-marrying your father, or post?"

"Pre, pre," Dad said. "It had something to do with Spaniards who came to Ireland when they couldn't invade England."

What was it about my family? Nobody ever seemed attracted to someone from the same group or of the same color.

"The name, Dad. This is a toll call."

"You won't like it. Forget it. I mean, you're living out there now. You made that choice. You're Indian. Okay. You probably want to choose an Indian name to make yourself feel more at home. I understand. Don't give it another thought. Whatever you choose, that's aces with me, sweet girl."

"The name." Sweet girl. I conceded, he won.

"Rose."

Rose. It could have been a whole lot worse. Rose. "Okay."

"You like it?" Dad told people I never failed to surprise him, but sometimes I actually did.

"Rose it is," I say. "Rose I will be."

I am brought back to myself by the honking of a horn and I crouch a little, protectively, just in case. But it's only Father Hurlburt in the mission van, slowing down. I bend my right knee, put on my brake, and when we both achieve a complete stop he leans over to roll down the window on the passenger side. If he's bothered by my sports bra he doesn't let on.

"I just got a call at the rectory from your father," he says. "He's in Havre—came early for the weekend festivities. I'm heading up there to have lunch with some people at the college if you want a lift."

"How long will you be in town?"

"An hour, hour and a half at the outside."

"Great."

"So, I'll see you at your aunt's in say, twenty minutes?"

"Excellent."

He smiles, nods, rolls up the window to save the air conditioning, and drives off—but not before putting on his left-turn signal. I look up and down the highway. Not a car in sight in either direction.

As I skate back to Mom's beat-up Volaré, my inheritance, I calculate the time. In and out. Hello, got to go. I've missed you, bye. Of course, I could have driven myself, taken the whole afternoon for a visit, but this way I have an exit not under my own control. Dad can't fault me. I haven't seen him since Mom's funeral a year ago—he's part of that general blur—and before that, not since the hospital the night before Mom bolted Seattle and drove us out here. An hour, hour and a half tops is plenty long enough for our first up close and personal.

Dad is waiting at Kentucky Fried Chicken, holding two prepaid tickets for the lunch buffet. He looks city-good, but out of place amid all the Chamber of Commerce types and tourists. His hair is clipped short, with a buzzed-in part, and his lavender silk shirt gives a sheen to his dark skin, sets off his green eyes. He has to be the only man in Montana wearing black pants with front pleats.

When he sees me he smiles. Relief, yes, but sincere happy. *Don't tell me I've grown,* I will him.

"You filled out, baby."

Yes.

He touches my cheek instead of kissing me. He has on some new cologne that surrounds us in a little haze of Elliott Bay jazz. Without quite meaning to, I inhale longer than necessary.

"Vetyver," Dad answers. "Some French root."

I even like the name.

He hands me a ticket and we move toward the chrome display that contains all the lunch selections. Our first stop is the hot table, kept warm by an overhead row of red lights that gives the food a science-fiction kind of glow.

"I wasn't sure how hungry you'd be," Dad explains. "Don't feel obliged to eat more than you want."

Steam rises from the well holding Extra Crispy thighs, the sticky barbecued Buffalo wings, the dried-up-looking health-broiled breast sections. The whipped potatoes are white as paste, bordered by a pot of brown gravy. I move on to the cold salads. It's amazing what the human mind can devise by taking ordinary things like iceberg lettuce and rice and Jell-O and marshmallows and various kinds of julienned vegetables and then mixing them up in weird combinations. I use the most colorful selections to decorate my plate like an easel. A beet-based concoction here, a pale green slaw there, a shimmering orange gelatin ambrosia next door. Dad, I notice, has gone for the traditional white meat-biscuit-milk gravy.

"You could have gotten that in the three-piece special," I tell him. "Saved a dollar."

"Call me a big spender. Besides, we might want dessert."

I look over at the cluster of butterscotch puddings, glassy

strawberry pie slices and brownie squares. I could achieve the same result by attaching weights to my ankles and wrists. "Right."

"Anyway, I like to give them my business," Dad goes on. "The Kentucky thing, you know. It makes me feel loyal."

Loyal. Our eyes don't meet. We don't want to touch "loyal."

I sit across from Dad in a two-person booth. He carefully takes each plate from our trays, arranges them in front of us as if we are eating in a real restaurant. He's ill at ease—I don't know if it's me or Montana.

"It's okay," I say.

"You know, it's just . . . I mean I'm not used to being so obvious. What do they do with the black folks around here?"

"What black folks? We're it."

"Yes, well. But I mean I feel as though I'm standing out, in the spotlight. Makes me nervous."

Tell me about it. "Don't worry. As soon as they see you're not going to smoke dope, start a riot or hold up the cash register, they'll relax. Besides, it could be worse. You could be an Indian. A black man in Havre is just interesting, an Indian is trouble."

He glances at me, a quick dart, but enough to let me see that he understands, he regrets, he apologizes for my screwed-up gene pool and for his long absence from my daily life. He means it, too. He always means it when you have him within your reach. Something glints on his earlobe.

"Dad," I say, and point.

He touches the stud, grins, rolls it between his thumb and forefinger. "Now don't diss me I'm too old," he says. "When I was the right age for this nobody had one. No man."

"Dad." I rip open the little transparent packet that holds salt, pepper, a napkin and a Handi Wipe. "It looks good." I page through my mental 1960s dictionary for a word that will be the compliment he hopes for. "Cool. Call you 'Shaft.'"

"What do you know about Shaft?" he asks, all strutty, but he likes the comparison. "Shaft!" he repeats. "Shaft."

While Dad feels good about himself, my attention is caught by a bright yellow card set in Plexiglas. There is one on every table.

The Buffet is a separate item we sell," it reads. *"This item is a per-person item for sale. Items from the Buffet can only be consumed on these premises by the person who has purchased it. The sharing of food with others who HAVE NOT purchased the Buffet is prohibited and subjects these patrons and yourself to each pay the FULL PRICE for the Buffet. No food from the Buffet can be taken from the restaurant (even scraps). Please DO NOT embarrass either of us by violating these policies. Thank you.*

"Hold on a sec," I say, and get up, go back to the hot table and pile a plate with drumsticks. On the way back to the booth I snag a handful of extra napkins. The Colonel's face is printed on them in red. His expression is trusting, maybe you could even call it startled.

"Get your appetite back?" Shaft inquires.

"For the road," I inform him, turning the little announcement holder facedown on the table. I can see the headlines in the Havre *Herald:* "African-American Female Apprehended. Embarrassed Local KFC Manager."

"So how's your Aunt Ida?"

"The same." If there is one right answer to his question, that's the one.

"Dayton?" Dad's voice tries to be neutral but it's roughed up by an edge of jealousy. Does he actually think Mom and Dayton had a thing going while she was in the last stages of liver failure? I mean, I give Mom credit, but not that much credit.

"Dayton is . . ." What *is* Dayton? Dayton is the only truly nice person I know. He's there when you need him to be and not there when you need that. He somehow manages to be smart and kind at the same time, not an easy mix, and Dayton made the last days Mom lived livable. "Fine," I say. "Dayton's totally fine."

Dad grunts, goes back to his chicken thigh. What does he want? *Dayton's moved to Hawaii? Dayton's a shit? Dayton, who's Dayton?*

I check the clock above the serving counter. Twenty minutes to blastoff.

"Dad," I say to fill him in, maybe to shock him. "I don't know how to break this to you, but Dayton, I'm pretty sure, is, like, gay."

"Gay?" Dad sits back in his booth chair, blinks his eyes. "You serious?"

Great. Now he's going to have an opinion. I nod.

"That explains it." Dad gives a broad smile.

What, is he feeling superior? "Explains what?"

"Just . . . all of it. I knew a guy a long time ago in the service and he was that way, too—was a good soul."

I stop myself from saying "That's a stereotype," because as stereotypes go, this isn't a bad one—and anyway it's true about Dayton.

"He saved my life, as a matter of fact," Dad adds.

I look at Dad's face. He never talks about his time in the army, but I can tell he's sincere. Yet just as he's changing before my eyes, becoming somebody I don't know as well as I'd like to, he changes back to being my father.

"So, you finished the school year here?"

Duh.

"But you're coming home to college?"

I raise my eyebrows. Where was home? For my whole life up till now, home was Mom—and now Mom wasn't home.

"The University of Washington," Dad says. "I got a packet from them the other day. Forms. Want my taxes. Wanted to know if you were an in-state resident."

"I had to give them your address. Sorry."

"No, I mean, I'm glad you did. But, are you? An in-state resident?"

I look out the window on Main Street, Havre, Montana. I think of the funky excitement of Pioneer Square in Seattle.

"Let's just say I've been on vacation here," I say. "A long, long vacation."

"Because the tuition shoots way down," Dad goes on as if he hasn't heard me. "It's a lot of money to make a point."

"There's no point."

"Because you triple qualify for affirmative action."

"Dad, I got good grades. My ACT scores are up there. Relax. This isn't going to cost you. I'll get a job after class."

"Where?"

He seems to think I have my life plan completely worked out. I haven't even decided for sure if I'm going to school next year. I haven't decided what I'm going to wear to Aunt Ida's party. I haven't decided for sure about the chicken legs. "A video store or something."

"School comes first."

My absentee father has me flunked out for being a mall rat before I enroll.

"The library, then. I'll study."

He's satisfied. Tick-tick-tick. Another five minutes off the clock.

"I guess I'll get a room here in town," he says. He seems unsure, as though he's waiting for me to have a better idea.

"Dayton wouldn't care if you stayed with him."

This isn't the plan he's looking for.

"Or Aunt Pauline."

He gives me a *get serious* stare. "Uh-huh."

"Maybe not."

"Well." He's weighing his options, preoccupied. His eyes go to the pay phone on the wall. I don't take it off the hook, but I do soften the blow.

"I am going to be Rose," I confirm to him as his consolation prize. "But I don't have any idea who I'm naming myself after."

"Me neither," he says. "She was, what, your grandmother's grandmother? I don't think there's even a picture. But there are stories. How she came from Ireland carrying a table and vase. A big woman, plump, whose hair turned from black to blond in her old age. There was this song my mother always claimed had been written about Rose—she used to sing it to me. To you, too, the time I brought you to see her in Louisville when you were little."

"I remember that!" I had been about ten and Mom was off somewhere in detox—so Dad was taking care of me. It was the only time I ever flew on an airplane.

"You remember the song?" He seems surprised. No wonder. His mother hadn't exactly been around much.

"Kind of." More than the song, I remember sitting on my grandmother's lap. We were in a rocking chair and part of me felt too old to be babied and another part didn't want her to stop. She smelled like talcum powder and her hair was a strange color—dark tangerine. Mom almost never touched me, so being so close to this woman made me nervous. She just took for granted that I'd like it, though, and the funny thing was, after we left and came back to Seattle, even when I didn't see her, my body could still feel hers every time I heard her voice on the phone. That rocking was memory I could get back to with instant recall. From a distance it seemed comforting, like thinking of being asleep when you're wide awake in the middle of the day.

Dad whistles part of a tune and watches my face.

"Right," I say. "That's it."

"She'll be glad to know it still means something to you."

"I'll tell her the next time I talk to her."

Now it's Dad's turn to look at the clock.

"Actually," he says, "that will be sooner than you think."

I wait for him to go on, but he carefully unfolds his Handi Wipe, pats around his mouth and cleans his fingers.

"See, when I told her what name you were taking—I couldn't talk her out of it."

Help me, his eyes beg.

"Out of what?"

"Okay." He takes a breath, lets it go. "She's flying into Billings at eleven o'clock. She wanted to be here."

"You are shitting me." My brains lock. But wait, this can't be happening. "She's too old to travel by herself. No way."

"She isn't by herself," Dad says. He looks like I feel. "She's coming with her sister. My Aunt Edna."

"She's even older!" It came back to me that Aunt Edna was not a toucher. She had sort of watched me from off to the side.

Dad knows this. He nods, not happy. "It doesn't stop her," he says. "Nothing does. They went to Ireland last year. Next they want to go to some Catholic shrine in Croatia. They said Montana will be a piece of cake compared to that."

We stare at each other, at a loss for words. We both turn to the clock: time's up. I wrap the chicken legs in two layers of napkins and slide out of the booth.

"Here," I say to Dad in a loud voice. "You'll need these for the drive to Billings."

I drag into Aunt Ida's just as one of her programs is going off.

"Would you ever steal a man from your mother?" she demands in Indian. For a minute I think she's making some reference to Dad's being here but then I look at the TV and see six women, three middle-aged with defensive expressions on their tight faces and three teenaged with frizzed hair and mean eyes, all of them sitting on stools and mad at each other.

I refuse to point out the impossibility of this problem.

"Look at them," Aunt Ida gestures toward the set. "Look at how they repay their mothers. And they're not even sorry. They don't even apologize. They think they can do anything, that there is no sin."

The camera stays trained on the women while the show's credits scroll up the screen. I try to imagine the three men who are being fought over. It's scary. I figure I might as well tell Aunt Ida my news while she's still busy with being pissed.

"My Dad's in Havre," I say, switching us back to English.

No reaction. She's glaring at the daughters.

"He's coming to the powwow."

That gets a twitch of her jaw muscles.

"And here's a surprise . . ." I have nothing to lose by trying to put a good spin on things. "His mother and aunt from Kentucky are going to be here too. They're flying all this way."

In old horror movies, the slow-motion shots always look phony, as if events happening in real time aren't menacing enough so you have to goose them up by inching them forward a frame at a time. In real life, however, slow motion is a very effective technique. If Aunt Ida had just swung around fast and shouted, "WHAT?" I would have known how to act—hurt and weepy, so that possibly she would feel guilty at frightening me and put the focus of attention back on herself. But instead her whole body moves like a door turning on extremely stiff hinges. You can almost hear the whine of strain. Sand drops into the hourglass. Hens lay eggs that hatch and produce little chicks who grow up into hens themselves. The seasons change—fall, a long winter, a short spring, a hot summer—before we're back to August again. Finally we make eye contact.

"A surprise." I echo my own word. My voice falls somewhere between a whisper and a squeak, higher pitched than I've ever heard it.

Slow motion again, but now in reverse. Summer, spring, winter, fall. Chicks going back into eggs that heal up. Sand sucked from the bottom chamber into the top. Aunt Ida faces me with her back. Nothing she could have said would have matched all she didn't.

"I'm sorry," I say.

The next program comes on. Three men dressed in panty hose and high heels walk out on the set, sit down and cross their legs. The studio audience is shocked but titillated. Aunt Ida reaches forward and turns up the volume.

As things works out, I could qualify as a guest on one of those shows, except my segment would be titled, "Children Whose Parents Turn Them In To The Cops." Would you believe that when the KFC manager, Mr. VonderHaar, followed Dad out of the restaurant and demanded to see what he had "concealed" in the napkins, Dad told him he had gotten the chicken legs from me?

"I'm sorry, baby." That's how Dad explains his betrayal of me as we stand in the parking lot. The line stops me—it could have been the theme song for our whole relationship. "I have to meet the plane in Billings," Dad says, "and the only way the dufus would let me off of his citizen's arrest was if I gave you up."

"How did you feel when your parent squealed?" I imagine the TV host asking me.

To my surprise, I hear myself answering, "I understand." Because I do. He had to pick up his mother and aunt. He was black and it was Havre. They'd go easier on me, he probably figured correctly.

"Community service," is the term Mr. VonderHaar uses when he calls the tribal police. Aunt Pauline, naturally, is in the building registering her car and so, milliseconds after she pulls up to Aunt Ida's, she is able to breathlessly report the conversation she has eavesdropped word for word.

"He promised that if you worked in the restaurant all day tomorrow your record will be clean," she recounts, her eyes wild with her exclusive hold on the news. "He said it will be a learning experience and anyway one of his regulars is off recovering from an accident at the waterslide near that state park where you used to work . . . ?"

She waits for me to supply the name. "Bearpaw Lake."

"Bearpaw Lake Park," she continues, not skipping a beat. "They turned off the tap when she was halfway down the Avalanche!" There's a moment of silence while we all picture this phenomenon. "Think of the insurance," Aunt Pauline finally whispers, awestruck.

I can relate to the woman. Somehow it seems appropriate that I fill in for her at her job. We both know what it feels like to hit the skids. And, too, if I'm in Havre tomorrow I won't be here, having to help Aunt Ida get ready for the powwow.

"What time do I show up?" I ask.

"He said *eight!*" Aunt Pauline is tingling so hard that every fact, every detail gets written in her mental italics. "He said *on the dot.*"

*   *   *

I wake up the next morning with the realization that I am slave-for-a-day to Kentucky Fried Chicken. Mr. VonderHaar greets me at the glass door, his pie-face stern. He wears a white short-sleeve shirt, a tie that stops two buttons above the ledge that his stomach makes over his belt. His too-black hair is combed straight back from his forehead and he has a widow's peak, like that kid on *The Munsters.*

"I hope you wore comfortable shoes, young lady," he warns.

We both look at my feet. Boots.

He hands me a uniform: a white shift dress and a matching red cap. There's a name tag pinned below the collar. LaVonne.

"LaVonne's the one who . . . ?" I ask.

He nods. I wonder what kind of sound she made when the water stopped but she didn't.

He points to the ladies'. "You can change in there. I'll lock your clothes in my office for safekeeping."

I snag on the word "lock." The old Sam Cook song from one of Mom's 45s pops into my head. *Uh. Ah. That's the sound of a man, working on the chain gang.*

"What do I do?"

"Tiffany will show you the ropes." And there—bam!—is Tiffany. On her, the uniform looks good. She can even afford to leave the top button carelessly open, there's that much of her to advertise. It occurs to me that in profile she's probably shaped pretty much like the Avalanche, swooping in and out in all the crucial places. She wears eyeliner, dark lip pencil with a pale plum accent, a necklace with a heart pendant. Her hair looks like blond meringue.

"You're going to love working here," she informs me. Oh God, she's peppy, too. "Every moment is a challenge."

The girl is certifiable, I think. She has overdosed on fast food. But I hide my perceptions, smile back at her, twinkly as I can manage.

"Oh yes, and this," Mr. VonderHaar remembers and hands me a green plastic shower cap. "For in the kitchen. We don't want your hair in the potatoes."

I look at the puff of the shower cap. Even pulled up and tightly packed, my hair will not fit inside it. My head will look like a spore, about to burst.

"I believe in clean," Tiffany confides in me.

She does. I watch as she takes a brush and scrubs the underside of one of the built-in tables.

"Ha," she exclaims, satisfied, and pries something loose. "Gum. They do that—can you imagine? Can you conceive of going into another person's home—and this place is like a home, really—and just sticking a wad under someone's . . ." She waves her hand with the incriminating pink blob while she searches for the most sacred possible object. "Television set?!"

I stare at her. How did she know I have committed this very act at Aunt Pauline's. Is there some aura at KFC that zeroes in on petty crime?

Nothing escapes Tiffany. She discovers a Kleenex stuffed into the corner of a booth, a line of graffiti—"Lonely in Malta. 555–2821" written with indelible ink inside the stall of the men's room.

"For now," she explains, and covers the message with an open menu she duct-tapes onto the wall. "This will give them something to think about," she decides. "Make them hungry."

Food selection, I learn at 10:45 when the doors open to the public, is the great stumbling block at KFC. Customers arrive in packs, push through the doors and then stall as they stare slack-jawed at the back-lit list of selections above the ordering counter. Each dish is accompanied by a color photograph of itself, sort of an inducement that tempts, "This could be sitting right in front of you in under five minutes!" Unfortunately, though, the visual aids seem to confuse people at least as much as they help them. Whole hungry families simply can't decide among the major choices presented them. Light meat or dark? Regular or Extra Crispy? The Buffet or à la carte? You can see from the expressions on their faces that they want it all. While they are trying to set their priorities—the thoughts flitting through their brains: *today, a sandwich, tomorrow night, a bucket*—more diners arrive, a crowd backs up, jostling unhappily. You'd think that while they were forced to wait the ones behind would spend their time making up their minds, but no. As each new wave of families or businessmen emerges at the head of the line they are as perplexed as the ones were who finally just ordered. I stand by the cash register, amuse myself by figuring out what a given individual wants before they do. Once I discover that I'm almost always correct, I have to fight the urge to grab a man by the lapels and say, "Don't fight it. You're going to wind up with Extra Crispy." Or whisper into the ear of a woman, just off a ranch and in town for a shopping spree, "You don't really want a salad, do you?"

My job does not engage the full potential of my brain. In fact, my duties directly contradict a chapter in my tenth-grade science book about the impulse for mastery that drives human evolution. I am in charge of watching the wire baskets that hold the various kinds of chicken and am supposed to alert the cook when a supply gets low so that he can pop another box of pieces into a pressure cooker. The first time I am called upon to do this, I open a little gray eye-level door in the wall that connects to the kitchen and squint through. There's a barrier of warming shelves between me and the stoves, each one holding The Product, as Mr. VonderHaar calls chicken. For a moment I am fascinated by the oddly cut-up shapes KFC favors—breasts, otherwise known as keels, cut along the bias, lumps of meat that could come from almost any part of a bird's anatomy. Could an actual chicken be reassembled from these assorted tidbits? Or would a whole new multilegged, multi-winged species emerge?

My gaze penetrates past the shelves and I find myself looking directly into the eyes of the cook—at least I assume that's who it is because what I see is a man who resembles a giant bunny—white and pink and twitchy.

"What?" the bunny asks.

"Honey-glazed," I reply.

The bunny nods, chuckles to himself, slides a tray of glistening brown blobs off the shelf and through a rectangular slot that opens before me.

"Wow," I breathe softly, but loud enough for Tiffany, who's operating the other register, to hear.

"Derek," she says. "Don't rile him."

It's not a warning I need to hear twice. I wait for her to go on.

"He's been sick," she explains. "They just let him out. But," she adds on a positive note, "he's real good at his job."

We get through the lunch rush—in Havre if you haven't eaten by one-thirty you wait till supper—and things quiet down so much that I can hear Derek, still chuckling off and on, beyond the wall. Tiffany goes back to her cleaning. Someone has scrawled yet another telephone number, this time on the menu she has left in the bathroom. It's a Dodson exchange, but whoever left it has failed to use a permanent marker. Tiffany erases the listing with a single sweep of her sponge. Mr. VanderHaar disappears into his office to do whatever he does in there. I, as Tiffany phrases it, mind the store. The chicken bins are almost empty but the scent of frying oil lingers, even, it seems to me, increases. I watch idly through the plate glass as traffic passes, pickups and moving vans going east and west along Route 2, a Federal Express truck, station wagons, a few people on foot. A car turns into the lot, stops, but no one gets out. Then three doors open at once. Dad appears from the driver's side. Simultaneously, the legs of two women swing stiffly from the front and back of the passenger side and grapple for the ground. Old lady legs in support hose. One of them has an aluminum cane. He has actually brought his mother and aunt here to see me.

I open my mental science book again. I think of this thing that measures radioactivity. A vacuum where ions attach to dust and you watch them bat around bouncing off each other, leaving their tracks. For the flash of an instant there's no mystery, no wonder how something got from here to there, no surprise appearances. My grandmother wears her eyeglasses as a necklace. She's dressed in a two-piece blood red suit and a silky cream blouse with a huge bow under her chin. The skirt is short for a woman of her age, which I estimate to be about eighty. Her mouth, bright with lipstick, seems to precede her toward the door of the restaurant. Behind her is a tall, thin woman bent at a slight angle at the waist. She uses a cane for support but looks as though she doesn't need it since both the top and bottom halves of her are held precisely straight. She moves slowly, her stance suggesting one of those paper fans opened to its widest extension. A dark violet felt hat squashes down a fringe of gray hair, and her eyes are suspicious, as if the KFC is not quite as it should be, as if it is an innocent front for something worse than it is.

I am so upset I shout without thinking at Derek behind the wall. "Will you shut up that laughing?"

Don't rile him. The words dance across my consciousness. I am surrounded, have eliminated my one available exit through the back door. Derek only becomes louder. *They just let him out.*

"What's all the yelling about?" Tiffany has been spritzing the display case with Glass Wax. She's listening to the radio with earphones so the only sound that has penetrated is my voice. She takes off the headset, which has miraculously not made a dent in her hairdo.

"He keeps laughing," I say, and gesture toward the kitchen. Worry blows across Tiffany's features like a bad smell.

"How long?"

"The whole time." It's easier to think of Derek than to hear the whoosh of the door opening. I smooth the wrinkles from my uniform, run my tongue over my lips.

"Look who's here!" Dad knows I have seen him. I hate the phony tone of his voice.

I stretch a smile across my face, turn around, confront my long-lost grandmother.

"Hello Ramona," she says.

"It's Ra*yo*na, Marcella," her sister corrects. She's more concerned about getting my name right than with me.

"That name." My grandmother shakes her head in annoyance. "Who could ever remember it?"

How did I get so lucky in the grandmother department? One out on the reservation, at this very moment wearing herself out in preparing to violate every known tradition of her tribe, and one who looks like she just stepped off the set of *The Brady Bunch* who can't be bothered with my name.

"Something's burning," Dad notices and sniffs the air.

He's right. Tiffany is knocking on Mr. VonderHaar's office door. "It's Derek," she calls. "I think he's having another one."

Mr. VonderHaar rushes out and passes us without a word. He disappears into the kitchen, Tiffany close behind. The fried odor is suddenly overpowering.

"Excuse me a sec," I say to my grandmother and great-aunt, and follow Mr. VonderHaar. My brain can't quite process what my eyes see: mountains of chicken pieces everywhere—in equal parts Crispy and Extra. On the sink. Packed onto the warming shelves. Strewn across sacks of instant potatoes along the wall. I've never seen so much chicken, and in the middle of it all, Derek, laughing, tears rolling down his bunny cheeks, laughing so hard he can hardly breathe, so hard he's crying. Crying, but laughing all mixed up. He's crouched on the floor and Tiffany is beside him. Derek is big, bald, heavy, and Tiffany is petite, but she's urging him to lean against her, to let himself be cradled in her lap.

"Shhh," she says softly, stroking his forehead. "It's okay." Automatically she reaches in the pocket of her uniform, takes out the sponge she was using and wipes the spittle away from around Derek's mouth.

"I'll call the hospital," Mr. VonderHaar says and runs back into the restaurant part. "Keep him calm."

"Holy Christ!" Dad says. I look behind me and there he is along with my grandmother and Aunt Edna, all goggle-eyed.

"Elgin. Don't take the Lord's name in vain," my grandmother says.

"What are those contraptions?" Edna asks and points to the

row of pressure cookers that line the back wall. They are all vibrating, their little vent-release caps twirling like miniature batons.

"God, does anybody know how to turn those things off?" Tiffany looks terrified, but she's pinned to the floor by Derek's body. What do the two of them look like, I ask myself. Oh yeah, that marble statue . . . what's it called? The Pietà.

"They're going to blow," Tiffany screams, waking me up to the fact that this is reality and not some *Saturday Night Live* skit that's actually taking place in New York, in another time zone.

I stare at Dad. He stares at me.

"Mom," he says. "Come back outside. Aunt Edna."

But Aunt Edna has other ideas. She comes forward, steps over the pile of Derek and Tiffany and approaches the shaking pots. She seems to be looking for something behind them, then below. The angle of her body becomes more acute as she bends over, reaches under the counter. Suddenly the bubbling noises begin to slack off, the cookers to calm down. Edna straightens to her original 160°. In her hands she holds a disconnected extension cord with the space for six electrical plug-ins.

We all relax, and I try for a joke while Derek continues to chuckle. Even he sounds more settled now.

"Well, at least we won't have to cook any chicken for the dinner crowd."

"We most certainly will." Tiffany, the highest-ranking KFC official in the room, is outraged. "That chicken" —she nods to the four cardinal directions. "We have no way of knowing whether or not it was prepared under conditions of quality control." She is reciting something out of the official company manual. Her eyes have a blank glaze, as if she is reading from the inside of her head. "We could lose the franchise."

Mr. VonderHaar is back, nodding his agreement. He turns to Dad. "Could you drive us to the hospital?" he asks, looking at Derek. "He's harmless. He just needs me to hold him, and that ties up my arms."

"Sure." Dad is happy to escape. I don't blame him.

"What do we do in an emergency?" Tiffany is suddenly aware of the heavy burden of responsibility that has fallen on her shoulders.

"Leave a message on my machine," Mr. VonderHaar tells her.

"Who has a pen?"

I hold up my hands, empty. Aunt Edna has still got the extension cord. My grandmother sighs, digs into her bag and comes up with a gilt-encrusted ballpoint and a gold leatherette address book. She flips to a blank page, gives Mr. VonderHaar a glance shaped like an irritated question mark.

"555–2821," he recites. She makes him repeat it twice. Tiffany won't meet my eyes on the second go-round.

By the time Dad and Mr. VonderHaar herd Derek into the car it's nearly four o'clock. We are approaching the hour of the wolf, that point in every twenty-four-hour cycle when a little pilot light goes on in the stomachs of Montanans and they believe themselves not only ready but entitled as American citizens to eat. When this condition prevails it is never a good idea to get between them and food, and even as my grandmother, my Aunt Edna, Tiffany and I stand together in the wreckage of the usually spotless KFC stainless steel kitchen I can sense, in concentric geographic circles—some as close by as the Conoco station next door, some as far distant as the tiny soon-to-be ghost towns of the high plains to the east and west—the pricking of a craving for fried chicken. It isn't telepathy, exactly, that makes me aware of this, but rather a survival instinct such as the one that makes wild animals raise their noses to sniff out a hunter in the act of sitting on the side of his bed, lacing his boots, about to set forth.

When it comes to not getting their chicken when they want it, need it, have a God-given right to it, no excuse is going to be sufficient. People have been trained in what they deserve to expect, and I imagine them now, like a whole town of "Village of the Damned," their pupils slot machines that show, instead of clusters of cherries or lemons, little bunches of thighs and drumsticks.

Any minute now a similar mob will descend on this very KFC, and they aren't in the mood for cole slaw.

"I love your hair," my grandmother tells Tiffany, who beams back her appreciation. "What do you use?"

"I find that over-the-counter conditioners work just as well as those you purchase in salons," Tiffany answers. "And they're much less expensive."

"But you have to make sure to rinse thoroughly." My grandmother grimaces, as if she has learned this fact from bitter trial and error.

"I always do. Otherwise you get buildup."

"Do you wash every day? I hope not."

Tiffany has no poker face. Her expression is an admission of guilt.

"You'll be bald by fifty," my grandmother predicts breezily. "I never wash my own hair. I have a beauty operator do it."

These women have over the years poured far too many chemicals on their heads, that's the only possible explanation.

"Isn't anybody but me worried?" I demand. "Customers are going to start banging on the doors and if we can't feed them the chicken Derek cooked, what will we do with them?"

My grandmother and Tiffany have been in deep denial and are suddenly stunned. Aunt Edna, on the other hand, has been thinking.

"You've got more chicken?" she asks.

Tiffany nods, slowly, reserving judgment about any idea that is to follow. "But I'm afraid of the pressure cookers. I'm afraid of them."

Aunt Edna makes a sour face, shakes her head.

"You've got flour, Crisco, skillets?"

"I guess," Tiffany says. "But I don't know the Colonel's secret formula, the exact mixture of thirty-nine herbs and spices. They only reveal that to the cook."

"Formula!" Aunt Edna scoffs. Her hands are on her narrow hips, her elbows pointing out like two sides of a Texaco star. "I knew Claudia Sanders. She was a client of my boss. Confided in me like a lot of them did. I tried to talk her out of marrying that man. I sat in her kitchen after-hours when her mother taught her how to cook."

"You actually knew the Colonel's wife?" I am totally impressed with this woman. First she saves us from being blown to bits and now she hobnobs with famous people of the past.

Aunt Edna hears the admiration in my voice and likes it. She gives me a twinge of a smile, the first real acknowledgment of me since she arrived. "Honey," she says. "She was just a human being like you and me."

"You know the secret ingredients?" Tiffany acts as though she has just met Albert Einstein.

"Claudia only had one trick to her flavoring," Aunt Edna announces. We all hang in anticipation and she draws out the suspense. Finally she breaks the silence.

"Paprika," Aunt Edna says. "Plenty of paprika."

I am unused to meeting somebody I am actually related to and being pleasantly surprised, but there is something about Aunt Edna that gets to me. Role models, that's what school counselors are always pushing me to identify with, but the people they parade out are all women astronauts or tennis players or homemaker/senators. I watch Edna, who has to be in her mid-eighties, has to be, take charge of a Kentucky Fried Chicken restaurant, assign us all duties, put on an apron and start rinsing chicken parts and patting them dry with paper towels. I can't imagine any of those type-A personalities with strings of college degrees after their names and resumés a mile long being able to pull this off. I mean, it's one thing to study, prepare yourself for a job, and then succeed, but it's another to just fall into an unexpected situation and then make the best of things. Fifteen minutes ago Aunt Edna was probably tired from her trip and now look at her, a whirl of activity in a white cloud of flour. It wasn't as though she liked what she had to do—but it wasn't as though she expected to like it, either. She simply pitched in. What was that about courage? How something wasn't real courage unless it was mixed with fear? Well, in Edna's case, work wasn't real work unless it was scrambled with annoyance but that didn't take anything away from what she accomplished. You could almost see her complaints rolling around inside her, poking out an elbow here, kicking a foot there, but that's where they stayed: inside.

She sees me staring. "What's the matter with you?" she asks, as if she really wants to know.

"Nothing," I say. "It's just that . . ." I'm embarrassed to say what comes into my head.

"That . . . ?" she prods without once pausing in her food prep.

"I don't know," I say, then chance it. "That I think I kind of take after you, if that makes any sense."

She looks startled. "No," she corrects me. "You would take after Marcella. She's the closer related one."

We both look at my grandmother who is still exchanging magazine solutions to common beauty dilemmas with Tiffany as they use ice-cream scoops to fill little cardboard cups with mashed potatoes.

"Right," I say, and then Edna surprises me again: she laughs.

"Sweetheart," she says. "Sometimes I can't figure out how I'm related to her either, but give her time. She's got a big heart."

"You do, too."

"Honey, I'm just big. Or I was before I shrunk. I've got one piece of advice for you. Don't get old. Now start deepfrying this chicken while I go outside and see if anybody's waiting to eat."

Since the pressure cookers are out of commission we've improvised, using a huge vat that normally contains gravy. Oil is bubbling inside and I carefully use a slotted spoon to ladle floured bits of breast and thigh into its depths. Without consciously thinking of it I guess I start to hum to myself, and as Edna moves past me she stops to listen. I look up and her face is quiet, lost in itself.

"That song takes me back," she says. "My grandmother used to sing it, claimed it was written especially for her by the only man she ever loved."

"Your grandfather," I nod.

Edna raises her eyebrows. "You had to know her," she informs me. "She was incapable of saying a sentence without a barb in it. To hear her tell it, she *married* her husband. She *loved* Gerry Lynch."

"She told that to her husband?" I am fascinated.

"Every day of his short life," she says.

"He didn't mind?"

"He hated it and she loved him for that."

I shake my head. I thought Mom's relationship with Aunt Ida was screwed up. "Nobody's normal," I say. "Are they?"

"Thank the good Lord," Edna answers, and then she's gone, her alone against a roomful of stomach-growling Westerners. This thought horrifies me. She's from the South where people are polite, where they please and thank you and write notes to each other on scented stationery. She doesn't know what she's in for. We are only cooking one kind of chicken and these people are used to variety.

"Turn the pieces when they brown," I call to Tiffany, then take a deep breath and go out to help Edna.

But of course she doesn't need any help.

"Darling," she's sweet-talking a man bursting out of a black Sturgis Biker Rally T-shirt. He has a skull and crossbones tattoo on each forearm. "You just *think* you want Cajun because you don't know about the one-night-only special."

The man looks at her as if she's a holograph, Princess Leia in *Star Wars*. His eyes are yellow, bloodshot. He could have just slashed a tire or something.

"And what would that be?"

Aunt Edna has turned into sweetness itself, transformed into a softer version of herself for somebody who doesn't know her better. She's unrecognizable. She reaches over, squeezes the man's hand where it rests in a fist on the counter.

"You just can't wait to know, can you, hon?"

Before my eyes, the man blushes. He looks as if he is having a stroke, that red.

"Well, I'm going to tell you." Aunt Edna lowers her voice and every person in line, which at the time numbers about twenty, inclines forward to catch her words. "Homemade Southern," she purrs. "My own treasured recipe."

"Your own?" The man knows a good thing when he hears it. Homemade is one of those expressions that perks up everybody's ears. It dawns on him that he has the opportunity to get more than his money's worth.

"I'll take it," he decides. My eyes sweep the room. Correction: everybody decides. Unanimous. "They have homemade," a whisper goes forth like a chain letter, snagging unsuspecting customers the second they pull into the parking lot. *"Real homemade."*

"I knew you would, sugar," Aunt Edna says. "You just didn't have a choice, did you?"

CHAPTER FIFTEEN

THE GIVE AWAY

Rayona

The four of us sit slumped at the counter. We share the calm of earned exhaustion, the camaraderie of veterans who have against the odds won a battle. Our clothes and hair and skin are speckled with dried drops of grease, smeared with dabs of mayonnaise, flecked with splattered brown gravy. We are too tired to move much, so we just swing our hips back and forth on the red vinyl stools, steady and effortless as the pendulums of those see-through, motion-run wristwatches. We are bunched in two clusters, Aunt Edna and me at the far left, my grandmother and Tiffany at the far right, the row of empty spaces between symbolic of the division of labor that has seen us through the night. We have been, each in her own fashion, in states of continuous activity for five solid hours and are, now that the sign on the door has been turned from "Open!" to "Sorry We're Closed!" slowly winding down. We don't talk, at least not in full sentences, because a shorthand has developed between us. Tiffany merely has to say "Mount Rushmore" to summon up in our minds the family group—father, mother, son, daughter—who wanted double-mashed, each of them dressed in a matching T-shirt displaying the carved stone face of a different dead president. As if they had been trained to do so, they lined up in exact order to create a kind of living panorama tableau of the Black Hills.

"We're from South Dakota," they announced proudly and in unison. As if we couldn't figure *that* one out.

"You're darling," Aunt Edna had complimented them. In their frenzy of self-appreciation they had purchased four frozen sundaes which previously they had declined by holding up their hands and shaking their heads, all in the same direction.

"You've waitressed before?" I asked her.

"My first time," she said. "But I'm a natural."

Now the Black Hills were gone, probably doing synchronized swimming in the industrial-green chlorinated waters of the Comfort Inn's indoor pool.

"Rapunzel," offers my grandmother, and before our eyes arises the vision of the old lady with straight white hair that reached below the backs of her knees. All she wanted was the salad bar.

"Lady Godiva meets *Nightmare on Elm Street*," I say.

"Miss Haversham," Aunt Edna nods. Neither of us understands exactly what the other means but in a general way we do, so we roll our eyes.

"What are we going to do with all Derek's chicken?" Tiffany wonders. We have bagged it in twelve jumbo sacks and ten tubs, turned down the emptied freezers to "cool" and stuffed it inside.

"It's a crime to let it go to waste," my grandmother says.

I instantly think of all the hungry people tomorrow at Aunt Ida's powwow. I think how happy they'd be to have KFC to go with their corn soup. Think of how full they'd get and how that would distract them from noticing what was going on.

I pass along my suggestion, speeding up the swing of my counter stool in my enthusiasm.

"I will not take responsibility." Tiffany is not about to get herself sued.

I stop moving, narrow my eyes in her direction. "Not doing something is just as much of an act as doing something," I say, quoting somebody. "If you're not part of the solution you're part of the problem." I see Eldridge Cleaver scowling down at me from one of Dad's younger-days posters that he still keeps in his apartment, even though Eldridge Cleaver now sells pants that have built-in pads in the crotch.

Tiffany is impressed by my logic, or rather, by the fact that I seem to be employing logic. "I guess I could look the other way," she allows. "But they can't be presented in official KFC packaging."

This girl has memorized the corporate manual. It comes to me that she must have career goals, and I'm momentarily defensive because I lack any clear plan for my life beyond surviving tomorrow afternoon.

"Deal," I say.

She smiles and I wonder why she has caved so easily. Then I get it: if we cart the chicken out of town it solves her disposal problem. She can have the restaurant eat-off-the-floor clean by lunch.

"Where did Elgin get to?" My grandmother rouses herself to search the four corners of the restaurant with her gaze.

"Is that the black man who brought you in here?" Tiffany asks.

"My son," my grandmother corrects her. "That black man is my son."

"But . . ." Tiffany begins to protest then stops herself. "Oh. Adopted."

"Biological."

"If you say so." Tiffany shrugs her shoulders, unconvinced but not interested enough to argue. Now that the crisis is over my grandmother and aunt have reverted in her mind back into the category of potential customers and at KFC you didn't argue with the customers no matter how wacko their statements.

"Anyway," Tiffany says. "He did call. I forgot to tell you. He said they had to take Derek all the way to Billings. The ward here was full."

Why did this not surprise me, the Havre loony bin having a No Vacancy sign at the door?

"He won't be back till all hours," Aunt Edna says. "I don't know about you girls, but I'm ready for dreamland."

"I'm too tired to sleep," my grandmother complains.

"No you're not," Aunt Edna says.

My grandmother looks at me as if to get my vote.

"Tomorrow is a big day," I say. I can't leave until she does.

"Maybe," she says.

Maybe?

"You go on," Tiffany urges. "I'll straighten up. I don't mind a bit."

One of those analogy questions from the ACT college admission test floats into my brain. "*Tiffany* is to *Not minding straightening up* as _____ is to _____."

"What's the matter?" Tiffany asks me. "You look strange all of a sudden."

"Madonna," I say. "Taking her clothes off."

"Whatever." Tiffany is anxious for us to clear out.

"Don't be disrespectful," my grandmother cautions me, but she's tired, her heart isn't in it. "Our Lady would do no such thing. The idea."

An anticipation of disaster sweeps over me. These two women—my grandmother, especially—are basically out of it, vulnerable, don't have a clue as to what awaits them tomorrow. I've got to issue a warning, I decide. After tonight, we have a lot of chicken between us, a lot of, as the Colonel would say, "fixin's." It's my responsibility to at least advise them to activate their shields and go into yellow alert.

"My Aunt Ida," I begin, and instantly feel a tug of loyalties. How can I explain Aunt Ida without seeming to put her down? "Sometimes she can be a little . . . moody. So, if she says anything, uh, out of line, don't take offense, okay?"

Both of them give uncomprehending stares. It's as though they can't believe what they're hearing.

"She doesn't mean anything by it," I say. "Down deep she's . . ." *What* is Aunt Ida down deep? That's a question I cannot answer at this moment and I drop it. "I just don't want you to get your feelings hurt."

Aunt Edna and my grandmother steal a glance at each other, quickly look away, seem to hold themselves at rigid attention. And then they lose all control, throw back their heads and laugh. Every few seconds one of them tries to say something, gasps a break in her hilarity, waves a hand in the air to attract the other's attention, but it's hopeless, no words will break through, she gives up and it's the other's turn.

"What's the matter with you?" Tiffany is worried that they've lost their minds. "Are you okay, or what?"

There is almost a lull, then my grandmother and Aunt Edna remake eye contact and that sets them off again.

"Well, pardon me." Tiffany is beginning to be insulted not to be in on the joke, and here she was, ready to be helpful. "Did I say something funny?"

Flushed, almost weeping, my grandmother's instinct not to be rude pulls her back.

"Oh," she says. "Oh, baby doll, it's not you."

"I'm having a spasm," Aunt Edna announces.

My grandmother turns to me, fights for calm. "You're a sweetheart, but honey, don't you worry about us having our feelings hurt by a moody old lady." She looks at Edna and they both seem as ready to blow as the pressure cookers had been six hours before. "We were weaned by the world champion," she says and slaps the table with the palm of one hand and pinches her own cheek with the fingers of the other. "Moody is mother's milk to us. Our mama invented moody. She coined the term. Meeting moody will be like breakfast on Mother's Day."

It's after midnight—tomorrow is today—by the time I pull into Aunt Ida's yard, but the lights in the house are still on. Aunt Pauline greets me at the door.

"Have you served your time?" she wants to know. "Are you free?"

"I've learned my lesson," I tell her. "I'll never embarrass anyone again."

Aunt Ida, who is standing at the stove stirring a pot of beans, makes a sound that indicates she believes my promise to be unlikely.

"It's good you're here to help us worry," Aunt Pauline says. "We don't have enough food if everybody who was invited comes. We'll run out."

"No we won't." I inform her that the entire trunk and rear seat of the Volaré are full of fried chicken, legally repacked in anonymous waxed paper and brown boxes.

"It's like the loaves and the fishes," she exclaims. "Like the little birds of the air who don't have to toil. Except . . ." She frowns at me. "You could have called. We've been toiling for hours."

I blink at her, relieved. She and my grandmother are going to get on like a house on fire. That's one less thing for me to dread. But no sooner do I mentally pair them up than the matching set occurs to me. Aunt Ida and Aunt Edna. I imagine a senior citizens version of *American Gladiators,* the two of them standing on platforms slugging at each other with padded lacrosse sticks. No nets.

"It's going to be great," I say. "I can't wait."

"Did you see your father?" Aunt Ida's shoulders are hunched and I know, without any doubt, that she is thinking of Mom. If this were an alternate universe I could go over to her, put my arms around her, and we could miss Mom together. We could tell each other funny stories about the stuff Mom got into, nod our heads over how impossible she was to be around, cry. But the closest I can get to this feeling with Aunt Ida is to simply not say anything, to simply let a silence fall around us like the gentle light of dusk, to be quiet with her for enough seconds that it's noticeable, to touch her with my understanding of what she can't do, what's impossible for her, no matter how much she might like to do it, and then let go before she pushes me away.

"It chilled off a lot," I say finally. "The chicken will be all right in the car. I put two bags of ice in the trunk, like a cooler."

Aunt Ida's spine relaxes and she starts to stir again. We've returned to real time, maybe a little less alone than when we departed it, but tonight this isn't good enough for me, I'm sorry. She's going to all this trouble—and not just for me, not just for her. She's doing it because she didn't do it for Mom and she's pretending it's not too late. And Mom, I know, would never have stood still for it anyway, even if Aunt Ida had tried—which is maybe why she didn't try. My role is to stand in, to be the daughter Aunt Ida didn't have so that Aunt Ida can be the mother she couldn't be. They're both behind this, pushing and pulling at me to get them off the hook of their guilt and regret, of their scaredness. My head buzzes. What the hell. I walk over to Aunt Ida, grab her around the shoulders and kiss the scar on her cheek.

"I love you," I say. She turns to me, shocked, frozen up, her mouth tight as if she's ready to suck herself inside out. "And you love me," I tell her firmly. "This ceremony is your way of showing it."

Her eyes flare, betrayed. By putting a definition on what's happening I have snuck some part of it away from her. She can't very well say, "No I don't love you," any more than she can get all sweet and cuddly and say, "Yes I do." Plus, Pauline has heard and has the nerve to nod approval. Aunt Ida is stuck, superglued to my explanation whether she likes it or not. Daggers. Mom would never have done such a thing to her. Mom knew the rules, played fair.

"My Dad is fine," I say, releasing my grip. "He loved her, too."

The powwow grounds are a circle with a circumference of bowers for shade. Since early morning, tribal employees under Aunt Pauline's stern direction have been threading poplar branches into the lattice that rides atop the poles, and the fresh leaves rustle in the wind as they dry. The circle is contained in a larger circle, a shallow bowl in the plains that doubles, in spring and fall, as a communal grazing land. Off to the west are a row of mountains so uniform in their sizes and shapes that they resemble a continuous line of linked capital M's or the blade of a handsaw, sloping toward the south. They're far enough away that they don't interfere with the open umbrella of pure sky that sails overhead, an airiness so limitless in its arc that it's as though the earth is looking up at an acrobat who has performed a perfect backbend. The wind is calm, alive enough not to be dead but missing the sort of push-you-over shove that often signals the end of summer, and the sun is low wattage, a flattering light that makes wearing a hat seem like an overreaction. Today is as pretty as it gets, the answer to somebody's prayers.

But not to mine. I have been hoping for a premature blizzard with tire-chain alerts, a rain squall that turned the high grass horizontal in long sweeps of fury, or a temperature so blisteringly scorching that all anyone can wish for is to be indoors, to run for available air-conditioning, to get this show on the road and over with as quickly as possible and then spend the evening talking about nothing but the disaster of global warming.

Before you put yourself into any pair of hands not under your own control, you'd better make sure that they aren't itching to be creative. I failed to follow this advice and as a result I find myself wishing I was still dressed in my usual civilian clothes—jeans, an oversize Mariners T-shirt, running shoes—as opposed to this Pocahontas nightmare that half the reservation ladies have been laboring over, under Aunt Ida's suspicious and no-if-ands-or-buts supervision, for the past month. The outfit is a definite mistake, but there's no way I can say so, Aunt Ida's intentions are that good, her expenditures that great, and her feelings, in spite of what she wants everybody to think and thinks that they do think, that easily hurt.

It's not her fault that she doesn't keep track of the ebbs and flows of powwow fashion. She hasn't gone out in public all that often, and when she has it's clear—from the composition of this dress and its accessories—that certain fads and touches have entered her memory banks at one time, certain items and notions at another, over the past twenty years or so. Put them all together and the ensemble she has personally designed and specified can only be described as a K-Tel collection of Crow Fair's greatest hits from the 70s, 80s and Today available for the first time on one bargain CD, a ragtag jumble from a trunk that should have long ago been donated to the Good Will or dropped overboard with a serious anchor attached.

Any single theme would be, by itself, plausible, okay, not too awful maybe, but when you start mixing up rawhide and satin and calico and tanned deerskin, when you make a red-and-black statement in a shawl and expect it to complement a turquoise and magenta zigzag in a dress, when you sew snuff lid jingles and tiny cowbells to any square inch that isn't otherwise occupied with neon yarn fringe, when you interchange floral and geometric in the same beadwork pattern, when you simultaneously push the traditional and the fancy dance buttons, when you give equal nods to plains, woodland, southwest, and northwest coast design motifs and then throw in a little *Dances with Wolves* glitz to spice them up, you get . . . well, you get what I'm wearing.

Warning: Viewing me directly without protective lenses at Grand Entry may be hazardous to your future vision.

And then there's the matter of my hair, which Aunt Pauline has taken as her special responsibility because, as she has told me more than once over the past two hours, "I had no daughter of my own to do this to." At its best my hair is Rae Dawn Chong wild, Afro-Siouxish. There are women who pay a lot of money to get permanents in order to achieve the hair I come by naturally, and after years of trying to make it straighter, blacker, easier to comb, I've accepted it, like it even. To Aunt Pauline, however, my hair represents a challenge to her ability to French braid—a challenge, I might add, that she has proven herself up to as I sat this morning in a kitchen chair while she worked on me. She used the sharpened end of a yellow pencil to prick out tiny oiled strands and then twisted them together along my scalp until they reunited like small streams merging into twin rivers.

When Aunt Pauline finally held a mirror for me to admire her success, I was stunned—and *looked* stunned because my hair was pulled back from my forehead so tightly that my eyebrows were in a constant arch of surprise. Loose or even bulky braided, my hair has all my life disguised a fact that now is undeniable: my skull is too small for the rest of my body. I look like a wet cat or as though I'm just back from visiting one of those South American tribes who specialize in shrinking heads, except that they have left the rest of me attached. Unfortunately, the basic pinto bean shape of my cranium is not made less obvious by the red ribbons, cowry shells, parrot feathers, otter tails and various carved stone fetishes that Aunt Pauline has intricately woven in here and there.

Finally, the jewelry—borrowed or pried away from a wide spectrum of the reservation's population. At least, I console myself, the earrings, belt buckle, bracelets, clips and rings have a couple of common denominators. They're all Hopi or Zuni silver, and they're all imprinted with some kind of stylized tracks design. The bad news is that these tracks have not been made by the same animal. Badgers roam across one part of me while bears, roadrunners, wildcats and wolves have left their paw impressions in others. I am decorated like the gray mud around some forest watering hole five minutes after rush hour.

If Aunt Ida and Aunt Pauline think that their efforts have made me look more like a full-blood, they're deluding themselves. True, they've created an effect that might be described as postearthquake Museum of the American Indian, but underneath the chaos I'm still Rayona-soon-to-be-Rose Taylor, too much of this and not enough of that to suit your average Nazoid quantum freak. And even if I could blush under all the makeup that's layered on my face, nobody would believe I was not at least a co-conspirator in assembling myself.

"Ramona?"

In a wind chime chorus of tinkles and clanks I turn around.

"Grandma."

"My," she says. "Don't we look cute. That's quite a color scheme."

She, of course, is wearing a tan London Fog raincoat. Aunt Edna, her head covered by a scarf sprinkled with bright green shamrocks, is right beside her and wins my heart.

"I liked your hair better before," she says.

I am so surprised by honesty that I don't know how to react. I've never known people, except maybe Dayton, who actually say what they mean.

"Do you always tell the truth?" I ask her.

"To those who can hear it," she answers, and now, on top of surprised I'm flattered, but still I won't let it alone, decide to risk a test—always a dangerous move.

"What do you think of my dress?"

She studies me. "Interesting," she begins, then sees my disappointment. "Look," she goes on. "What do I know? I mean, I can't see you wearing it on the street, but maybe here, today . . ."

I shoot her a give-me-a-break look.

"Well. All right. You have my sympathy."

"Edna!" My grandmother is scandalized. "Somebody made that. I've always loved clothes," she says to me in an aside.

"Marcella, she asked me and I told her."

"It's okay," I say. "I can take it." And in fact I am relieved, I am set free to laugh inside, I am transformed into a concealed audience of myself with somebody I can nudge with my elbow rather than being stuck alone in the spotlight. Aunt Edna gets an A.

"Elgin dropped us off there after the continental breakfast at the motel," my grandmother tells me, pointing to the entrance to the grounds. "That's why we're early, but we got tired of waiting and Edna thought that was you over here, so we walked." She waits to be praised. "Besides, we wanted to be a little early so that we could give you your present." She holds out a box wrapped in flowery paper. "You can open it now or later. It's special for the occasion."

"Thanks," I say. "Later would be better." The gift embarrasses me and I tuck the box under my arm. Nobody has told my grandmother that at a give-away the person honored gives-away instead of gets. I change the subject to distract her. "It's a good hike."

"It was hard on Edna," my grandmother worries. Aunt Edna makes a dour face.

"Where did Dad go?"

"Over to pay his respects to your Aunt Ida and to see if she needed a lift."

As if on cue, there's his car, churning up dust, approaching the powwow grounds as steadily as if it were being pulled in on a pulley rope, hand over hand. I squint to see if he's alone. He isn't.

"I'm so looking forward to meeting Ida." My grandmother plants an expectant smile on her face. "I've heard so much about her."

"You have?"

"Oh, oodles, thanks to your mother's friend, Mr. Nickels. I understand she's very devoted to the Church. And of course your uncle was killed in Vietnam, just like my Earl in the European theater. Loss forms a bond."

I wonder, suddenly, if it's also a bond between Dad and me. Him losing his father, him losing Mom, losing me. Then I do a mental double take: *him losing Mom, too.* But before I can process this concept, the car slows to a stop and I steel myself. It's as though I've been dropped into one of those cheesy Japanese horror flicks—*Rodan Meets Godzilla* or when that giant flying turtle sumo wrestles Mothra. Tokyo never survives these encounters. Subways are flipped around like jointed wooden snakes, crowds of commuters run screaming as live electrical wires crackle and writhe on the sidewalk, anxious TV anchors around the world— New York, Paris, Moscow—broadcast the bad news to viewers clustered around TV sets with rabbit-ears antennas.

But when the big moment arrives it's a total anticlimax. Dad hops out, runs around and opens the passenger door, helps Aunt Ida—who *lets* herself be helped!—from the car. Her fingers rest on his arm longer than they have to. She thanks him. She walks right up to where we are standing.

"I'm glad you could come."

Wait a minute. She's polite? She's speaking English? Aunt Pauline must have slipped a Valium into her coffee.

"We wouldn't have missed it for the world," my grandmother

gushes. "It's wonderful to finally meet. This is my older sister, Edna. We offer our condolences for your loss."

Aunt Ida holds out her hand to be shook. Aunt Edna shakes it. More than shakes it. Something is going on! They are having a squeezing contest, these two old ladies, they are each pressing down on the other's bones for all they're worth and neither of them is about to cry "uncle." How did they recognize the stubbornness in each other so fast? How do I break this up before one of them is on her knees, begging for mercy? I stare into the sky.

"What's that?" I say to divert them.

All eyes turn up, grips release.

"Is that a bald eagle?" my grandmother asks.

"A red-tailed hawk," Aunt Ida declares. "A good sign for today. Luck."

Aunt Edna simply gives me a sharp look, and I have learned a new fact: neither Aunt Ida nor my grandmother can see objects far away, Aunt Edna can. Or rather, she can't. The sky is just as cloudless and empty as it was thirty seconds ago. I offer an apology by way of a private shrug, just between her and me, and she accepts it, silently declares herself the winner by default, folds into one of the canvas chairs Dad is setting out. Round one is over. A gong sounds in my head.

I, trussed up as I am, cannot sit down, and until more people arrive I am the only show for Dad, my grandmother, Aunt Ida and Aunt Edna to watch. I pretend to adjust my shawl but I can feel their eyes on me, almost sense their thoughts dissecting me, dividing me up as if I'm a bag of peanut M&M's and they each like only one color. "Don't blame me," I feel like telling them. "I'm just you, strung together in a DNA lottery." There is a magnifying glass effect at work on this on the reservation: details that would go unnoticed in the outside world are brought into highlight, underlined, written in Day-Glo. So big deal, I'm hard to place, I don't fit into anybody's wish-book, I require an explanation. I make a mental note not to haul out this microscope on my children, assuming I have any.

"I had a nun friend who worked among the Indians," my grandmother announces to Aunt Ida, who has no comment.

"Who?" Aunt Edna asks.

My grandmother ignores her. "She said they were most pious."

"Mother?" Elgin interrupts, but then he can't think of anything to say. His impulse is good, though. Somebody needs to save my grandmother before she really puts her foot in it.

"Dad said you were in Ireland," I prompt her. "Did you have fun?"

There's a long pause while the two sisters weigh my question. Their silence has the effect of making their answer potentially interesting.

"I wouldn't call it 'fun,' " Aunt Edna decides at last.

"It was very beautiful," my grandmother says. "And the people were so friendly."

"What was wrong with it, then?"

"Sometimes when you travel you come back more confused than when you left." Aunt Edna's voice is dark with hidden meaning.

"I have been to Denver, Colorado." Aunt Ida is making her bid for the center ring but she gets no takers.

"Like what?" Now I am hooked.

"We spring from peasant stock," my grandmother says, but from her tone I can tell that this was not the bad news.

"Our grandmother was wanted by the police," Aunt Edna says. "That's why she left."

"Only the *British* police." This distinction is clearly crucial to my grandmother.

"What did she do?" Now even Aunt Ida is curious.

"It depends on who you talk to." Aunt Edna is in no hurry.

"Wait a minute," I say. "Is this the Rose I'm naming myself after?"

They all look at me, each with a particular reaction. My grandmother and father are afraid, but for different reasons, that I'll change my mind. Aunt Edna approves of my question. Aunt

Ida . . . she's simply intense, anything I do or say will poke her, prove her right.

The false floor drops out beneath us. I realize, I don't have to wait for my possible children to use the microscope: I can reverse the polarities or whatever they are. I can refract, can reflect like a mirror. If they can see me, oh wow, I can see them. And there they are. Two frail old white ladies still doing their sister thing with each other, and the rest of the universe can go fish. Outside their tight circle of competition and power trip everything else is just . . . evidence, just material for one of them to get a leg up against the other. Aunt Ida is not so different, except for all the terror she inspires in those who have to deal with her on a regular basis, you take her out of context, you plunk her down, say, on a checkout line in a Seattle supermarket or a roller coaster at the state fair, you put her on the radio or ask her to discuss an issue of national importance like health care, and before your eyes she'll evaporate. And Dad, still a temp at the post office and he's practically ready to retire. Never got a regular route, never established a neighborhood. Still eager when by rights he should be, well, familiar. Still apologetic, still . . . charming, when by now he shouldn't have to be. Going out, according to Mom's last surveillance report, with some airhead named Arletta who's young enough to be my sister. Dad who couldn't handle Mom. Dad who let me go and doesn't know what to do about it.

The house lights are on: I can momentarily observe them all as if I don't know them, as if they have no authority over me, as if they are a crowd scene I never have to be lost in. I can see them as the rest of the world sees them and they're . . . ordinary, not scary. They're needy, they need me to take them seriously, to believe in who they want to be. But it's my choice. All this bluff is an act depending on some kind of unstated agreement between us. I *make* them them, allow them to be them, and in return they make me me. Is it a fair exchange? Without them, without their opinions and their rules and their shocked reactions, free, who would I be?

The breath goes out of my body into a vacuum of loneliness.

Nobody. I'd be nobody. Important to nobody.

They sit there, the studio audience, expectant, waiting for me to do something that they can fight with, fuss over, recoil from, grieve. My job here is to give them cues, to spark them into their next ideas by either being "nice" or "bad"—like a computer program that's + or -, but at least it goads the processor to the next command. They're hanging, ready to return with interest whatever I throw them. And the thing of it is, I, too, have a turn. I matter. In this small pond of big frogs, I am an equal player, I have rights, I can make real trouble or bring real joy or call the game for rain. I count. I am counted upon.

I count *on*. The breath floods back. Atmosphere restored.

"Tell me about her," I say, providing them an opening. "Who was this Rose, anyway?"

It's as though a flag has dropped, as though somebody has flipped the circuit breaker. They're back, charge each into the spaces they've worked so hard to perfect. They all talk at once, so relieved that the dangerous pause has ended. They've got stuff to convince me of, stuff to contradict each other about, stuff to reveal.

I am all ears. We're in the same room. And now I know the big secret: being a family is a voluntary duty. We're none of us here against our will.

Most of the time. But not me, not today. Not dressed like this. Not such an easy target. Mostly I go along, let the world take its best shot and it doesn't faze me because what other people see isn't me, though they may think it is. It's some version of me that I've approved of, like a new shirt you buy with "Inspected by #79" still in the breast pocket—and *you're* number seventy-nine so you've got nobody to blame for you but yourself. But standing here decorated like a trading-post Christmas tree I'm exposed, too ridiculous to bend it into a joke. I watch as the trickle of people coming to see what Aunt Ida has cooked up turns into a stream. They approach in a seeping tide, an expanding puddle that widens and thickens and any minute will engulf us. Once they get a load of me, they won't forget the sight for years to come.

There used to be a special class of warriors you hear about—dog soldiers—who were the final line of defense in an enemy attack. They didn't go out looking for trouble, but they didn't run from it either. They were the last wall between danger and their families. They'd stick their spears in the dirt, give the bad guys an "over my dead body" glare. They weren't going anywhere soon.

I moisten my lips with my tongue, hold my breath, test my balance, close my eyes in concentration. People can say what they want about me, but if they rag on Aunt Ida or Dad or my aunt and grandmother, I'll have to answer them back. No fooling around.

My first customer is Aunt Pauline's gross son, Foxy. He saunters up to me and the way he walks announces that he's thought of a comment he thinks is a killer.

"I didn't know they made another sequel to *Halloween*," he sneers. "But you have to be the star. Ray-groana."

"Eat shit and die," I say pleasantly. "You'd better take off. The powwow grounds are a drug and alcohol-free zone. You might explode."

Foxy's brain whirls, searches in vain for a comeback.

"I will not," he says.

I roll my eyes.

"At least I don't look like . . ." another pause while Foxy consults his mental computer . . . "Freddy!"

I could point out that he's blurring his horror movies, but what's the point, and anyway here's old Henry Stiffarm who is much more dangerous because he's a genuine elder, somebody I respect.

"It's wrong what she's doing," he whispers at me in Indian and glances at Aunt Ida but makes sure she can't hear him. "She doesn't know about these things."

"She means well," I tell him. "She misses my mom."

He shows me a disapproving face. He remembers Mom from when she was a teenager here.

"My mom just died," I remind him. "Behave yourself."

He is shocked, he can't believe what he has just heard, he can hardly wait to tell his buddies what the black girl has dared to say. Imagine. I've made his day.

Beyond him are a group of grade-school boys from the mission. They're pointing at me and they're laughing. I turn away, see a bunch of older guys, basketball players from my class. They're doing the same thing.

I look at the ground. I will not cry. I will not cry. I will not cry. The box under my arm is all pointy angles, digging into my ribs.

A weight enfolds on my shoulders. A warm, soft weight. I look down at myself. I am draped in a gray queen-size Pendleton blanket. I focus and make out an understated turtle design in simple earth tones of green, coral and tan. I raise my arms and draw it close around myself. It's as near as you can get to being a designer blanket and still be Indian, the kind of blanket you'd find tossed across some natural wood bed in a Crate & Barrel catalogue, the kind of blanket Robert Redford or Ralph Lauren probably sleeps under on their perfect ranches, the kind of blanket most of my relatives would reject as being boring, the kind of blanket that can't make a mistake. It's a little black dress and pearls of a blanket, a Starbucks coffee of a blanket, an acoustical, unplugged MTV special of a blanket. If this blanket were food it would be steamed fresh vegetables. If it were liquid it would be bottled water. If it were a movie it would star Emma Thompson. If it could talk, it would prefer not to.

There's a hand at the back of my neck and I turn to see Dayton.

"I dropped over to Aunt Ida's yesterday and was granted a showing," he says. "Of your dress."

I blink, speechless.

"It occurred to me you might get chilly out here today."

Dayton and I are pretty much the same height, so the spark of electricity that passes between us doesn't have to turn any corners. His middle-aged face is getting slightly lopsided. There are shaving cuts on his neck. There's some gray hair in his eyebrows. His mouth doesn't smile and that tells me that it's okay with him if I play dumb. He doesn't want any more of me than I'm prepared to give.

"This isn't happening." It's all I can say because I'm too inflated by strong feelings.

"Hey, we breeds got to stick together." He keeps his mouth steady but now his eyes smile.

I look away. It's too much, being helped out.

"Excuse me," he says. "I think some of this stuff is coming undone. Wouldn't want to lose it."

His hands move on my hair, gentle but insistent, and in a matter of seconds they are full of fur and feathers and rocks, every foreign object Aunt Pauline has plastered me with. He deposits them in an open backpack at his feet and extracts two long rectangles of red flannel. He sticks one under his arm and unwraps the other to reveal a dark leather snap-lid box.

"This was awarded to your Uncle Lee," he tells me, and shows me what's inside: a purple heart from the army resting on a white satin backing. "They gave it to your mom and she passed it on to me. She'd want you to have it today, kind of as a keepsake. I'll hold it for you till later." He slips the box into the backpack.

Just his mention of Mom puts her next to me. I can sense her listening the way she always did, managing to give the impression that she was daringly eavesdropping even when something was said to her directly. Now, she's nodding, proud of herself for thinking of all this, for not forgetting to remember me on a special occasion.

"You were real good to her," I say to Dayton. "You saved her life." I remember how he was at the end of her sickness when she was up all night in a bad mood, demanding, furious at the universe. Dayton could always talk her down to normal. She'd look at him so hard it was as though she was holding on with the grip of her eyes.

315

He shakes his head. "You got it backwards." He pauses a beat. "This one's from me." He unwraps the second slim bundle. An eagle feather. "It came down to me from my mom's side," he says. "Do you mind?" He holds the quill end up to my head. I don't move as he fastens it at the top of my braid. I feel the wind tug at it, but it holds in place.

Dayton steps back, cocks his head and nods once.

"You look beautiful."

The sounds of the powwow wash over us. It's as though a close-up shot suddenly turns into a wide-angle. My shadow stretches out from me on the ground, and the blanket makes the contours of my body as smooth as the sides of a shell. Its plain gray elegance conceals the noisy chaos of my clothing, and that in turn masks the even greater tangle and confusion inside me.

"What's that you're holding?" Dayton asks, and I remember my grandmother's present. It's in one of those boxes where the top and the bottom are wrapped separately, so all you have to do is open it, and while Dayton steadies the blanket on my shoulder, freeing my hands, I do. Inside is a cut-glass vase.

"It's older than we are," Aunt Edna whispers from behind me. "An heirloom that by rights now comes down to you straight from the first Rose."

"All the way from Ireland," I hear my grandmother brag to Aunt Ida.

I turn the vase in my palms, letting each facet catch a distinct light, its own individual color of sky or earth. It's like looking at a thousand faces, each different from all the rest.

"Here," I say to Dayton. "You take care of it for me. Go sit with the family. I brought an extra chair, special. Yours. There's room for everybody."